For Margaret Mainwaring —
It's lovely to have you as
neighbor and friend.

Virginia Gavian Rivers

PRELUDE TO GENOCIDE:

Incident in Erzerum

Virginia Gavian Rivers

ARCHWAY
PUBLISHING

Archway Publishing books may be ordered through booksellers or by contacting:

Archway Publishing
1663 Liberty Drive
Bloomington, IN 47403
www.archwaypublishing.com
1 (888) 242-5904

Because of the dynamic nature of the Internet, any web addresses or
links contained in this book may have changed since publication and
may no longer be valid. The views expressed in this work are solely those
of the author and do not necessarily reflect the views of the publisher,
and the publisher hereby disclaims any responsibility for them.

Any people depicted in stock imagery provided by Thinkstock are models,
and such images are being used for illustrative purposes only.
Certain stock imagery © Thinkstock.

ISBN: 978-1-4808-1873-6 (sc)
ISBN: 978-1-4808-1874-3 (hc)
ISBN: 978-1-4808-1875-0 (e)

Library of Congress Control Number: 2015944120

Print information available on the last page.

Archway Publishing rev. date: 09/03/2015

Dedication

*I*n memory of Marjan, my grandmother, who still wept, years later, in telling my father of escaping to Russia nailed in wooden boxes.

In memory of Martiros Kavafian, who was shot to death with the other males in his family near Erzerum in 1915.

And in memory of my great aunt Zevart Kolligian, Martiros' granddaughter, whose love, faith and hospitality stand as a beacon to those who knew her.

And finally, in memory of my father, Sarkis Petros Kavafian, whose determination and courage brought him to this country, where he earned college and graduate degrees, met and married my non-Armenian mother, and never tired of telling how he came to be here.

Marjan Kavafian

Preface

T his book grew from family stories told by my father Sarkis and his second cousin Zevart long after they became Americans. Basic elements of the novel are theirs: an uncle's death in the Incident of October 30, 1895 in Erzerum, the family's salvation by a Muslim neighbor who was an Army officer, and my grandparents' escape to Russia, the mother and children hidden in coffin-like boxes. The remarkable horse, transposed from my father's military service in 1917 to his neighbor's military service a generation earlier. The family's business in shoes and imports. The hours spent at worship in both church and home. The large household under one roof. The Kavafians' friendship with a bishop, also transposed. The book ends before my father's birth in 1899 in Kars, then under the Czar's rule. He remembered sitting on that bishop's knee as a child; he met him again just before sailing for the States.

October 1895 brought suffering, violence and death to Armenians living in eastern Turkey, the historic homeland of Armenians. Set off by events in Constantinople in late September, the government's retaliation moved progressively with military and para-military (hamidieh) personnel through the villages, towns and cities where Armenians were most populous. The incidents continued after the Oct. 30 event in Erzerum and were recorded by foreign observers. They were an important precursor of the Armenian genocide that began throughout Turkey in 1915.

What captured my interest are questions similar to those asked about the Holocaust: Why don't people see what is coming and flee to safer territory? How does a diverse community that has been functioning cooperatively become, abruptly, violent? How can relations between diverse elements grow back together? Can the scars heal?

I've used fiction to explore these questions, while staying as close as I could to what I know of the circumstances of Turkish Armenians, particularly of my family, in Erzerum in the 1890's.

Three narrators tell the story. **Hamed**, a captain in the Fourth Army, lives with his family in a mixed Muslim-Christian neighborhood of comfortable houses near the foreign consulates. **Martiros,** his close friend, is the second of four brothers who live with their extended family next door. **Marjan** is the wife of the third brother, Petros Kavafian. They are my grandparents.

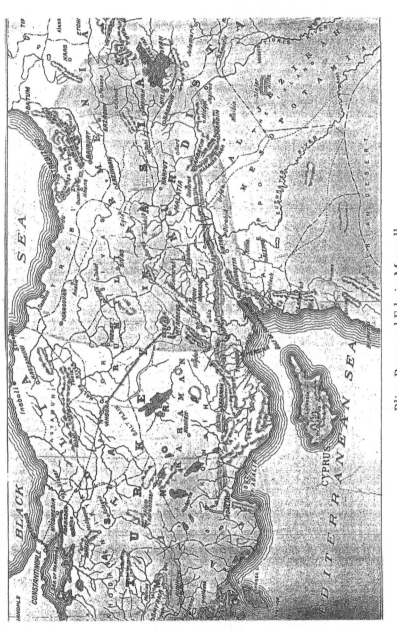

Bliss, Reverend Edwin Munsell,
Turkey and the Armenian Atrocities, Philadelphia, 1896.

A Brief History of the Armenians through 1895

The Armenian homeland is an area bordered by the Caucasus and Pontus mountains in what is now eastern Turkey and the Armenian Republic. Its people trace their roots to early Urartu, near Mt. Ararat and Van.

Located as they were on an important route for trade and conquest, Armenians look back on a long history of domination by stronger neighbors: Syria, Egypt, Greece, Rome, Persia and Turkey, among others. Those conquerors often allowed Armenia self rule; however, it has been a fully independent nation only during the reign of King Tigran the Great from about 95 to 55 BCE; under Bagratid kings from 886 to 1045 CE; and from 1198 to 1375 as the Armenian kingdom of Cilicia in an area along the Mediterranean to the southwest, populated by Armenians who fled repeated invasions of the eastern plateau. Armenian Cilicia provided essential help to the European crusaders.

Armenia became the first Christian state in 301, after its ruler Tiridates III, newly converted by Saint Gregory the Illuminator, proclaimed Christianity the official state religion. When Armenia adopted its own alphabet a century later, a golden age of Armenian literature followed. The Armenian Apostolic Church was established in the sixth century and still exists independently of both the Catholic and the Eastern Orthodox churches. During its later political eclipses, Armenia has depended on the church to preserve its unique identity.

The Armenian people remained Christian during centuries of Turkic-Muslim dominance and Ottoman rule that extended from about 1520, or 1639 for the eastern plateau, until WWI. Ottoman rulers allowed non-believing religious minorities self government, providing their religious leaders maintained order within their millets (religious groups, primarily Armenian, Greek Orthodox and Jewish) and collected required levies. Each millet saw to the schooling of its own and settled internal disputes.

The subject minorities were not allowed to testify in Muslim proceedings and this fact meant special difficulties for minority members—and special opportunities for criminals. Although millet members were restricted from military service and forbidden to own firearms, Armenians could and did serve as government officials and advisers. Many Armenians were merchants; they were also disproportionately represented in the practice of medicine and law and in the business of banking and finance because they tended to be well educated.

By the 1850s, some 2.5 million[1] Armenians were Ottoman subjects, living predominantly in Turkey's eastern provinces. The number dropped after the Russo-Turkish War of 1877-1878, when thousands of eastern Armenians emigrated to Russia in expectation of a better life—and protection from Kurdish raids and discriminatory rule.

A nationalist fever spread through Europe during the 19th century, sparking the creation of three nationalist Armenian organizations (Armenakan, 1885, Hunchagist, 1887, and Dashnakstutsiun, 1890). This added to the suspicions of Sultan Abdul Hamid and his advisers as to the loyalty of Turkish Armenians. With some justification, Turkish Armenian subjects were already seen as preferring Russian to Ottoman rule; some numbers had cheered the Czar's soldiers as they marched into eastern Armenia in 1877 and some 25,000 Armenians had followed the retreat across the border at war's end in 1878.[2]

Although the Ottomans had adopted a liberal constitution to satisfy foreign objections in 1876, it was not implemented. In fact,

---

[1] *Ubicini and Dulaurier, cited by Hovanissian,Richard G., Armenia on the Road to Independence, 1967, p36.*

[2] *Hovannisian, Richard G., Armenia on the Toad to Independence, 1918,University of California Press, Berkeley, 1967, p. 12.*

Sultan Abdul Hamid II, who came to power the same year, imposed further restrictions on the minorities. He rankled at ongoing pressure from foreign diplomats to grant Christian subjects equal rights with the empire's Muslim majority, including protection from Kurdish raids on their farms and villages.

Ottoman leaders had long feared Russian expansion. Sultan Abdul Hamid II felt especially threatened when the Treaty of Berlin (1878) gave Russia control of Kars and other formerly Ottoman territory on the eastern plateau. He was angered by diplomatic efforts on behalf of religious minorities and was aware that three secret Armenian parties were trying to advance nationalist goals.

The autumn of 1895 was fraught with anxiety for Armenians living in eastern Turkey, their historic homeland. In 1894, the Armenians of Sassun had been slaughtered by military forces for refusing to pay taxes (see note). [3] Intervening months had seen an increase in assaults on Armenian villages by Kurdish tribesmen and militia (hamidieh) armed and encouraged by the Sultan.

In late September 1895, Armenian demonstrators[4] in Constantinople were routed by police. For several days following, mobs wreaked violence on Armenians and in the Armenian quarter of the capital. Anti-Armenian violence erupted soon after as the Fourth Army moved south through the eastern provinces where Armenians were concentrated,: on October 8, Trabizond and neighboring Armenian villages, then Erzincan on October 21, Bitlis and Gemush-khan and surrounding villages on October 25, Baiburt on October 27 and Urfa on October 27- 28.[5] After Erzerum's "incident" on October 30, violence came to Diyarbekir and Arabkir on November 1-3, Malatia on Nov. 4-9, Kharput on November 10-11,

---

[3] *The Kurds collected extortionary "protection" taxes while increasing their depredations on Armenian farms and villages. Dashnak organizers encouraged the Sassunlis' protest.*

[4] *Led by Hunchaks.*

[5] *Urfa now endured a siege without food or water, culminating in extended massacre during the final days of November.*

Sivas on November 12, followed by Amasia, Aintab and Marsovan. Kayseri suffered on November 30,[6] and more violence struck Urfa in late December, with many Armenians killed. Nor is this list complete.

Again, foreign diplomats and missionaries decried these events, pressed for an end to the depredations and to secure equal rights for the Empire's Christian subjects. Again, they heard promises which were not implemented. Britain, France and Russia participated in diplomatic protests in 1895. It did not serve the national interests of the European powers to confront the Sultan with military force. Their threats added to the Sultan's anxieties about the Empire's security.

An estimated 100,000 Armenians fled to Russia, Greece and other countries following the "incidents" in 1895-96.

note: Erzurum was the ancient capital of Armenia and was the capital of Erzurum province during the Ottoman Empire. Along the course of its history it was also known as Garin, Theodosiopolis, Erzen-el-Rum, Arzerum, and Karin. Many contemporary sources refer to it as Erzerum. Similarly, various names and spellings are found for other cities, towns and villages such as Sassun.

---

[6] *As chronicled by Walker, C.J., Armenia, 1980. He relates that a bugle call began and ended each period of violence.*

Kavafian family and household

Patriarch: Nazar — Matriarch: Toumia

Nazar's sister Maxime — Toumia's sister Flora

Levon — Sahad — Rafael

Sarkis (Sako)
m Dela (died 1892 with two daughters)
m Henzanant 1895

Astghig Arsen Karin Yetkine

Martiros
m Yiri

Petros
m Marjan

Heranoush   Artashes   Vagram

Miton
m Sara

Krikor   Hamajah   (son born 1899)

Virginie (b 1897)   Sarkis (b 1899)

Servants: Ephraim   Verkin

Added to household: Nerses & sister Arsha (refugees from Trabzon)
Not in household: Marjan's mother
                  Marjan's older sister Nora m Sempad Halebian
                                         four sons

Marjan's younger sister Zari m Asadur Melikian
                              daughter Gavnee
                                          son

Berci family

Pasha ——— Hannum

Hamed
m Khadijah

Khalil

Marta Souren Rupen

Ehsan   Hüru   son born 1896

Marjan's friend

Varti m Karekin Meserian   his brother Manik & wife

                               Rebecca   Zeput (twins)

Cook: Husneh

One

Before

September 20 to October 29, 1895

A Troublesome Tenant

※ · ※ · ※ · ※ · ※ · ※ · ※ · ※ · ※ · ※

Hamed   September 20-25, 1895

His plan to oust our tenant worried me. The fellow might be a spy, trouble for us. Eviction was inevitable, but why this urgency?

Father chose the better course, said later he'd foreseen it. Anticipation was beyond me, with upheavals still weeks away.

The wife was all courtesy to us. Poor woman, she'd a bruise under her veil. They'd all be better off back home: the boy at school, the girl near her cousins and aunts.

Her husband was clumsy, pouring coffee. Puffy flesh around his eyes meant poppy paste, for sure. No wonder he'd paid no rent these seven months. Who buys cloth from such a merchant?

Deftly, Father wove his net: a harsh winter ahead meant many scarcities; raids by Kurds; a harvest half the usual; and even dung fuel would be in short supply. His friend the military supply officer, a recent visitor, foretold famine for the eastern provinces. This pricked our tenant's ears. Topol alert now, like a hungry cat.

Too many foreign mills drowned shops with cheap yardage. Buyers here in Erzerum were ignorant and easily misled. He'd have better prospects closer to the capital—that is, home in Gebizeh. Topol could trade with us now to make good on the rent and buy passage home with what was left.

Our tenant swallowed, scratched, and then stared at his feet and the carpet beneath. He wiped his mouth with a sleeve and then rubbed his forehead with snag-nailed fingers. He struggled for words as if foreign born. We waited. He finally gave out a sigh loud as a belch.

"Need some time…maybe… two weeks."

"Three days."

"No!" then, "Yes, if they…if I can sell…" His face took on a scheming look. "My rent for a quarter of my stock?"

"Let's see what we can do." Father motioned me in: the negotiations were now mine. Father preferred hunt to kill, strategy to tactics. He kept both ears cupped for new investments and gave his younger brothers lesser details. My uncles ran his farms and caravansary. That work never caught my desire.

It's well to prepare on all fronts. I'd visited dry goods shops, fingered textiles, tried prices like a buyer. Also, I'd discussed it with an astute businessman, my friend Martiros. Fully armed for this meeting, I got a fair division that satisfied both me and the useless tenant.

First the fellow tried to put specifics off, reluctant as to inventory and loath to show the spare room. Goods were stacked high there, some tight woven stripes of blue, red and palace gold, others plain but serviceable. The remaining bolts were too flimsy for dew. It's a crime to sell such shit to the idiot who buys it.

We argued back and forth. I knew he'd cheat me if he could and he knew I knew. That may explain his tenacity one moment, acquiescence the next. Opium also makes men unpredictable. In any case I felt relieved at this game's end.

His unpaid rent was on one side. On the other, 30 bolts of his best fabrics, along with his house furnishings and his wagon. With what remained, he'd settle other debts and get the family home. I'd arrange travel papers with the mayor's aide, Abdi. My old school friend and I traded favors fast as a blind beggar plucks up a coin. I'd get Topol two pack mules, his to sell in Trabizond, an even deal.

Riding home, satisfied, Father and I waved to friends and traded quips like schoolboys on holiday. We cut through the Christian sector west of Blossom Quarter, clearly out of place, not the noon patrol. We forgot to moderate our voices, causing a frightened housemaid to drop her broom and hide behind a door. The next street over, my uniform scared a priest. He tripped and fell knee-deep into mud.

No wonder Armenians were wary. A soldier meant trouble, even before Bab Ali and what followed. A few traitors deserved blame but every Christian in their millet was now suspected. Arrests were far too many.

Even my child-brother Khalil noticed our happy mood. "Why your smile, Papa, is it a feast day?" His afternoon at the Kavafian shop was already forgotten.

My boy Ehsan took his chance and cajoled a ride on his grandfather's mare after prayers. We watched the sunset from the hilltop. Our Erzerum city turned to shadows.

My wife read my face and understood best. "I can see you're glad to get your old house back from those people," Khadija said.

That evening Martiros and his father stopped in. We were eager to report the day's bargain. I set myself to best my friend at backgammon and felt victory pulling my fingers like a flag.

Father always chuckled when asked about our "impure" neighborhood. How could we bear to share a garden wall with infidels? Yet the Kavafians were our close friends. Not the Muslim ship owner on the north side of our house or the Muslim tax accountant at the rear.

I was born in Blossom Quarter and was happy there. Understandably, I balked at our move to Iron Foot Street after the Russian retreat, until I discovered four brothers next door. What matter if playmates are Muslim or Christian? My brother Khalil and I played soldiers with them in their yard one day, ours another. Their roof was somewhat higher, better for some games. Martiros and I soon became fast friends. We were born the same month, a special bond.

We were all still boys, we found mischief together—innocent mischief, mostly. As we got older—well, one episode mortifies me still. Martiros and I were not yet 16. Was it our idea or his older brother's? We likely mustered it together, sneaking a woman into the stable behind my house. She was a willing small woman from the streets, an able teacher, patient with our inexperience and smart enough to conceal amusement. She initiated us most skillfully, working from eldest on down: Sarkis, nickname Sako, first, then Martiros, then me, then Petros. The amazing wonders she accomplished with her little mouth and tongue and hands!

We'd planned it for a certain day when their mother would be at the baths, their father in his shoe shop, mine at his caravansary. Surprise! my father returned prematurely. He caught us all hot and disheveled, Petros with his pants down, the whore just rising from her knees. He took in the scene and knew the story. I wanted to disappear, unable to speak, my tongue heavy as stone. We all were quivering with embarrassment and fear, the brothers mute as does.

"So this is how you waste your time, for shame!" he scolded. He made sure we paid her fairly. Then he lectured us: first on discretion, its value in consorting with lewd women, then next, on the merits of abstinence. Yet he understood our curiosity and I doubt he truly disapproved. The brothers seemed hardly to breathe until he said he'd say nothing to their father so long as we did nothing like this again. *Never never* in the neighborhood, he warned us. Knowing Nazar Kavafian's temper, I nearly shouted with relief. Then my father sent them home, poor Miron still an innocent. Father never spoke of it again. He earned the brothers' lifetime devotion.

We never repeated this sort of misbehavior, that is, not together—we found other mischief. Then Sako went off to study pharmacy and I started at the Academy. We still had summer escapades, sometimes pretty reckless. We survived by fools' luck, as lucky children do. Not that we thought ourselves children! We thought we were smart—and we were, each in different ways. Sako was the story-teller, singer and thinker, supplying new ideas. Petros was the bookish one, less attentive to others. He did best in school, though the rest of us did well enough. Miron tried to keep up and sometimes surprised us. Miron knew a lot and could do a lot. Martiros and I competed in everything with everyone but especially with each other. We took turns at math problems in our schoolbooks, teased one another with new words. Even then my friend favored long sentences and often talked about himself.

When Father stopped by Topol's shop the next day, he found the assistant sorting fabrics into three piles. He was annoyed to see light-hued stuff spread on soiled, unswept matting. Father well knew the assistant Pohar's repute for cheating.

"And what are you doing?" Father inquired.

"This pile for the master, that pile for me, that pile for you, Effendi." Pohar didn't look up from his task. "It's the master's request."

"And did he tell you to put all the best in your pile? I can see you're giving mostly crap to me." Seeing him, Father first thought of a wolf's head on a duck's body: crafty eyes, a narrow face, short neck, slight chest and a large pot belly. The odd-looking creature straightened up.

"Master's paid me nothing since last spring. I've slaved for him. He owes me," Pohar whined.

"And how many bolts have you sold?"

A shrug. "Some come just to look, not to buy."

"So you'd take the best cloth. Cloth you did little to sell. You preferred drinking coffee with friends…"

"Yes, effendi." Insolent, a smirk crossing his face.

"You'll take nothing. Not a scrap until your master and I agree. Nothing."

Father made Pohar follow on foot to the house on Blossom Street. Some laughed to see him pacing his horse so the fellow had to trot, his knees knocking the full way. The distance was less than a mile with no great hills to climb.

Father found Topol and son loading stock, mules hitched and ready. The guileless boy flushed dark red, but Topol pretended nothing was amiss. The hoof beats had warned him.

"Good, you're in time to help us with the carpets," was his greeting to my father. Sure enough, the heavy things were rolled and ready by the back door.

"You've forgotten. We agreed you'd leave the carpets here. Just as they were." It's from my father I learned to stand firm without accusing, to keep tight hold of anger.

"Ah! It's well you remind me, it drifted from my mind." Topol's quick answer proved its falseness. "I thought we'd bring them to your house, effendi. So you don't want them there, but here?" He spoke with no hint of chagrin. The boy looked miserable with shame—to his credit. Father took Topol's duplicity as unremarkable, knowing he'd no idea of honor. As he said later, "This fellow is the kind you must watch when he asks to use the privy."

Not blinking an eye, Father directed Topol, "The fabric goes there, the carpets and other furnishings here. As was decided yesterday."

"Wait," said Topol. He clapped hands to summon his wife. "Bring refreshments for us, while these two" (a nod to the boy and the assistant) "load the wagon." Topol turned back to Father. "After our coffee, of course, we'll bring the wagon to your house." Our tenant had grown smooth as a silken cord. He thought he was smarter than he was. Father was certain Topol meant to cull the best bolts for himself. Still, it was encouraging to see this idler trying to whittle a whistle, as we say. His energy and guile might get them home.

"We'll select from your shop's stock, as we agreed yesterday," Father told him. Topol stuttered and fell mute. His landlord's stern tone forced thought of consequence: how cheating Father would surely reach the Military Supply Office and dishonor his family name. Such men as Topol and Pohar lack honor but crave respect.

At our tenant's shop, we saw improvement. Topol was cooperative, even hard-working, running from stack to stack, pulling out the finer goods, proclaiming their merits, estimating prices. He talked knowledgeably about his stock now, no longer stumbling. His hands were fairly steady, his eyes less red. He seemed more careful to conceal his scheming, but unabashed. Perhaps this misfit from Gebizeh was suited to spying, after all.

Father and I examined, discussed, sipped coffee, tallied. At the end, we got what we wanted: virtually all the best merchandise, well woven and dyed. While not what the richest pasha takes to his tailor, the stuff might be worn in public or spread on divans. We also took lesser goods easy to sell.

We left a few high quality fabrics with Topol and Pohar. The rest was everyday stuff, middling or cheap. Topol himself stacked our share in the wagon, praising this bolt's weaving, that bolt's dyeing, another's strength. He seemed well satisfied.

My friend Martiros later sold some of these goods and we shared a healthy profit between us. It was a congenial arrangement, no effort on my part, small trouble for him. He'd many customers in and out each day. He was a trader by nature, like many Armenians. Yet my father's a match for any.

We saw our tenants off on schedule, and Pohar was in the yard as well. Topol's lad was hopping with excitement, his new sandals tied to his mule's belly strap, awaiting the first hard climb. Through the braying and clatter, his mother laughed, the first I ever heard. She was nuzzling the baby.

Topol circled his travel papers above his head, grinning. "No one can stop me now! I'm all set to go!"

As if anyone wanted to stop him! He sounded like the young man we'd met the year before, well-spoken, clear-headed. A defined course of action keeps a man healthy, whether soldier or civilian. It's invaluable.

Sharp shouts, brays of protest, and they were mounted, Topol astride one mule, his wife on another with her infant. The boy with his sister on a third. Two last mules creaked and staggered under innumerable burdens: food sacks, cook pots, clothing, bolts of cloth and bedding. Pitiful mules! I also pitied the family for lacking saddles or cushions. They'd cut cloth for padding within two hours, I expected.

At the gate Father handed Topol a small sack. "Buy sweets for your kids in Baiburt," he said.

Topol was startled into grateful babble and Pohar's mouth fell open, muted by the coins. No spy'd malign us after such generosity.

Pleasant relief to their riddance! Yet I envied them the journey. It was a cool morning with cloudless sunshine, still perfect weather for the trek. Continuing to the barracks, I mused on the pleasures of riding to Trabizond. Four days on horseback, if unburdened; twice that long with pack mules.

Topol and his family would cross fertile plains nourished by the Euphrates' full-flowing teats. Next, they'd pass through fragrant forests musical with birdsong. Then, climb great mountains to gaze like eagles on the world below. From Trabizond, they'd have a restful voyage visiting ports rimmed with trees in autumn colors. Then at last, they'd reach the magnificent harbor at Constantinople.

Constantinople itself was a marvel to me. The Sultan's palace is one glory among many. Visitors see beauty the city's residents are blind to. It surpasses Baghdad's, makes Berlin dull in comparison. Constantinople's setting on the Bosporus is perfect.

My last visit was in '91 for a review marking the Sultan's birthday. Already one heard furtive queries, was he mad? Yet his governing seemed sound enough. Army matters had their own logic or illogic, worry was pointless. I was working to make colonel and be posted there.

My good mood at Topol's departure improved further at the fort. New guns, promised so long we quit hoping, had at last arrived. It took a new commanding general, although even Zeki Pasha got us less than requested.

Fifteen camels instead of a hundred didn't stop the boasting as crates were untied. How the troops craved new rifles! Some lucky soldiers would get their officers' castoffs.

With everyone talking of new guns, I supposed my superior's summons related to them. So much of what was ahead was unimaginable...

The major stared out the window. Fifteen kneeling beasts chewed placidly while sweating drivers detached their burdens. A few soldiers helped but most watched idly, as if unprying knots was best left to a djinn.

Major Rustem read off lading bills while his aide set figures in columns. So many U.S. Peabody rifles, so many six-cylinder German pistols, so many cases of shells for each. I expected he'd have me check paper against opened crates to make sure all was in order.

"Your stallion Keyif is in good health?" From the Major's greeting I knew I was bound again for Trabizond.

My horse is a remarkable creature, smart on mountain trails and fast on level stretches. Unique, the very best, and much too fine for a mere Fourth Army captain—unless very wealthy or very lucky. I'd been lucky. Keyif was given to me by a rich and grateful Englishman I'd escorted—safely—through a bandit-nest on Kopdaghi. The Inglesi was about to set sail and trusted me not to sell his darling to a dealer. He knew Keyif was something rare—as does everyone who sees him.

His gift made me famous. Visiting officers will ask, "You're the captain who rides the stallion Keyif?" They know his name, not mine! I'm teased for keeping a horse finer than the Commandant's. Some say it will hurt my advancement, while some contend he's too high-bred for military service. They'd buy him gladly but could never pay his worth.

"Pick some men and prepare to leave for Trabizond after first prayers tomorrow. Get yourselves new firearms. Make sure you sight them properly—they'll be different from our Mausers. Flush snipes for practice."

Major Rustem's an exceptional soldier. His strategic skills went underutilized these years of peace in Erzerum province. He turned to gunning game with passion, hunting in any weather, far up in the mountains or below on the lower plains. More often in nearby marshes, where his short stature lets him disappear among the grasses. We've had excellent eating of his quail and pheasants—a welcome change from lamb and mutton.

The Major continued his terse instructions: a new German consul was arriving at Trabizond port, I was to escort the family to Erzerum. I knew the routine back and front.

"Harm to him, we're mud! We can't have another foreigner murdered! You make sure they ride *horses*, not infernal foreign machines! *Horses!*" The Major rubbed a spot on the glass with his sleeve and studied it, renewing calm. Grey strands in his dark hair glinted in the sunlight.

Two summers back, a foolhardy American meandered alone in the nearby mountains. After he got himself ambushed, foreigners in the capital bellowed like bulls and caused double investigations: first by our provincial governor, then by an imperial commission. They learned this fool was riding some two-wheeled device that terrified the mountain people. They're superstitious—and unaccustomed to strangers with strange contraptions. Surely the devil's own workshop produced this monstrous thing! So they smashed both man and machine.

"Get back before the passes close. And keep your eyes open!" The Major advised me on the fastest safe route, then renewed his list-reading.

I went to find my junior lieutenant. Shakir is truly among the best. He keeps a level temper and sound judgment even under fire. He fought with me in '77 at Kars against the Czar's Cossacks and earned an ugly face wound when not yet 20. These things are never fair. A missing hand or eye can be concealed but a half-nose cannot. Strangers flinch at Shakir's disfigurement, draw away as from a leper. It's hurt his prospects as an officer—and a bridegroom. Yet he's forever well-mannered, uncomplaining and soldierly, a top-rank man who deserves better.

Together Shakir and I chose our detail, then collected new weapons. I gave my discards to one of the escort. His passed to a fresh-cheeked recruit whose Mauser was heavy as a small cannon and rusted useless.

The summer past I'd twice escorted dignitaries between Erzerum and Trabizond, had also done this the preceding spring when snowdrifts were still bothersome. Our assignment was an Englishman, a professor of antiquities. His arrogance created inconvenience, as did his wife, brother and young nephew. None of the four was accustomed to mountain riding. The professor insisted we leave prematurely and then dawdle along the route. Thus a storm caught us, so it took eight days instead of three, simply getting from Erzerum to Baiburt. It was a truly hateful trip for my men and our horses. The man loved himself too well to admit his error.

Whether northbound or southbound, the journey between Erzerum and Trabizond is always risky, but especially so in blizzard season, from early October through mid-May. In any season it demands strong lungs, a sure-footed horse and a good rifle eye against bandits. Yet I'm always glad to leave garrison routine to lead an escort. At best such varied duty affords companionable evenings with men of some importance. At worst the travelers are arrogant or boring. In any case, I've Shakir and my men for conversation and it's over in about a week—usually.

Other officers were capable of getting a party safely back from Trabizond in early October. Major Rustem chose me because I've lived in two capitals, can converse with foreign civilians. The Major prided himself on assigning us by our particular abilities. He scorned the common practice of treating subordinates as interchangeable.

"Before battle, be sure each officer is suited to his post. There are as many levels of defense as attack," he'd say.

Not that he never made mistakes. In my division, he promoted a fellow from junior lieutenant prematurely. The man Fikret was the army-college type, born to a well-connected family and full of himself. Not especially smart, merely clever at making a good impression with his elders, and not so good at dealing with soldiers. He created problems.

I looked ahead to the pleasures of this journey: riding again up into the Kopdaghi, mastering a rutted, rocky path from the Erzerum plain; visiting the famous old fortress at Baiburt; penetrating the conifer forests near Macka, rediscovering the spectacle that rewards the hard passage at Zigana. One particular outlook to the sea sets me braying a jolly song my mother taught me, deaf to my men's complaints.

Already the mountains would be aflame with maples and oaks prideful among dull ranks of evergreens. The Consul would see our mountains at their best, within our great Empire, magnificence. The thought filled me with patriotic pride. No better place on earth was possible, no uniform better than mine.

Martiros gave me a list of purchases in Trabizond: an ornament of polished ebony for his wife; silver clasps for a child's saddle; a few tanned goatskins of glove quality, if reasonably priced.

"Any more gifts and you'll have to come with me," I told him. Laughing, Martiros recalled the time we set forth for Erzincan as boys, with so much paraphernalia our two old mares could barely move. We spent all afternoon reaching the great Armenian monastery beneath the Khachapayd Mountains. It took us hours more to find a decent overlook for camping. By then we were leading our weary horses and wishing we wore thick-soled boots instead of sandals. We ate most of our food, then rolled ourselves in blankets and stared at the stars. So near, so far, so bright! A long time passed before our excitement let us sleep. The next day we turned around and came home.

When I go off on such a trip, Khadija hides her fears, as a soldier's wife must. Twice she reminded me to bring gifts home for Ehsan and little Huru. Twice she suggested I tell Father not to leave the old house vacant, lest mice or worse invade. She prattled on, some clever question of Huru's and Ehsan's answer. To gain some peace I finally said, "That's enough talk now, go to sleep." Then I lay awake planning the quickest route to Trabizond and thinking how to handle Topol if by bad luck I overtook him. At last sleep came.

I woke early, eager for the journey. Yet in the pale dawn light, Khadija's face was lovely in girlish sleep. I drew her to me with caresses like a bridegroom. She was warm and pliant, and came awake quickly. It was well we took time to enjoy each other then, for a long while passed before that pleasure was repeated. They are right to say it –"Best to leave a wife happy."

When I kissed Mother's forehead in farewell, she cried out for me to stay, clutched me so I couldn't leave. She looked tired. Her face was puffy, her skin damp. Her spirits had been sinking with her health a year at least by then. Even so, it wasn't like her—yet she insisted it was not her illness. While Shakir waited with my horse, I coaxed the reason from her, wiping her tears. At last she confessed her bad dream: Some terrible accident would befall me on my journey. My reassurances failed to wash anxiety from her face.

"If Mother had her way, there'd be no soldiers," I said to Father. "It's a routine trip."

"Your mother's dreams are true more often than false. Be careful how you ride," he answered.

"Keyif will take good care of me." With new weapons, a clear sky, my best men and my fine stallion, I set out with perfect complacency.

Marjan Visits

Marjan   late September 1895

Surely the Almighty forgave my small deceit. My husband's mother said visits wasted time. She made up work to keep us home. Toumia only let us out Christmas and Easter unless we'd special reason. As if a daughter should ignore her widowed mother the rest of the year! Secretly I called her "Sour Tongue Toumia" and "Mean Old Mother" and held in my thoughts.

God knows I never turned from work like certain others. That same morning, while the rest of us cleaned up from breakfast, Sarah put her infant to the breast twice the same hour. The whole time watching Henza and Yiri green-eyed their husbands got born before hers. Sarah hadn't learned to swallow what can't be spit—or to be thankful for her Miron's patient nature.

As we set off behind our men folk, my daughter asked me, "How did Grandmama hurt her back, Mother?" Her words put heat in my face and fog curls in the air.

"Her note didn't say. I only know she wants my special back-rub." A truth meant to conceal. Heranoush was only 13, too young to know some lies may be forgiven in Heaven.

"Can I tell her about our new fabric? The dress we're making?" She took a skip-step and before I answered, said, "Grandmama won't make me scrub cupboards again, will she? My hands are sore…"

"No more cupboards 'til spring, I think." I let her whining pass. She missed school, thought she was overworked at home. Most of all she missed Zeput and her twin Rebecca. Church gave no talking time and it was months since they had a good visit.

Autumn was the hardest time for women. Kneeling for prayers, I was wrapped by sleep, so heavy with it I'd half fall, chase thought-tails 'til my senses cleared. Special washes took doing after summer in the mountains and Toumia disliked hired hands. "Such a woman, what's she care for fine embroidery?" from her was not a question.

Avoiding laundry was what two of my sisters-in-law did best. A baby to rock, a bottom to clean, Sarah and Yiri found ready excuses. Henza and I made sure their hands got wet—we left their underclothes out of our washing.

The day Henza and I got to the last basket, we asked no one's help. We understood without words that it was nicer to end the chore by ourselves, without them dragging about like whipped dogs.

Henza hugged me when we hung out the last sheet. We treated ourselves to a glass of mulberry juice and a few dates from the pantry cupboard. "Next year, let others do it!" I said, knowing she and Sako wanted a baby even more than me and Petros. We laughed and hugged again. Toumia was resting in her room, so we sat talking a while before the schoolboys got home.

Endless though they seemed, the food tasks of fall were more pleasant than laundry. Together we labored through September, preserving the season's fruits before they spoiled. We sliced and chopped, boiled and stirred, squeezed and poured, spread and turned, morning until night, day after day. We smiled as the pantry shelves filled with jars of jam, bottles of juice, baskets of apricot paste and dried cherries, quinces, raisins, pears and apricots. At last, after weeks, we could rest.

We were just settling down to toast the end with tea when a muleteer arrived with barrels of over-ripe figs and grapes from Smyrna. Sarah looked so sorry for herself I almost laughed aloud. Her little Hamajah was sleeping in the cradle so she'd no escape. We began again.

After the fruit came eggplants, onions, beans, tomatoes. After the vegetables, meat. Then we made cracker bread, before insect eggs spoiled the flour.

Most of the work was agreeable. Apricots simmering in a heavy copper kettle smell sweeter to me than roses. Firm cherries and plums, softened slowly in hot juices, are delightful. And tasks change. Now slicing, next stirring, now straining, maybe sun-drying. In the sun I moved slowly, my face upturned.

While we worked, Aunt Maxime and Heranoush would start us singing or we talked about the children, no matter whether birth child, niece or nephew. Mostly we praised them, even Arsen. We loved planning games and outings. Time passed pleasantly unless Matriarch was there.

Mother-in-law never let a task be. She liked to cut in, instruct you, find faults. She called you over, grabbed the paring knife from your hand and showed you her way of using it, her knobby fingers bent out from the handle like grasshopper legs. If the pitcher dripped, your pouring was wrong, just watch how she did it, so... She set herself on a stool with her knitting and gave one order after another. *Bring this. Put that aside.* Even Aunt Zabel and Aunt Maxime with their half-gray hair had to serve her.

Toumia was hardest on the girls. Her scolding gave Heranoush stomach pains, though the old witch said she imagined them. Sometimes I took the girl a cup of thinned yogurt as comfort before Matriarch's next task.

When she asked, "How's your weaving?" you felt like a mule getting kicked to go faster. If you finished your looming, she found a brass coffer for you to polish, a quilt to mend. At least we had Verkin and Ephraim for chamber pots, shoes and stable.

As a bride I ached for my family and Varti without hope, until I found a way to get around old Toumia. My mother had a real backache the first time, and then I came up with more. Or I used my nephews' name days. Another time I must teach my niece Gavnee certain stitches of Toumia's. I was careful not to overuse such flattery.

I think Petros caught on, though he didn't interfere. He saw how the outings softened my mouth and warmed his bed. Best not to talk of me fooling his mother.

I understood Aunt Maxime longing for her nephews in Constantinople although she'd two grandsons here to mother. I loved my husband and children yet I still needed to see my mother and sisters and Varti. One family shouldn't have to be all there is.

"Look, Heranoush, at the big load that little donkey has to carry!" I was excited and happy as I watched my husband and Sako striding ahead with their men's strong backs. My daughter's eyes were on her feet, sharp for a stray tassel. I had the habit, too.

A water carrier hurried past, his twin jugs bobbing from their pole. We moved aside, taking care not to step in waste. I pulled at my daughter's shawl to hide her pretty face. "Mother, I can't wait to sing Reba and Zeput my new song... I wish they lived next door!"

"And if wishes were horses..." Before I could catch it, one of Toumia's sayings. My daughter scowled, annoyed. She hated teasing—only Sako was allowed. All the youngsters adored his playful ways, starting with toddling Krikor on up to Astghig, now 14. Leave out Sarah's infant—he knew nothing but his mother's breast.

A stranger seeing Patriarch's four sons in a crowd easily picks Sako and Petros for brothers. The two were built alike and they crossed a room with the same quick steps. They shared the long Kavafian nose and bushy brows. Both were partway bald, well built and strong. Even handsome, Henza and I agreed about this! Martiros was taller and broader in shoulders, with a wider mouth and an eyebrow that went up when he talked. He liked to talk, one reason people used to mistake him for the oldest. Long before that job fell to him, he was telling others what to do. It was his nature, he even bossed his older brother sometimes. Sako didn't seem to mind—he got along with almost everybody.

Anyone seeing Toumia bend to Sako could tell he was born first. Whoever cooked his favorite foods, she made sure her hands served them. His shirts must look fresh or get passed to a younger brother. Poor Miron with his blinking, maybe his eyes were fighting envy. His bulk made him slow-moving and shy. So unlike the others, so lacking backbone. Nagged by Toumia, nagged by Sarah. He never said much, though his fine deep singing drowned the other voices when we walked mountain paths in summer.

I watched my husband walk arm-in-arm with Sako and wondered what matters filled the air between them. For as long as I knew, the two were fond friends, easy together, each ready to help the other. Like now, this escort duty.

A misunderstanding came about it still chokes me to remember. Just before Sako and Henza's wedding, Petros mistook a moment shared by Sako and me. Dumb foolishness!

It was late, and dark. I was leaving the outhouse when I noticed a man standing by the gate. His face was turned, but moonlight showed me it was Sako. Gripping my shawl tight, I walked over to say I was happy for him, and how glad I was about Henzanant joining our household. He replied with pain in his voice, how Dela and their girls must forgive him. "It's wrong to remarry, I know it!" he said. I saw tears shining.

"You're wrong, dear brother, it's God's will you marry again. The living must live," I told him.

"I fear…they deserved a better husband, a better father. I spent too little time with them."

"You did as well as any man. You were a good father and husband."

"I loved them."

"They knew. They know you love them forever. Forever and always, Sako. Just the same, dear brother, three years mourning is enough," I told him. I wanted to help him push away the past. "Now our Father in Heaven is giving you and Henzanant His blessing. He wants you both to live again. It's time."

Tears slid down his cheeks. Tender feelings filled me, as any woman feels for a brother at such a moment. When he was calm again, I reached up with my fingers to wipe the wetness from his face. He took my hand and pressed it on his lips.

"Thank you, dear sister Marjan. You've given me comfort beyond all measure," he said. Sako was still holding my hand when a shout came from the kitchen doorway.

"Marjan, come here!" It was Petros. "What were you doing there in the dark? Why were you with my brother?" He held a fist up as if he might knock me down, then let it drop. He was on fire with rage. I kept trying to explain, but he didn't listen—instead he grabbed my arm so hard he bruised me.

"Don't be angry with your wife, Petros, she's given comfort to a troubled bridegroom," Sako told him. But my husband held onto his jealousy like bitter sumac under his tongue. Not until the third day of celebration did he show me any small affection. He made me suffer for doing nothing wrong.

When Petros is ill-humored, I wish I was born a male and not a female, along with other foolish thoughts. I grieve for my daughter, I want to sleep and not wake up. I remind myself Petros is kinder than most men in this world. He's been good to me more than not. And I thank God he's better tempered than his parents.

Watching for tassels meant my daughter and I sometimes missed other things. An oxcart carrying twin kids and their nanny passed. "Look how their legs wobble, the kids are so cute, Mama! They aren't going to the butcher, are they?" I was glad she didn't wait for me to answer.

"…Oh, look at the boy with the pony!" The outing was good for her. We only got out for church that fall, and maybe twice to the baths.

We were passing ruins a good mile from home when a boy ran out and stood in our way. His size made me think of Vagram but his face wanted scrubbing. His jabber made no sense until I caught the words, "Bread! Please, bread!" and later, "Christian lady!" Pleading.

His feet were bare, pants torn, shirt thin and filthy. A chicken-liver sore oozed on his throat. He panted his plea again, pulling at my hands. Beyond him a bunch of ragged refugees squatted in the rubble. They seemed pinned into place, barely alive. How could this lively child belong with them? I felt ashamed of my warm cape, my wool dress, my well-fed stomach. Ashamed of flinching like a Persian princess when he touched my arm with his dirty hands. I was ashamed of wanting to run away. I didn't breathe until our sturdy escorts turned back. Sako asked the boy questions, then handed him a few tin coins to buy bread. The boy ran crowing to his group, jumping over wall-stones like a kid.

"Mousagh! Remember your manners, say thank you!" Sako called after him like a good-natured uncle. He was smiling as he explained, "A Muslim name, the little liar, claiming to be Christian! Not that it matters—they're starving."

"I couldn't understand him."

"He's from one of those rock-rich, one-tree villages on the plains, I've heard the dialect before. He's started picking up Erzerum Turkish," Sako said. "The boy tells a sad story. Hamidieh killed his father. They stole their sheep and all they owned."

"Couldn't his family...?"

"The village was burned. So they came here. Those who survived."

"It's awful!" I said.

"You can't tell the Christian beggars from the Muslims, half the time," said my husband. "One will beg you, if he sees your cross, 'Please, alms for a starving Christian,' and he'll tell the next person, 'Please, alms for a starving Muslim.' They're shameless, you can't trust –"

"You can't really blame them for it, Father." Sometimes Heranoush showed wisdom beyond her years and I'd forget she was half child. That same morning, Artashes set her sobbing by calling her too dumb for school.

"Brothers always say these things. Pretend you've no ears," I told her, and got only a sigh. Then Henza, blessed bride, drew her aside and somehow made her giggle.

It was only five months since Sako brought Henza to our house, but already I loved her. Each night at prayers I thanked the Almighty for His gift.

Talk slowed our feet. A pair of soldiers swaggered past, crying out a crude insult that made me flush. Heranoush and I pretended we were deaf. We walked faster, eyes down, her fingers warm through my sleeve. My temples throbbed and the next minute I wanted to weep for Petros and Sako, imagining their shame. Yet all Petros said about it later was, "It's nothing. Words can't hurt us."

We went on quickly around the garrison, saying little. We passed soldiers on patrol three times and heard no insults, saw beggars but didn't stop. When at last we reached my mother's little house, I said a quick prayer of thanks. It seemed a long time since we met the beggar-boy Mousagh.

The men left us at my mother's door. They'd a good way still to the bazaar. Their route home from there would make a sort of triangle.

Most everyone we knew lived in the Armenian neighborhood under the west and north walls of the garrison. My sister Nora lived on the next street south, my other sister about three streets further, toward the bazaar. My friend Varti lived not far from Zari at the edge of the quarter, up the street from the holy grave of the wet-nurse St. Barkevadu. We girls were happy growing up there. The world seemed a safe place for Armenians, most of the time.

Our news upset my Mother. "You can't be making new dresses to wear when others are hungry!" Her words surprised me and made no sense. There are always beggars. It wasn't good for her to live alone, she was getting things mixed up.

Mother seldom went out any more. One of my sisters came every morning and brought what she needed. She refused to come live with any of us. "I'm not lonely, I like my kitchen to myself!" was all she'd say about it.

Nora said Mother was smart to live by herself. "Once the boys get home, it's all noise and confusion! It gives Sempad headaches," she said. Between Sempad and his brother there were nine boys in the Halebian household. Mother would need cut fleece around her ears.

Mother knew she'd be unhappy living at my house under Toumia. My younger sister's home was no better. Zari kept pressing our mother to move in with them, but who'd choose to live with such a difficult son-in-law? Zari supposed her husband's hand would lighten with Mother there, though I thought, if his own mother can't calm Asadur, how can ours? He seemed to dislike females, even his two daughters. Maybe he'd change if a son was born, maybe not. "We both bear crosses on our shoulders," I used to tell Zari. "You have Asadur, I have Toumia."

Heranoush longed to be with her friends one minute, the next minute wanted to live alone like her grandmother. "Her life's so nice and peaceful," she gasped when we were half-way to Nora's. We were almost running to keep up with the Halebians' crane-legged house-boy and I was too short of breath to answer. "I wish..." She began. "It would be wonderful to eat lunch at the Meserians' instead of Aunt Nora's."

"It would break Gavnee's heart." Zari's elder daughter was a quiet nine-year-old who glowed when she looked at Heranoush. Her right eye sometimes drifted. Gavnee's sister Zevart was five and still clung to her mother.

"I'm not even hungry."

"Me neither, after your grandmother's boreg. They'll be happy to see us, just the same."

And they were. Nora delighted Heranoush with a red silk tassel cut from an old tablecloth. We sat gossiping and laughing about nothing important, until Zari asked after Aunt Maxime. In a cat's blink, the mood changed. Forgetting small ears, we started on rumors and frightened the girls without thinking. Seeing their pale faces, I took the next pause to tell about our neighbor riding to Trabizond. We were all glad for easier matters. We talked of the mountains and snowstorms, remembering differently the worst ones, and which summers had the prettiest flowers. Before I left, we fixed on a sledding trip with all the children at the first good snow. I was joyful, knowing Toumia wouldn't interfere where so many took part.

When Varti and I were growing up we planned our children's wedding, the way young girlfriends do. Her son, my daughter, or my son, her daughter—we weren't fussy with our matchmaking. It was only wishing in the wind, for God in His wisdom gave us daughters before sons. Yet He also gave her twin nieces as a way to join our families.

We matched Artashes sometimes with Rebecca, sometimes Zeput, and even both, once they all converted to Islam!! We'd be silly as half-wits together. Her big house with its fine elbow-courtyard had private places where we could talk about anything. Her family was smaller than ours. Like most.

Varti was more mother than aunt to the twins. Their mother had kept to her bed for many years with imagined ills and voices. A sad thing for their father, with less than half a wife. Yet he was proud and loving of his daughters and they seemed to love him, their mother and their aunt as much as any parents are loved. They were happy girls, full of good spirits. Varti and I rejoiced at their friendship with Heranoush.

We watched the three girls shriek and take hands and skip laughing through the Meserians' garden. "Your nieces are graceful as does," I said.

I told her how Heranoush was getting stomachaches. I'd need to explain to Sara or Yiri, but Varti understood without me saying. "I hope we're doing right, keeping them home."

"Let's hope we're doing wrong and worrying over nothing! Do you know what worries me? It's the way I love Reba and Zeput just as much as I love Marta and the boys." Her daughter Marta was three years older than Heranoush. Her Souren was born a year before my Vagram and her Rupen came soon after.

"Why not? They need you just as much, love you just as much as daughters! You know this!"

The frown left Varti's forehead. I went on boldly. "Hear my confession! Sometimes I want my father-in-law to pass on so Sako can be head of the family!"

"It's allowed, so long as you don't wish it out loud! You know this!"

We were sitting beside a fountain edged with tiny tiles that told the story of the loaves and fishes. We told stories of our own. A bit later, our girls lined up in front of us and sang "Frere Jacques" in a round from school. We clapped.

"Sing more, lovely songbirds!" Varti said. I whispered that I was glad for the change from war games. She laughed and answered, "Girls are too smart for war games!"

Heranoush started begging again for an oud. "I could play for the children!—and the refugees, I can teach them songs! I can help Aunt Maxime stay on tune!"

The twins took up her plea. "Please let her get an oud! Heranoush is so musical!"

"An oud means lessons," I warned.

"And practice," added Varti.

"I want lessons! I'll practice! Please!" from my songbird.

"We'll see what your father says." Petros would agree if Vagram's schoolmaster was her teacher. Matriarch no longer complained about our daughter's singing, it was so rare now.

"Let's teach the little ones Frere Jacques!" said Zeput. She was the liveliest and usually led the three though Heranoush was sixteen months older. I remember thinking Zeput would make a fine teacher when she finished school, if she could stay unmarried. Unlikely, given her looks.

Rebecca was just as pretty when she smiled. Like Heranoush, she'd rather read than sew. I was the same at their age. I taught myself to read from my uncle's schoolbook. When I nagged Heranoush to finish a quilt for her wedding chest, I heard my mother speaking, like the echo at Tort'um cave. Some 12- and 13-year-old girls may love quilting, but they aren't in Varti's family or mine. "I'll sew tomorrow!" was what we heard.

"Tell me, Reba and Zeput, how are your quilts coming? Anything finished yet?"

"I won't need quilts, I'm going to marry a famous pianist who gives concerts all over Europe. We'll live in hotels!" said Zeput.

"And I'm going to marry a famous scientist and live in Athens where it's warm all year," said her twin. They giggled.

We waited for Heranoush. "I'm going to marry…" she began.

Zeput burst out, "Your Uncle Sako! You say he's perfect!"

"He's too old!" My daughter blushed. "Besides, he's already married."

"You should marry Dajag Shabanian, he's the smartest boy in Sanasarian! And he's handsome!"

"I'm not going to marry anyone!"

The girls ran off hand in hand, laughing. "They have it all ahead of them," I said. "Growing up, getting married…"

"Getting married, growing up…"

"Mothers in law…"

"Fathers in law…" Hers was short-tempered with children.

"Sisters in law…"

"Childbirth." Varti grew thoughtful. She smiled in a sad way and said, "Families and friends. Especially best friends. Forever." It was part of an old pledge between us.

"Forever." We hugged, eyes wet with looking back. Then, hearing warbles from another room, we went to find our girls.

Doing chores the next morning, I kept smiling, recalling our visits. I made a silent promise to stay cheerful, no matter what rumors came home or what Sour Tongue Toumia demanded. But of course it wasn't that simple.

Hamed's Journey

❋ · ❋ · ❋ · ❋ · ❋ · ❋ · ❋ · ❋ · ❋

Hamed   late September – early October, 1895

Nothing outside Paradise can attain perfection. Yet it was unmarred pleasure from Erzerum to Baiburt, despite stretches too steep to ride. We barely stopped to water our horses that first day. Whatever banter we managed was dead by the time we made camp near Kop, high on Kop Dagh. We spent maybe two minutes star gazing before talk ceased. I recall thinking the Germans might enjoy Ilidja's hot springs if the skies held clear for our return.

We started our descent early, through a wooded cut into Baiburt. Soon bells signaled a caravan. The sounds came at us deep-toned first, then mixed with jangling, tinkling noises—a concert of close and distant notes. We began overtaking heavy-laden camels: packs of seven, each led by a drover, another at the tail—an endless procession of beasts and men moving steadily forward through light rain.

The caravan claimed the trail ahead as far as we could see. An hour earlier would have meant frustration. Being stuck behind a line of small-brained camels on a narrow mountain path is true misery, made worse by the way they move: slow, ungainly and impossibly ugly from the rear. Yet at a distance they remind me of the sea, their motion as perfect as birch trees in wind.

From the Baiburt citadel ramparts, we watched them reach the caravansary. One of my troop counted 650 camels, perhaps 800 animals all told—a bestial army.

Passing the caravansary, a sickening smell made me doubly glad for different trails to the seaport. I saw one desert mule forced to kneel by shouts, tugs, slaps, sticks and curses as two Arabs struggled with a loose crate and a white-beard tied barrel to pallet. A wheezing, runny-eyed drover explained their cargo: dried fruits, goatskins, fleece and linen. From Trabizond harbor it would go to Germany. He was well informed for a camel-drover—he even named a Berlin bank. His hide was black, an African.

A fair road eased our ascent from the valley until colder air brought stretches of hoof-deep slush. We slogged through Khadrack, a hamlet offering fetid subterranean hostelry and fine, broad views to the Paryadres Mountains. Patchy snow and ice surrounded us now, our beasts advancing easily. The stream was hard-frozen, so we avoided the worm-eaten bridge at Murad-Khaneh. Allah o Akbar! That thing collapsed a few weeks later, tossing a horse and rider into fatal flight.

Where the road levels out north of the stream we came upon our former tenants. The woman was cooking their noon meal. She looked up in fear at my approach and I glimpsed a red, swollen nose before she veiled. The boy shouted, "It's the Captain!" His father scrambled to his feet and trotted toward me. I was ready to refuse him money, but Topol asked only for bulgur and I'd plenty in my saddlebag. His hands as he held up the bowl were steady, his eyes nearly clear and without ill will.

Topol grinned at learning our destination. "My cloth should get a good price in Trabizond, they'll see it's not that cheap English stuff," he told me. I wished him success and meant it, aware that a few days outdoors could not transform him to a salesman. Still, his merchandise ought to buy their return to Gebizeh. His family would rejoice to have their grandchildren back, whatever they felt when Topol left. His wife's situation was sure to improve in a larger household.

My thoughts turned to my mother. Her habitual kindliness had been overcome by complaints and I hoped her grandchildren still felt affection for her. She'd not want to be remembered at her worst. If I end up an invalid—a risk soldiers take—I pray not to be self-absorbed.

The trail became icy for difficult miles. We trotted where possible to make up time, so that one horse stumbled descending a gully and pitched his rider. No injury, but a warning against hurry. Speed and safety are poor friends, as sit-at-homes like to remind us.

Our urgent pace was rewarded that night with crisp air and bright star-fields, good appetites and easy sleep. The final day, we pushed through Zigana Pass and north to the ridge, little noticing the scenery. We climbed hard before sighting the vast grey sea.

We reached Trabizond garrison shortly past dark and worn by three long days' riding. Stable boys competed to help me dismount: was this for the honor of stabling Keyif or for the few piastres? Either way, they knew us—and were quick to report their news.

"Did you hear? There's been fighting in Constantinople! Revolutionaries killed!" said one, stumble-tongued by the long words.

"Our Sultan was saved!" exclaimed the other. The two babbled together nonsensically and I shut up one so his smarter comrade could tell the story.

It seemed typical barracks rumor: mere hearsay passed from a sergeant who'd overheard two officers, their source possibly reputable and possibly not. My mind was on the excellent bathhouse down the hill. Nothing is more gratifying after hard mountain trails. We proceeded there promptly, grateful our weight was on our feet, not our saddles. Afterwards, much refreshed, we moved on to Trabizond's abundant pleasures.

Aristo's is my favorite Trabizond café. Best not ask much in a thriving port beyond digestible food and lively music, a decent class of clientele, and a reasonably friendly proprietor. Aristo was an affable man generally, yet bigoted and a rumor-monger. When offended, he was ill-tempered. On the other hand, he was invariably congenial to Shakir, treating him in a natural way, without regard to his disfigurement. He kept watch on both help and customers, blocking provocations and brawling. Many times I saw him throw rowdy sailors headlong into the muck-thick street, one after another.

Aristo welcomed us with his usual cordial shout, setting out glasses and a bottle of Greek wine, bread and olives. It's pleasant to be treated like old friends, even if we're simply good for business. Officers in a café attract civilians, strangers venture in—and we also spend more freely, a distance from home. Having once owned a café, Father taught me to see beyond welcoming smiles.

"You've gotten thin, have you been ill?" My teasing provoked a laughing roar along with a heavy slap on my back from Aristo's massive right hand.

"Sick as an Arab sailor!" Many laughs rose from my men. We always enjoyed ourselves at that café, glad to mix hearty food and drink with easy banter.

The night started out as well as any. We soon finished a third bottle and mopped our gravy, when Aristo produced a bottle of anisette. "For you young lions, may you triumph over your enemies," he cried.

We raised our glasses, laughing and calling out, "To the lions!" Soldiers enjoy thinking they're heroes, yet an awful scene from ancient Rome lit my head.

"You must drink a glass with us," said my first lieutenant, his eyes shining and his face flushed from unaccustomed wine. Shakir knew when to be serious and when to enjoy living. Sometimes I forgot he was eight years younger, for his judgment at 27 surpassed that of many older officers.

I counted on Shakir more and more. Where another junior officer first assesses his prospects, he considered honestly; he was a fine horseman as well. I planned to recommend a promotion, for some day he'd want his own command.

Aristo signaled for another glass, calling out, "To the destruction of our enemies, Sultan Abdul Hamid's enemies, one and the same! May they vanish from the earth!" Others toast this way to impress spies, yet Aristo seemed sincere. Hearing the Sultan's name, I asked his news of Constantinople. Our host now became an actor strutting beside our table.

"The stinking Armenians tried rising up and got beaten up and beaten down! The police sent them scurrying like sheep—what they are IS sheep!" He bleated, laughing at his own wit.

Glancing about uneasily, I saw no Armenians wearing their provincial headgear. At one table, western trousers worn by men whose Turkish held the sharp accent of Trabizond. It was impossible to tell whether city men are our race or another.

Aristo pulled a chair beside mine and settled his bulging hind quarters, his contented sigh slapping our noses with garlic. Our guts were gassy with it already.

His face sparkled with glee and sweat as he related how Armenian conspirators tried to destroy the government. This very day in Constantinople—incredible! A mob attacked the palace but was swiftly routed, the perpetrators killed: no further details. His story echoed the stable boys', else I'd have dismissed it. Now I'd wait and weigh.

Aristo swore on his improbable tale: true! unembellished! straight from someone who knew someone in the telegraph office.

That Greek took a boy's delight in rumors of murders and misery. Such tales thrive around a waterfront. He'd dress a pickpocket's words as a governor's announcement and finally believe it himself, its source forgotten. Stories demeaning Circassians, Yezedis, Armenians or Europeans, he liked most.

It's discouraging to hear such prejudices from a Greek, as if he was a Muslim Ottoman. A small man resided within that overlarge body. In any event, fatigue drew me to the garrison ahead of the younger men. A few—among them Shakir—made visits that evening to women. His was respectable and he didn't talk about her. I gathered they cared for one another, for Shakir was always glad to go to Trabizond and always sorry to leave.

No more rumors of Constantinople came my way that evening and I slept well before visiting the mosque. Outside in the morning, examining trinkets on a blanket, I overheard a copper merchant tell a story like Aristo's. His supposed source was a telegram from the capital. Now my interest in trinkets was replaced by unease.

I feared it augured badly for Armenians in Erzerum province. Already, Abdul Hamid was mistrustful—with cause. Certain Armenians safely distant in Moscow and Paris had been agitating for a separate Armenian province, to be carved from our eastern provinces! This treasonable and absurd concept was being spread throughout the Armenian millet. Spies kept our officials informed.

Now this, now that incident was creating mistrust. Other minorities were sometimes involved, but most often Armenians. One recent case: Sassun village refused to pay taxes. Raided by Kurds and left starving, the village asked for government protection. It was blind to necessity: how can authority overlook taxes? This Sultan was never known to bargain—especially, not about his Treasury. Sassun was duly decimated.

Since then, fear spread among our minorities in the eastern provinces: not only Armenians—also Greeks and Jews, who displayed their loyalty like captive brides. How could Armenians forget their lesson so soon, and in the Sultan's home city?! If rumors were true, I pitied them.

One heard reliable whispers that the Sultan was mad, imagining brigands lurking in cupboards, eating nothing before his taster. Whispers that the Sultan banished or hanged his best ministers on whim, was moody, vindictive, and frightened by wind-gusts. It was said he carried a pistol despite guards everywhere, and one morning shot a gardener walking towards him, like a horse who startles and bucks at a waving banner—that same poor fellow tended the Palace rose beds every day! Hearing these rumors, I prayed for our exalted ruler to find wise guidance. Unless he learned to sort innocents from devils, Constantinople's Armenians were doomed like Sassun's.

※　※　※

The commandant was now thinner, but still held himself like a cannon aimed skyward. He expounded on the merits of Berlin's Imperial Officers Military College, where we both trained.

Next, he turned to my mission. He insisted our profitable relations with Germany were risky and depended on the Consul's safe arrival at Erzerum.

"You'll need spare horses, good rifles and dry ammunition. Take extra fuel in case the khans run out." As if I lacked experience. With fresh interest he added, "You should stay tomorrow afternoon. Greet Bahri Pasha at the troop review. Know him?"

"I had the honor when he was governor of Van. Regrettably, my orders deny this opportunity. They require the swiftest possible return."

He grunted, distracted. Two telegrams topped a stack of papers on his desk. He followed my glance. "A military situation has arisen in Constantinople. A rebellion by Armenian traitors. Already executed, or about to be. Death to traitors!"

"Death to traitors!" My echo almost matched his fervor. He dismissed me with parting words that made sense only later.

"We may have a bit of action here soon. Too bad you'll miss it."

The commandant saluted, ending the interview. Throughout, he never softened his jaw or posture, and I'd shadowed his stance, mindlessly stiffening my back and shoulders. I stayed a carved wood soldier to the stairs. There I finally flexed knees, spine and elbows, to become a normal man again. Even a German-schooled officer must let himself bend, descending stairs.

Trabizond consulates stand near the main square. I easily located the German building, then met both consuls. Erzerum's new consul was a rosy-faced, cheerful man, as unlike the usual board-backed German as a ripe fig from a rock. He presented me immediately with a fine German harmonica in a red plush case, reciting a verse extolling music's beneficial effects on the mind. The Erzerum consul was undeterred by my ignorance of harmonica-playing and offered to instruct me on our journey. I felt the gift augured a pleasant trip ahead.

I never anticipated Consul Behrmann's female trio, each as yellow-haired and light-browed as the other. The wife's young sister was pretty enough, round of face and bosom. The wife was bony-jawed and altogether too thin, her shoulders sharp, with hands always waving about as she talked. The child's misfortune was to resemble mother more than aunt. Behrmann said they celebrated her sixth birthday on the train from Berlin.

Because little Heidi was tall, we expected her to act older than she could. The girl was too young for the trip and too indulged. She caused difficulties both directly and indirectly, yet I grew fond of her.

Less leggy children often ride in horse baskets balanced on either side, truly uncongenial travel except for infants. Worse still is the tachtravan, rare now even for invalids: the victim rests inside a narrow box that's slung on poles between two horses. It's almost impossible to maneuver—and terrifying on steep trails and switchbacks.

Once the females retreated, I advised the consul that a sure-footed pony would be better for the child, far safer than sharing a horse. Also, I remembered my Ehsan's delight riding his own pony before he grew too big. Thankfully, the consul agreed.

"Take plenty of blankets. It's already October," Behrmann's host said. He seemed a nervous sort, one of those Europeans with three steamer trunks of heavy clothes and bedding, even in July. Goose down comforters were some place unknown within the Behrmann's luggage, so they'd buy blankets for the trip. That decision was smarter than they knew, as blankets are more easily cleansed of fleas.

"In that case the Consul must purchase extra pack animals," I said, in futile hope of diminishing my service as guide, interpreter and animal-trader for Behrmann. His Turkish was no better than my German.

We examined many animals before selecting a calm-mannered pony, three strong horses and six pack mules, three of them for the women's trunks alone. My knowing the livestock traders proved helpful. As my father says, first find an honest seller, then study the goods. Next find a price that satisfies both parties: neither should bear regret.

Next I proceeded with gifts for my family. A favorite mule-trader pulled me to his brother's stall, where I bought my mother a carved rose of redwood.

Frau Behrmann and her sister joined us at a well-known woolens shop. They bought gloves, socks, under-garments and scarves. The proprietor was a short, swarthy Armenian with broken front teeth and a large household to support. His family was likely slaves to their spindles and needles. Whoever made each muffler or mitten, he identified, "My nephew Gorba's pattern" or "My girl Risima's work." I lost count after the fifteenth name.

Frau Behrmann asked later, "Do Armenians always have large families working for them?" I thought of Martiros' sizable household (were there twenty-five? perhaps twenty-eight, with the latest babies) and told her they liked to live together if circumstances allowed, whether or not their labors were required. It's much the same for us.

It's simpler to buy mittens than horses—haggling was brief, delivery easily arranged. We still required candles, blankets and various foodstuffs, so I hurried the Germans along. The shopkeeper caught my sleeve.

"A pair of warm gloves for you, Captain. The best in the city, knit by my wife herself. For a distinguished officer of the Sultan's great Fourth Army. A gift from a loyal subject of the great Sultan Abdul Hamid."

He refused payment until I said, "Thank your wife for knitting these fine gloves. Buy some sweetmeats for her," and pressed a 20-piastre piece into his hand. "May you and your family prosper." To showed I understood his fear, I added, "A long distance separates Trabizond from Constantinople."

"Perhaps. I hope so. I pray to God it's distance enough." The capital was perhaps a thousand miles away, it was unreasonable for Trabizond's Armenians to be alarmed, yet his face wore deep worry.

Unveiled European women were not unusual on Trabizond's streets, for many ships dock there, yet they always distracted me. Who'd want to shepherd two unveiled ladies around a city's bazaar? Whether veiled or unveiled, a woman takes too long deciding.

Experience has taught me that traveling females extend preparations, require undue comforts and prolong the journey. The wife's insistence on some purchases proved fortunate, however, despite delaying us.

Some visit Trabizond only for special sights, its ancient holy places as well as extraordinary sea views. Provisioning done, I excused myself. Mistakenly, I mentioned my plans to see the Fatih and the Gulbahar Hatun Mosque, near the citadel, and perhaps also the Great Mosque on the outskirts.

Solitary sight-seeing allows contemplation: the sweep of time, the vagaries of war, what qualities separate men from horses and sheep, women and one another—if any do.

Without consulting her husband, Frau Behrmann said, "Such a delightful idea! Don't you agree, Gustav?" She asked their host, "You'll come with us, won't you, Herr Consul?" I'd no way to refuse her, as I wanted.

So we went together to the Fatih, she talking freely as we walked. Her manners appalled me and I hardly tried to understand her. She finally stilled her tongue, at my request, entering the mosque.

It was not the restful, meditative afternoon I sought, to clear my head for the trip back, yet we did look down on the sea from the hills. Our excursion helped me decline the woman's invitation to dinner. It surprised me she left none of these formalities to her host: other European women are more feminine.

Rumors concerning Constantinople were spreading fast, most barely credible. By sunset, Trabizond teemed with excited hearsay from cafes to citadel, from hilltop to waterfront. The few Armenians in sight looked fearful. The woolens-shopkeeper's face woke me in the night.

After morning prayers, the Plaza thickened with loiterers. The *Trabizond Gazette*'s front page saluted their whispers, proclaiming that armed Armenian revolutionaries had besieged Bab Ali Palace and murdered a mounted officer in their way. Sadly, I recognized his name: Major Server Bey. That distinguished officer reviewed my class at military college. Premature death is one risk of this career, as students are always warned. The circumstances were shocking, nonetheless, for the Palace was heavily guarded and not where a major expects to die.

His assassins had been felled at once. Police and cavalry routed the Armenians, pursued traitors through their quarters, flushing every niche. More arrests were underway and anyone guilty would be punished. Our government was in control.

Armenians in the capital must be numb with terror. I recalled an acquaintance from college days, a relative of Martiros who worked in the public debt ministry, had sons in school, would never join a mob. He and his family should be safe.

When Shakir read the account his expression changed. "It could be bad for my friend here," he said. Beyond that only, "Her name's Rosa and her lips match her name. Ask no more, for I'll not say!"

The Consul's family was not ready after breakfast. A travel pass needed revision, the women must buy a few things, a horse required fresh shoe nails. Inconveniences bombard travel in company, military or civilian. Added to my agitation from the newspaper, these delays annoyed me unduly. I thought longingly of my pliant Khadija and the order of my life at home.

We finally started out just before noon. In the main square a loud hail delayed me again, and who should run alongside Keyif but Topol!

"Cap'n, before you go, I need your help!" Panting, he grasped at my foot in the stirrup. I signaled Shakir into the lead. Topol's son waited nearby with a laden mule, dancing to show off his sandals while his father regaled me.

He'd met no great problem since our meeting on the trail, yet Topol was now panic-ridden lest his money run out before getting home. He'd sold a single bolt of cloth, was paid only half its worth by a tight-fisted Armenian, his words. He was too discouraged to continue: true to character.

"You've plenty of time before the boat sails. You should get a fair price for what's left," I told him, with poorly controlled impatience. I reminded him the mules would bring a decent amount, providing he fed and rested them properly, and I named two honest mule traders. My advice set him whining about the costs of feed grain, his family's food and shelter. Setting my principles aside, I offered a loan—and handed him two gold lira, an over-generous sum, simply to be rid of him

"As Allah is great, I'll pay you back!" He tied the pieces into a crumpled handkerchief and slid this into his shirt. He reached for my hand to kiss it. I drew back.

"I must catch up with my party," I said.

"Wait!" He pulled a length of woven wool from the pack mule and thrust it into my hands. "A gift for your wife. A lovely color. Mauve."

The encounter left me uneasy, less from two lira lost than from his manner. He was not only excited, but seemed to expect us to meet again. An unreasonable premonition lingered, bothersome as a spider bite.

Hay Carriers

Martiros   early October 1895

I'd say their fate was an early omen. The hay carriers reached our shop late, the sun almost touching Mt. Kohanam, the faithful gathering beside the mosque. That sentry at Olti gate kept them two hours because he could, for flies relish biting. The two would get home well after dark.

I was relieved to see them. You're never sure with new arrangements, and it was two weeks since I'd made them. Between the army's growing appetite and recent depredations, hay was getting scarce, so you must take it when you could.

Father had me guide instead of an apprentice, for our work was almost done. I was glad to leave, as I like getting home before the others, to have some minutes at ease before the evening prayers and meal. A businessman needs to weigh events and plan ahead, even in normal times. Already I doubted these times were normal.

I led the pair the shortest way, striding briskly past the dry goods and iron mongers' shops, between the cafes near the big mosque, along Iron Street. I could tell from the dark woven head cloths they were Armenians born to a particular village on the nearby plains. Their mirrored features—high cheekbones, narrow foreheads, deep-set black eyes—marked them as father and son. One face was wrinkled and gray-bearded, but from neck down, their bodies could be switched with no one wiser. Both equally lean, thick-necked and hard-muscled. Bodies meant for work, not rest.

Peasants must of necessity be strong, but the hay got heavy for them once we passed the American Mission and began the long climb up Customs Street. When the old man fell too far behind, I shortened my pace. Even the young one was panting, dripping sweat below his headband, by the time I pounded the gate. They waited bent and motionless, staffs forced into the ground by the weight of the hay. Patient as mules. Finally my nephew Artashes put eye to gate hole and slid the bolt.

Arsen ran over, other youngsters trailing. "Papa, I've captured three prisoners!" he bragged. Then he shouted at them, "Go back to jail, infidels!" His grandfather wouldn't have let that word by but I still remember how boys like showing off. It pleased me to see my older boy playing well with the young ones.

"Go tell Shapundi his hay's here!" I told the children. They raced to find the mule, nearly knocking the carriers off their feet.

"Take care, boys!" one of my sisters-in-law called out. "The men have heavy burdens."

The children were circling the mule, hopping with excitement as the carriers set their hay in the stable. My brother Petros' wife Marjan brought out food and a water bowl for washing.

"Bless your kindness and this meal. It's our first today," the old man said. He rinsed and dried his hands carefully. His son did the same.

"Christians must help Christians," I replied, using my father's expression.

"Some Christians do not do so," said the son. His tired face held lively eyes that suggested intelligence beyond his station.

They spoke no more until they'd cleaned the yogurt bowl with the last of the bread. Only as he ate did I notice the young man's crippled hand. Its clawed fingers seemed carved of stone—not ugly, but no more useful than a stick. I thought it accounted for the bitter edge to his voice.

His father nodded regretfully at the pasterma. "My teeth are too few for meat," he explained. I could see three on his bottom jaw and four above, only one paired to meet another.

I sent Marjan back for soup and more bread. "Tell matriarch it's my request," I told her. Mother watched our larder as if Russians still held the garrison. During those 14 months, only two caravans came through. There wasn't a sack of grain, much less a lamb or she-goat, to be bought, begged or stolen. Our hidden stores kept us and others alive that year, when thousands starved.

It was exciting for us children, with soldiers advancing and retreating right along our street. My brothers and I watched from the roof—until the day a bullet drilled Sako's cap. We had to stay inside after that, so Father put us to shoe-making to keep us out of trouble. I took readily to the business and this was my last year of school. A man learns plenty on the streets and can outsmart you, though he can barely write his name. I tell my sons to study so someday they can outsmart their rivals.

When the hay carriers were done eating, I saw the young man eyeing what was left on the tray. "For my wife and child?" he asked.

"May your sons be sturdy," I told him, the traditional blessing. We Kavafians were fortunate—our storage cellar was amply stocked. Many were hungry that autumn after a poor harvest and relentless raiding.

At my suggestion, they each put a few pieces of pasterma and bread inside their shirts. They divided the coins I paid and slipped them into the rags around their feet.

"We must hurry to cross the bridge before nightfall," the young man said.

"You'll make better time without that weight on your backs," I told him. I directed them towards the city's west gate, over the hill and around onto Customs Street, past the British consul's house and the Public Health building. From the west gate it was only half a mile to the bridge they must cross.

The route to their village went past an encampment of ruffians, mostly Circassians, on the far bank of the river. When we took the boys this way to fly kites at the monastery, we hired guards for safety. Even daytime could be risky on the roads beyond the city.

"Be careful passing the thieves' camp!" I warned them.

"I told my wife not to worry, we've strong poles to fend off dogs and robbers!" the young one replied with a confident smile.

"Just the same, walk quickly."

Artashes asked as they disappeared up the road, "Uncle, are Circs going to hurt them?"

"They'll be all right. Men that poor aren't prey to robbers," I told him. None of us realized how things were changing already for our people. I never thought to invite them to sleep in the stable and I doubt they'd have done so.

Rumors are like gutter stench in Erzerum, you wave them away. When the subject's distant, say in Constantinople, they last longer. Lately there'd been talk of Christians storming the Palace, a preposterous notion. I thought only lunatics would take on the Palace guard, because even nationalists have brains. It was kin to the tale about a ewe birthing a heifer—nonsense invented for imbeciles. Besides, the capital was farther away than Jerusalem, what went on there was small concern in Erzerum. I considered these good reasons to dismiss idle hearsay.

In short time I learned differently.

Our stable boy Ephraim brought us the grim news with next day's lunch. A soldier riding near the Circassian camp across the river came upon the remains of two laborers. Their skulls were crushed, their bodies stripped of clothing but for a bloodied headband on the younger man. Whose withered arm (this sent a chill through my lungs) was bent unnaturally behind his back.

"Filthy devils! Killing honest workers, for what? A few piastres? It makes me sick! What sort of human being murders harmless hay carriers?" Miron asked, indignant, his eyes blinking fast. As the youngest, he was protected longer from the outside world.

"Circs despise Armenians, that's reason enough," said Petros, our brother in between. He was generally more practical than the others. Of the four brothers, we two most often agreed, although he argued from reading history, while I learned from observation and analysis. His bitter tone surprised me.

"You sound like one of our Misery Armenians," I jabbed. Certain acquaintances railed endlessly on their hardships, oblivious to their good fortune, as if they dined on table scraps, not lamb and baklava.

"Hear me out, Martiros. Consider what people are saying, that Hunchaks tried to kill the Sultan…"

I interrupted. "Rumors. Senseless. Crazy. Totally untrue."

"Senseless or not doesn't matter! Since Sassun, every mischief gets blamed on Armenians, maybe Dashnaks or Hunchaks or Rumgevars or some other crazy idiots. The looks we catch on the street as if we're traitors! They hear ridiculous rumors and decide Armenians are enemies, no matter how loyal we are!"

My younger brother had to stop for breath. I saw something in him of our father, enraging himself like a flagellant. Petros lowered his voice so it nearly hissed. "It's a ready-made excuse for those Circ thugs to rob and murder…"

I came round to Petros' thinking as we talked. Whoever the murderers were, they figured Armenian peasants made good targets, killed them more for manly show than the paltry pickings. We sat in gloomy thought. I regretted not hiring a guard for the hay carriers' journey home, though such a thing was almost inconceivable. I know that should haves are best ignored.

At length I said, "We must find out what's happened in Constantinople. When Hamed returns, he can tell us –"

"The military version."

"You need wheat before you sort out chaff," I told him.

My good friend Hamed was due back any day. While I waited, I meant to ignore stories about Constantinople. Father used to say rumors are like rotten meat, bad even for dogs. The fate of our hay carriers was troubling enough.

Word of the murders rushed through the bazaar. Within the hour, the wood-carver Berj strutted self-importantly into the shop.

"You've heard? Armenians killed near the river! Penniless peasants, murdered for their rags!" Berj stood panting, his small eyes bulging beneath a shallow brow. His agitation made the fleshy wattles below his chin bounce and quiver, and his long beaked nose was yellow in the light. Poor homely man, he'd been called "Rooster" since a child. A girl with those looks shouldn't go to the baths, as they say. Fortunately his half-sister, our friend Krikor Shabanian's wife, looked nothing like him.

Rooster was elated I could add to his story, which he flew off to spread through the Armenian shops. With rumor mongers, bad news is a love potion that makes them fervent.

Minutes later, Sako's boss ran in, shouting for me. I was in the back room, teaching an apprentice to stretch boot leather.

"Martiros, since you saw the unfortunates last, tell me what you think caused their murder? Were they wearing new clothes?" the pharmacist demanded with his customary directness. "Well then, did they look weak?" he persisted, "Or simple?"

Once I replied, Khagorian wasted no time speculating. "Easy targets, that's what they were. Men armed with poles are no match for ruffians with knives. Even one could overpower them... Their misfortune was being Armenians in a dangerous place at a dangerous time." His smooth-shaved face took on a wry expression as he turned to leave. He paused at the curtain only long enough to say, "We must all be watchful." His tone sent another chill through my frame.

That evening our bishop stopped in, as he often did. It was our privilege to be the holy man's unofficial family during the two or three years he was in Erzerum. Any unmarried man of gregarious nature will be lonely, coming new to a city. Father took a liking to Bishop Shishmanian the first time he presided over St. Asdvadzadzin's lay council, invited him home and encouraged him to make us his family. We were honored—and in time, we Kavafians and the Bishop became genuine friends.

He relaxed with us. He courted the old women, teased the children, spent hours with us in amiable conversation and play. I'm certain he enjoyed himself. Nonetheless, the Bishop carried himself with dignity and authority, as suited his position. His bearing and full whiskers made him look older than his years. Most people were surprised that he was about my brother Sako's age, not yet past 40.

The Bishop turned from pleasantries to questions: were the hay carriers definitely Armenian? As provincial Bishop, he must oversee the welfare of the entire Christian millet within Erzerum province, from newborn peasant to dying pasha. If the hay carriers were Christian, he must write a report to the Catholicos in Jerusalem. I believe his concern went beyond his position, for he often reminded the Lay Council of its Christian duty to aid unfortunates. Father thought his advice was pointed at a few complacent Council members, yet he addressed them all. The Bishop was a man of great compassion.

On this particular visit, our Bishop spent a long half hour discoursing on the Lord's words, "as ye feed a little sparrow, so ye feed me," while our stomachs moaned for supper and children sneaked to the kitchen to tear bread. He declined our meal but was slow to go home to his own. Perhaps supping late added to my agitation, for I slept poorly, fretting in the dark about what befell the hay carriers and what I might have done to protect them. Guilt is like one of those rare night-blooming bulbs that requires attention. I was glad when daylight came.

The next day Father Ashod prayed for the souls of "the humble murdered laborers of our Millet" and the Bishop talked of God's love for the least among us. Leaving church, Marjan said it was sad none of us knew their names. "Our Almighty Father knows, that's what matters," Yiri replied, drawing little Yefkine into her arms while she spoke. Several acquaintances stopped me to ask about the hay carriers, unsure Berj had told it right.

Through the next week we waved the coffee vendor in so often that he grumbled, "Give me time to buy more beans, you've drunk me out!" Every Armenian we knew and many we didn't came asking about the hay carriers, seeking not gossip-fodder so much as reassurance. They wanted to hear the pair were careless, such fate avoidable. A few whispered of finding the killers. "We must retaliate! We must not let this go unavenged!"

I shrug at vain threats. The thing was hopeless unless the police acted. When a bird gives milk! For Muslim peasants, police might spend half an hour asking questions, half a day tracking their murderers—for penniless Christians, pretense at most.

Gathered in one or the other Armenian shop with no Muslim present, we puzzled matters over. We'd start out on the murders and soon be discussing Constantinople. Every hour brought another version of the trouble there and I doubted any was reliable.

Day by day the tales got bloodier: now mobs rampaging and burning, now blows and thrashings, now arrests and executions, now slaughters, until only Roman Catholics remained alive of the Armenian thousands in the capital. Father disparaged rumors, but after a week of this, even he feared something terrible had happened. Yet we knew nothing! We told the women the stories were foolishness. Some of my brothers must also have been wakeful, for I heard steps creak in the night.

Our first reliable informant was the mayor's aide Abdi, who knew whatever the mayor knew and probably more. He was sharp-eyed, a former gendarme. Some people faulted him for using information to his advantage, yet he'd no call to be better than the next. I never found him false. I see no failing in a man who looks out for himself.

Abdi talked with complacent authority while I measured his foot. "So, yes, Nazar effendi, there was an incident," he told my father. "The mayor's kept fully informed in case a similar situation should arise in Erzerum." He drew a handkerchief from his jacket and blew his nose, returning it with points neatly displayed. He looked at me, then at my father. "You doubtless know our city's home to certain revolutionists—most now in jail. Let me tell you what took place in Constantinople.

"A howling mob of Armenians tried to storm the Sultan's Palace. Think of it! Traitors marching en masse, waving axes and cudgels, across the Plaza with the sun overhead! Shouting threats, heading straight for the great entrance! Of course, our soldiers routed these scum instantly! Crushed them to paste! Washed them into the gutter! So, yes—the last day of holy September was their last day as well!"

It seemed inconceivable, absurd, play-nonsense from a lunatic roving jester. Could Abdi be serious? I'd never heard him disparage Christians in numbers like this, and what put the relish in his voice, how could he tell these lies, and gloat? It upset me so much I couldn't think straight, nor flex my cold fingers. To lift my thoughts, I imagined myself walking through mountain woods on a summer day, inhaling fresh air with each stride. The last thing I wanted here was to listen to this hateful, stupid nonsense. I forced myself to pay attention.

"... assaulted a policeman near the Palace and attacked another near their cathedral. Fortunately both policemen survived, or who knows how deep infidel blood ..." Abdi let a clamor on the street subside while he re-wrapped his big toe with its ingrown toenail. My head was throbbing as I motioned to Khalil to find the coffee vendor.

"So, yes, naturally the public was aroused. They wanted the perpetrators punished! Business stopped, stores shut for days until they tracked the traitors down!"

I thought of the steep streets of the capitol's main Armenian quarter, crowded to the water's edge with houses. I shuddered to imagine the searches and terror. I could not dwell on these grim images, for Abdi spoke now of new boots, and we returned to matters of trade.

He studied the leathers my father showed him, weighing them in his ringed hands, crumpling and pulling at them like a Persian before finally selecting one. He tossed it to me. "...Calm's been restored, the shops are back open. They've got the traitors locked up." He accepted a coffee and continued placidly, "They'll be executed, of course, after trial."

Now Father spoke out. "As they deserve, misguided fools! Let them go to hell and stay there!" From the first day he heard of them, my father despised Armenian nationalists.

Abdi sipped, smiling agreeably at Father as at a favorite uncle. "We'll purge them from Erzerum. We've got orders. Every last revolutionist in the Empire will be locked up before long." He set the cup carefully back on the tray. At the curtain he turned, adding, "Our Police know their job. Yesterday they caught three more, hiding in the Armenian district. Dashnaks. A bad lot."

"A bad lot, indeed," said Father. He flashed me a warning look. He was right, I had already concluded it was the wrong time to inquire as to an investigation of the carriers' murder.

Blizzard

Hamed   early to mid-October 1895

We started well enough, in bright sunshine, my men joking and eager to go. With Keyif all prancing energy under me, I was relieved to set out at last, elated to exchange Trabizond rumors for clear mountain air. I vowed to waste no thoughts on Constantinople. In a week we'd read about it in the Erzerum paper.

The Germans were in cheerful spirits, too. They teased Heidi about her pony's name, pretending it was "Play Mate."

"His name is Brown Eyes, not Play Mate!" she protested each time.

Two hours along, Heidi tired of her play mate. Riding with her mother proved uncomfortable for both. She returned to her pony, next rode with her aunt, then her pony, then her father and again her pony. Her parents and aunt apologized for her whining. They assured me she was normally tranquil and simply lacked experience riding.

At one point, Shakir joined me at the head of the column. "They indulge the girl too much," he said.

"The child's only ridden on a lead 'til now," I replied. "They should have prepared her better."

"They should have left her with her grandparents. She delays us," Shakir said.

That night we spent at a shabby khan in Djevislik, an Armenian village. Its merits consist of grazing, water and sweet plump grapes. Fortunately the Germans had bought waterproof sheets as I suggested, and were spared most of the vermin khans offer travelers.

We rose early to ascend Khamsikui. Wirh a good road and the aunt letting Heidi share her saddle, we reached that settlement late morning. Khamsikui's station was a popular stopping place, for good reason. The Germans especially savored the keeper's quince and mutton stew. They would have lingered if allowed.

Travel grew difficult that afternoon. The mules required beating to climb the steep trail. Excepting a single patrol, we walked to spare the horses. The women complained of headaches, being unaccustomed to thin air. I spaced us amongst the Germans and their mules for safety. Near Zigana Pass, men in Kurd headdress watched us from above. I was relieved to reach Zigana without incident an hour after dark. Its well-managed khan provided tasty fare, strong coffee and a good night's sleep.

Zigana's road rewards with spectacular views, bright with reds and yellows in early October. Although morning fog slowed our descent to Ardast village, it blew away to show off the valley's rich, wild beauty. The consul was curious about the silver mines and the women asked to visit a local silversmith, but we lacked time with Baiburt still distant. Fortunately our route now was fairly easy as well as beautiful. We sided a winding stream to our midday rest at Gumesh Khane.

A level stretch let the Consul and me converse. Our own odd mix of his Turkish, my German and our native tongues created absurdities and laughter. He surprised me, saying farm girls learn to read and write in his Frankfurt province.

"They must make difficult wives," I remarked—immediately chagrined to have impugned Frau Consul. Another European might have showed offense.

We talked of trout fishing near Erzerum city. Hearing me describe favorite spots, the Consul grew eager as a boy. The best may be Lake Shamik, at a northerly branch of the Euphrates, parting the plains above the city. Fish and waterfowl abound there, as do mergansers, ospreys, egrets, loons and more. Some names he recognized with delight, while others took struggle to translate, flapping arms and drawing diagrams in air. We might have talked longer on these safe topics with the usual diplomatic restraint. Instead, he asked about Constantinople, having heard before sailing for Trabizond that Armenians planned to demonstrate. He understood the Sultan looked unfavorably on protests. In response, I pulled out the Trabizond newspaper and pointed to the account. He insisted I translate every word and regretted its brevity.

"Newspapers publish what the Ministry allows," I replied. "We must guess the rest."

A patrol rode up with word the child was crying. We led our horses against the flow to find her, this stretch fortunately broad.

"Papa, I'm tired! My saddle hurts! Brown Eyes isn't nice!" Heidi greeted him.

"Well then, you'll be happier down with me, Heidi-chen," he responded. He lifted her free to walk beside him. Heidi was content maybe six minutes. Then she stumbled on loose stones and whimpered until he lifted her onto his saddle. She sat agreeably with her father walking beside her, his hand gripping her leg. A bit farther on, we had to remount. They rode quite a distance together, girl fronting father, little comfort possible for either.

My detail rode three hard days from Erzerum Citadel to Trabizond, the shortest way. Travel with civilians meant a less demanding route: five days with able riders, more with others. Having been delayed, I hoped to make time up early on. An hour from Trabizond my hope disappeared, for it was clear these Germans were not practiced riders. Easier trails, when possible, took us more than three days reaching Baiburt. Already the German family was exhausted, and Frau Consul Behrmann insisted on a half-day's rest. At this rate, Erzerum was another six days off.

My men groused among themselves at their campfire. "It'll be November before we get back." "We'll have nothing left to eat." And so on.

I reminded them our task was bringing the Consul's family safely to Erzerum. "It will take the time it takes. Be patient," I told them.

In the morning I took the family to see the ruined castle on the north ridge, above the river. Marco Polo praised the massive fortress, hospitable then and sparkling in sunlight. That traveler was on his way to China.

My half-invented story delighted the Behrmanns. Silently, I resolved to bring Ehsan next summer, then pondered including the Kavafian boys he played with. Could their fathers also get away? If so, good company, but I must then invite my father. A simple trip for two thus would become a field maneuver, requiring plans, logistics, negotiation. The prospect dimmed.

My soldiers were cheerful, idling, some fishing the Tchoruk upstream. The sky then was bare of clouds, the air warmed by sun. The scene called for music, but my harmonica gave only croaks.

I chose the safest route from Baiburt to the plain. It's a gradual climb first, then steeper after a couple of miles. Nearing Kop Dagh pass, it's almost vertical in places, with innumerable switchbacks. Shifting rocks add strain but toughen a rider's seat. My great dread was meeting a caravan coming the other way. A loaded camel can't pass a pack mule along narrows that sometimes extend half a mile or more. My group might be stuck without warning from bell sounds, depending on wind and terrain.

The women were fearful their horses might slip. They pleaded to walk, yet obviously four feet give twice the balance. The Consul convinced them. "The horses know these trails," his half-truth. Few Army horses recall every trail, and a new-bought horse may never have been here.

Frau Consul Behrmann set her shoulders like a soldier. She rode close behind me, her face stoic, pale, and anxious. She controlled her fear. I admired this (if little else) in her character.

By mid-afternoon the females were fatigued, so we halted at Kop, a post-horse station with a few dismal huts at the edge of the tree line. They arranged themselves on blankets and took turns massaging each other's backs. Heidi ran off to explore the meadow and soon the three were gathering mountain flowers. Again I tried to blow a tune, and then, discouraged, I asked Consul Behrmann for instruction.

"You must call me Professor, as my student. And promise not to practice when I'm trying to sleep." He taught me step by step to get clear notes. Before long no one winced at my playing. Myself hoping to enchant my wife and children—with practice.

Presently, Heidi offered me a fistful of mountain asters and bluebells. She giggled at my question. "Your German makes her laugh," her father said. "She's picked a flower for your cap."

"Jawohl, danke shon, fraulein," I told her, bowing as I wound a stem around a button on my tunic. Then I bade the group remount.

Two hours were spent climbing a trail around Kop Dagh. Along its western face the wind shifted and clouds roiled. Snow crystals began stinging our eyes, nostrils and throats, so we pulled blankets from saddlebags to cloak the shivering females. Shakir drew alongside to ask, "Who thought we'd meet snow so early in October?"

"Mighty Alexander lost 30 soldiers here. Frozen animals and slaves, a great blizzard. Xenophon wrote of it."

"This early?"

"Fear not, it was December." Best not admit it may have been earlier.

Snow pebbled our faces. "We must wait out this squall!" I shouted, and reminded Shakir of an outcropping at the next turn: better than no shelter.

"At least escape this whirling dervish!"

"If it keeps on, set up tents. Take the lead while I ride back to tell them."

"Yes sir, Captain Hamed. I'm on my way."

The snow kept getting stronger as I worked down the line, explaining the plan. Long gaps between riders needed closing and I urged them to close ranks. The snow now covered hooves with each step. The trail narrowed to single file. Just east of this point, I waited for Heidi on her pony. Digging into my saddlebag, I withdrew Khadija's gift from Topol and wound it around my neck.

Heidi's pony advanced slowly, its big head bent low. When my horse whinnied, it looked up. Seeing an apparition clouded by snow, the pony twisted away in fright. In one awful moment it lost its footing and fell over the edge. Rolling, then flying in a terrible curving arc into whiteness. A strangled scream, pony or child? Just then her father rode into view. I informed him quickly.

"Don't worry! I'll have her back in two minutes. Safe and strong!" I brought Keyif behind the Consul's horse and dismounted.

"I'm coming with you!"

"No, you don't know this terrain! I can get her faster by myself. Go join the others up ahead." Military authority was needed. "You'll have her back soon!" I patted Keyif's strong neck.

Taking a deep breath, I hurled myself down. Now sliding, stumbling and slipping on icy rocks to where the child was lost from sight.

"Heidi! Heidi! Where are you?" No reply. My own feet now invisible, snow falling fast, wind whipping my face. As I tightened the wool around my head, I wished I'd looked for the gloves wasting in my saddlebags.

I searched methodically, 10 paces right, 10 paces left, guessing where she likely landed. I imagined my Huru lost, Khadija's anguish. Unexpected sorrow seized me, for my parents, for what all parents suffer. My mind was on my family every minute of searching.

"Heidi! Answer me! Where are you?" Yelled over and over. I saw a shape, fought gusts, came to a boulder. Heard only my heart and wind. Another shape, another—I fell face-down into snow. Precious moments getting breath, forcing myself upright. Was the trail behind or to my right? I longed for the cave where others already were warmed by a fire. I imagined breaking leg or arm, dying frozen in this snow—a summer meal for vultures. I preferred Major Server Bey's death, on horseback, under fire. An officer's death for a purpose: order restored. My death here would be only stupid, matching those revolutionaries at the Palace, dying from bad judgment.

With these reflections, stumbling forward. Shouting in the wind, my tongue tasting blood. Stopped at last to listen, deafened by my pulse. Still now, hearing nothing. A long shout. Waiting. First silence. Then the child's high wail, faint, yet from close by. A minute later, I almost stepped on the girl's small body in a drift.

I crouched beside her. "Mama! Mama!" she cried. I freed the cloth from my head, wrapped it around her, then gathered up the sobbing child.

"I've found her! Heidi's safe! I'm bringing her back!" This I shouted to reassure the girl, for no other ears were within range. How I wanted to hear a mule's braying! Instead, hearing her sobs, my own gasps and the wind. Heidi clung to my neck and soon stopped crying, soothed by my thumping heart.

Our eyes are what guide us, not our feet. Yet our eyes are useless when snow clots the air. Blind men could be sent ahead into blizzards, to map the ground underfoot: a proposal for Major Rustem.

A struggle, ascending, with false steps, almost blind, and the girl's inert weight. Loose rocks hid under snow. My balance often faltered and I stumbled, twice fell to my knees. Had I crossed over the path? My nose and ears and hands ached with cold, while I gave thanks for good boots, for the friend who gave them to me, Martiros then close in heart and mind. A closer brother, though a Christian, than my own. We understood and trusted one another without explaining, as if we listened to each other's thoughts.

I remembered Father's lesson: such a friend is a gift from Allah and a gift requires responsibility, it means accepting an obligation. He was chiding me for playing with the Kavafian brothers instead of studying. Our sons do likewise, running between our courtyards in a pack, like puppies. Tireless, until—put to study—they fall asleep with books in hand.

Later, asked to explain why I risked my life for a foreign child, I was startled. Never did I think to do otherwise. It was a responsibility, as well as a matter of honor. Stumbling with freezing fingers and numbed feet, I knew and understood my father's truth: Family, Friends, Country and Honor, these alone matter. Everything else is trivial. Dissolute worms like Topol the Gebizehli were insignificant, and so were the martinets competing for attention at my garrison. My son's schoolwork was less important than this lesson.

A while the child rested against my chest, then she wept for her mother. I sang to comfort her, panting verses as I clambered upward. At last I needed both hands and had to set her on her feet.

"Follow me, Heidi!"

She clung, begged to be carried.

"It's too steep. You must walk it."

I started forward without her, called back to her, "Come on! We'll see your Mama in just a little while!"

That good child struggled along behind me. After 30 or 40 more steps, I pitched forward, caught my fall. I realized we were climbing no longer—we were on the trail at last!

Elated, I embraced the girl and swung her half-way round. "Your mama and papa are waiting for you, little Heidi. We'll reach them soon!"

"I'm cold!"

"I know. Me too. We must be brave." She shivered as I gathered her against me inside my cloak.

The blizzard was drowning us and rushing thrusts of snow blinded me. Was I still east of where I'd left Keyif or had I circled? I called his name. If he was downwind, we might be half way to the cave already. If upwind, we'd surely come upon him soon. Guessing, I forced my legs forward into the wind. Every few steps, I yelled, proclaiming our location. Meanwhile, I hummed to soothe the whimpering child.

"It's all right, you're safe now," I told her, hoping this was true.

Time after time my shoulder scraped rock along the inside of the path. My bare fingers were dead-numb, my face and ears stiff-frozen. Wherever I touched, hurt.

"Wriggle your toes and fingers, you'll get them warm," I told Heidi, and tried to do the same. My toes refused to curl. I forced my hands into fists, tried to open them, fighting the stiffness. Pain replaced numbness.

Moving heavily, I trudged forward. My shirt stuck to my chest, damp with sweat. Snow melted at my neck, froze my collar, my shirt cuffs itched and I was sure I'd lose toes, fingers, ears to frostbite. I thought back to the winter Ehsan was fresh born. We'd had maneuvers on the plains in air as cold, or colder. Yet we were well clothed, with wool cloaks, hats and gloves. Our bones never throbbed from chill. Now I yearned greatly to lie down and sleep. The girl was limp and silent, breathing softly: I mustn't let her sleep long in this cold.

A dark shape moved a few steps ahead. A mirage? A familiar whinny. "Keyif!" I croaked. "Keyif, you noble stallion! You're the best horse in the Empire!" True, true!

Somehow I lifted the girl, hoisted myself onto the snow-clad saddle. After this I recall little. Probably I dozed while Keyif lumbered forward. Next I remember someone pulling me down. Wrapping me in blankets, massaging hands and feet, slapping me when I drifted. My face, ears, fingers and feet prickled and burned. Pain stabbed one place, then another. I recall sleeping by a fire and waking to a tin cup of gruel pressing my teeth. A voice saying, "He's hot with fever." Another saying, "He's shivering. Get another blanket." Words in German, too, perhaps an argument. I recall a woman crooning.

Slept a night or two before they woke me to say it would storm again. I recall being heaved onto Keyif, then a lurching descent, icy winds. Another warm place, sleeping and then moving on again, conscious only of daggers piercing my lungs with each breath as I crossed miles of plain to home.

Vagram The Brave

❀ · ❀ · ❀ · ❀ · ❀ · ❀ · ❀ · ❀ · ❀ · ❀

Martiros   second week of October 1895

I saw that despite Abdi's confidence, not every Dashnak and Hunchak was chafing in Erzerum's jail. At night they slipped leaflets under shop doors calling Armenians to the struggle for a homeland and citing the murders of the hay carriers. "You see how criminals go unpunished, how Armenians are killed at will," one said.

I wondered how many mad and wild writers cranking unlicensed presses were spawning these crazed and dangerous pieces of paper. Some sheets made little sense, others were coherent, a few mixed reason with a deaf ear to realities. Some denied any assault on the Palace, instead claiming unarmed students were petitioning the Sultan to grant Christians the same rights as other citizens. They were blind to the damage this would inflict on our Holy Catholicos' authority and to the general impracticality of their proposals.

One day I noticed Khalil idly folding and refolding a printed page. "What's that?" I asked. "A boat," he answered. I found a fleece ball for him and traded. It was yet another broadside, saying, more or less, "These innocent students, so wantonly murdered, were the pride of their families. We must not accept injustice like sheep!"

I knew it must be revolutionists writing this, of course they wanted us to believe the so-called mob was merely some students with a scroll. It's easier to sort out a fistfight between school boys than learn what truly happened at the Palace.

"Anything worth reading?" I asked my older brother. He was seeing the same fliers at the pharmacy before Khagorian set matches to them.

"Probably more true than the government story," Sako said.

"You think they really were unarmed?"

"You mean, every single one?" He was grinning. I remember thinking that since his remarriage, he smiled readily.

Along with the rest of us, Father doubted the official story. How often were government reports reliable? You learn to infer from what's written. I doubt any government's different. Why expect men to be better than they are? Why replace a known with an unknown? This is why Father abhorred nationalists.

On a raw and rainy afternoon soon after, two of these leaflet-writers slunk into the shop. They looked like university students: immature, underfed, serious. They wore no coats despite the weather. They spoke to Father in low voices for a few minutes before he erupted.

"Extortionists! Parasites! Idiots!" he shouted, and began shoving them through the curtains. I left my task in time to see him spit at their feet. "That's my donation for you!" he called out as they escaped stumbling down the street. "Misguided fools," he complained, "Worse than broken spoons—Those clay-headed Hunchaks are dangerous."

At home, Patriarch described this encounter standing proudly, legs planted like a warrior primed with courage. Mother's face froze, recalling the doctor's warning. Aunt Maxime assured him he was right, entirely right, we Christians owed more problems to ourselves than to Muslims. She merely rekindled his rage. None of us managed to ease him until Sako's bride Henza put a glass of brandy by his hand. Not that Mother thanked her for it.

The next day Berj ran in to report mounted soldiers entering the Olti gate. "Hamed's back at last!" I cried. But from Khagorian's roof we made out 40 cavalry in double file, too many to be Hamed's company. For cheer I said it meant more business, though we'd no need of new customers. We were making shoes, boots, saddles, boxes and gloves as fast as we could already.

We deposited a hefty sack of coins at the German Bank every day or two. Nazar talked of making an especially generous gift to the church. "We're on earth to serve God," he reasoned. Who could argue?

We couldn't block the children's eyes and ears: they were frightened by the murders. They heard rumors, felt our nerves. We did our best to conceal our fears.

Like any children, they played soldiers.

One day an errand boy brought a message: Petros must come to the school at once on account of Vagram.

"Is my son hurt?" He stood so quickly he nearly knocked over our lunch.

"The principal didn't say," the lad replied.

"Tell me what it's about!" demanded my brother, his voice as sharp as Father's.

"He may—perhaps—have got into trouble. I can't say."

"This messenger speaks like a diplomat." My words put a smile on the lad. I guessed his accent came from one of the Kurd-beset mountain villages to the east. He told me his parents sent him to Erzerum to learn a trade in safety. A good prospect, I thought, for our next apprentice.

At day's end, brother and nephew still weren't home. The other boys knew next to nothing. Artashes had heard his little brother "was put in jail," but not the reason for it. Marjan grew pale. I reminded her of Arsen's day in a dark school closet.

"What better opportunity to reflect on one's errors? It won't hurt him," I told her.

"But what did Vagram do?" Levon's son Sahad pestered. Children relish knowing what mischief their playmates have concocted.

"Whatever he did, he'll be punished, be sure of it," said Father. Sako appeared from the next room then with little Rafael on his shoulder. These two sang a patriotic ditty while the child waved Sako's fancy handkerchief like a flag.

"Vagram's a good lad, it won't be anything too serious," Sako said. He reinforced his point by whirling Levon's child in a circle, the boy shrieking with pleasure. He set him down and carefully folded the silk, a birthday gift from Henza. I pinched Rafael's cheek, smiling to cover my growing anxiety.

"We'd best go over to the school," I told Sako.

"I was thinking the same," he said. Since the murders, we rarely walked alone. Even in groups of three or four we kept our eyes open.

Weeks earlier we'd stopped letting the women walk unescorted. Unruly characters, some in tatters, some in uniform, were everywhere. They showed small respect for Christian women, veiled or not. Our daughters weren't safe. The two big girls pleaded, "Can't we just go to the fountain? We feel like prisoners!" They begged to see their friends. My Astghig was 14, her cousin somewhat younger. Plenty old enough to help at home and master wifely work.

I was pulling on my second boot when Petros appeared with his mischief-maker. The father was solemn, the boy subdued. I'm sure the entire household was holding in its breath. Little boys and baby girls waited open-mouthed as fledglings for the story. Maxime helped old Aunt Flora into the main room so she wouldn't miss anything.

Petros started to speak, then looked at Vagram. "Tell your family how you got yourself into this trouble," he said.

The child took a deep breath and swallowed. "I only wanted to show the big guys they couldn't scare me, I can look after myself!" he exclaimed, his voice growing stronger as he spoke. I noticed his small hands were clenched in fighting position. "It's for honor—the honor of Armenians! To show we're not cowards!"

"Yes, but now you must tell our family what it is you did," his father reminded him.

Vagram's bright dark eyes flashed. "When the big guys pushed me down on the rocks, I told them, 'You can't kick me and call me *giavour*, I am a brave Armenian!'"

"Are you leaving something out?" Petros's tone was stern as a schoolmaster's.

Vagram hesitated. My wife tried to tell Flora what he'd said. "What, what?" the deaf old woman kept asking.

Explaining was hard for the child and his little shoulders sagged. I could see his confidence fading. Just the same, he told his story. "I pulled your dagger out of my shirt and shouted at them, "I'll kill you mean Turks!"

"Oh, Vagram!"

The boy flinched at his mother's alarm, then took a deep breath and added, almost defiantly, "I scared them! That's why they ran to get Teacher." He looked determined and apprehensive at the same time. I caught Sako's eye. We were both forcing our mouths down, doing our utmost to look stern.

Patriarch growled, "Your father's Spanish dagger?"

"Yes."

"And where did you get it?"

"I took it from Papa's box in the cupboard." In a small voice.

"Who gave you permission?" Father shouted.

"Nobody." In a very small voice.

"You've done a bad, bad thing!" Father yelled at him. He brought his hands together with a loud clap. "Get me the sharpening strap, Marjan!" he commanded. Then, "You must learn obedience, boy! Bend over!"

The child was clearly frightened, yet he made his father proud. He bore his first stropping without tears. Father beat him hard, as was his practice. The strop whipped across the lad's buttocks, five, six, seven times. I could see Father's fury rising with each blow. Mother seemed to be holding her breath lest Father collapse from another seizure. Petros flinched each time the leather struck but held himself back. It was Sako who got Father to halt the beating. He stepped in, catching the upraised wrist in his hand.

"Give your heart a chance to slow down," he told Father. It was a command made in a conciliatory tone. Sako's special status allowed what I wouldn't have dared. Hadn't he gotten to study pharmacy while the rest of us made shoes? Yet how could we resent this good-natured brother with his aptitude for treating our illnesses? He'd make a good patriarch when the old man was gone. Nonetheless, I half-expected Father to hit him.

Instead, the old man let his arms drop. The next moment he

ordered the child to bed, glaring at him with all his force. He seemed unaware as Mother took the strop from his hand. Vagram fled, Petros and Marjan following him to their room. I supposed that once the pain eased, the boy might find that missing supper was no high price for avoiding evening prayers.

My doubts about Principal Drikian increased. He treated Vagram like a delinquent, imposing an extended penalty on the child and ranting at the father for letting it happen. Embarrassing the man. No matter that Petros always kept the knife hidden, Drikian blamed him along with the boy. The bureaucratic mind is not confined to government officials. Why he slighted our family's generosity over years, I can't imagine.

The boy wasn't allowed home for lunch but must stay in the classroom. Moreover, he was banned from the schoolyard until New Year's. When the other boys raced outside, Vagram must do extra lessons for Teacher Tarbasian. Neither boy nor teacher would have chosen what proved a light burden. We'd arrive to lead the delinquent home from the empty school and find the two singing from a music book.

As it turned out, my young nephew was spared most of his sentence. What's more, his misbehavior made him a hero to the other schoolboys. And to their fathers, who'd stop at the shop to congratulate Petros on his son's bravery.

Words of honey flowed to the family. Often someone asked me or Miron or Sako, after church, "Is that the boy who fought the soldiers in the school yard?"

Onnik Bedoian shook my hand, laughing. "You'll be known as the Dagger-boy's uncle, I predict it. A credit to the Kavafian name," he told me, beaming with affection for our family and happy anticipation of his first grandchildren. "He's given us all courage."

At home, the children paid Vagram fresh respect. Artashes and Arsen started letting him play the gendarme. Sometimes they called him "Brave One"—his uncle Sako dubbed him this, and Vagram took it as his due. He began to walk with an odd, childish swagger.

"If he's this ready to fight at 7, just imagine what he'll be at 17," I said to Petros. The child made us all hold our chests out, even his grandfather, though he never admitted it.

Patriarch and Sako

Martiros October 13, 1895

W e call ourselves religious, but I doubt any of us pay full attention to the black-robed emissaries of the Almighty during services. I found myself thinking about Vagram's boyish defiance and pondering whether it takes a child's mind to act a hero. Are Hunchaks, too, boy-brained, uncaring as to risks? At sight of Rooster skittering towards us after the service, I expected more compliments for our little hero. Instead, Berj seized cousin Levon's arm with his scarred wood-carver's claws. "My sympathy to you," he intoned. For a moment I thought he referred to the hay carriers, yet that was old news.

"But what for?" asked Levon. His mother Maxime was beside him, leaning to hear.

"You haven't heard? Then I must report a misfortune. A tragedy..."

This set the women shrieking, "What's happened? Who's dead?"

Berj took his time, enjoying the attention, like a cock. "Yesterday, my brother-in-law's uncle arrived from the capital with a newspaper. You know our papers here tell us nothing, nothing!" He paused to make sure every ear was attending. *Get to the point!* I wanted to shout, before he went on.

"This newspaper's listed the dead. From the mob, you know, at the Palace. Last month. All those killed." He adjusted his sleeves, then his collar, and continued, "Your cousin Hagop's name was there."

"Hagop Mesvanian? My uncle Torig's son?"

"Exactly so. Sorry." What should be said first was for Berj an afterthought.

Aunt Maxime screamed and collapsed against Mother, who'd have fallen except for Flora's grasp.

"What's wrong? What's happening?" Flora was quivering with apprehension and Mother held her fast while the younger women ministered to Maxime. Levon stood by helpless, stricken and silent. Sarah sent Miron for water from the churchyard well. Other families clustered around, offering help, curious. Before long Maxime woke from her faint and let herself be propped against the narthex wall.

"My sister's only son, a scholar! …How can it be? A good boy, so thoughtful! My poor sister! Her husband! How can they bear this?" On and on she moaned, gasping and sobbing, Levon and the women trying to console her. A futile effort. What solace could we provide for that young man's death? That evening we prayed for his salvation three times, first with Father Ashod, then the Bishop, and last, past time to retire, with my father. We spent the better part of Sunday on our knees. If our prayers that month reached Jesus, young Hagop must sit in Heaven.

Since we knew by then Hunchaks were to blame for the so-called uprising, Father took the lad's death as yet another folly by misguided revolutionists. He saw Hunchaks and Dashnaks as equally disloyal and not worth the bother to sort.

"Those Hunchaknaks are the Devil! Dangerous! You don't so much as say 'Hello' to someone mixed up with them! Keep your distance!" Nazar warned his sons and grandsons at dinner, stabbing his prized Sheffield fork into the table for emphasis. "You avoid these stone-heads! Stay out of coffee shops! If one approaches, turn! Cross the road! Don't give gendarmes excuses to arrest you!"

The Patriarch's fierce black eyes skewered the "big" boys: my son Arsen, whose 13th birthday we celebrated at Khachavan in August, his little brother Karin, barely 10, and his cousin, Petros' son Artashes, full 12 and growing fast. The warning did them no harm, nor the little Brave One sitting nearby. Yet Nazar meant mostly to instruct Sarkis. Not long before, they had a tense exchange.

"They tax our earnings to pay for their schools—and spend

nothing on ours. It's flagrant oppression." This from Sako. I caught Petros's eye and winked—we knew what each would say next.

"We can support our own schools. We aren't destitute!"

"Armenians paid as much last year as all Erzerum's Muslims added together! I have it from my friend in the Tax Office! And they outnumber us four to one, as we both know!"

"Most Muslims are poor, except the officials –" Miron's quiet voice was drowned in the duel.

Patriarch was scowling at Sako as if no one else was present. "You hear me complaining? We've money enough after taxes—"

"Kurds can kill our peasants and no one bothers!" Sako began to stride about in agitation.

"Mostigo was put in prison!" Patriarch was referring to a notorious Kurd chieftain.

"He's back with his bandits."

"Not our concern."

"Whose concern is it when our hay carriers are murdered? Are their lives worth nothing?"

"The police are looking…"

"The police only pretend to look! What do they care there's two less penniless infidels? They do <u>nothing</u>!" Sako stopped walking and faced our father. He could worry an issue like a barking dog but I never knew him to argue with Nazar so persistently.

"What about our people? Is it only Kavafians you care for? You expect police to help when one of us is attacked?" Sako's temper could be a fair match for the old man's rages.

"Leave well enough alone, Sarkis!" Father thundered. "Steer clear of those radicals! Keep your nose clean!"

As a flush rose in Father's face, Sako shifted tone. "It's all right, Father. I won't join them. They're too fond of violence and too impractical," he spoke slowly, choosing his words. He looked into the distance, then back at Father. "…but I believe there's some truth in what they say."

An inflection in these last mild words reminded me I'd heard a secret group was looking for the murderers. Sako's scientific logic was well regarded—of course that group would ask his help. I resolved to speak with him. Anything to do with the Circassian encampment would be perilous. Yet surely Sako's love for Henza would keep him from risking his own safety—of this I was quite certain.

They'd been married just a few months. She was a pretty young widow from a well-regarded family. Her father ran a profitable business in bricks, her late husband's family were jewelers with three shops, well-respected. They were perhaps more well to do than we. With Sarkis a pharmacist, and first born, both sides judged the match "good". All the mothers and grandmothers who make it their job to weigh out these matters praised it.

Both deserved happiness, if it's ever deserved. Three summers back, cholera filled the city's cemeteries—Apostolic and Mohammedan, Greek and Jewish, Protestant and Catholic. Most of our family stayed in the mountains, but Sako's wife and daughters returned early to keep him company in the lonely house. The hapless female creatures perished within a ghastly four-week span. They were only three of nine buried the same September morning. I recall seeing the widow Henzanant on her knees nearby, her eyes swollen, her face pale against her black wool shawl. Her husband had died a day or two after their child.

We thought Sako might never regain his spirit, might starve to death, he grew so gaunt and weak. I think it was Khagorian saved him. His boss kept him long hours at the pharmacy, forced his mind onto problems different from his own. Gradually, Sako found the strength to turn from mourning to living. He was fortunate. So was Henza. Perhaps God's grace helped them discover the route back. Or call it character, or luck. In any case, they taught me a valuable lesson.

The two families knew one another, of course. No one thought to attempt a match during two years' mourning. Then Henza went to hear her brother-in-law sing with the men's chorus. Sako sang a solo part in his fine strong baritone that evening.

We weren't surprised at the steady advance of their courtship. We rejoiced at their wedding and especially at their happiness. Shared bereavements didn't account for the way he looked at her, or she at him. It was something fine to see.

A few months into the marriage, we started the usual bridegroom-teasing. "How come your bride's still slender, brother, are you too shy?"

He'd reply, unperturbed, "Why should we want a crying brat to disturb our bed at night?"

But Sako had doted on his daughters—I thought he said this for their memory. He played games with his nephews and nieces, told them stories, led them on butterfly and spider hunts after Sunday church. The youngsters followed him like ducklings after their mother. His joyful use of his talents made me sure he wanted his own.

Glad Tidings

Martiros October 14, 1895

Every day we asked Pasha Berci for news of Hamed. We reassured him he'd be home soon and safe. I reminded him of his son's expert horsemanship and his familiarity with the mountain trails, for I'd learned long past of his proficiencies.

We spent endless summer days together exploring the mountains before he went off to military school. When we were both 11 I was able to out-race him, not by better riding, but by pushing my horse to its limit. The next summer, our races tied or put me second. In shooting, I never matched him. I gave up striving to best him—I was smart enough to realize he was getting better, while I was tethered in place like a goat. I settled into admiration. By then I knew my strengths were in mathematics and commerce.

By this time, Hamed was almost a week overdue. We took heart that no travelers had entered the city's north gate in some 12 days: It meant a storm had hit Kopdagi. That pass is two miles high and fiercely windy. Its unpredictable blizzards have turned countless inexperienced horsemen into lifeless statues. Though we mark Easter as the end of winter and All Saints' as the start, snowstorms can fell a traveler even in mid-May and mid-September. Experienced voyagers take extra food and fuel and blankets when they head there. Most likely Hamed and his company were waiting out bad weather in relative comfort and would be home when it stopped. Like any such assurances, these hid unspoken fears.

This evening, my father's crony declined refreshments. He was agitated. "Hamed didn't take his heavy coat—nobody expects a storm this early! They weren't prepared for it," he lamented.

"The consul will have trunks of winter clothes and comforters," I told him.

"Soldiers always pack a blanket for the mountain nights, even in summer," said Sako. "You mustn't worry."

We persuaded him to smoke with us, and while we chatted, Sako's wife came rushing into the room. In her radiant excitement, she spoke directly to Hamed's father, bare-faced as she was. "Pasha Berci, come at once! Your grandson came to find you—your son's come home!"

With a joyful shout, Berci bolted home in his socks. I picked up his shoes and trotted after, eager to greet my friend. But when I entered the house, I found no rejoicing. Slow-witted Khalil was face to wall, crying loudly.

Hamed's son Ehsan explained as he led me in. "He was caught in a blizzard. They were stuck at the pass. Sergeant Shakir said they ran out of firewood. They almost froze!" Ehsan was a bright lad with long legs and big feet that promised he'd grow tall like his father.

Hamed lay limp on a divan. His wife and father were kneeling beside him, eyes fastened on his face. My friend was pale, rough-bearded, gaunt, his eyes sunken and unseeing. Each breath made a ghastly and exhausting wheeze. The mere sound would have convinced a blind man death was near. I thought Hamed's case beyond my older brother's skills.

"Let me fetch Dr. Tashjian. He cured my daughter when she nearly died. I'll have him here in 10 minutes," I said.

"Let _me_ go, Grandfather! I know his house," said Ehsan.

"Yes, do it!—Run!"

I went home to pray with my family for my friend's recovery. Although we worship differently, One God hears us, when He chooses.

He answered, but slowly, as if battling forces of darkness. That night and another Hamed lay delirious with fever. The second morning, his skin was cool. He slept without waking, though he swallowed the nectars his wife spooned onto his tongue. The third day, he sat up and made us laugh. He grew stronger by the hour after that.

Later in the week, our holy friend the Bishop arrived just as the family was assembling for evening prayers. He was breathing heavily, his hands bustling with energy.

"Dear friends, I beg you, don't scold me for not coming Monday, there's been much work to do, many headaches, many troubling matters…"

Indeed the Bishop looked distracted as he paid his customary attentions. He kissed Mother's hand, murmured words that made her simper like a girl, repeated his courtesies with her sister and niece. I noticed moist droplets glistening his thick black beard as he greeted each parent and child in turn. This done, His Holiness turned a great smile on Father. "You're the first to hear the good news!"

The Bishop had rushed directly from visiting the Consul to tell us about a telegram. We assumed he referred to the French Consul, knowing the two friends shared interests in literature and philosophy, the Bishop being fluent in the Frenchman's tongue. We were confused, for it was the British consul Cumberbatch showed him the telegram.

"Not only have Armenians in the capital reopened their shops at last—the Sultan's promised big reforms! It's just what the English were asking! Fine news! The consul told me, 'This proves our diplomacy's effective!' His very words!" Bishop Shishmanian paused for breath, beaming at us with hand raised as if for benediction.

"And I say to you, my dear Kavafian family, this answers our prayers! Just imagine the righteous joy of our Most Holy Patriarch at this! Recall how he stood up to the Sultan, telling him, 'My people want only to live in peace, we live on bread and olives, I've no room in my house for your decorations!'" The Bishop rambled around about the Patriarch in Constantinople for a time before returning to the news at hand.

His excitement spread quickly to the women and children. My

mother-in-law actually wept for joy, while Yiri kissed the Bishop's hand in happiness, the boys cheered, and the littlest shrieked in elation without knowing why. As for the men, the Bishop was blind to our indifference as he continued to expound.

The words "the Honorable English Consul" and "Most Honored Consul Cumberbatch" floated so often on his breath that I found myself meditating on the sin of pride, despite my respect for our prelate. To summarize, the holy Ghevont said Cumberbatch credited England alone for the Sultan's decision. "The Sultan mistrusts France, its petition serves French economic interests, and the Czar only wants Ottoman land. It's England carries moral weight." Seeing doubt on some faces, he added, "His country's been pressing the Sultan for some time, you know."

Right about then, the women brought in refreshments and the Bishop helped himself to pastries with one hand and to a cup of juice with the other, talking all the while about Cumberbatch. "Our friend's quite proud of what they've done. He keeps the ambassador well informed when Christians are mistreated in eastern Turkey. Those murdered Armenians two weeks ago, he wrote a long dispatch…"

The Bishop halted. "No need to dwell on sadness when reforms are coming. The Honorable Consul expects these reforms to follow Britain's list…"

While His Holiness was talking, I recalled an experience that illustrated our need for reforms. Years back, Father saw a thief enter the shop, take shoes and run. He gave chase without success—no one stopped the fellow. A week later, Father spied the thief wearing those shoes! Yet he was powerless, the man was Muslim and a Christian can't testify in a Muslim court.

The Bishop went on, "As soon as he's informed, I'll let you know. The moment he tells me." He then ate the pastries in two large gulps, with a sigh of pleasure.

I think we all remembered how our Christian millet rejoiced some years back (soon after I finished school) over a fine long list of reforms announced by Abdul Hamid. He cancelled them before anything changed. Promises weren't enough this time to make us celebrate.

"Take the guns away from your hamidieh, then we'll believe you, Abdul Hamid," Sako whispered to me and Petros, standing behind him.

Much as we valued the Bishop, he was a man who enjoyed his own voice. His sermons were like spun sugar, agreeable before melting to nothing. His prayers were much the same—Sako compared them to the miller's donkey that endlessly circles a single patch. I wasn't disappointed to hear him plead a surplus of church business to address, we must pardon him if he now led only a single prayer.

True to habit, he praised God the Almighty, the British government, its ambassador, Consul Cumberbatch, his family, all British consuls and their families residing elsewhere in our country, the French and Russian ambassadors, various members of the Apostolic prelacy, the directors and principals of the Sanasarian, Heripsimian, Ardzenian and other Armenian schools, and so forth, repeating the inventory in case the Almighty's attention was elsewhere the first time, while Kavafians tried to think only of God and not our knees. We were grateful to stand to see him out.

Father's prayers were lengthy too, but he served a meal to chew on. He prayed for the future, for the Sultan's good will toward his loyal and patriotic Christian subjects. He prayed for Constantinople's Christians, living and departed, and especially for Hagop Mesvanian and his parents. He prayed for the murdered hay carriers and for all the poor of the city. He prayed for harmony between Christians and Muslims and for an end to revolutionist activity.

I often thought my father had the qualities of an outstanding priest. He savored the Biblical texts, quoted long passages of Holy Gospels from memory, and recited each Psalm by heart. His prayers and sermons were invariably superior to Father Ashod's, due to intelligence and passion both. I think he was more content leading his family in evening prayers than he ever was at lasts and hides.

We stayed at table discussing the news, with insufficient care to ears in the kitchen. When they brought our coffee, Henza and Marjan wore gloomy faces. "They've overheard us, speak more softly," Petros said.

Despite our doubts we poured ourselves brandy and toasted every proposed reform we could imagine before we went to bed. "No special taxes on Armenians!"—"The right to keep a gun for self-protection!"—"The right to testify in a Muslim court of law!"—"No stealing sheep and women!" and so forth. Sako offered a refrain that we repeated before each swallow: "May we live to see the day."

I detected no real joy, only pretense. Yet it was human to hope and I couldn't help feeling a grain of it under my tongue as we laughed at our irony.

We were all a bit drunk by the time we ran out of reforms. Sako wobbled to his feet and held his glass high. "To future generations of Armenians! To our sons and grandsons!" he said. It convinced me Henzanant was pregnant. Yet when we whispered in the darkness later, Yiri dismissed this notion. Henza would have told the women if this were so. I felt my wife's soft, warm flesh under my hand, and let no more words be said.

Home

❋ · ❋ · ❋ · ❋ · ❋ · ❋ · ❋ · ❋ · ❋ · ❋

Hamed   circa October 18 through October 22, 1895

T hey tended me while I struggled against fever. My wife feared I'd cough both lungs out my nose and my father said my hair smoked from heat. I heard Ehsan weeping. Peculiar dreams pulled at me: in one, my feet were missing and I limped along on stumps so heavy I could hardly lift them. Looking down, I saw my legs were gravestones listing dead soldiers. One carved name was Server Bey, yet strangely, Server Bey was watching me from close by, mounted, battle-ready, watchful as I read his name. These things I dreamed without surprise.

They say I cried out now and then for the lost child, and Keyif. Called for Ehsan, Huru, Khadija, Martiros. Yelled odd, incomprehensible things about Armenians, soldiers and shooting, and snow.

Everyone expected me to die. Yet one morning I awoke and knew it was dawn. I flexed my fingers and toes, felt my beard and wanted a bath and shave, fresh bread and a cup of tea. With joy, I embraced my wife, my father, my sweet-faced brother, my son, my daughter.

"Welcome back!" they said.

"The child. Heidi—is she all right?"

They told me she'd recovered quickly, as children do.

"And Keyif? Is he—?"

"He's well—so well, your good Shakir tells me he's seeded a young brown-spotted mare. He's truly the Sultan of stallions, as you deserve," my father said. He added an unexpected compliment: "You came through this with honor."

You can imagine my happiness! Then I noticed my mother

asleep on the divan nearby. She looked old, pale and lifeless. Father answered before I asked. "She's gotten worse, but she still eats. She'll rejoice that you've awoken. She asks every hour."

"Your Khadija also rejoices." My wife was kneeling beside me. She pressed her lips to my hand.

"She's been a faithful nurse through long nights," Father said. More than once he's warned me not to underestimate Khadijah.

"Thank you, good wife, for nursing me to health," I told her. She flushed with embarrassed pleasure. I saw dark circles beneath her eyes, lines of fatigue beside her mouth. She looked much the same when Ehsan nearly died of cholera.

Father and brother helped me walk a little, for my leg bones were weak as a baby's. I was soon glad to lie down.

Before long, my friend Martiros arrived with his brothers and father. "You look perhaps better than yesterday and its day before— perhaps not. Do you know what day it is?" Martiros teased.

"It must be Sunday, since you're not at the store. So, why aren't you at church?"

"Because it's Friday. We've declared October 18th a full holiday to honor your rapid recovery—" Martiros replied, before his older brother interrupted.

"And since you no longer require Epsom salts and leeches," said Sako.

"Not leeches! Get them off me!" I pulled my shirt up to look while my visitors chuckled. Retaliation was required. "Your boots were no good, my feet nearly froze. You must've used cheap leather. I'll report you for selling shoddy stuff to the military."

"Spare us!" responded Petros. "We promise to make you a good thick-skin pair for the next time you choose to amuse yourself in a blizzard."

"They may be bulky, but your toes will smile," said Sako. "I can see you riding through South Gate at the head of your battalion, your feet wrapped in fleece like a mountain shepherd's. You'll set the style! Everyone will want Kavafians' footwear!"

Khalil and Ehsan laughed along with us. Our noise awakened Mother, who lifted her head and gave a slight smile.

The sound of laughter's a fine tonic. So is music, so I had Khadija find the harmonica among my saddlebags. When I tried to play a marching call, everyone groaned and giggled.

"Please, Papa, let me try!" begged Ehsan.

"If you can play a tune by bed time, it's yours." He caught the harmonica I tossed and ran off to practice alone.

"It's a fine gift for the lad. I'll say thank you for him," said Khadija, stroking my hand. I handed out the other gifts, saving her scarf for last. Mother held the carved rose in her palm and touched fingers to each petal, smiling. I turned to my wife. "Our tenant the Gebizehli sent this for you."

"It's a lovely color—but look, here, it's torn –"

"A momento of my trip." She frowned as I showed how I'd wrapped it around my head first, then the child's.

"It will please me to wear it, knowing this," she said.

The next day Consul Behrmann came to thank me for rescuing his daughter. With him was the Consulate's secretary and interpreter, a trustworthy fellow, but antiquated. Weak eyes, a deaf ear and a habit of formal phrasing typical of a one-time schoolteacher. Still, he eased our conversation considerably.

"My wife and I are forever indebted to you for your perseverance. We've all prayed every night for your recovery. I've told your commanding officer of your heroism," Behrmann told me.

"He may reprimand me. We prepared for bandits but not for a blizzard."

"You did well to bring firewood from the khan in Baiburt. Without that, we might have frozen."

"We've all been fortunate."

"We left Trabizond just in time." With rising agitation, Behrmann told of violence in Trabizond while we were locked at Kopdaghi Pass. Armenians—illegally armed—had tried to kill the Commandant and a former governor of Van. This from a consular telegram, most likely a reliable source. Worry, even fear, lined his face as he described the dreadful episode. He supposed the attackers were anarchists, and he reasoned that a German consul was likely the next target. Although I assured him this was almost impossible, he left me reflecting uneasily that any army officer might be mistaken for a Commandant by an excited revolutionist.

Soon Shakir cheered me. Knowing I let no one else mount Keyif, he'd got my stallion onto a lead and tethered him near my window. He told me to quit lolling, as Keyif detested rope-led exercise. Although thought of a saddle exhausted me, resting kept me weak. With Keyif now here, Ehsan could look after him while I regained strength. Shakir helped me walk into the next room and back, then I lay down almost breathless.

Shakir offered news from the morning's briefing. The crowd in Trabizond's Plaza was evidently infuriated by the would-be assassins' escape. A mob began assaulting Armenians, and a few days later stormed the Armenian quarters. Searching out traitors was predictably followed by looting, shooting and fires. It sounded much like Erzerum saw five years back, only worse. Officially 200 perished. Major Rustem told his officers this: likely half again more Christians died and twice that number fell maimed.

Shakir was like me in many ways. Without his speaking, I knew we shared fear for friends in Trabizond: his red-lipped Rosa, and (for me) the woolens-shop family. We were both sure the Armenian sector was devastated.

"Something puzzles me," I told him. "The commandant advised prolonging our stay in Trabizond 'for the action.' As if he expected something…"

Shakir shrugged my question off. "Maybe he meant the review. Or maneuvers—who knows? He never expected getting shot at!"

The next moment he was grinning. "You know what puzzles me? Telegraph wires! Our generals know what's happened in Trabizond before the Trabizondlis. We hardly need post riders anymore."

"Still, orders need a signature! What comes by telegraph could be forged!" We found no solutions that day or when we picked at the puzzle later.

Further news lacked explanation: two regiments from Aleppo were now quartered in Erzerum's south garrison. We speculated about training, exercises, a review. We agreed there'd be no outbreak here. Yet if Armenians were fomenting violence in Constantinople, attempting assassinations in Trabizond...

I needed to see Major Rustem, learn what threats our government faced. I called my wife to help me dress. I must walk, lift, bend. <u>Ride.</u> I was impatient for the central garrison after nearly four weeks away.

School Boys

Marjan   October 18, 1895

A rtashes came panting in ahead of the others as we set out the scholars' lunch. "Teacher 'basian's in jail! Soldiers arrested him!" he shouted.

"It can't be!" I told my son, as if arrests have rules. Tarbasian should sit last on any list, I thought, his head held only tunes and 10s. Out of his classroom he was helpless, tongue-tied. People thought him a good teacher though at home he did nothing but practice and read about music and numbers. His mother said it was good Boghos has no mule, since it would starve before he thought to feed it. Senseless to put such a man in jail. Besides, we needed him for music lessons!

The other boys ran in. "Principal's gone to City Hall!" Arsen called out. The next moment, he snatched a beanbag out of Vagram's hand and tossed it to Artashes, laughing at the child's yelp. Arsen was as childish as his little brother Karin, though born three months before Heranoush. A first-born son and grandson is sooner spoiled if a girl comes first.

"Good, he'll get them to let Teacher Tarbasian go," said Yiri as she served the soup.

I doubted this but only said, "They've already got enough Armenians in jail without poor Boghos."

After school we met the boys with questions.

"Principal missed closing prayers!" said Arsen.

"He's out collecting money with Teacher's brother and all the fathers have to give!" my 12-year old announced. Most Ardzenian families should have no trouble filling a purse for the police chief.

The Kavafians would be generous. So many people wanted new boots and shoes, they couldn't keep up. They stopped making saddles because it took too much time. Goatskin gloves sold as fast as Miron could draw out the basting. Too fast for us at home—the two skins Petros saved out from his trip to Tiflis ended up on strangers' hands. Our old gloves would have to do another winter. A sign, at least, the business was healthy.

The moment the men got home, the schoolboys raced to tell their news, proud and excited. The men didn't let on they knew it already.

"So, a teacher's locked up the same day as six innocent Armenian businessmen. Good law-abiding, tax-paying church members like us!" My father-in-law got angry as if it was fresh news. "Stuck in jail with filthy stinking riffraff! It's a disgrace!" Nazar punched a fist into his palm.

Arsen was bouncing on one foot, then another. Martiros frowned and put a hand on his shoulder to stop the hopping. "I hear they've jailed 22 Armenians on dreamed-up charges. Decent men, not criminals…"

Sako spoke without letting go Henza's hand. "It's not criminals they're after, it's Armenians."

"It's a wonder they've jail space for a teacher," said Petros.

"Underfed teachers take no room, it's the fat effendis who have to sit." With his hands Sako shaped a barrel so huge Miron couldn't take offense, and everyone smiled.

Sako went on, "Anyway, jail's less crowded now—Luivik Duzian's been let out, Rooster says. Fined 30 gold lira, no extra charge for the bruises."

"The godfather's free, that's wonderful! That means they'll have the christening!" Yiri burst out with what I was thinking. We hadn't been to a party in months, and this (if they gave it) would be one to remember. The Shabanians hired cooks and musicians for it long before their first grandchild—a boy—was born.

Martiros could be irritable. He turned on her. "So when a man gets free from jail it means you can go to a party, foolish woman? It's so important, a party?"

"I didn't mean…I didn't think –"

"I think you never think –"

Blessed Henza cut in before he said more hurting words. She gently asked how anyone could pay a fine so steep. Thirty lira would buy a flock of sheep back then.

"Money's no problem when your father-in-law's been City Treasurer," Sako answered, smiling at her. After six months of marriage, their eyes still glowed for one another. It was a fine thing to see. When I was tempted to envy their happiness, I reminded myself it followed much sorrow.

The bridegroom's good humor did little for Martiros. "Don't forget it took Krikor Effendi Shabanian two weeks along with 30 lira to get…" he broke off as Arsen darted in, tweaked his brother's nose, gave a pig-grunt and then ran away chortling. Karin chased after. Arsen ducked behind his sister and Heranoush, busy talking. Youngsters nearby squealed.

"Children, be still!" Matriarch clapped hands for quiet.

To comfort Yiri, I said, "Martiros has a lot on his mind."

She gave a small smile, eyes brimming. "We must forgive," she whispered back.

Then the Bishop came in, warm with good news. The Sultan was promising reforms! Look in tomorrow's papers! Christians get the same rights as Muslims! Yet Henza and I read doubt on our husbands' faces. While the holy man led us in thankful prayer, I puzzled and fretted. If the Sultan was sincere, why jail innocent Armenians and let murderers go free?

Putting the children to sleep, I did my best to hide my doubts. Heranoush asked why I was sad and I told her I was only tired. In the kitchen, though, I said, "Why do we feed our wishes this way? Things are worse, not better."

Aunt Zabel was hopeful as ever. "Why would the Sultan promise reforms unless he means them?" she asked. No one had a good answer. We overheard the men toasting the Sultan's promises, saying, "May we live to see the day." They were laughing without happiness.

Toumia and her sister were upstairs by then. I poured wine and we toasted the Sultan's reforms ourselves. Henza and I ended up giggling together like schoolgirls and Aunt Maxime smiled for the first time since Sunday. She kissed me on the cheeks after I lit her lamp. She was humming when she went to the room she shared with Levon and her grandsons.

As we got ready for bed, Petros asked the reason for my rosy face, guessed about the wine. "Good woman," he said, and pulled me to his side. We laughed together, a fine thing.

Punishment came promptly for our joking toasts. The stable boy Ephraim—our family spy—brought unhappy news with our morning bread. Four dogs lay dead in the street at the foot of our hill. Shot by some soldier for sport.

Dogs can be mean, and even bite you when you feed them—we keep a safe distance. I can't see keeping one for company like a songbird. Still, we were fond of some neighborhood dogs and felt sad at the news. Five-year old Sahad cried for his favorite, a big long-haired bitch with a short tail and a wide backside. We always laughed at how she wagged her whole rump when he threw her table scraps. Levon tried to comfort his son by saying other dogs would move into our neighborhood before we knew it.

"It won't be the same! I want my doggie!" wailed the boy. "They are bad soldiers, BAD!!" He turned to his hero. "Vagram, I want you to shoot them!" We had to smile, down-hearted though we were.

Two Waifs

Martiros   October 22

I expect no patients died from Aunt Zabel's sumac soup. She swore it cured ailments quicker than any powders and insisted on giving it credit for Hamed's recovery.

I saw Hamed's will beat back his illness. He tired like a puppy at first. He'd blow a few strange squeaks from his German instrument and fall back on his pillows in cold sweat. Bit by bit, through persistence, he grew stronger. Once the redness drained from his eyes he went walking outdoors, then even rode a little. He bested me twice in backgammon, his fresh-shaved cheeks oddly pale.

"You see your friend Hamed's invincible," he crowed as he cleared the board in triumph.

"If the world were a tavloo board and I your only opponent, perhaps."

"How much pleasanter the world would be. Everything clear and orderly." I heard regret there.

Hamed rode by in uniform as we walked to the shop one morning soon after. My heart lifted to see my pale-faced friend on his splendid horse again, his back a post. "Work hard on those new boots!" he called to me.

At mid-day we chanced to be standing outside, enjoying the sun, when my father said, "Look at this, Martiros, the shoes on those young beggars—see, coming towards us." They were made of good cowhide.

The boy led the way, the girl a taller shadow keeping up. Both about Karin's size, though leaner. Brother and sister, I surmised. Hungry.

"Please, e-e- effendi, are you the sh-shoemaker?" asked the boy. He was at once shy and purposeful.

"You see our stock, it's not sheep's cheese!" Father retorted, pulling open the curtain to show our loaded shelves. His words were brusque by habit, but Father was already beckoning a pastry-vendor. We could tell the children must come from comfortable circumstances, for they were dressed much like our own. Though torn, her frock and cape, his coat and trousers, were of good sturdy fabric and well made, like their shoes. Their family would be well off, or sheep lay eggs.

I was surprised by their condition—miserable, empty-handed and unprotected. If children from good families are orphaned, relatives or neighbors take them in. They've no need to walk some great distance.

The girl stood mute, shivering while her brother struggled with his tongue. Both looked near collapse. At last the boy managed to say they came from Trabizond and his mother spoke of an uncle who made shoes in Erzerum. Were we the only shoemakers, or was there another Armenian shoemaker in Erzerum? Father's answer didn't ease his trembling. While ours was the city's only Armenian shoe shop, he knew nothing of a relative in Trabizond.

Family or not, Father was about to invite these waifs inside when the boy got ahead of him. "Please effendi, we're hu-hu-hungry, we've eaten nothing bu-bu-but snow all week."

"So you've followed the blizzard! You've got courage!" I said, and waved them inside.

They folded onto a single cushion, hand in hand, eyes sewn to the tray. To settle their stomachs we had them sip sweet tea, slowly. Then we gave them bits of plain pastry, like you'd feed a baby. They'd have cleaned the tray in a blink if we let them—and then vomited it onto the floor. I made them wait before getting more. "You can rest here today," I told them, and bade the boy tell us about their journey. I must say it was an almost unimaginable route on foot at this time of year.

"It was d-di-difficult to walk. Es-es-pecially for my sister. We en-ca-ca-countered a huge snowfall. We ne-ne-nearly perished." He chose his words with a stammerer's care. I guessed from his vocabulary the boy was 12 or 13, like my nephew Artashes.

"I fell into a step-hole," said the girl, almost inaudibly. She looked more weather-beaten than her brother, her lips worse scabbed, her nose more burned, her glowing brown eyes sunk deeper. Her tangled hair would take a magician to uncomb.

The boy's name was Nerses and his sister's, Arsine. Only later did he say why they left home. We surmised some catastrophe occurred.

Nerses told us they overtook many other fleeing Trabizondlis in their first haste, before being slowed by painful blisters inside their socks. Trudging dawn to dark is a sorry business, and they carried nothing that might have helped, no food, no coins. A couple of times, riders heading north gave them bread and raisins out of pity. Lacking money for the khans, they slept beside the road. At Baiburt they camped with 40 or 50 other Trabizondlis in a churchyard.

"I was se-se-sleeping beside Arsine. We were under my ca-ca-coat when a man t-t-tried to pull it off. I sh-sh-shouted out and held it fast so he couldn't g-g-get it. He was kk-kicking us and cursing –"

"He hurt me here," said Arsine, pointing first to her back and then to her hip.

"—two women chased him away."

They were too frightened to get back to sleep. In the morning, they learned their two protectors and a few other refugees were heading to Erzerum. Nerses recalled his mother once mentioned a second cousin's cousin with a shoe-shop in Erzerum. Without knowing the relative's name, he decided on this destination. It proved how much a child's faith can accomplish.

"No one had f-f-food to spare, they warned us we'd g-g-go hungry. We f-f-figured we could beg from t-t-travelers. B-b-besides, it was only supposed to take four d-d-days," Nerses said. Nobody noticed the distant whiteness. A day past Baiburt, (I guessed, near Zaza Khan), the trail disappeared under snow. The refugees struggled on for a mile or so before realizing they'd lost their way and must backtrack. Even then, it was two days before riders appeared, heading for Baiburt. The walkers waved and called. Great relief when the riders stopped! The men gave the group a little bread and, most important, tracks to follow.

I asked how they kept from freezing.

"A lady let us under her blanket," the girl answered.

"I'm glad you met a good lady." I chose not to ask their reasons for leaving home. It could wait. I cleared space for the exhausted children to lie down, and they slept the rest of the morning.

We kept our voices low as we explained the situation to Petros and Miron. It was Petros sparked my forebodings by saying, "Yes, I've heard that Armenians are in peril." When pressed, he spoke of newly-come refugees and hearsay of attacks on Armenian villages.

Ephraim arrived with our lunch basket and tempting odors brought the children back to life. We let them eat small bits of bread and stew to start. Once these settled in their bellies I had more for them, but they were already yawning. They were back asleep before we finished our meal.

Customers came and went that afternoon, a dog sniffed their faces, an apprentice dropped an anvil, their eyes scarcely flickered. Between customers I sorted through a pile of hides until I found a match for my mother's missing glove. I set our best apprentice to fashioning a mate, glad I'd resolved that one small problem. Father was easing his feet on his old divan when Berj rushed in, panting to give us bad news.

Oblivious to the sleeping children, Rooster burst forth. "You've heard what's happened in Trabizond? The Christians murdered, their shops and houses plundered! Women killed in the baths, babies butchered like lambs!"

Before I could shush him the youngsters jerked upright, Arsine wailing as if she was lashed. My father, startled from his nap, called out, "What's this fuss? Why's the girl crying?"

"Because Berj was talking about Trabizond, Father. Berj can tell you," I replied, as if my indirection could shield the children from what they already knew. The commotion brought Petros from the back and he helped me quiet them while Rooster repeated his story for Father.

Before he finished, the girl started speaking in her high child's voice, almost too faint to hear. "…and killed her, we saw! They grabbed …Mama screamed … with a hatchet... her face!" She paused, sobbing.

I found myself gripped by pity. Strangely, I could hear noises from the back room, hear street vendors, see Berj had left and know tasks waited. Yet what filled my mind was the picture her words created—and Christian feeling for these two impoverished waifs. I made a silent vow to succor the pair as best I could. Since becoming a father, I've grown fatherly feelings toward children generally, although I must struggle not to favor my own in cousin-squabbles.

Her eyes did not see the tea I offered. Instead she went on whispering her story. "Her blood made a puddle on the road." She spread her little hands to show its size.

Her brother put his arm around her shoulders and stroked her while he spoke. "N-n-now she's in heaven, Arsha. She's ha-ha-happy with Papa and Mida. They're s-s-safe in heaven now." The girl's weeping slowed into silence. She rested her head against his narrow chest. I watched my broad hand rise and fall on the boy's shoulder as he breathed. I thought he was young and slight to be so able a comfort.

When Arsine was quiet, Nerses fixed his dark eyes on me and started to speak, carefully, as if reading from a page. Sometimes he gave us a whole sentence without stammering.

"It was afternoon, we were playing outside. Windy, in-and-out sun, mostly clouds. Cold. That's why we had our coats on. Then we heard screams and rifle shots around the corner. We were scared! Father called us in and took us to the roof to hide. We crouched down low so they couldn't see us. Mama had the baby in her arms. Mida…" He took a deep breath. His face reminded me of our picture of the Holy Mother with the crucified Son across her knees.

"We heard soldiers breaking in next door. A lady was screaming... Through the rain-holes I saw men with clubs running up the street. We heard lots of shooting... and shouting...

"People broke in across the street. They killed our neighbor on the steps. We heard screams. They came running out with stuff! Taking what they wanted! Soldiers and boys and men with knives! Their arms full of clothes and rugs and sacks..."

One of the cobblers took Petros aside while my father glared.

Arsine's high voice broke the silence. "Why was Mida crying?" Her red-rimmed eyes were turned up to her brother's face.

"I don't know. Mother couldn't get her to stop. You remember she tried nursing her, only her milk wouldn't come. Mida just kept screaming. We were scared they'd find us."

"Bad men broke in our house, didn't they, Nerses?"

"Yes, and Mida was making so much fuss that Father took her from Mama. But still she wouldn't stop crying..."

"His handkerchief!"

"Yes..." The lad looked at me uncertainly.

"It's all right, Nerses. Go on," I said.

"...Papa pushed his handkerchief in her mouth. He held it there so she couldn't cry, so they wouldn't find us... But then..." He paused. In his face I saw the features of the adult he'd become. His voice was very faint when he continued.

"But then he took his hand away. He pulled out the handkerchief and jiggled her. He put his ear to her mouth, to listen. After a while he put her down on the roof and said, 'She's stopped breathing." Nerses closed his eyes and fell quiet.

Arsine spoke next. "And Mama just looked at him –" Tears ran down the girl's cheeks. She pressed her face against her brother's thin chest. He coughed and then picked up the story.

"Then Papa said, 'I hear them. I'm going down. Stay here. Lie very still so they don't find you.' He said to Mama, 'Take care of them. May God in Heaven watch over you all.'"

Nerses was fighting sobs now. He took deep gulps of air, his eyes focused somewhere distant. I held my breath and waited, trying to imagine how my Arsen might tell this story. He is old enough not to cry, I thought. After a while, Nerses continued, "...Papa kissed us goodbye and lifted the door and went down..."

"Somebody shouted," Arsine prompted, her voice partly muffled by her brother's shirt.

"We heard noises from our room. We waited. ...all of a sudden, Mama lifted up the baby –"

"She was already holding the baby, remember?"

"She bent down and picked up the baby, then walked over to..." His voice grew flat, as if he was reciting a lesson in school. His stammer stopped. "She didn't say anything. She didn't look at us, even...she just lifted the hatch-door and disappeared. Like Papa..." Nerses bent his head into his hand, covering his eyes.

"...Like Papa, except Mama got out to the street. She carried the baby and walked right down the middle as if nobody was around," he said. His voice was unemotional. I remembered the way Sako sounded after his daughters died.

"They used hatchets on her. Once like this, and here, and here..." He pantomimed the blows with his free hand. "Later someone dragged her out of the way. Soldiers on horses were carrying things from our house..." The boy looked at me as if only I was listening. His face was nothing like a child's.

"It got quiet. Two soldiers rode up the street. No one else came. We didn't know if anyone was alive inside the houses. When it was dark, we went downstairs. We had to feel our way along the walls. We were scared to stay there. We tried to go to my grandfather's, we got part way there, only we saw soldiers –"

"Dead people lying in the street..." said Arsine.

"We walked up the hill and kept walking. We met people from our church. They said Armenians must get away from Trabizond. They called it a place of death."

My father's face was sorrowful and Petros's eyes were wet. He motioned me outside.

"We can't let them sleep on the street," Petros said.

"I was thinking the same." Together we spoke to Father.

As we expected, our wives swiftly brooded these chicks, clucking and bustling with motherly care. Mother was dour. Already that day she'd given over one side of our stable to an Armenian family, two young widows and a boy. She'd helped find spare bedding, overseen their nourishment. Adding two refugee children was too much to ask of her in a single day. I could tell that Mother's head accepted the duty to shelter the three villagers, without her heart. Whatever comforts our stable provided, she grudged.

"We're doing what good Christians must," she told me. She meant but didn't say, "Other so-called Christians don't do enough." I suppose many good deeds are owed to self-righteous pride and I'm sure honor is due her for many good deeds. All the same, those objects of her charity stayed apart from us, in our unheated stable with the mule and hay. Yet I can't fault her for not bringing them into our family life.

Were we now proposing to take two homeless orphans into our home as if they were our blood, treat them like members of our family? Relatives so distant she'd never heard them mentioned and didn't know the family name? Maybe they made up this fairytale of a shoe-maker uncle! She wanted them out in the stable with the widowed peasants.

"Let refugees care for refugees! They don't belong with us!" she said, looking at Father for agreement. He stared impassively ahead and I spoke up.

"They've well-made clothes, they're from a good family—and they've no one else," I said.

Sako got her to let Nerses and his sister stay the night before deciding whether to put them outside. We figured time would help change her mind. Our strategy succeeded after two events. First, Father thought back to a distant female cousin—I think his mother's sister-in-law's cousin—who'd married a man from Trabizond. Mother gave a snort on hearing this, as if she only half-believed him. Then, to our surprise, little Arsine won her heart before bedtime.

Arsine did it, Yiri told me, by asking Mother to teach her to knit. The girl saw the old fingers working the needles, understood Mother's pride in her skill. Some children learn ways to bend their elders at an early age. In our house even small boys know better than complain to Matriarch of itchy socks and mittens and know to kiss her scolding mouth good night.

I know what I saw that evening: the girl and Mother back to front, kneeling child straight-backed between heavy legs, gnarled hands teaching supple fingers to master yarn and needles. After that we heard no more of the stables for Arsine and her brother.

Pressed to Serve

Marjan   October 22

Before our refugees, I hardly thought past my family and Varti's. Politics was something men talked about. They say a fox makes you look past your feathers to the flock. That fall our everyday frets were blown away by bigger matters.

Suddenly my eyes dripped for two orphan children from Trabizond. Not ragged peasant beggars like Mousagh or the family in our stable, but children like our own. They were our secret nightmares come alive.

Aunt Maxime started keening half-way through the story, and soon little Rafael in her lap was sniffling with her. Really she was mourning her beloved, unlucky nephew. His buried future.

The tale Martiros told left even Toumia and her sister Flora wet-eyed. The crying baby, her desperate father, his guilt and despair. The mother's blind and careless grief, the orphans' terror. Our hearts ached for them all. And if we asked how God could let it happen, we found His hand in sending the children to us.

Their parents in heaven must stand proud knowing they raised their children well. I tried not to brood over what the father, the mother, might else have done, for what will any of us do in the darkest hours? Finding Heranoush red-eyed, I told her, "Better to teach them your songs or some lessons from a school book." We were fortunate the children came when our home and hearts still had space. We were never sorry. Slowly they melted in with our own and became much beloved.

Petros agreed to take Nerses and his sister into our room,

close-folded as we were already. How could they possibly sleep well in the same room as tiny Yefkine, even though Martiros' space was larger? We put them along the far wall near Heranoush. They fell asleep in a breath, though little Vagram was jumping like a hop toad to play with them. To still him, I told a favorite story about David of Sassoun, embroidering it thick and long. At the end his eyes still shone. I expected a question about David, or heroic Vartan, or perhaps about his new playmates or the family in with our mules.

He startled me by pleading, "Mother, can I please come to the Baptism party?" He knew the answer—only the four oldest children were invited. To console him I said he'd see the baby baptized.

"I wish I had a little brother," he whispered.

"If God chooses," I told him, as if I hardly cared.

Since it was a baking day, the Bishop was in the sitting room, as usual surrounded. He was a solid man who liked good food and he often said Aunt Maxime's boreg would tempt a saint. He always accepted an extra, wrapped for his breakfast. In my head I called him Bishop Belly. We enjoyed his company. The old women came in the moment he arrived and he charmed them with compliments.

The smoky air was buzzing with talk of some woman living in a house too large for her. It took a while for me to figure out she was Berthe Sharopyan, a widow of means who often helped the poor. Some faulted her for not letting Father Ashod or the Bishop spend her money for her. Once I heard my mother-in-law say, "Too independent! She ought to know a woman's place!"

It seemed the widow filled her home that day with homeless Trabizondlis, as Bishop Belly asked. Now she wanted helping hands. Many of these refugees were sick or else too young to be much use. Without asking anyone, Toumia already told the Bishop we'd help. Our women's labor was hers to give, so long as our husbands approved.

"Sarkis, the sick ones have only colds and flu, nothing dangerous. They don't need nursing, they're looking after their own. Your wife needn't get near them at all!" said the Bishop. He was always definite, right or wrong.

"Then I don't object," said Sako. Later we heard there was cholera in Trabizond. The story caused much fear before we learned it was made up to keep travelers from finding out what went on there.

"I can always count on you, dear friends. As solid as St. Asdvadzadzin's itself. Unfailing in your Christian duties. Your love of our Savior shines like a lamp in the night."

The Bishop beamed at Patriarch and Matriarch, then at Sako, Martiros and Petros. He nodded at Henza, Yiri and me in order. "Let them come right after the boys leave for school. Mrs. Sharopyan will be glad to see them. The other good ladies, Mrs. Bedoian and Mrs. Avedian, will be there already, most likely. Excellent, excellent."

"Pardon me—may I ask who will go?" I supposed it would be Aunt Maxime and Aunt Zabel or Henza and the older girls, Heranoush and Astghig. I doubted Matriarch would let me miss another day of home-chores so soon.

"Why, you and Heranoush and Henza, of course," Matriarch answered, as if telling a foolish child. "Astghig can go next time."

"But my sewing –"

"It can wait until the children are sleeping."

Pointless to say I'm too tired to sew at night. And it was better than staying home.

The Bishop would write the Bishop of Trabizond to find out if Nerses and Arsine might have closer relatives to care for them. The two were sure to stay here until Easter thaw at least.

Bishop Ghevont took a pastry Toumia offered, then forgot he was holding it. Flakes kept dropping onto his lap while he gave advice on caring for the family in our stable.

"Work, work is the key for refugees!" The good Primate talked an hour about mankind's need to labor, as part of God's plan of righteous toil in fields and kitchens and factories like Kavafians'. For each place Bishop Belly tapped a finger on his left hand with the boreg in his right. When it finally fell in two he looked at the pieces with a puzzled tilt of his head. A moment later they were in his stomach. Although Martiros and Nazar both started to speak, it was Toumia who made herself heard.

"You're so right, dear Bishop, all of us have our appointed tasks, however lowly. You are called to the work Our Father holds most sacred."

"On the contrary, mine is just one small part of the great clock. It cannot keep time without its many and various parts. No part holds more importance than the other, for each is essential and depends on the rest," he began. The whole Book of Holy Scriptures was in his head, I think, for he braided one Bible story into the next as if he'd go on forever. Finally he pulled a watch from his robes and said how quickly hours passed.

After he left, Toumia pulled me and Henza over. "You must take the peasants with you. Make them do useful work. Their idleness is unhealthy," she told us. Then she turned away and bade the family good night. We got no chance to answer.

Henza's face was troubled. "Matriarch's got no idea of their misery…It will be difficult." She reached for my hand. "Pray come with me to talk with them, Marjan! We'll be doing God's work—and getting fresh air, as well."

We took lamps and a few sweetmeats to tempt them into eating. Henza feared they were letting themselves starve. Now, meeting the three villagers in that mule-stinking stable, I understood her worry.

The two young women—thin as children, though already widows—were sitting beside the sleeping boy on blankets spread over straw. They made me think of ghost games my sisters and I once played. We took turns making scary sounds in the dark with a candle under our chins. Shadows cut and bent our faces and our eyes glinted like a cat's. This time it wasn't the lamplight—which did no harm to Henza's beauty—that made faces into ghosts. It was hollow cheeks and eyes so deep with suffering that I felt ashamed.

They said their names were Arpineh or Arpee, and Oskinee or Oskee. They were sisters-in-law and the child Serop was a brother-in-law, eight years old. They whispered together when we asked their ages, agreed on "maybe 16, maybe more, maybe less." They looked twice that, at least. It's custom on the plains to marry girls off at 11 or 12.

Seeing the widows, you knew they'd been misused. Dark scabs and bruises marred both their faces, though these would fade. Oskinee had worse wounds hid by bandages and a broken tooth in front where it showed. Later we saw scars she'd forever need long sleeves and high-necked dresses to cover.

Henza's words, though slow and gentle, set them trembling. They drew away, saying "We can't!" and "Please, no!" and pointing to the boy. Henza kept at it while I ached for bed. They'd be safe, protected, there was nothing to fear. They were needed. Matriarch wanted them to do this. The unfortunate girls couldn't help but finally give in.

In the morning we took the girls cloaks and the child a jacket for the walk to Widow Sharopyan's.

At Widow Sharopyan's

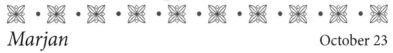

Marjan   October 23

O ur refugee family never went inside a city house before or met so many strangers. They were scared to raise their eyes when Widow Sharopyan opened the door. She eased their shyness by showing where the great earthquake of '53 cracked her front steps. It was a small miracle the house stayed up, and the Prelacy next door.

The boy's eyes got big as we went inside. Where I saw dark rooms wanting whitewash, he saw riches. Glass windows, brass braziers and carpets still soft underfoot. Berthe Sharopyan herself wore a silk head-cover trimmed in gold and a white lace collar. Dressed for church, except her skirt showed wear. Her handsome clothes surprised the little family as much as the house and all the strangers in it, I think.

Berthe led us to a sitting room crowded with women. They sat or lay there silently, too ill or tired to meet visitors. Two lay still, faces feverish from influenza, perhaps old, perhaps not. A gap-toothed, lumpy woman was sewing with much effort. Beside her, a four-year-old played with a piece of wool like it was a doll. A loose-haired woman about Sarah's age sat staring into space, and another young mother nursed a small baby. Now and again it let out a tiny wail that I took for a sign it might survive. The healthier women were looking after the sick ones then, though within a week they were all ill from being shut in that close room.

While Henza and I said friendly words to the women, the child (I now saw, a boy) came over. He held his wool toy out to Serop. "Kitty, my kitty," he said. When I meowed, he laughed and put his hand in mine—and became mine for the day. As we passed through the empty men's sitting room, he acted like any four-year old, pulling free, climbing onto a divan and crowing. He smiled at me and Serop before sliding to the floor.

A door opened to a large kitchen where a flock of women were preparing food. It took me a moment to find Berthe's famous sink-tub near the rear door, for there was little light that day from the windows.

Father Ashod's wife greeted us warmly. "It's wonderful you've come—we need you!" A voice called, "Watch out—she's bossing us all around, you have to do whatever Elmas says!"

"Keghvart Bedoian! How nice you're here!" I was delighted we'd have the company of the sunniest person I'd met in my 32 years.

She waved a hand above her head and two hairpins flew onto the table. "Lovely Heranoush, my girls will ask to hear everything you tell me! Come sit with me!" She offered my daughter part of her stool and set her peeling potatoes.

Others working in Berthe's kitchen somehow reminded me of women from our church although their faces were new to me. It puzzled me until they spoke. Then I understood their dresses were cast-offs like our refugees were wearing.

Across from Keghvart and Heranoush was a red-nosed lady with thick black eyebrows and teary eyes, her hair in a braid that fell to her waist. She was chopping sage and parsley. Close by sat an old woman wearing a black scarf over what looked like a hairless head. A clump of white whiskers stuck out of her chin. She was carefully peeling garlic.

The potatoes Heranoush peeled Keghvart was cutting up and dropping into a water-tub. She ignored the growing circle of mud-puddles around it. Two infants crawled nearby, muddy but content. Their mother, barely taller than a child herself, was showing a girl of about 10 how to slice turnips, without success—the knife was far too heavy for their small hands.

I asked our hostess for a lighter knife and she found one with a strange handle shaped to fit a hand. "Best knife in the world for turnips. My late husband's father shot the caribou," Berthe said with a smile. The short woman looked it over, then smiled as well. "Perfect, perfect!" she said.

Just then two youngsters pounded downstairs into the room, calling for Mrs. Sharopyan. "Gorbo's throwing up again, come!" the girl shouted.

"He's really sick! You told us to get you!" the younger added, as if no one heard the girl.

"She already knows that, Setrag, don't tell her again!" scolded the girl.

Berthe invited my sister-in-law to go with her. Henza's wink reminded me she'd cleaned up after Yefkine a few days earlier. Sarah was nursing her infant at the time.

"You've picked the right person. I'm good at this," Henza told the widow. She went off before I could remind her we were supposed to stay out of sickrooms.

My little friend by now was splashing in the mud. Elmas calmly handed him a wooden spoon and found another spoon for Serop, who wanted to join in. She chattered pleasantly at Oskee and Arpeh and then set them to stringing a basket of beans. Another young refugee brought over a second basket and stool, and with effort got them to talk a little. She asked them something and waited for one, usually Oskee, to answer. Then she asked something else. They spoke too softly for me to hear, but the stable girls did all right.

I got a good look at Berthe's new sink of carved soapstone. It was better in every way than a tub and a bucket. I damped a rag to wipe off the muddy boys, wishing. Then since I wasn't needed in the kitchen, I collected children for stories.

We sat in the quiet sitting room, the young ones at my feet. The girl who wanted Berthe upstairs leaned her head on my knee. I couldn't tell if she stayed awake, but her brother's eyes never left my face as I told Vagram's favorite tales. "Some day I'm going to ride a big white horse like Vartan's," said Setrag at the end. "Me too," said Serop. The two boys were serious and proud, like my Vagram.

Meanwhile two little ones were getting wriggly as minnows in a pond. It was clear they couldn't last through another story. "Let's play outdoors," I said.

"Yes, Yes!" half the group responded. The rest soon followed. When we passed through the kitchen, Serop ran straight to his sisters. My daughter Heranoush was glad to be done peeling potatoes. She helped us play hide and seek, then tag and apple toss, until every child but Serop was jumping, dancing, throwing, running. Serop went outside just before we quit for lunch.

Mrs. Bedoian left early with a promise she'd bring some flannel the next day to make into clothing. She was happy to be useful here, she said, her marvelous daughters-in-law took care of everything at home. She enjoyed being head of her household, free to do what she pleased.

Henza and I guided Oskee and Arpeh as we fixed cheese noodles and stewed beans with tomatoes for the evening meal, boreg and bulgur pilaf for the next morning. They'd no knack for these dishes, except the beans—we'd have done it faster alone, but we were trying to give them friendly company, sympathy, understanding. At the very least, to distract them. I think we partly succeeded. They'd brood all day in the stable.

Maybe Short Mama thought to ease their suffering by talking about her own. They hid in a storage cellar for hours, listening to shouts and footsteps overhead. First Kurds, then Muslims looted their home. She said they weren't discovered because "We prayed to the Almighty and He listened." The Almighty was deaf to their neighbors. It made me tremble to hear it. Seven entire households put to death, even infants. "You can't believe the screaming! The bloody paws of those hamidieh!" She pressed with both hands on the bone-handled knife, forcing it slowly through a peeled turnip.

"Be careful, Mama!" her daughter warned.

Oskee and her sister-in-law were staring at her with frozen faces. In the silence, I explained. "It was hamidieh who attacked their farm and burned their village. That's all they've told us."

Short Mama nodded. "Yes, monsters! May the devil burn them!" With harsh grunts she chopped turnip slices into shreds too small for stew, as if they were enemy fingers. Now she began naming the victims, one after the other like a tax collector. Grandmother this, Grandfather that, Grandaunt so and so, down to the smallest child in each family. She spent a long time on her list. She wanted us to hear every single name.

"Killed for being Christians, just for that!" she kept repeating, rocking on her stool and wiping her eyes. In a strange way she got pleasure in telling the story. Not that she was glad her neighbors were killed—her grief was real. Yet her sorrow was stitched, I thought, with pride, for surviving. For being chosen. Short Mama seemed sure God's hand reached down for her family. As if He judged them more worthy to live than others. Something self-satisfied about her made me nearly ask her if her neighbors didn't also pray? My tongue can be sharp when I'm tempted. I took a deep breath and decided to save the question for Father Ashod or the Bishop.

The entire time she was speaking, Oskee and Arpeh barely moved. We weren't sure how well they understood the Trabizond accent, yet their eyes showed they were following the story. Poor girls, they already knew death strikes unfairly. Now they found others also suffering.

At the end they talked together softly and nodded to the woman before returning to their work. When we left, instead of staring at their feet, they looked around and whispered goodbyes. "See, Henza! You did well to make them come," I said.

"Don't say I made them—but yes, I think it's done them good. Like Matriarch said. It's been good for Heranoush, too—Look!" My daughter was holding Serop's hand and counting out their steps. Every fifth step, they skipped together. I wanted Petros to turn around and see her mother him, see our daughter wasn't all sharp edges.

Henza caught my arm. "The men," she said. "Did you notice how grim their faces are?" Usually I took in such things, but I was thinking about the refugees. We tried to guess what was wrong, agreed it must be some new tax or penalty.

We learned the awful news when we got home. That day the police put our Primate in prison.

Our Bishop's Arrest

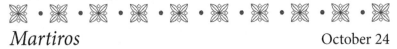

Martiros   October 24

B usiness was good for the Kavafians. I'd be fitting one pasha or
Army officer for boots when a second would appear seeking
gloves or shoes. Father and I stumbled on each other's feet serving
them. All day our ears rang with a shoemakers' concert from the back
room, where Petros, Levon and Miron and a rat's nest of cobblers and
apprentices cut and stretched, hammered and stitched our dwindling
supply of leathers. We'd started using skins of lesser quality, certain
nothing prime would arrive until spring. We dropped our prices no
more than necessary. As we told customers, these prices were low for
such fine workmanship. Which was true as far as it went. We were
the best boot and shoemakers in Erzerum and most knew it.

Competition kept Sako's boss nervous and lean. Two Muslims ran
pharmacies close by the Great Mosque, doing considerable business,
though one was too old and the other too young to instill much
confidence. Enough customers had the sense to prefer Khagorian's.
Sako stayed busy producing powders and tonics for their rashes and
fevers, coughs and gasses.

We weren't the only ones making good money, for plenty of
shopkeepers treated their families to French snails and African
chocolate that season, and dreamed of expanding their inventories.
Yet at night we paid with sleepless hours for our prosperity. What
brought these extra soldiers here? The news from Constantinople and
Trabizond chewed at our thoughts like maggots eating flesh.

Everyday difficulties multiplied for Armenians here. More often
now we'd hear mocking jibes from soldiers and school boys, see

a digger or carrier tripped by a gratuitous kick that left him slop-soaked and bruised. Vagrants grew more numerous, bolder, more desperate. We kept our eyes keener now for thieves, and though I put our best goods out of reach, some sneaks were too fast for me. Any merchant must be watchful, the difference was in numbers. Worse for us were the tin-badge hamidieh who swaggered in, snickering as they helped themselves. We set our jaws and covered what we could with canvas.

I did better than many that season, for I lost less than seven lira to sneak stealers. Giragos lost 30 lira worth of gold and silver jewelry before resorting to a floor hole. Unfamiliar customers got to look at cheap ornaments made of base metals. What they didn't see, they couldn't steal. Temptation's the mother of thieves.

Another fear was trumped up charges. Of some 25 or 26 Armenians already jailed, three at most might be fairly suspected, coming from Hunchak centers in Russia. Half the rest had no status—a few vagrants, a driver, an itinerant tea-seller, a scrivener—with no ideas beyond earning enough coins to survive. The remainder were respectable men like Kegham the potter and Dertrad the tailor, skilled tradesmen working to feed their families. They'd no notion of sedition, merely respectable hopes—for selling at better prices, for cheaper materials, for lower taxes, contented wives and many sons. We knew these men, they no more wanted violence than we did.

We tried to push fears aside, perform our daily work as though oblivious of how easily a Christian might be jailed. We'd done nothing to create suspicions and we were careful with our competitors. No other course was logical.

When a shotgun blasts a flock of chickens, a few birds fall and the rest flutter off. The hunter doesn't touch the cock, a leader's needed. We saw our Bishop as the cock. We were naïve to assume the authorities considered him essential.

One evening, our holy friend enlisted our help for Christian refugees sheltered at the widow Sharopyan's. That same day, as it happened, we ourselves took in five. This benevolent priest insisted, rightly, that leading families set an example of charity. Without charity, what claim had we to Christ Jesus? What sort of city would Erzerum be? Yet the very next morning, gendarmes marched our Bishop to prison "as if he was (my father's words) a shoemaker!"

It was inconceivable. Lawyer Blabilian termed it an appalling and unprecedented assault on the Armenian millet of Erzerum and undoubtedly a violation of the second Ottoman Constitution—as Blabilian informed the Lay Council in pompous tones. The Bishop was given no warning, nor was his secretary permitted to send word to the Patriarchate for five full hours after he was taken.

Many Christians closed shops at the news, forfeiting income. We'd an advantage, having Petros and Levon, even Miron, to manage things while Father and I attended an emergency meeting of the Council.

Armenians were already gathering outside the Prelacy when we arrived, for a new rumor of violence in Erzincan was adding to everyone's distress. Our father was breathless from hurrying uphill and Onnik Bedoian, too, was panting and red-faced. Father Zaven persuaded both elders to sit while he brought them cups of water and the other lay councilmen fretted and gossiped like schoolgirls.

Father Ashod turned naturally to Nazar for guidance, much as the Bishop had done. My father's age, clear head and intolerance for nonsense made him effective on the Council. His signal kept discussion from wandering too far and long. Many of the councilmen were agitated, confused and inclined to long outbursts. Shabanian would have helped keep the group in harness, but he sent word he must meet with government officials that morning.

Berj proposed we talk in confidence with the bishop's friend, the French consul. The more I reflected on it, the more this made sense. I often underestimated Berj. By the end, the Council decided a few things worth noting. Principal Drikian was persuaded not to dismiss school - his first plan—so as not to exacerbate anxiety. Father Ashod and Father Zaven were also convinced to continue their usual routines.

One councilman was Asadur Melikian, husband of Petros' sister-in-law. As canny as he may have been at trading kerosene, the man was nonetheless a conceited ass short on common sense. The fellow proposed Armenians gather at the Government building on the Bishop's behalf. Nazar argued—as should have been obvious to a blind man—that this would probably provoke another bloody rout like the recent nightmare in Constantinople. Then he turned to his trustworthy friend Giragos for support. The jeweler was well liked by his fellow councilmen and gave the impression of independence, but in fact looked to our father for direction. He was quick to guess what he should say.

"They may be waiting for an excuse to kill us," he said. "We must not give them the opportunity." Others voiced assent and Asadur's rash suggestion dissolved in air like alms to a beggar.

The Council and clergy nattered over how to proceed. Each man had a different view and half had several. The miller Sempad changed his mind three times. After long argument, consensus: The Bishop's release must be arranged, using utmost care and discretion, and enabled by a generous sum from the church treasury if negotiations warranted.

It took less discussion to assign my father and Onnik the task of taking the Bishop some necessities and, while at the jail, learning what they could. Two old men were presumed more apt to succeed than younger men, who anyway were afraid to go. The elders were to report back to the Council that evening. Meanwhile, at Nazar's suggestion, I was to work with Councilman Shabanian on finding out what we could from other sources.

Within the hour, I met with Krikor Shabanian at the bank. As I looked around at the simply clothed clerks who labored over ledgers, my burly friend approached me with his pocket watch in hand.

"Is it the Bishop?" he whispered.

I nodded. "We must talk."

He conferred briefly with two men as formally dressed and clean-shaven as he before they parted with cordial handshakes. When I saw the pair again at his grandson's christening, I learned they were agents from the Sultan's treasury.

Krikor and I spoke little until the Plaza fell behind us and we entered the Armenian quarter. We walked the half-frozen mud of St.Mesrop and Holy Shrine streets to Poplar trading conjectures, both sure the Bishop was innocent of wrong doing.

"Some censors allow nothing. A Christian hymnal with 'Armenia' and ..." Shabanian mimed a knife cutting his throat.

"I'm sure they wouldn't jail a Patriarch for a dust speck!" My fear was larger. "The question is, what makes them take our leader now, after the bloodshed in Trabizond, after what occurred in Constantinople? Do they plan to destroy us all?"

What we knew of events elsewhere came from refugees, and having heard of nothing like our Bishop's arrest gave us vague hope. Yet I had to consider his jailing ominous. It was plain to me that we Erzerumlis were now, without our Patriarch, acutely vulnerable.

A café sits on Poplar Street half way up the slope between Iron Fist Street and the bathhouse, and here we found a quiet corner suited for confidences. Sunk in gloomy thoughts, I watched the proprietor fix our coffee and set it before us. The moment he left Shabanian said, in a low voice, "There is news this morning from Erzincan."

From a reputable source on the governor's staff, another official story, not much different from Constantinople's, nor from Trabizond's. Erzincanli Armenians had flagrantly assaulted some government official or building, maybe both, causing much loss of those rebels' lives and property. Erzincan refugees must come 140 mountainous miles before we'd get more reliable information.

Shabanian was confident we Erzerum Armenians were safe. I reminded him that our city produced its own rampaging mob just five years earlier. It taught us to secure our stock in trade as well as our receipts. Planning underlies survival, I told him. He understood me.

By now the café was filled with people, noise and tobacco fumes. We had to raise our voices to hear one another. "Allons," said Shabanian, pushing back his chair.

"Allons," I concurred, glad to recall that bit of French from school.

We could do nothing about Erzincan, but we might be helpful to the Bishop. How best to proceed was the question. We speculated and walked, walked and speculated. Near the westerly gate leading to Erzincan, a lanky boy approached. Greasy hair fell over his eyes like a yak's, and a cluster of little beggars trailed him. I noticed Shabanian's fingers move over the buttons on his jacket, making sure his watch-chain was out of sight. The gesture gave him away, though I doubt he realized it. Soldiers patrolled within earshot so we'd small cause for worry, yet it's wise to satisfy beggars. I gave greasy-hair coins, saying, "Buy bread for your pals." The gang ran off shouting.

Shabanian turned to face me. "We must do like them. Make nuisances of ourselves until we get our Bishop freed." Thus we advanced from explanations to strategy as we went from the bank to the café and back to Thirty Mills Street, discussing every approach we could imagine. Finally we decided on the best.

A dough-faced flunky tried to deter us. "Monsieur Consul's not available. Unless you've got business with France…" He spread his arms like sails across the doorway.

"This is not our purpose—" I began.

My companion stepped forward. "I am Krikor Effendi Shabanian. With me is Martiros Effendi Kavafian," he declared in a forceful tone. "Kindly announce us to His Excellency Monsieur Consul Bergeron." He stood impassively, no flicker of hesitation in voice or posture. His impact was immediate. Pasty-face collapsed into apologies, bows and hand-wringing. Such a creature inevitably capitulates to an authoritative manner.

Bergeron received us graciously, calling at once for tea. I was satisfied to see the expression on the flunky's face as he withdrew. After a few words from us in French, the consul tactfully suggested we converse in our native Turkish in order to help him improve his proficiency.

Despite his courtesy, it was plain Bergeron lacked the good spirits of prior occasions. Concern for his imprisoned friend surely was part of it, but I think his gloom arose from loneliness. The man was stuck in an alien city, without familiar friends, required to speak an alien tongue. His wife and child had departed two weeks before, leaving him alone in this large residence with only pasty-face, a secretary and house servants for company.

"My dear family will appreciate a mild winter. A felicitous change, from Erzerum to Paris! Yet you will understand that I miss them already. The walls are too quiet. A situation quite different from yours, Krikor and Martiros." His face was sorrowful, though he gave a small smile. "Well, then. Perhaps I can guess the reason for your visit this morning. Does it concern our mutual friend, the Bishop?"

Though cheerless as the room itself, Bergeron was attentive to why we chose him, a European, to consult with Raouf Pasha, the Governor. He considered our proposal solemnly, eyes half-closed behind his spectacles. He first resisted, "Are you not overly cautious? Armenians are important to the city…"

"We are more vulnerable than you may realize—especially with our Most Holy Primate in shackles." I'd resolved to speak bluntly. "At any rate, I am merely a family friend of the Holy Primate, without office. I'll raise funds for his release, if that's useful."

I looked about at the French silk draperies and gilded armoires that had inspired so much comment after the consul's first reception. I could imagine Yiri's envy if she saw them.

The Consul's thoughts, as well, seemed to drift. Nonetheless, I continued, "Our good Krikor Effendi, on the other hand, holds a position of substantial influence. This allows him to bridge the distance between Muslims and Christians, both professionally and socially, as a grandfather."

Now my companion surprised me by saying, "Until today, yes, I've wanted to help create a bridge to bring Erzerum's Christians and Muslims together. Two communities, joined by a family celebration. But now, with our Bishop—" Shabanian sought the right word "—taken, and outbreaks in eastern Turkey, there may be those

Christians, those Muslims, who'd be uncomfortable at mixing with the other race."

He sighed, turning his eyes briefly towards me, then back again to the Consul. "I'm not sure this party we've planned is wise. Perhaps, Monsieur Bergeron, you will be so kind as to advise me."

The Consul polished his spectacles slowly before replying. His eyes were pale and watery, like a rabbit's. "It's a central principle of diplomacy that social occasions improve cooperation in other areas that might be troublesome. Your celebration provides a worthwhile opportunity, well worthwhile." He adjusted his eyepiece into place on his nose, then looked again at my companion.

"Moreover, to withdraw the invitations now might cause offense to some and create worry for others. *N'est-ce pas?* Would you not agree that anyone uncomfortable at mixing with the other race will understand he may gracefully decline? *Certainement!*"

"Your advice is sound," said Shabanian. "What's more, my family has looked forward eagerly to this gathering. I'd not like to disappoint them."

"I, too, anticipate it with pleasure. My regret is only that Madame Bergeron will be unable to congratulate you and your family in person. You must accept me as her delegate."

"Now, forgive my question," the Frenchman went on. "Please take no offense. You know the Bishop is my dear and valued friend. Such an excellent command of the French tongue—like a native-born *francais.* An exceptional man. But tell me in confidence—do you know any error that might account for his arrest? Might something he said in all innocence have reached the wrong ears? His extensive library—was he conforming to the censors?"

Impossible, we insisted, certain our Bishop's arrest was one of those perverse and irrational official vagaries that separate the powerful from the powerless. We knew examples of a censor, or another of the governor's marionettes, naming an innocent as a criminal on whim, perhaps for a personal reason—or none. A luckless man's face or suit or swagger might undo him. We also knew of legitimate prosecutions. We doubted our friend had done something he should not.

"You're an outsider, our city officials respect the French. Armenians are suspect here, particularly members of the Bishop's church," I told Bergeron. Shabanian added more, yet the Frenchman was not easily persuaded.

The consul finally overcame his reluctance, but insisted we accompany him. At length we convinced him to see the governor alone, as soon as possible. Shabanian and I exchanged a triumphant glance, glad for both the Frenchman's friendship with the Bishop and human vanity.

Shabanian and I returned to our employments through streets that seemed more hectic than usual. The shop, too, was clamorous, and though I did give a quick nod to Father and Petros, I found no good time to explain what was accomplished. That day I thought hard about the current troubles and what opportunities might arise, not only for holding on, but for advancing our business. Secretly I began to develop new plans that excited me.

Father was impatient for my report, yet kept interrupting with opinions that delayed me. He was never inclined to listen and wait. I wasn't surprised at his pursuit of information, his persistent dismissal of my sound arguments for leaving matters in the Consul's capable hands. He stood watch at the doorway like a cat, ready to seize any acquaintance. He asked customers their ideas on the situation before attending to business. One afternoon I chanced upon him at an olive seller's, conferring with Asadur Milikian. Our father, who always castigated rumors, was inviting them in futile hope of finding answers. He listened and learned from these bits of hearsay and it did him good. He became interested in what people were saying, whether factual or not.

Although I doubted the change would last, it encouraged me to tell him my proposals for our business. We talked at length while the others prepared for bed. Before we joined our sleeping wives and children, Father assented to my proposals, indeed, endorsed them with a few suggestions.

What little help we could provide our unfortunate friend, we gave. We took the Bible and a prayer book, slipped coins into the proper palms to see they reached him. Each day we sent Ephraim with a basket. Coins changed hands, but whether our stews and boreg warmed our Bishop's belly was a roll of dice. Each evening we prayed fervently for his well being.

Our prayers now included the Trabizond children, the refugees in our stable and others pleading at our kitchen door. Beggars beset us at the shop and church and on the street, trying to sell some sorry remnant, a shoe (rarely a pair), a cap, a clump of buttons, an icon salvaged from a ruined home. We prayed for them all.

Many evoked pity, but none seized our raw hearts like Nerses and Arsha. Most were filthy, unkempt, ragged and rude. They'd push their way into the shop. They interrupted business. Yet where once we might have turned them out with nothing, now we responded kindly. Our two young Trabizondlis softened us to stories we'd no wish to hear. We gave a few piastres, sometimes food. One consumptive, limping man, toes black with frostbite, got sandals a customer discarded. Others got scraps of hide to tie around their feet. If we were not always good Samaritans, we at least were ready with small alms.

Every day more refugees, many now from Erzincan, made their way past the sentries at our city gates. Some found a brief resting place in the yard behind the boys' school, until the principal chased them off. They begged at mosques and churches after services. They pestered every shop. They formed packs like dogs, gathering wherever they found space: by the south gate, in front of the ancient chapel at St. Asdvadzadzin's, behind the baths, in the rubble strewn by earthquakes at the foot of Poplar Street and at neighborhood fountains. We'd see them squatting behind fires too scant to set an egg. We thanked God for our comforts.

My friend Krikor considered my proposal with a sharp eye, going over my calculations in his methodical fashion, challenging me on choices and quantities. He persuaded me to add financial backing from other sources for several good reasons, most especially as protection once our caravan arrived.

While we awaited information on our Bishop, rumors churned from the mouths of bankers and teachers, shopkeepers and shepherds, carriers and idlers. Even Protestant apostates spoke fearfully, for our Holy Patriarch's arrest threatened Christians of every lineage. For a while Apostolics, Protestants and Catholics were like sharp-edged stones cemented by a common interest. A good from bad, as sometimes happens.

To demonstrate the uselessness of rumors, one day Rooster had the Bishop set for release by nightfall. He swore our Holy Primate in Constantinople had intervened. The next day Berj declared our Prelate faced imminent trial and predetermined execution, claiming indisputable sources, some aide of the Governor's or a spy of Ayatollah Nayim. I rejected the tale, yet even hearing such things was troubling. I hailed Krikor Effendi as he walked by the shop to learn he'd no word yet from the Consul. Our Bishop had endured four days and three nights in prison before Bergeron summoned us.

Meanwhile I worked as one lashed. I applied spare moments to arranging—discreetly—the purchase of grains and other foodstuffs. I spread my orders among several reliable traders, Greek, Syrian, Russian and Jew. I chose no Armenians.

Worry weighted my chest at night. Sleepless one night, I wrapped a blanket around my shoulders and walked out to the privy. The courtyard was quiet, the stars half-clouded. It was a moment of peace, before I glimpsed a dark figure near the garden wall.

"Who's there?" I called out, making my voice gruff, threatening. I seized a stick we kept nearby.

"Only me, Sako!" was the reply. "I've just evicted a mouse from our bedroom. Silly pest wants to share my bed." We laughed together in the darkness. The incident seemed inconsequential.

At breakfast I noticed two black-nailed and swollen fingers on Sako's hand. "You look like an apprentice new to awl and hammer.

That's not from grinding arrowroot. What happened to your paw?"
I said, as his wife set another plate of cheese near Father.

"I dropped a pestle on it. Like a novice, clumsy," he responded
lightly, dismissing my inquiry. Father wore a strange expression and
started to say something, then closed his mouth on a piece of cheese
instead. Henza was holding her arms flat against her sides like the
ancient statue of St. Bartholomew and staring at her husband's feet,
avoiding everyone's eyes. That struck me. Yet at that time I saw no
significance in it, or in Sako's hand and the fatigue in his face.

Berj stopped in at the shop, his small frame twitching with
excitement. "What do you bring us now from your reliable sources?
Taxes returned and censors in jail?" It was easy to needle Rooster and
he rarely noticed if I earned a chuckle.

"Good news, my friends, good news!" His voice dropped to a
hiss. "Revenge has been taken! The scum who murdered the hay
carriers! Tracked down and paid back! A Circassian!"

Smug at dispersing news our ears craved, he aired details: A
corpse found stabbed that morning near the river. A paper with one
word, "JUSTICE," stuffed under the victim's knotted belt. Three men
seen running over the bridge towards the city midway through the
night.

Rooster's story came from a trustworthy source this time, the
so-called "vagrant's telegraph."

"You bring welcome news. And the police, are they
searching for—?"

"The Circassians say nothing. They'd no fondness for the man.
Or so they say." With that, our informant rushed off to spread his
story. We resumed our tasks. Father took up his ledgers, speaking
little.

On the way home, I told Petros, "The tale can't be true, it's a
daydream."

He answered, "True or not, it will give the boys courage."

Karin ran up first as we entered the courtyard. "Did you hear?
The hay carriers were avenged! A beggar boy told us walking home!"

It could have been the last day of school, the way the children kept shouting and chasing, inattentive to their supper and evening prayers, fidgety as flies.

Father showed surprising patience, considering. Only after family prayers, when the women set out our meal and retired to the kitchen, did he confront his eldest son. In the quiet preceding grace he seized Sako's wrist and displayed the hand with its injured nails.

"Where were you last night, Sarkis?" he demanded. His manner surprised me, there seemed no reason for his anger at his first-born son. I learned the explanation later from my wife, for women often know such household matters first.

It seems that late the night before, the old man had rapped on the bridal door to ask a remedy for his (he claimed) sour stomach. Sako often provided medicine for our family, though we tried not to bother him at night. But instead of Sako answering the knock, Henza, flustered and embarrassed in her nightclothes, offered a story. "He's gone for a tonic to help me sleep." Her slight excuse served to magnify our Father's suspicions, for he'd been listening in the parlor and heard no doors open and close. Why would Sako leave by a window on that honest errand?

"Don't ask more than it's wise to know." Sako's jaw was set firm. He and Father glared at one another.

"You killed that man!" The accusation exploded from Nazar's mouth with drops of spittle.

"As it happens, no."

"You were there! Say yes or no!"

A long pause. Every eye on Sako, breathing held.

"Yes, I was there." Sako looked steadily at Father, then at each of us. Saying without words: *My life will be in your hands now.* He looked back at Father as he spoke. "My job was to kill the other murderer, but I failed." He paused, eyes closed, before going on. "He got away." A sigh, a grimace. "After a struggle."

"You fool!" Father spat words like rocks against an enemy, one by one. "You arrogant fool! You reckless, stupid, thoughtless…" He checked himself just long enough to fill his lungs again. "You'll have us all destroyed!"

"No one saw us."

"Except the man who got away. And the man you went with, the one who slayed the Circassian."

"Neither will talk."

"Don't be so sure!" He flung his fist open and slapped the table. "Others may have seen you!"

Sako said nothing, but stared back unblinking.

"How could you!"

"Someone must do these things, or we live in shame. We merely exist –"

"Revenge is not for men, it is the Lord's!" Father thundered this at him, pounding the table with such fury that Miron and Levon flinched. He began a harangue as long and passionate as his prayers, vituperation replacing entreaty but no less eloquent. Finally, voice rasping, he proclaimed, "You put us all in danger! You will NOT go out again!" He fell into a fit of coughing.

His lips set firm beneath his mustache, Sako gave the slightest shrug and began to ladle stew—by now, barely warm—onto his plate. Father thought he'd acquiesced. I did not. It was not Sako's character to yield on such a matter. He held intense political conviction, a patriot fired by passion. He loved life. And like the Bishop, he loved some principles more than life.

While we ate, Father let his anger fade. I could see thoughts working behind his eyes, perhaps as contradictory as my own. A while later he looked up from his game with Pasha Berci to chide Sako, "You have a treasure in your bedroom, don't neglect it."

Sako's reply was quick and manly. "We make up for my time away. She's not neglected."

Return to Duty

Hamed   week of October 21

O bediently Khadija pushed the boots onto my feet, her slowness signaling reluctance. She grasped my knee to get upright and frowned at me. "You're sure it's not too soon? You're strong enough? ...You'll get tired..."

"I can't stay home forever, woman! I feel fine!"

She drew back at my words, dismayed at offending. I reached for her hand. "Don't worry! I've recovered, I need to get back. You've others to care for." Thinking: *Look after Mother, Khalil, Ehsan, Father. Leave me alone.*

Mother demanded most of my wife's attention. She taught me to treat servants kindly, yet now muttered "dirty peasant" after the servant girl. She called only Khadija's name, even with Khalil or Ehsan in sight. Her voice held strong as her body weakened. She kept Khadija moving day and night.

Khadija said Khalil and Ehsan took less time but more thought. One an adult with a child's mind, the other a child with a nearly adult mind. Khalil forgets what he's learned. My sweet-natured brother wanders out the gate, follows a cart or a dog or a cloud. Forgets his way home. Khalil must be watched. One June day the gate was poorly locked and Khadija was distracted by our newborn Ehsan. Khalil wandered downhill, then across the city to the river. Its waters were running high and fast, its banks were loose. Khalil might well have drowned. Luckily, Nazar Kavafian was passing and saw the danger. Coaxed my brother with a sweetmeat. Led him home, arms linked like old friends.

A good Armenian. Next day, he proposed a job for Khalil: mostly sweeping at the shop, sometimes an errand close by. My father hesitated at this burden on his friend. Khalil overheard us and jumped about so eagerly! A short trial was agreed to, and Khalil adapted with surprising ease. Meager pay, yet a huge gift, a place in the world of men. Now he felt worthy.

Our nine-year-old son took attention those hours he was home. So did (and still does) his grandfather. Khadija managed well, considering. A good woman, docile, loving, gentle-tongued. I'd never take a second wife, I've no appetite for female jealousies and bickering.

My restlessness baffled Khadija. A week recuperating left me bored, disliking her doting and my own inactivity. Domesticity cloyed, I wanted purpose. Military duty has honor and simplicity: I'd command my men, carry out my orders. Besides this, I must learn what was going on. Was there reason for our neighbors' apprehensions? I wanted to get back to the garrison. I missed the company of my friends, my men, Shakir, and I missed riding Keyif.

My first morning back in the saddle, was I ever more elated? Perhaps when Ehsan was born, but the memory has faded. A physical pleasure claimed me, overcoming my fatigue, pains in my thighs and aches in my backside. It kept the Major's news from gnawing: news of outbreaks in Trabizond and elsewhere were put aside for later. This day was mine, for soldiering, for activity, for muscles, not thought. Saddle set, my touch shifting Keyif's pace, I became a Sultan. For the thousandth time thanking Allah for my stallion and wondering again if that Englishman knew what he was giving away.

My men greeted me with cordial shouts and jibes of a predictably ribald sort, the rescued child being female. "So you snagged a virgin for your harem" was typical of their nonsense.

Their welcome was sincere—they'd had to bend to second captain Fikret in my absence. The man's rank outshone his intellect. Like many novices fresh from military school, he was strict on trivia such as the proper stride-length on parade, most ignorant of leading men to a purpose. Time might teach him to give respect to lesser ranks, but I'd not wager on it. Meanwhile their posture and grooming showed signs of improvement—sufficient accomplishment, perhaps.

That day Major Rustem gave us none of his customary easy humor, no talk of hunting, horses and parade grounds. His manner was brisk and efficient, as if pressed by duties, even preparing for battle. He said Consul Behrmann regretted the difficulties created by his family's inexperience with mountain horsemanship. The German had praised my conduct and my men's, moreover, had written the Commandant about my heroism (Behrmann's words). Thus the Commandant discussed me with the Major, reflecting well on the garrison. Behrmann was distantly related to the Kaiser and worth cultivating. The Major meant to take him hunting when the current situation eased

The Major leaned forward across the desk to ask the hour we departed Trabizond and whether we sensed impending trouble. He listened intently as I confirmed Shakir's account.

We'd left before the troop review was disrupted. Later reports blamed unknown Armenians for nearly killing the former Governor of Van. That Governor was said to be a harsh man hated by Christians. There seemed no clear reason for their other target—possibly shot by mistake, possibly a personal grudge. Any judge should best avoid ceremonies on platforms.

Fortunately the hopeful assassins were inept. The bullet wounds were superficial, despite bleeding that created hysterics from nearby females. The crowd yelled itself hoarse with righteous fury. The faithful showed commendable control, with only three elders and a child trampled. Unfortunate developments were seen over the next few days, however. A general rage soon grew beyond control, causing a rampage through Trabizond's Armenian quarters. A mob stripped the entire row of silversmiths' shops and many others. It looted dwellings, large and small, burning some. A number of Armenians died.

"Every mob's a baby screaming for its tit," the major told me. "It must be satisfied."

He awaited official specifics as to casualties, knowing that hearsay exaggerates most numbers.

"These hothead infidels send schoolboys against the Palace guard and don't blink when they're killed. They toss their own people like slops into the gutter!"

Major Rustem called the revolutionaries "peace destroyers" and blamed them for upsetting balances between Muslims and Christians.

"They beget war!" he said, his chest heaving. A button flew from mid-tunic to the floor and he retrieved it before resuming.

"They're plotting with the Russians, stirring up revolution! Christians with Christians! They'd drive us off the earth!" He struck the desk with his fist. "The Czar's learned nothing from defeat, he's promised them a <u>province</u>! He still covets our eastern territory!" He wiped sweat from his forehead with a handkerchief. "These revolutionists hold hands with Russia's Minister of War, no question!"

"They can never defeat the Fourth Army. They failed in '78. They'll fail again," I said.

"Infidels!" He looked out at the parade ground and then turned back to me, his face determined.

"We must stop them starting anything here! These traitors belong in prison! If we must shoot them, so be it! If we must hang them, so be it!" Abruptly, he checked his outburst. He scratched his neck and looked past my shoulder, preoccupied.

"My Armenian neighbors agree. They detest these revolutionaries," I put in.

"Your friend with the shoe business? Good. We depend on loyal Armenians, loyal Greeks, loyal Syrians. They help us prosper—just as we help them prosper by crushing rebellion into the ground!" Voice rising, he was standing now, a straight-backed man without excess flesh, unlike most men of 50.

"Our job is simple. We can outsmart these fools with our eyes shut. They agree on nothing, one group wants this, the other wants that. Dashnaks, Hunchnaks, what's the difference? We'll block them before they can blink! We have the men—" Twice the Major sliced hand across palm. With a fresh breath he declared, "We have the arms—" He grabbed his sword, thrust it high like a banner. "We have the power. We will stop them!" He transferred the weapon hand to hand and back, weighed it and set it on the table.

Foot patrols tramped through the Armenian sector day and night. They also patrolled public squares, bazaars, wherever people congregate. Each soldier was instructed to watch for outside agitators and bring them in.

The Major's tone changed. Brutalities must be prevented. During my absence, two penniless Armenians were killed in sight of Ghezmahali Fort. Murders were hardly unusual in that location, yet Armenians were apprehensive. Any recurrence would be most unfortunate: therefore a "Hawk Watch" was to begin today. All captains, with selected riders, were to crisscross troubled areas, keeping eyes and ears open for anything unusual. Such to be reported at once. He'd have me start patrolling tomorrow if my strength sufficed.

"Look at No Man's Land as well?" This notorious camp of thieves lay just beyond the city walls.

The Major considered a moment. "Affirmed. But watch your flanks once you've crossed the bridge. Warn your men the camp's dangerous." He stroked his scabbard, then pushed it away, relaxed now into a jocular tone. "My mare prefers Keyif undamaged."

My men needed re-training. They held equal distances in straight lines yet lagged at turns and otherwise. All afternoon I drilled them hard, my displeasure showing at times. I strived for patience. At last they responded as a unit to my voice. My implicit criticism affronted Fikret, inevitably. I was absorbed by the task but fatigued by the saddle. Every muscle ached—a welcome payment for recovery.

My two junior officers were a clear contrast at afternoon drill. Mounted to my left, my faithful Shakir was a perfect mirror to my commands. Mounted to my right, Fikret was a half-hearted, inadequate reflection, his face a map of prideful resentment. *"Child, go home to the nursery!"* I thought as I glared at him. When he flinched, I turned away. I'd no strength for dealing with him—nor strength on the route home to notice numerous changes.

The next days showed Armenians' unease was well grounded. Ruffians clustered in unaccustomed places, especially near Armenian shops and the edges of Christian neighborhoods. They jibed crudely at passing Christians, taunting an Armenian beggar near the Grand Mosque, and more, as tensions throbbed the air. Now it was obvious why Christian merchants kept close to their storefronts, why my neighbors no longer walked alone nor let their women and children go unescorted.

One episode stands out. A sorry-looking bunch of women, children and weak-armed old men were huddled in a dugout shelter near the Poplar Street horse-trough. I was patrolling with my men when the refugees called to me. They were not begging coins or bread but seeking attention to their story. We listened willingly. An old woman talked most.

They were Armenians from Gemush Khaneh, a valley town some miles below Zigana Pass and some 50 miles south of Trabizond. Violence cast them flying with little but what they wore. Thankfully, the old woman foresaw trouble, so she sewed silver pieces and a gold ornament into her underclothes. These valuables were traded in Baiburt for necessities: spoons, a cook-pot and grain, plus three blankets of local weave. The Gemush Khanehlis found Baiburt costly, unsafe and crowded with refugees from Trabizond and elsewhere. They agreed to push to Erzerum, and fared decently until a blizzard (my own!) held them at Kop Khan for hungry days. The khan's food and fuel ran out and they lacked means for it in any case.

This morning they were robbed of their few possessions by Circassian thugs. The Gemush Khanehlis shivered violently as the old woman talked. Hunger magnifies cold. It's said shivers warm the body but I doubt it.

They begged us to retrieve their goods. Perhaps this was

impossible, but I promised to try. I led my men across the river to the Circassian camp downstream. Further along the bank were smaller encampments of Lazes, Kurds and Yezedis. A ways upstream lay the oldest camp, infamous for its thieves and murderers, avoided by other camp dwellers. The camp was well protected by marshy ground above that fishing birds filled in season.

Our Russian border's no blessing for our eastern provinces. Immigrants beset our city gates three or four years back. Scores sought work, houses and farmland here, mostly Circassians and Lazes. One time a Laze blocked my way.

"Your Sultan sends liars to betray us!" Although his rant and wild eyes surprised me I spoke to him patiently, as to a madman. Finally he calmed enough to explain himself reasonably. He insisted our Governor's representative enticed and misled them into quitting their mountain villages. The Laze blamed false promises for their present misery. It seemed an implausible claim—yet how else do we explain those misplaced Lazes?

The Circassian camp had grown fuller since my travel. Where there had been mostly men and perhaps 20 women, now twice that many were gathered around cooking fires. Unkempt children raced among tents, excited by our arrival, while the men eyed us silently with tight, hostile mouths. Mistrust was strong both ways. You'd not let those men shovel snow off your roof—my father's saying. Even the Governor never passed here without a military squad.

Our detail stood guard while Shakir and I searched. We found the blankets quickly, two at one site, the third at another. Baiburt's red, brown and black pattern stands out. "We're cold," one man whined. I lost my temper.

"You're no invalid! You've two strong arms, get honest work! Nothing's wrong with carrying! You can sweep!" I said, disgusted. He was a healthy young man, although white-haired, his eyes strangely colorless. Shakir discovered the kettle close by, half filled with bulgur.

The Gemush Khanehlis smiled to see the bulgur. "It's baksheesh for your hardship," I told them.

Another day, patrolling grain-sellers' row, I arrested an agitator I saw pull a sheet of paper from under his cloak. On noticing me, he stuffed the page back in his shirt and—looking frightened—stupidly began to run. As if Keyif was an ordinary horse!

Half-way down an alley, I overtook the fellow, a heavy-set man by then breathing hard. He knew his luck was ended. When he handed the shaking paper over he could barely whisper his name, "Memmik."

I could read enough Armenian to know his broadside inveighed against the growing number of official censors. An especially fervent censor was assaulting Christian libraries in Erzerum, black-lining Christian bibles and song books. The Christian millet hated this interference, of course. Their archbishop was trying to end it through diplomatic channels, while radicals printed broadsides.

A policeman led Memmik off after telling me he'd confiscated an identical sheet nearby. An Armenian lamp seller had called him in, afraid to touch it.

Relaxing with a pipe that evening, I told the Kavafians about the Gemush Khanehlis. We talked about street thugs and refugees and soon agreed the Circassians should return home, as should others surviving by thievery. Every city shares like complaints, yet it was worse now. We tossed remedies around but settled nothing.

Nazar roused when I described catching the agitator.

"Worthless trouble-makers with their broadsides! Put them in jail or hang them, it's all the same to me!" he fumed.

His sons half asleep, murmured agreement. I remarked, "You confirm what I told Major Rustem. Our Armenian neighbors are loyal subjects, as loyal as any believer!"

※　※　※

The Major greeted no one in the paddocks early, as he preferred attending fully to his mare. The next morning, he surprised me by beckoning me over, then complimenting my arrest.

"Anyone suspicious invites us to act," he said. "The Commandant says arrest them all, pack the jail solid. Keep the city calm. Don't let trouble-makers wipe their asses."

He looked admiringly at my stallion. Keyif was whinnying to me while a stable boy held his lead. "Last week, he bred my mare, and if it takes…"

"If it takes, you'll be astride a fine young horse in a couple of years, chasing quail just when my good Keyif goes lame and blind." What if Keyif understood me! We disparage what's most precious as if we truly fear the Evil Eye.

"Even so –" He stroked Keyif's muzzle. My horse didn't jerk back. I thought to myself, *You're a disloyal beast, Keyif, but I'll bring you round.* I hoped he'd done his job well on the Major's mare.

※ ※ ※

Market streets were bustling as I rode past with eyes half open, my mind on Ehsan's schooling. With its endless recitations, Old Erzerum Boys' School bored him. Mother said boredom was alright as long as he mastered the Koranic syllabus. I knew the New School studies were modern, better suited to him. She insisted the New School was for upstarts, not for sons of established families. Inflexible—and Father let her have her way.

"Captain! Captain Hamed! Come, help me!" Calling from his shop front, Father's friend Giragos. His jewelry was unmatched in Erzerum, nor was any finer craftsmanship to be found in Constantinople or Berlin—I've looked. Some hold such beauty requires an ugly artisan, as if appearances must balance, and certainly Giragos was especially homely. His eyebrows joined above a lumpy purplish nose, a paltry beard pushed his chin into his neck and his body was egg-shaped.

Giragos was struggling to hold someone almost as homely. "This man's a thief, arrest him! He tried to sell me this ring here! The very same ring…" The goldsmith took a deep breath as Shakir took hold of the captive and forced his arms back. Giragos opened his fist to show the circlet.

"I myself worked gold beads into a circle around this jade! My own design, the only ring of its kind!" He looked proudly at it before tucking it into his waistband. "Somehow he thieved it and now he tries to sell it!"

The younger man protested, "You're wrong! I won it at dice from a fellow at the café. It's mine! I didn't steal it!" His sallow complexion and beady rat's eyes were familiar from somewhere.

Two policemen idling nearby over coffee came quickly when I signaled. One nearly tangled with his stool in his rush to make another arrest. He'd taken my Armenian revolutionist to jail the day before.

Trying to explain the charge, I said, "Giragos says this fellow's a thief. You must talk with the buyer. Make sure the ring was stolen." The policemen looked confused.

"Look at my fine work! No other goldsmith can do this!" Giragos thrust it under their noses. "Made to order for a special customer, someone important—Abdi, the mayor's first assistant!" The jeweler described rare features that made this ring unique.

"It took me years to learn this fine work, and I am teaching my son so that someday he can work by my side, though he does not yet have the patience," said Giragos. The boy was a couple of years younger than my Ehsan, I recalled—he had years to learn his father's skills, and patience.

Meanwhile, the accused resumed his protests. Whining in a way I finally recognized: he was Pohar, Topol's knock-kneed shop assistant. Untrustworthy still.

"I'll take him in, you'll get no more stealing." The policeman tied Pohar's hands with cord, then marched him off. I advised Giragos to find Abdi and learn how the ring changed hands. Giragos sent a boy for me the next day.

"I was right, that ring was stolen! I know my customers! Such a special design, no one parts with. Not unless…." He lowered his voice and winked "...it's a gift for his mistress! Goldsmiths learn these things! What did I tell you!"

"You must have talked with Abdi..."

"As surely as nanny-goats suckle kids. He's joyful, amazed, a grateful man! Calls me the world's most honest jeweler!" Giragos did a little dance that set his flesh bouncing.

"He's rewarding me! A fine gift!—" he paused to be certain of my full attention. "Lambskin boots for these small feet! From the city's best boot maker!"

Bath

Marjan   October 23 - 26

An empty stomach doesn't make an appetite any more than bearing a baby makes a mother. Your mind must be right. That night's meal tasted to me like lint. One bite was all I took, though the stew was thick with vegetables. The short Trabizondli's story kept repeating in my ears, perhaps in my daughter's and Henza's too, for they ate nothing that I saw. We were too stirred up by worries.

Yet the outing was a tonic for our stable girls. They said they were too tired for supper in the kitchen, yet it was only shyness. They ate as much as young Serop from the tray I took out. They nearly emptied their bowls.

"Now they'll start feeling better!" said Aunt Zabel, scraping scraps for the stray mewling at her ankles. Her remark was so perfectly cheerful and ordinary, I stepped over to hug her, saying, "I'm glad you're here!" because it was true. Yiri beamed at her mother and me while Aunt Zabel hugged me back, saying, "Good! Good! Our kitty's glad, too!" She and Aunt Maxime both spoiled it for mousing. It filled out quickly, though Toumia wanted it kept hungry.

Sun was jabbing through the early fog and drying the path to the outhouse. Meeting Oskee, I saw promise of a nice face, once healed. I felt sweet hope for her. Serop squatted at the stable door with his bony knees pulled under his chin, smashing fleas, deaf to my call. Later, when Heranoush was reading to the little ones, he crept close enough to listen. It was a good sign.

The next day Serop and his sisters-in-law went readily to the widow's in the rain. We were hardly there two hours before the men turned up to take us home. They were grim and tense. It seems Armenians were shutting their shops and closing schools early due to a great many soldiers marching through city gates. We were all frightened. Even our fearless Ephraim was afraid to go out, saying, "It's the most soldiers I ever saw!"

What reason for soldiers, if not to hurt us? The men bolted doors and covered windows while we hung our cloaks to dry. We lit lamps and kept the children in the kitchen, away from the street. We spoke in whispers and listened for gunfire. Sarah started crying and Toumia came close to slapping her. Without dough to mix I might have wept too.

Then our neighbor came smiling to the gate between our courtyards. The soldiers, Khadija said, were in the city for a peaceful reason. It was a special secret! Her handsome captain husband was being honored as a hero! Her kind wet face was proud as can be.

Even so, we fretted until the boys shouted down that troops were leaving by the Erzincan Gate for the forts above the city. We hugged each other with floury hands before we finished the shaping. They say baking is the nervous woman's comfort. If there's a better remedy for nerves, I'd like to know it.

When the last troops marched from sight the men uncovered the windows. It was dusk and thankfulness filled me as we knelt together to pray. Later Henza and I got the children playing guessing games, then Heranoush set the aunts and children singing, and Nerses and Arsha taught Vagram a new verse to "Pretty Bracelet". Our men took a tray of fresh-baked pastries to our neighbors to sweeten their celebration, with Patriarch Nazar leading the way.

The next morning Patriarch called Ephraim from the kitchen to ask about the streets. All was calm, so Patriarch decided to open the shop. "No reason to neglect our business," he said. He always went when he could. Better than staying home with women and children!

The women gathered in the front room, all eager to go for our Saturday bath. As usual, we'd filled baskets with towels and underclothes, fruits and pastries and extra treats to share with friends. Sako and Petros were waiting to escort us.

All this was wasted—Toumia declared the trip too risky. We must bathe in the kitchen. Her sister Flora was as disappointed as the others.

"No bath, you say? Ah, ah! The child is ill?" She pointed to Arsha. "No, no? You say it's the soldiers? Why should they take over our bath day, it's not right! Ah, dreadful!"

We gave up trying to explain, and simply smiled over her head at her confusion. Her bad hearing gave us fun again when Toumia said the refugees in our stable were ignorant peasants. "Presents? Someone's brought presents? I hope it's candy, I do like candy…" Flora said, and Toumia answered crossly, "Never mind!" instead of giving her sister a sweetmeat then and there.

We thought only Toumia's bad temper stopped our outing, though later her caution looked wise.

"But I was counting on getting out!" wailed Sarah, like a disappointed child.

We did our best to console the children with promises of sweets and stories after their tub baths. Sahad's howls made Heranoush quit sulking. She gathered him in her arms and comforted him like a mother. "Think how hard the bath ladies scrub you! Your Auntie Maxie will be lots gentler," she told him. He thought this over with his head on her shoulder. When he wriggled to the floor she got him laughing with peek-a-boo. Another sign she was growing up.

"Martiros said there'll be rainstorms today. We'll be glad we stayed home." Yiri also was at her best. Even when Matriarch left the room, Yiri kept still about missing her only outing all week.

Ephraim and Verkin did a hard day's work as best they could. The buckets were barely half full by the time Ephraim hauled them to the door, then Verkin made a puddle where she pushed them inside our steam-tent. We'd hung sheets from ceiling hooks around the stove. Of course Toumia checked every sheet before letting it go up, then every overlap. The first kettles were steaming before we finished the tent.

The old ladies got to bathe first, then the younger women, then the girls and children. When we went to the stable for floor-straw, we tried to talk Oskee and Arpeh into bathing. My saying they'd feel better did no good. Henza told them they'd get sick if they didn't bathe. "Then what would little Serop do?" They gave in finally after we promised no one would peek while they bathed.

Mud was oozing up through the straw by the time Heranoush went for them. They brought fresh straw, their heads sparkling with raindrops. Within minutes a storm sent rain flooding past the kitchen windows. The wind rose, shooting cold drafts through every crack and tumbling loose twigs against the outside walls. Bits of dry straw blew in and dropped with odd knocks and patters inside the kitchen door. I felt grateful to be snug at home.

We went through our trunks and cupboards for things to fit the three refugees. Aunt Zabel turned up an old black dress of homespun wool, Sarah a dark muslin skirt, Yiri a faded calico shirt with long sleeves. I dug out two flannel nightgowns and a few underthings. Yiri donated some pants and underwear of Karin's. We stacked these on a bench and shoved it through the curtains without looking.

Toumia settled Arsine beside her in the sitting room, facing the brazier. Nerses kept it stoked, telling us proudly this was his job at home. Though we sweated from his zeal, it was pleasant, sitting together, chatting while we sewed. Toumia relaxed as she knitted with the girl. Bathing brings contentment, wherever you do it.

Serop came in shyly wearing fresh clothes and smelling clean. I took him by the hand to find my nephew Sahad and left them playing in the next room. Heranoush and Astghig were braiding each other's hair while they watched over the young ones.

"It's getting dark. They'll be home soon," Yiri said. If she was worried about the men and schoolboys, she didn't show it.

This made me say, without thinking, "It's going to be a cold night. Perhaps we might let the child and his sisters sleep in the kitchen."

At once I wished my tongue was gone. Toumia never ignored something you said by mistake. She made sure you were sorry. When she showed a bit of sweetness, vinegar followed. Looking back, I think her kindness to Arsha and Nerses pulled her out of balance and now she saw a way to even things.

"Winter's almost on us. It's time we got those refugees out of the stable. They need another place to live," she said. "They can't stay here any longer."

"But –"

"Don't you think –"

Before Henza and I could say more, Toumia ended all talk. "We can't have a gang of peasants in our kitchen. We don't want everyone sick. We've already taken in two orphans—" here she patted Arsine's cheek "—and that's enough. Other households have space to spare. We don't."

Henza gave a tiny cry and I was close to tears. Moments later her face changed. "Let me write a note to my first husband's family. They've got a large house—maybe they'll take them."

"Good. Ephraim can deliver it on his way home," Toumia said at once. "Mrs. Baronian can let us know at church tomorrow." Lips pressed firm, she left the room.

I burst out, "They're just starting to feel safe with us! It's not right to send them away now! Our kitchen's big enough…"

Henza knew how I felt. "You were right to suggest it. Don't feel bad, Marjan." She patted my arm. "The Baronians will treat them well, if they say yes. They're good people." She was fond of her dead husband's family, and they of her. She left the room, returned with pen and paper. While we watched her write, I tried to think where else the three might go.

"If the Baronians don't take them, my sister Nora's family might. Or my sister Zari's. I can ask them after church."

"They'll be happier in a smaller family. Being shy," said Yiri.

As always when someone's discouraged, Aunt Zabel said, "Things work out for the best, in time." Yiri and her mother found marrow in any bone. I held my tongue and counted the tucks I was putting into a new nightgown. A few days earlier, Martiros gave us our pick of some lovely dotted cottons he bought from his friend next door.

Henza took my hands. "Let's pray the Baronians will take them," she said.

When she warned Ephraim to keep the letter hidden inside his shirt, he laughed. "They never stop me. They think I'm another Believer."

We found the young women sitting near the kitchen stove, combing knots from each other's hair. They listened calmly, their faces sad. We didn't have to speak so slowly now for them to sort out our Erzerum accent.

"You'll be better off in a warm house, you can shiver to death in the stable," Henza told them.

"We're already packed tight or I'd take you into my room," I said, as if it was up to me, not Matriarch.

They were silent awhile. Then Arpee amazed us with a reply two sentences long. "You know, we can spin and weave. We had a loom, before."

"And we can help with children and animals. And washing," put in Oskee.

How they spoke no longer puzzled me. "We wish you were here for the fall wash," I said. With a smile I handed her my broom.

Together, the four of us swept the dirty straw into the yard and tidied the kitchen. Then I set the sisters to shelling nuts on a blanket with Nerses, Arsine and Heranoush. My daughter got the Trabizondlis singing, then Maxime arrived to add her strong alto voice. For a short time we thought of nothing but music.

A Military Ceremony

Hamed October 26

We'd but a day to ready every soldier in Erzerum's various barracks. Zeki Pasha, Supreme Commander of the 4th Army, was coming from headquarters in Erzincan to review our ranks. As usual at such assemblies, he'd award medals for meritorious conduct. Among those honored, Major Rustem ("for outstanding leadership") and me ("for heroism, bravery and perseverance").

My award would be all well and good in other circumstances: another brass disc for my jacket, a brief surge of self esteem. In this case it was swiftly dampened by reflection. First, I knew of far braver acts by others (and by me) that went unrecognized. Second, my so-called heroism was nothing without my second lieutenant's bravery and skill. But for Shakir I'd have missed the turn-off, died with Heidi in the blizzard. His ability likely saved the group. Later, while I battled pneumonia, Shakir advised Fikret invaluably in settling two intricate disputes. Otherwise that callow junior officer would have failed his temporary command, as I pointed out in my request. The upper ranks were wrong to pass over my adjutant and it embarrassed me to be honored when he was not.

Third—this rankled most—two awards defied common sense. One went to a notorious informer despised by other soldiers, who called him "Blackmail Bekir." This rat-like runt turned in three decent men for selling a military rifle. The three got flogged while Bekir was rewarded.

Yet most recruits would starve without selling equipment from time to time. On arriving in Erzincan last summer, Zeki Pasha learned the troops were unpaid nearly two years. Zeki got the governor to make up their wages, while at the same time starting regular counts of military issue at all garrisons. It worked reasonably well in deterring illicit sales of army issue—although civilians soon were complaining more about thievery. Soldiers need pay continually, a truth the government forgets.

Equally appalling was a posthumous award to a junior lieutenant of unusual stupidity. Apparently he couldn't tell a she-camel from a he-camel, so he often wiped camel spittle from his face while his men smothered smiles. What's more, despite five years' duty he needed help reassembling his rifle once he cleaned it. This fool died appropriately of inept horsemanship, after riding within close range of a hunting party on Kop Dagh. Their gunshots panicked his mount into bolting. It fell some 30 feet onto a rock pile—the end of a useful mare, unfortunately. Were they honoring this joker for expiring with his horse? It was incomprehensible. Absurd.

Misjudgments are staples of military life, arising from misunderstanding, poor information, carelessness. Under fire, they cause needless casualties. These honors were misguided: why reward a blackmailer, or a nitwit killed by his own incompetence? My head throbbed at what this taught our soldiers.

Using all my tact, I pressed the Major. Shakir deserved special recognition.

"General Osman chooses not to dilute the honor paid you," the Major responded. Discussion was closed, yet he missed the point.

The bemedalled Bekir would be another captain's problem. Every unit's got at least one such doubtful character who needs reminding what's right, what's wrong. Men learn from bad examples as well as good and my company was no exception.

I drew no pride from my new medal, although it occurred to me that this kind of honor, fair or unfair, helps make captains into majors. If the Almighty One chooses. Nor did I share my misgivings with my father. *Let him enjoy the occasion*, I told myself.

One jail window was barely eight horse lengths from me. The two criminals I put there were probably watching with envy and hate. One revolutionary and one thief, kneeling on one another's shoulders to see the dignitaries standing under a makeshift canvas roof: Governor, Mayor, Commissioner, Commandants, Colonels, Consul Behrmann, a few others. Behind them, a glimpse of my father, bench-seated between my friend Abdi and a father who traveled three days from Izgir for the ceremony. He'd honest pride in his son. The sergeant pulled two children from the river in an August thunderstorm, his heroism a credit to the Army.

They'd see me standing with the other recipients: Major Rustem on my right at the end, the Izgir sergeant on my left, next the runt, last the brother, another junior lieutenant, vacant-faced. The Army'd lose nothing if he, too, tumbled over a cliff.

Soldiers in huge numbers thronged the parade field, perhaps 2,000 rain-soaked men. Regiments marched in from the forts around: Remedli, Ghezmahali, Djebri, Aziz and Medjidle. Standing with them, soldiers from the Citadel and forts on the city's eastern perimeter: Kavak and Ouglou Vairan. Some were careless of their stance and untidy in attire, poorly trained both at rest and marching, grumbling at a rest day in formation, enduring rain and wind. Still, ordinary soldiers rarely glimpse a commanding general—it improves their fighting spirit. Thankfully, the rain ended before their march back.

Fighting spirit is improved by martial music, as well. Our military band thumped and tooted, sounding a little better at the close perhaps than at the start. Having learned to appreciate the German style years back, I was flooded with patriotic sentiment by the music and the scene. Whatever shortcomings beset Abdul Hamid and his ministers, I was proud to be an Ottoman, a Muslim and a soldier. Everyone there surely felt something similar. On display for the dignitaries and our troops I felt honored, important and confident of future success, depite my medal's irrelevance.

The Commanding General was an imposing man, built tall and heavy. His eyes never seemed to blink. Even Rauof Pasha must feel skin-scraped by that gaze. In Zeki Pasha's presence, the air itself quivered with pride and striving. A man of such bearing can never lose a fight—total perseverance grinds any adversary into dust, as the Sassunlis learned too late.

Some say it was his idea, arming Kurds to help us control the eastern provinces. The Sultan's hamidieh were excellent horsemen, so useful warriors against the Russians, though difficult to manage. They enhanced Zeki Pasha's influence with the Imperial Supreme Commandant. Unfortunately, Commanding General Zeki did not inform himself as to our province's particulars. His error is familiar throughout history. His decisions grew from his preconceptions and what he heard from certain unreliable men, among them an ayatollah with his own motives.

The band sounded reasonably martial outdoors. When it lost its rhythm in the reception hall, it compensated with still louder noises. Fortunately, it was dismissed before officers and guests shouted themselves entirely hoarse.

Orderlies passed trays of refreshments. The two visiting colonels moved among the crowd, exchanging comments where appropriate and speaking at length only with majors and up.

Fikret saw me and started to turn away, thought better, nodded, then looked elsewhere. His peculiar little dance suggested jealousy.

Moments later I came upon the Izgirli with his father. After introducing them to my father, I said, "Sergeant Mohamed, I'll be following your progress with great interest and expectation. Call on me if I can be of assistance." He thanked me gracefully.

At one point Shakir Pasha conversed closely with Governor Rauof, most likely on events in our provinces, for Commissioner Shakir was preparing a report for the Sultan. Neither official lingered to meet us. Commandant General Osman stayed tight to General Zeki, looking uncomfortable throughout. Osman disapproved unnecessary bloodshed and had earned praise across the city for aborting a bloodbath back in '90. The host's temperament was quite unlike his superior's.

My father seldom boasts, but when I led him to the commandants he held his chest forward as if it bloomed with medals. The German Consul was extolling (through his interpreter) the great variety of migrating birds in the region. We heard Zeki Pasha respond, "I trust the vultures looked fat enough, Consul—they feasted in Erzincan this week."

This puzzled Herr Consul Behrmann, who failed to hear the Commandant's ironic tone. "You slaughter livestock at this time of year?" he asked.

"Only pigs and dogs," the Commandant replied. "The kind with two legs and ideas of rebellion."

The consul gasped.

"Why so surprised? Don't you execute traitors in Germany?" Commandant Zeki looked smug.

The Consul took a moment to respond. "In Germany we put such men on trial. If convicted of treason they are executed," he said carefully.

"Just so do we have men awaiting trial in our prison here –" General Osman's tone was sharp as he tried to guide the conversation from mishap.

"There is a time for trials, and a time for cleansing the country of traitors. Let the Armenians beware."

No mistaking Commandant Zeki's meaning. Stories of his ruthlessness roiled my memory. I no longer doubted him capable of the most brutal exercise.

A pause let me introduce my father. He accomplished what Osman desired, a shift to safe topics bearing on travel and horsemanship.

The festive occasion left me disillusioned and brooding. Arresting traitors seemed futile. Mass violence was ahead for Erzerum regardless, as General Zeki held the entire Armenian millet disloyal. He hadn't bothered sorting rotten meat from fresh in Trabizond and Ak Hissar, he wouldn't bother here. Our vigilance could not keep loyal Christians safe.

Our good neighbors celebrated with us that evening, bringing trays of homemade pastries and apricot brandy from Garmir Vank monastery. "May it make us all holy!" We laughed as we echoed the eldest brother's toast.

They treated me like a bridegroom with joyful strikes on the back, toasts and embraces. Nazar congratulated my father for his success in raising me. The two old men foresaw my triumphant military future. Ehsan bragged about my medals, too young to understand their insignificance.

Sako took my son aside to test him with riddles. Ehsan tried to catch me.

"What has a wet tail when its head's on fire?"

"What field grows again after it's been harvested?"

I pretended to think hard before replying, "A lamp" to one and "A head of hair" to the other.

Our neighbors' courtesy was extraordinary. They never mentioned their holy leader's imprisonment, though it must have weighed heavily. The charges had to be most serious. It seemed likely he'd be tried in Constantinople before the Imperial Judicial Tribunal. Our conversation stayed on lighter topics, as fit our celebration.

Ehsan and Khalil amused themselves with the harmonica. Our conversation stopped while Ehsan played a song, proficiently. My brother sang along, some words right, some wrong. Everyone praised them. Ehsan smiled at my pride in his performance. During the hard times that followed I drew comfort recalling this.

Throughout the festive evening our neighbors concealed any uneasiness, as did I. At its close we watched the moon rise over the courtyard and I assured Martiros and Sako we'd keep Erzerum calm, that loyal Armenians need fear nothing. Yet troublesome doubts made me sleep fitfully, disturbing poor Khadija's well-earned sleep.

In the morning we were both short-tempered from fatigue. She wept when I scolded her for nagging.

"You've got a new medal, you care nothing for an old wife," she said. To placate her, I stayed all morning with her and Huru in the garden, and twice attended my mother, since idleness wears on me. She was weak and spoke little, but my attention raised her spirits. She asked again to see the medal, beamed at its weight on her palm. At least it gave her something other than her burdensome flesh to contemplate.

My half-day off duty failed to lighten my anxiety and I returned to barracks resolved to talk with Major Rustem as soon as possible.

Bergeron's Surprise

Martiros   October 26 - 27

Having seen the man almost daily for years, at church, at meetings, at my home and in my shop, I became confident I knew his character. We Kavafians were proud of the Bishop's friendship and we admired his leadership and probity. Now, astonished, I was forced to recognize that Ghevont Shishmanian, for all his abilities, was a man of flawed judgment. Like any of us, imperfect. Unpredictable.

From anyone else, I'd have scoffed at what Bergeron reported. Even then, only his discouraged and downcast demeanor convinced me.

"Our friend has made two serious misjudgments." The Consul's face was grave as he poured our tea. He said nothing more until he'd served us.

First, he confided, the Bishop wrote a secret letter, describing recent events in the eastern provinces and asking that England make every effort to protect his people. The letter was addressed to the British Foreign Secretary and intended for the English government. Before it reached London, his letter was discovered.

Our church leaders looked to England for help in those days, exactly as England's diplomats encouraged them to do. Oh, they were fine friends, those diplomats; the Bishop was sure of their sincerity. How full of sympathy they were! They spoke of us as "fellow Christians" in letters to the Sultan protesting mistreatment of Armenians. It was only <u>words</u> they gave away so freely, nothing more.

"Meat that's free may be rotten," it's said. Things would have gone better for our people if the Englishmen ignored our troubles, kept to neutral matters in their missives to the Sultan. Who knew that, then? What the Bishop did was understandable, although unwise.

"Second, he would not deny composing it."

With alarm I contemplated the probable consequences. The Bishop executed. Before that, tortured: feet, hands, eyes, manhood, as the Governor or Commandant chose. And others: his assistant, his secretary…perhaps the priests. Property confiscated. The Bishop's possessions, maybe the Prelacy building, conceivably also its orchards and pasturages. Indeed, every Catholic and Protestant church in the city could be rendered penniless if the Governor chose. The Armenian millet in Erzerum might be hard pressed to survive. I glanced over at my companion. Shabanian's face was lifeless, as sickened as mine.

The Consul continued in a sad voice. "Our friend Ghevont admitted dispatching this report by messenger to Kars. Then he reconsidered, sent a second messenger to overtake the first. But there were difficulties at the border. Either the first horse was too swift, or the second, too lazy. The document was sent. A great misfortune for our friend! Who could have known it would be intercepted in Paris and published in *Le Figaro*? Incroyable et tragique."

"I know that paper. But this is incredible!" said I.

"The Governor showed it to me. The Bishop's letter was there for all to see."

M. Bergeron waved away my questions with a tired hand. "In fact, the Bishop pointed out small errors in the printed version. Rhetorical changes the Figaro editor made for dramatic effect." He turned from us with a snort. Moments later he gave an odd laugh and continued his story. "As you imagine, he made his situation worse." The Consul shook his head regretfully, biting his lip.

"But how did the Governor—?"

"A gift from the Russian Consul. You know the sort he is. A soft-spined man, forever trying to ingratiate himself—the greatest of friends, the perfect envoy of brotherhood, while Cossacks threaten the border." I'd recently attended this man's reception for a Russian string trio headed for Paris, a city beloved by Russians.

"If only he'd called it a forgery!" I exclaimed.

"Ghevont is a man who lives by morality," the Consul said. "Our friend is unable to toy with truth, as a matter of Christian principle. It is his fiber. If all Christians…"

Krikor interrupted, indignant. "So it's treason to ask for help protecting your people? To ask the English for a diplomatic letter?"

"You offer a reasonable defense. Perhaps he said the same. If so, it was *inutile*." Bergeron sat motionless, his face without expression. "I gave the same defense and failed. The Governor, his staff, the mayor, the Commandant, have all agreed. Treason, they contend. Nothing other than treason."

"But they cannot dare harm him! They must not—!" burst from me.

"He is too prominent. We can be grateful for that." The Consul's voice was strangely flat.

"What will they—?"

"Exile. Immediate exile. Tomorrow he leaves under armed guard for Jerusalem. We are to speak no word of this. I believe the Governor plans an announcement. We must await the town crier. Do not tell even your families."

We sat stunned for several moments. After a time I was able to say, "Thank God for His mercy."

"My friends, I must tell you something else. Alas," Bergeron said, ruefully. "My usefulness in Erzerum has ended. I've become *persona non grata* from this incident. I must depart within the fortnight.

"No, no, it was not my inquiry, you're not to blame. Not at all." He sighed, and drew a deep breath. "Rather, they hold I helped the Bishop write the letter. At the least that I knew of it before the Governor." His voice lacked any note of indignation. I tried to read his eyes behind the glasses, saw neither denial nor admission of complicity. We had to form our own conclusions. I felt a renewed affection for this Frenchman.

In view of the circumstances, he considered it impolitic to attend the Shabanians' celebration. He'd no wish to compromise his friend

Krikor, nor to make an awkward situation for other guests. With that, Bergeron opened a drawer and withdrew a small beribboned parcel wrapped in shiny paper. He handed it to Krikor. "A small token as a momento, for your new grandson."

"You may be leaving at a good time. The events our Bishop wrote about have only gotten worse. You are aware of our apprehensions," I said.

"This is a trading center. Bloodshed here would damage economic affairs throughout the eastern provinces," the Consul said. "Although the same logic should hold for Trabizond." I nodded in grim agreement.

"I think…speaking unofficially, the climate for Christians is not healthy now. Disturbing things are being said, things I haven't heard in my four years in Erzerum until now. Not only said, but published. I hear there's a book just out in the capital, reviling members of your millet. And articles in *les magazins*…"

He broke off as if uncertain, then spoke again. "Please, should you need my protection while I'm still here, then do not hesitate. I'll gladly shelter your families. And if you should want French visas to leave the Empire—perhaps you'd find life more congenial in a Christian country? Russia is close. Or perhaps Greece—?"

"No, no! Thank you!" we both exclaimed together.

"Greeks and Russians share a single creed and pope. To them we're sinful heretics," explained Krikor.

"But do they do violence—?"

"From time to time, not often. But who can say it would be safer for us under a Czar or a king?" said Krikor.

"This has been our home for generations. It's our place—and we prosper here," I told him.

"I understand," said Bergeron. "I pray you continue to prosper here. Yes, I will pray…" He paused, smiling. "But let's not be so gloomy! Surely you'll be fine. Just keep yourselves warm when the snows arrive. Your magnificent, enormous snows! I won't forget them.

"And I won't forget you. I regret leaving my friends in Erzerum." His gesture included us. "However, it will be a pleasure to rejoin my family."

"No one can blame you for preferring your lovely Paris. It was my great fortune to study there. A beautiful place," said Krikor.

"Beautiful indeed. Yes, it will be good to see my city again." He bade us call on him, should we visit Paris. I hope to get there someday.

We saw him again the next morning at the Garrison gates, waiting for the Bishop to appear. Although it was early, several vendors had already spread their wares and now sat on their haunches, eyeing every passerby.

My father (I told no one else) would have embraced Bergeron in gratitude but the Consul stepped back. "You must not act like a friend or you could catch my illness," he warned. "It's best they don't see us talking. Allow me instead to thank you all—(here he bowed his head in turn to my father, Krikor Shabanian and me) for your friendship to me and your loyalty to our dear friend Ghevont Shishmanian." His eyes glistened as he moved apart.

I was startled to see the Bishop bare-headed, displaying an unfamiliar bald spot. One cheekbone bore a red sore edged with black, plainly a burn. Owed to a cigar, I guessed. A shameful insult to this holy cleric. His wrists were shackled. The Bishop's mount was a bony mare secured by a lead to a rider in front. He was gripping the mare's mane, for he did not ride often.

"Farewell, your Holiness!" "Farewell, dear friend!" "We wish you a safe journey!" we cried out as he passed.

"My blessings on you, dear friends. May God be—" The rest of his words disappeared in the clatter of his escort. At the next turn, the group swung toward the south gate.

In subsequent days his assistant took on the Bishop's duties with trembling hands. When I went to Father Ashod to discuss my donating some fabrics, he listened with bewilderment. Routine matters required unusual effort from him. In due course, the callow priest did learn to make decisions. Eventually he proved himself a reasonably competent leader, though always lacking confidence.

Almost a year passed before another Frenchman came to occupy the consulate.

Tears

Marjan

S ome noise woke me. Most likely it was Arsine crying out from a bad dream again. Nerses was close beside her with an arm around her shoulder, crooning a lullaby to her the way a mother does. The lantern in the corner flicked shadows across their bed.

Heranoush must have woken, too. She padded after me as I headed to the outhouse. At the door to the kitchen, we met darkness filled with wailing.

Someone's beating them was my first thought. But my lantern shone on them alone.

The two girls lay curled on a mat behind the stove, the boy sitting at their feet. All sobbing like keys on an accordion—when one slowed, another cried louder. Their noise made kettle lids clatter and brass trays hum. In our kitchen was a concert! It was my fault for telling them Toumia's order, yet I thought their sobs were from something else. My heart went to little Serop, how could he help but add his tears to theirs?

I knelt beside Serop and called the girls' names sharply. "Stop crying! Tell me what's wrong! Please, we want to help. Talk, tell us. We want to know –" I guessed they needed to explain their wounds and bruises, guessed the story would be painful to tell—and to hear.

So it was. After a time they pulled themselves up, facing Serop. The light shone thru their nightgowns in places, as if their bodies were naked. They looked like children, not young women. Their sobs gave way to groans, then mumbley sounds, then words. I should have sent my daughter back to bed, she was too young to hear their story. It haunts us still.

Oskee spoke first, eyes down. Her voice caught. "We were… we were working in the field. My husband, his brothers, Arpee. We heard shouting. Men. Kurds. They came on horses…" She paused.

"It's all right. Take your time." I didn't want to hear her. I wondered if Oskee's broken front tooth cut her tongue. Once when I was learning to cook, I licked a knife and could only eat plain bread and cheese for days after.

"Our husbands told us to run for home. My baby was there with his grandmother. We ran…"

Then Arpeh picked up the story without lifting her eyes from the lantern. "The Kurds were yelling, frightful cries, like wild pigs, to scare us. They fired a gun—they had long ones, rifles. I heard my husband scream. We were still a long way from home. I fell and got up again. We kept running for our house. We heard them coming after us, their horses ran so fast…" She took a deep breath, then another.

"You must leave now," I told my daughter. "Go back to bed."

"No, please, Mama! I'm not a child anymore!"

Perhaps she should hear this, I thought, to know why we keep her and Astghig home.

Arpeh went on, "We'd nowhere to hide, just fields on either side…" Arpeh's voice trailed into silence and her sister-in-law picked up the story.

"They knocked us down there on the footpath."

"Seven of them."

"Five, I think." Oskee's voice was faint.

"Five, seven, it doesn't…" Arpeh wept. My daughter made a retching sound, nothing else. Then Heranoush handed Arpeh a kitchen rag for her nose.

Heranoush, you shouldn't be here, I wanted to say, and in the same moment I recalled how ignorant I was of such thugs at her age. It took my older sister Nora to tell me these things when I was already

17 and promised to Petros. My mother never spoke of anything between men and women, bad or good. Girls must learn young to be wary. Nora scared me with her stories, but they helped keep me safe. When a stranger said something, I pretended I was deaf as Aunt Flora. I didn't look up.

"They cursed us for struggling. They laughed at us. They enjoyed themselves..." She waited for some time before going on in a quiet voice. "They hurt us. When they were done with us, one of them threw dirt all over us. He rubbed mud and pebbles into our..." Her hands went to her lap. "His face was like the Devil's! He had pointed ears and a forked tongue! Oskee saw it too! Forked like this!" She wriggled two fingers to make a serpent's tongue. "...Then they rode to the village. We heard screaming and shouts."

Arpeh was breathing hard. Heranoush and I were both too upset to cry, though our eyes were wet. Some say a husband changes a girl into a woman. It can be. Yet I say it's when her ears open to another's suffering that a girl grows womanly. Heranoush heard more and saw more after listening that night.

Oskee spoke now, in a tone like death. "It hurt so much. Every step hurt. Pain all through me...But we had to hide in case they came to hurt us again. We took the path to the orchard. We pulled ourselves up into an apple tree and hid there. After a while we saw a fire. The village was on fire! Our house was burning! We ran to get there..."

"No one was around. It looked like everyone was killed! Our neighbors lay dead on the path. Yalena—her skirt was up to... They took her jacket and headdress—Oskee, you saw?"

"I had to find my baby!"

"Oh, Oskee!" Now Arpeh clasped Oskee's hands, tears falling. We saw her struggle to go on. "He was alive, little David, in his cradle. We got him out. He was choking from the smoke... Father called out to us. He was slumped against the wall-post and his head was bleeding..."

"We dragged him out, away from the fire. Then I tried to nurse

the baby... I couldn't make my David suck. The dirt on my... tits..."
Oskee's voice choked. "He was wheezing as if he had no air. I squeezed
my...tit so drops fell into his mouth, but it made him gag and cough.
At last he fell asleep. At least he was still breathing." She gulped for
breath, gulped again and gave in to weeping.

Heranoush was swallowing. She looked ill. I almost wanted her
to throw up, to stop this story-telling. I didn't want to hear any more.
Like Artashes when he was little, pretending he was sick to stay home
from school. It meant more schoolwork later, and if I put off the story
now, I'd only have to hear it another time. And I admit, I wanted to
hear it, it was like looking through a doorway into someone's private
sitting room. You weren't supposed to look, but you couldn't stop. It
was exciting.

"Father-in-law saw our torn clothes, our cuts and bruises, the
dirt on us... He hissed at us..." Arpeh stopped in tears.

"He called us whores. Better dead. Said we ruined his honor.
Disgraced him and his sons. He called us worthless, and other awful
things. He spit at us. Then he shut his eyes," said Oskee.

"Your mother-in-law?" I asked.

"Dead. Stabbed with daggers, here and here." Oskee pointed to
her chest. "We left her in the house."

"The village kept burning. Twenty-one houses take a long time
to burn. An orchard burns faster. The wind blew smoke in our faces.

"We went looking for our husbands in the fields ...we were so
scared..." Here Arpee stopped and whispered something to Serop.
He was watching her as if she was the only person alive. She wiped
his nose with his nightshirt. We scold children for that, as if it's not
natural. We should let them be, I remember thinking.

"All killed..."

"Except me." Serop's first words that night.

"Little brother was hiding in a haystack, our clever boy! We
were so glad to find him!" She squeezed him around his narrow
shoulders. "We stayed there all night. David cried and cried, but he
wouldn't suckle. In the morning we got him to swallow a little water

and we washed ourselves in the stream. Everything was quiet. It was strange… We looked for someone to help us bury the bodies. No one was left."

"We found a broken spade and scraped out a place in the field. Serop helped us gather stones…"

"I found some big ones. Heavy ones," the boy put in proudly.

"We spent all day putting rocks on the grave so dogs … We saw dogs with someone's arm –"

"The next day we picked all through the ruins. We found raisins and a jar of oil half-buried in a storage pit. A small cup, nothing else. We ate a little and saved the rest, it wasn't much. We walked west towards the next village. We took turns carrying the baby, and sometimes we carried Serop." She stroked the child's cheeks with the back of her hand, the way a mother strokes her infant. A moment's softness in her face reminded me she was not much older than Heranoush..

"The baby wouldn't suck. My milk was gone. He was going to die… At the well, we met a woman who gave us bread and a little soup. She had goat's milk inside to give the baby. 'I'll make him strong,' she promised. She let us sleep in the hay pile." Oskee stared at me without seeing. She scratched the back of one hand, then the other, with rough fingers. Even in the dim light of the lantern, I made out new stripes on her skin.

"In the morning she gave us bread and olives. Then she told me my baby was dead…" Her voice had gone so faint I had to strain to hear it. "I said, 'Bring him to me! Please, let me kiss him goodbye! I must bury him!' She answered, 'He's dead and buried!' and she slammed the door in my face." Oskee's voice got shrill as she went on.

"She was lying to me! I pounded on the door, I screamed and pounded! Is he dead? Let me see him! I don't know, is he dead? Show me!" My daughter gasped. Her eyes were full of pity. I wanted to put my arms around her, protect her from the story, but she was too far to reach. My heart pounded from remembering the time Toumia kept my little Artashes from me when he was wailing to be fed. She wouldn't let me have him, made me leave him screaming. "He has to learn!" she said. *Learn what?*

Oskee's voice turned low and quiet again.

"I shouted and waited, I kept shouting, waiting. What else could I do?" Oskee was staring at me now as if I had an answer. "What else?"

"We stayed. We waited…we shouted. Then her husband came out. 'Get away!' he said, 'Your baby's dead. Armenians live in Erzerum, go there.' He told us who to ask for travel papers. He said we must leave, they didn't want us." Arpeh was weeping softly now. "The Kurds should have killed us, too."

"If not for the boy…"

"Oh, Oskee, Arpeh!" burst out Heranoush. Tears dripped down her cheeks. "It wasn't your fault!"

Oskee turned to me. "They should have shaved our heads. It would be better."

"Oh, no, your hair is beautiful! It shines like obsidian, I wish my hair was like yours, not plain brown –"

Love for Heranoush poured through me. She was learning to be generous.

"We…we… Tell us what to do," begged Arpeh. In the flickering light her right eye with its puffy, drooping lid gave her a madwoman's look. Yet her cheekbones were well formed and her neck was graceful and slender. I glanced at Oskee's scabbed lip and nose, the wound on her throat, and thought, her eyes are as lovely as Henza's. Once the sores heal, the two girls will look fine.

I wondered what Henza would say to comfort them. She seemed to find the right words easily. Dear Henza, who proved that losing your husband and child might be—for all your suffering—a boulder you could get around. Henza and Sako started a new life. Surely these two unhappy young women could, too. They were still very young. If…if only they were lucky.

"Don't give up. God kept you alive because He's got work for you." Just then Serop sneezed so loud we all blinked. "You're young, you're healthy," I told them. "Your lives aren't over. Not with these nice clean faces, nice clean bodies, nice clean feet. Good clean nightgowns. A fresh new life. Be patient, wait. You'll be happy again. I know it." I tried to sound more sure than I felt. My heart ached for them, and for my daughter, too young to hear what she heard that night. Maybe my words helped, for their breathing slowed. Arpeh yawned. I told them to sleep while they could. Serop was already dreaming.

Church Troubles

❀ · ❀ · ❀ · ❀ · ❀ · ❀ · ❀ · ❀ · ❀ · ❀

Marjan   Sunday, October 27

I twisted to catch Zari's eye through the female flock, then I waved her to the back of the balcony. I explained the problem in low whispers.

"You've got that room behind the kitchen and they need a home so badly! They'll do housework, they won't be any trouble. You'll like them, Zari, I'm sure of it," I ended. It was not the best home I could think of, but it would do.

"You're a kind woman, big sister. You try to look after everyone in the world!"

"They need a place. And you'll be glad to have them around."

A crease between her eyebrows showed Zari was thinking hard. Finally she decided, smiling. "I'll talk to Mother Varsenik. If she likes the idea, she'll have to talk the men into it. The whole family's a tangle, who can guess what they'll agree on?" I squeezed her hand in thanks.

Berthe Sharopyan slipped in beside me. One of the sick women had passed on, but others were getting better. The little boy had caught cold so he was sleeping by the stove. Happily, Zari's Asadur had donated a barrel of kerosene and other members of the lay council were helping with food. The miller Garmir sent two big sacks of bulgur and one-leg Vartkes sent a crate of dried figs.

"I think they mean it as a church offering," the widow whispered with a small laugh. Her air of well-being made me see she took to managing things, like Toumia. The one, kind and thoughtful, the other not. Before that I never saw the two were alike in character.

The next blink, loud voices under us burst through the Sunday drone. Something was happening in the main space, we'd no idea what. The women at the front of the balcony were leaning forward on their knees to peer below. A few women stood. Aunt Zabel and Yiri, holding hands, pushed forward so they could see the main chancel. Heranoush and the twins used the commotion to dart to the rear. They knelt there chattering, heads close.

"What is it?" "Is it soldiers?" "Who came in?" asked voices.

Someone said, "I think it's a priest, the fat one –"

"Did they arrest him?" another asked.

Sarah's little Krikor started crying. We heard men talking, though their words weren't clear. Had soldiers come? Were our priests getting arrested, too? No one knew what happened to halt the service. Whispers passed around the balcony, causing small cries of alarm. Excitement mixed with fear. For several minutes my worries for our refugees faded. Then I looked about for Zari, deaf-mouthed to her, "Don't forget!"

Hand bells rang for silence. Our priests went on with the service. We tried to keep our thoughts on prayer, but we were uneasy. Had some misfortune come to someone? My other worries kept me almost calm.

Babies know when their families are nervous. Little Garen screamed at the first drip of holy water and didn't stop until his godfather poked a sugar bag into his mouth. An old woman near me chuckled.

"He'll have good health, that baby, he chased the devil out," she said, her words slurred by missing teeth. Her twinkle showed she wasn't truly superstitious. Many women that age hug odd notions close as Jesus. My father's mother always left small gifts for the Magi at the fountain and Petros remembered his grandmother making him and his brothers carry blue beads in their pockets against the Evil Eye. Varti's mother would cover the mirror at nightfall, and my own mother never baked bread if she had her monthly because it would taste bad. Such foolishness! Toumia herself never stepped over a sleeping child. She made a cross sign when an owl hooted, too, though she frowned at what she called "peasant customs." As for me, I won't look in a dead person's eyes. Also, I'm careful never to praise a child's looks in his or her hearing, though this is sensible whether or not there's an Evil Eye.

Zari caught up with me as we went down the steps. "She says. 'No, two women in a house are enough.' She says we can take the child if you want—"

"They need to stay together, Zari. You understand…"

"I'm sorry." Her face showed it.

By now a huge babble of voices overflowed the church lobby, as families reunited.

"What happened?" "Tell us what happened, we couldn't see!"

We felt foolish when we learned. What lit our fears was only a bat swooping near the men's heads. We guessed the great noise of the church bells scared it from its roost. Some say you'll have sorrow if bats' wings touch you. It can't be true, but still I shudder if a bat flies close. When Heranoush was little, she dreamt a bat caught her by the hair and carried her away. The dream scared me, too, and for some weeks I slept poorly.

Zari's answer didn't bother me, for I was sure the little family would be happier with Varti and her family. I hurried to catch up with my friend. Varti, though, said 'no" at once. They'd already taken in two homeless families, as the Bishop asked—their house was full.

"I wish we could, I know we'd like them. Especially the twins, they miss getting out…" She caught my arm. "Don't look so worried, Marjan dear. You're sure to find a good place for them."

The women Varti suggested both gave me excuses. My hope was wiped away like spilled brine by the time we started home. My sisters, my friend Varti, the good Mrs. Avedian, Henza's first husband's family and two others—no one was willing. How much easier if our stable family came from Trabizond, I thought. Most city people are ill at ease with peasants.

"We'll ask around at the party. Someone's bound to take them," Henza said as we walked to the Shabanians'.

"The Shabanians may take them, they've such a big house! It's perfect!" said Yiri.

"It is indeed," I answered. I'm afraid I used the same mocking tone that Martiros did with her, and I was grateful Yiri didn't seem to notice. I doubted the Shabanians would care to add to their household now they had a fresh-christened grandson.

Christening

Marjan Sunday, October 27

From Souren Shabanian's glow, you knew right then this baby was the prize of her life. She went on about him like a cat that can't stop purring. Aunt Flora muttered an oath against the Eye.

Souren was dressed like a queen, with gold everywhere—ears and neck, wrists and fingers, head band. Her head scarf, too, had gold threads woven through. Her dress was new, of dark rose watered silk. Her husband and their elder son Mesock wore matching silk handkerchiefs of grey and green in their chest pockets. They need color, those dark suits in the English style that our men sometimes wear. School uniforms look nicer, with their rows of shiny buttons marching up the front. My mother's ear caught Heranoush's little sigh seeing Dajag Shabanian, handsome as a prince in his Sanasarian School uniform. As if it wasn't the same dull grey her brothers and cousins wear at Ardzenian!

On the sideboards were heaped olives and grape leaves, cheeses and pastries, nuts and sweetmeats, set between punch bowls and carafes of wine. Flowers filled every corner. Musicians were playing in a side room and extra servants worked in the kitchen. The Shabanians were known for giving marvelous parties, but this was the best ever. Not just because of musicians and flowers, music and food, but because of Souren's joyful face. Her pride in her grandson was something to remember. It made us happy despite our worries.

Party guests are expected to celebrate and I think most of us were cheerful. Yet feathery chat kept dropping to serious matters. Some mention of the cold would draw words on homeless beggars, a remark about the summer would bring up raids on nearby fields. We kept thinking of our Bishop and other good Armenians in prison, the Trabizond refugees, the troubles in Constantinople, the extra soldiers on the streets. Even the milky Eksa in her bed asked what we heard about the Primate, though in a moment Henza and I turned her to her birth-labor and its precious result.

Garen was a fine baby with a tight little mouth and small dark eyes that stared calmly up at mine while I held him. He wailed when I handed him to Heranoush and she shoved him back like a hot stone before he got used to her scent. Henza declined to take him, saying he wanted his mother. She wanted a baby of her own too badly.

Sounds from downstairs made the new mother say, "It's not fair to make the baby's mother miss the celebration. I did the work!" In fact, Eksa seemed content to see a stream of female visitors.

Because she'd miss the gift-opening, Eksa begged to know our family's christening gift. It was a child's saddle, beautifully tooled, with bright brass fittings. I wanted such saddles for my sons if we had ponies. Eksa had no notion of the work put into it, yet she gave a charming comment. "So he's to be a horseman like his godfather Luivik! How wonderful!" she said.

We no sooner joined the other guests than Souren's gap-toothed brother Hamo tapped me on the arm. He was a cheerful, gossipy man without airs, forever slipping sweetmeats to the children at church or on the way to school. Since Hamo's trade was selling tobacco, not banking, he wasn't used to European clothes. He kept poking a finger inside his collar as if he was choking, then pulling on his jacket. His fez was the brightest in sight so he must have bought it for the party.

Souren's brother stayed close, whispering names. Three Americans from the Mission School were there, wearing serious faces. Nearby stood the mayor, his assistant, a judge and the treasurer, said to be the richest man in Erzerum. Heranoush started to giggle when she saw them, and I hissed, "Mind your manners!" at her, but they struck me as funny-looking too, the assistant Abdi like a heron beside three puffy pigeons. The judge was even wider than the mayor, the treasurer wider still, and each had a sort of cow-horn mustache with waxy-pointed ends like cousin Levon's. Maybe it was the latest Erzerum fashion for important Muslims, I don't know. Hamo pointed out two officials from the capital who he figured were spies, and both were smooth-faced.

Most Christians never invited Muslims to family celebrations, but it was different for us and the Shabanians, living in a mixed neighborhood. You naturally try to make friends with your neighbors. Also, certain Muslims had to do with Krikor Shabanian's bank. Nazar Patriarch said Krikor Effendi was the most important Armenian in Erzerum, after the Primate. Hamo whispered that the Governor was also invited, although everyone knew that Raoul Pasha never went to Christian gatherings. Think how nervous we'd feel if he came!

Captain Hamed, his father and another Muslim neighbor were sharing jokes with Sako and Martiros. The Captain was so pale and haggard I only knew him from his uniform. It hung loose from his shoulders. He left early, apologizing for having to return to the garrison. None of the Muslims stayed to the end except his father. The three Americans left soon after the mayor.

The Muslims avoided our eyes. We made them uneasy. Of course their wives were at home, the Muslims don't like other men seeing their womenfolk. Captain Hamed never brought Khadija over, the many evenings he and his father visited, until after his mother died. Except once, for condolences.

Women can visit one another, though. Sometimes when we were outside, watching our children play, Khadija invited us over. We invited her, too, but she'd only come for a moment because her mother-in-law might need her. The old woman was bed-ridden and Khadija nursed her for years.

Many important Christians were there, too. Souren kept glancing over to make sure the Americans were content. They spoke our language poorly, but better than other Europeans. I overheard them talking with Principal Drikian and his wife. Mrs. Chambers was trying to find chalk for their school's slate boards. I'd have told them Stoljk's just got some in from Damascus, if not for the Drikians. They held themselves apart from ordinary people, as if Ardzenian School was better. Yet everyone knew Sanasarian exams were harder and Hripsime's girls were as smart as the boys both places. The Sanasarian and Hripsime principals were polite to everyone, the Drikians just liked to keep their noses up.

We all pretend we like to watch other people open gifts, but it makes me uncomfortable. Some gifts will be better thought out and the fine gifts shame me with envy. Some of us stayed a bit apart whispering. This was when Principal Babayan invited Heranoush and Astghig to Sanasarian School's chorus concert. It was thoughtful of him and they were eager to go.

Some women you learn to dislike at the baths—the ones who are loud or whiny or too lazy to pick a towel from the floor. I always cringed to see Yegisapert Popgian. She'd find any excuse to come near when Heranoush and Astghig were naked, as if they were bride prospects for one of her dreadful sons. Other women you came to admire for their tact and courtesy. Mrs. Soghikian was one of these, and her friend Mrs. Madatian another. At the baths we shared lively talk along with our juices and fruit pastes. It was natural to ask these ladies if they might take in our three peasants. I told them all the best reasons, but both said their houses were already over-crowded. I prayed silently for God's help and felt discouraged.

We went on to talk about summer school-camp and how else to keep children busy out of school. I noticed their husbands locked in close conversation nearby, looking around to make sure they weren't overheard. We guessed they were talking about the new rules for Christian schools. Berthe Sharopyan had warned me not to teach lessons to the refugee children, as this was forbidden.

Spies could be anywhere, and now and then a husband hushed his wife for something said openly at home. Big ears didn't worry two couples speaking a strange tongue that Hamo called French. The women wore smart silk dresses, tight on top, rounded in back below the waist. They talked so fast, I wondered they could understand each other. Their husbands were the German and British consuls. Hamo said they asked his advice about shipping tobacco from Trabizond. Everyone smokes in Europe, even some of the women!

Yiri was talking to a short-sighted young man, one of our sons' teachers. He looked like he wanted to switch places with the Bishop. Taking pity, I led Hamo over. The teacher escaped and Hamo got the pleasure of pointing out to Yiri the various notables present.

Dr. Tashjian stopped to chat with Toumia. It still angered me to see her preening like a well-fed cat. She <u>was</u> a kind of cat, I decided: wily, selfish and half savage, protecting her own, with no pity for others. My inside ear heard my mother remind me to fix my own eye before finding fault in Toumia's. Better to use my mind to find a home for Oskee, Arpeh and Serop. Matriarch Toumia had cares of her own.

Dr. Tashjian was moving from guest to guest, shaking hands and bowing, missing no one. He changed easily from Turkish to Armenian for the women who knew only our ancient tongue. Gracious, tactful, reassuring, popular with Muslims and Christians, like our host. A physician makes a lot of friends if he doesn't kill too many of his patients.

Keghvart Bedoian motioned me to her group, her face beaming with pride at her good-looking sons. They stood listening politely to a lanky, red-nosed man talk about the Bishop's arrest. None of us had any idea that our saintly friend was exiled because Martiros and Krikor Effendi (it turned out) promised to keep it secret. The news came the next day.

"It's clear they want to humiliate us." Red Nose looked about before resuming in a lower voice, "It's a brilliant start to turning us back into slaves. Without our holy leader, we're powerless!"

Keghvart and I both gasped at hearing this, while Red Nose took on a smug face.

"They'll have to release him soon, I think. He can't have done anything," Garabed Bedoian reassured his mother.

"They don't care <u>what</u> he's done, they want us to tremble! I think—" Red Nose might have kept on, but my brother-in-law broke in with some business matter.

Keghvart Bedoian seized Martiros' arm and filled his ears with questions about the Bishop. He wouldn't answer. "We'll hear something soon, that's all I can tell you," he told her firmly.

She went on as if she hadn't heard him. "Such a good man, I'm sure they'll let him go soon! They <u>must</u>! He's promised to christen the babies." Her frown became a smile and she winked at me in her merry way. "Such a happy new year for Bedoians! Already Garabed and Aram are planning a party for our friends! You and your family must come!" A bit later, she promised she'd think of someone who'd make room for our refugee family.

Petros was talking close with Father Ashod and took no notice when I joined the priest's wife Elmas and a pretty Greek woman with her. Sophia Bjalian's face was smooth and perfect as a cameo. When she spoke, her features danced—I never saw a face come to life so fast. Yet when she was quiet, her face was sorrowful. I soon learned Sophia was only five weeks wed to one of the rug-trader Bjalians. Her family was far away in Smyrna and she was homesick.

Sophia and her husband came on the new railroad as far as Konya. She called it a featherbed compared to the oxcart they had the rest of the way. Someday the railroad's supposed to reach Erzerum, though Martiros said only luck will get it as far as Adana by the end of the century.

Sophia heard one of the American women, Mrs. Chambers I think, say Palestine in summer was even worse-smelling than Erzerum. She asked me was this so, and the next minute I invited her to visit us at our mountain place as if she was a close friend! Already I was thinking the Bjalians might take our refugees. I liked Sophia as soon as I saw her.

By now the guests were mostly familiar faces from St. Asdvadzadzin's. Talk became easier. People were congratulating the baby's godfather—he was Eksah's brother Luivik—on getting out of jail. He was enjoying the attention, pushing up his sleeves to show his sores. He said others got beaten worse, that Teacher Tarbasian had both eyes swollen shut. Luivik guessed they'd let the teacher go when his face looked better. Poor teacher! He couldn't walk around the prison yard without Luivik guiding. At least their feet weren't beaten like young Memmik the Knifemaker's.

People were happier in the next room. The musicians played a round of "Pretty Bracelet" that set Garabed and Digran dancing. All the girls were watching the handsome brothers as if they were still bachelors. A couple of old men joined in, then younger ones, until a jumble of men raised hands above their heads, showing off their footwork for the ladies. Sako danced as well, his lucky silk handkerchief stretched between his hands, his eyes shining for his smiling Henza at the side.

The music drew the young like flowers draw bees. Soon Souren's schoolboy Dajag, her niece Hasmig, Artashes, Arsen, Heranoush and Astghig all joined the circle, clapping hands at every beat. It was good to see them enjoying themselves. Especially Heranoush.

Most of the older men ignored the music. They stayed together, whispering, trading rumors. Where usually they talked politics and business, this Sunday it was the Bishop, the extra militia, the bloodshed in Trabizond and Erzincan.

Aunt Zabel closed her ears to their talk. "Invented by beggars to get your coins," she called it. Yiri and her mother looked out the same roof-hole, as we say. They wanted to think all was well, and pretended it was. They chose to speak of easier matters more fitting for a party. Who could blame them? It made no difference what we talked about, we'd no way to change anything. We might as well enjoy ourselves.

Yet I couldn't bear chatting on about bridal chests and baby clothes and baking. Too many more important things were being talked about that day. And not only by men, for women were scattered among the men folk. I tucked myself into one of the groups, next to Mrs. Madatian.

Her husband Masis, Eksa's uncle, was a man with a scowl carved into his face and one claim to fame: He sought payment for carpets stolen from his shop five years ago that turned up later in some offices at City Hall. Petros said the man was too self-important to imagine he'd be thrown in jail for this. His ransom cost as much as the carpets. Why his family paid it was another question, did they think his ill temper would get better? The son brought in customers and the father got rid of them.

They talked about a village girl who renounced Our Lord to save her life. She pretended to become Muslim, but she kept on praying to Christ Jesus in secret. When she was rescued, she told the priest she never turned her heart from Jesus, but held fast to Him. The priest called the poor girl an apostate.

"Unfortunately, our priests are not all wise," said Father Ashod. He felt the girl was still a Christian. I always liked Father Ashod. He was a good man, unselfish and sensible, strict with children. The youngsters made fun of his lisp and the way his eyebrows jumped when he made the signs, as if that mattered. Most of us respected him for his kindness and learning.

Masis entered in by declaring he'd kill his daughters before he'd let them be kidnapped. I couldn't keep from gasping. "Couldn't you hide them instead?" I asked. Several people agreed with me, but Masis and one or two others said they'd kill their girls first.

"They'll be killed anyway if they won't renounce Christ!" said my homely-faced cousin Berj, who was Souren's half-brother.

"I'd throw myself from the roof!" declared his wife, although she was way too fat to climb through a roof hole.

His voice low, Father Ashod said he'd had Elmas and their children practice hiding behind a false wall. "Find a safe place for yourself and the other young women at home," he told me.

If someone else said such a thing, my face would turn red. Even Sara is hardly a tempting young woman any more. He was right, though—it's best to avoid harm's way. A memory fell out of the air, of the secret closet where Petros and I sometimes made love half the night, before Heranoush was born. Before the Kavafian grandchildren were so many we moved up the street to a larger house. It was a joyous place, that closet. The memory caught me by surprise, and I felt a flush travel from my belly to the top of my head.

The group went on arguing while I slipped apart to let my color settle. I looked for Henza to ask if she'd thought of any good hiding places.

"I can think of something better."

"What?"

"Shave our heads." She was half smiling.

"I thought of that, too, but I know what my daughter will say. She'd rather hide."

"We must do both." Henza gazed at me steadily. She was as serious as I.

"All right." We embraced to seal our pledge.

A familiar laugh made me turn my head. Aunt Zabel was beaming at us. "What did I tell you? Souren invites our little family of three! She says it's what they need so their grandson won't be too spoiled!"

"Has she asked Krikor Effendi?" Perhaps it was too good to be true.

"He gave his blessing."

"Bless you, Aunt Zabel!" We both hugged her, our eyes overflowing with relief. She chuckled with delight at what she'd done.

With my heart thumping I hurried to Souren.

"Now the baby's named, it's time to look out for the unfortunate. We Shabanians are ready and willing."

"Shall we bring them some day soon? Perhaps on…" I hesitated at whether three days was time enough to wait.

"Today's fine! We've so many little cakes and sweetmeats—won't the boy like those! And look at all the flowers! We'll put flowers in their room!" Her heart was truly generous that day. She might have taken three blind lepers if someone asked.

On the way home, my daughter and Astghig skipped along, giggling together like children. "Mama!" Heranoush called back to me, "I think someone likes me!" More giggles. "His name is—- No, I won't tell you!"

"I'll tell! His name is Dajag Shabanian!" put in her cousin.

"He's a nice looking boy. His mother says he's a fine student," I said, trying not to sound pleased.

"He's going to sing at the concert!" No pretending the music mattered.

When we were done putting the children to sleep, Petros noticed I was smiling. I couldn't help it, I was so happy that our village-refugees were in a welcoming home.

"You should smile more, it makes your face beautiful," he said.

Instead of answering, I touched him. Then he put both arms around me and we kissed, behind the curtain tied on the bedposts. He stroked my neck and breasts. We nearly made love then in the dim light except our neighbors had sent for Patriarch just an hour before, and we needed to find out why.

Preparations

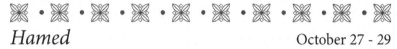

Hamed   October 27 - 29

A grown man's face can be hard to read. Not so a child's. Ehsan's disappointment flashed when he opened the gate. I checked my tongue; far heavier matters than his lessons weighed on me.

"Tell your grandfather I must see him. Hurry, I'm due at the Citadel!" I said, drawing my horse inside.

Already Keyif was trading whinnies with our mares, his ears up, head turned toward the stable. I knotted his reins, sent him trotting with a fond whack.

"Go to it, boy, while you've the chance!" The blizzard showed me no one knows what time is left. Best use it well.

Slippers slapping across tiles, Father's breath heaving. "Bad news? Something wrong?"

Indeed. With Zeki Pasha to review all garrisons the next morning, everyone was pressing to prepare. Explaining, I guided him to the bench beside the fountain. Ehsan knelt on the far rim watching the goldfish flash and bob, avoiding his books.

"It's got to be—what we've talked about." Uncertain my son could hear us. "Nothing else would bring Zeki Pasha back so soon. As you said—bad news."

"You've been told—?"

"Nothing officially, but it's clear what's planned. This commandant leaves blood behind him."

"Rebellions bring bloodshed. It's inevitable." He shrugged. "Sassun's Ermeni had to learn that. Or would you let them light fires—and start a revolution?"

"Father, you know they were living on chaff! The Kurds stripped them bare! How could they pay taxes? All they asked was protection."

"They threw their lives away."

"Along with their women and children and elders." I stood up, agitated. "Father, the slaughter was avoidable."

"It earned your general every honor."

"Don't call him my general, not Zeki Pasha!" A faltering melody cut into my argument. Ehsan was making progress with his harmonica.

"Admit at least, Sassun brought him fame. Heroic General of the Fourth Army! Follow his model, the Sultan's pet!" Father threw out his chest in a military posture.

He was playing with me; I started pacing to regain some calm. The conversation was not proceeding as planned. "Drills and discipline—fine. Soldiers need it. But as for its present purpose..."

"To fight Cossacks!"

"That's what we're told. But you see what's happened since the trouble in the capital! Trabizond...Baiburt... Erzincan! Ermeni hamlets..." I could see he wanted to speak, yet was too heated to stop myself. "We've refugees camped a mile out the Trabizond road. And the Erzincan road. And the river banks. Beggars all over the city! Sneaking in at night through Olti gate, clambering over the cemetery wall, desperate for..." I paused, distracted by a splash. Drops shimmered in a bit of sun above the pool.

"You'd let mobs storm the Palace? Threaten the Sultan's life? The army shouldn't dig out revolutionaries?" His tone contrived to draw me on.

"You know what's going on here, Father!" By shifting sideways I could see his eyes. "We've locked up those who matter. The rest are too scared to blow their noses. Granted, some Ermeni don't care if it's us or the Cossacks so long as their trade's profitable. That doesn't make them traitors—or collaborators. They aren't working to bring the Russians here." Aroused, I pounded my right hand into my left. Father raised his eyebrows as if doubting my logic.

"We both love our country, we don't want it hurt, we don't want our Sultan harmed. Those trouble-makers who'd damage our Empire should be shot! We can't allow it! But these are loyal citizens and we both know it, Father! Look at Petros, look at Krikor Effendi Shabanian, look at your friend Giragos! They want a peaceful life, a fair living. Safety for their families." My father's face was still impassive so I fired another volley.

"Erzerum Ermeni aren't a threat, we've no reason for pogrom!" Since I was a boy he'd talked of our eastern neighbors and their harsh hands with their minorities.

"So, Hamed, you say this review means Erzerum's in for trouble too? The Sultan's favored butcher came this distance to lead jihad? Our city's calm, it makes no sense."

My father paused at familiar sounds from a window: a ringing bell, Khadija calling, "I'm coming, Mother, coming!"

"Your wife gets no rest," he said. He was kind to her. Lately, if he woke early, he'd see to Mother's bell so Khadija could sleep. He leaned forward, elbows on knees. "We've heard the mayor, the governor. They've said it won't happen here. They'd look like... liars—or puppets." He mused aloud, perplexed. "You're telling me our mayor and governor have no say?"

I shrugged. He knew as well as I whose spoon went first in the pot and whose second, as they say. "We're wasting words. You're right, it will embarrass Raouf Pasha and Shakir Pasha. It makes no sense— just the same, it's going to happen." I paused, reluctant to continue, and determined he hear my gravity.

"Soon. Ermeni will die."

His face tightened. His next words seemed a plea. "Surely Iron Foot Street will be safe, at least! We've more Ottomans and foreigners for neighbors than Ermeni..."

"You taught me, Father, not to mistake a hope for probability. Once a mob gets going, start praying for Armenians! Well off ones like the Kavafians and the Shabanians..."

My daughter's laugh from inside startled me: Huru and Khadija in a hiding game even as we struggled with this desperate matter. A soldier must avoid thinking of his family. "The rabble aren't stupid, Father. They'll pluck grapes from the vineyard if they get the chance...assuming soldiers don't strip it first."

"I gave no ear to the ayatollah on Friday. You know I dislike his ranting. But he was plainly calling for bloodshed: infidel blood. Without remorse."

"I've heard him. He favors breaking, not mending. Some blame him for the slaughter in Sassun." We agreed on this point. He went on, pausing only to breathe.

"He screamed like a madman, 'We must perform jihad against these infidels!' They cheered and he yelled it out again and again! Four times or five, until the entire mosque was shouting, 'Jihad upon infidels!' Everyone hopping with excitement like schoolboys playing leapfrog. As if bloodshed's a game!" He sighed before continuing.

"This ayatollah gains much from jihad and loses nothing, like the people he leads. For the glory of Allah, Mohammed and the ayatollah, destroy the infidels! Enrich the mosque, enrich the mob!"

His words rang in my head before I spoke.

"We must consider our friends."

The old man stayed quiet while I breathed deep to slow my pulse. At length he reached a decision. "This evening I'll speak to Petros. He must bring his family here if trouble comes."

With an effort, I lowered my voice. "Listen, Father! Once it starts, we won't have time to save them. Imagine the crone-face sisters hobbling across their yard to our back gate with 40 thieves breaking their door! They'd never make it!"

"We can leave the gate unlocked –"

"Father, think what can happen. One of the women can't make it, or someone spots her coming through our gate, and the mob goes wild! They chase their prey, invade our house!"

"You're saying they'd follow the Kavafians into our house?"

"And do who knows what harm to all of us," I told him.

"I've seen mobs do ugly things. Civilians or soldiers, it hardly matters, once they start. Before long there's a crazy kicking a half-dead dog, five corpses, and 10 men too lazy to swat horseflies hauling all the loot they can carry. They'll deny they've done wrong. By suppertime they're your neighbors again." I thought of Topol with his shifty bloodshot eyes and his thieving helper, Pohar. They'd slide into a mob and out again smooth as eels.

"Even if we're not invaded—say the whole family makes it here safely and no one follows them here—their house will be stripped. Emptied out with nothing left!"

"I suggest they store their valuables here, ahead of time. And make ready to get out of their house and into ours, in a blink…" Father's voice trailed off. "The problem remains—can they get here fast enough? Perhaps you'll know beforehand, Hamed?"

"Possibly. Mostly we'll have to guess from deployments. We may have a day to prepare, we may have two hours…We may get no warning at all."

"Then we should tell the Kavafians to come here soon. This week."

I frowned and shook my head while I looked for a way to lead him further without opening objections. "Father, think carefully how it can be managed. We don't know when the violence will come. It might be this week, or weeks away. We can't tell how long they'll need protection. One month? Two? Imagine us all together in this modest house, imagine our discomfort!"

During this conversation, my son had been pebbling the goldfish, defiant. The fountain was faced with fine old tiles of faded yellow and deep blue. My annoyance flew.

"Ehsan, STOP THAT! You'll chip tiles and clog the drain!" My harsh voice startled us all. I've always held shouting is the wrong way to lead. One must show self-control to earn respect.

Ehsan stared at me a moment, hurt and sullen. Then he pounded into the house, dragging his jacket. Ashamed, I pledged to show more affection next time I was home.

"They can't stay at home and they can't come here…" My father was drawing me back to the central issue. "So. What superior solution do you propose, my Captain-hero son?" His tone fatherly, bemused. With relief I realized he'd hear me out.

"Simply this."

My father anticipated every element of my proposal. He suggested safeguards, got us tossing details about like bullets. Catching some, letting others drop. We chose not to speak of risks to ourselves and to my career; we both knew these were intrinsic to our plan.

If our plan was known I could forget promotions and strategic postings. A high price, yet unavoidable. A necessity, for Martiros was my brother. His father, his brothers, mine. Their family was my family. A man bears obligations stronger than personal success. I still believe this, despite an unfortunate estrangement.

My father, too, faced risks. Our family could be denounced, castigated, his enterprises strangled. Yet he didn't hesitate. He imposed one condition only. I must keep my part hidden, protect my career. He chose to carry the risk alone. A model of courage, my father.

Relieved at our decision, I cantered Keyif half way to the garrison. Father worked most of that Sunday night seeing the scheme through. And tired as he was, spent the next few days covering for the Kavafians at their shop.

※ ※ ※

An early morning drizzle on top of a downpour two days earlier made soup of our parade ground. Imagine 1,800 soldiers with their feet mired in muck, every face dirt-spattered. Imagine as well three mounted squadrons, each 140 strong, mud-speckled like drovers. Another commandant would have called off this review, but not Zeki Pasha. He took no notice of the mess or the animal stinks. Nor did the men. Excepting the usual grumblers, the men were content to slog in muck as a fair trade for riches close ahead. From time to time a buzz escaped the ranks. The men were impatient for action: for plunder.

"Eyes forward!" I made my squadron sit straight in their saddles, heads up. The most important rule is discipline. When the order came, I must maintain command. Men do shameful things when they run wild.

The troops fell out of step, sizing up houses along the way to their forts. Few Christians were out and most of their shops were closed. What with whole battalions marching to and fro, and the many Kurds and toughs idling about the Plaza, the Ermeni had good cause to be apprehensive. The idlers watched my patrol with hard faces; many carried cudgels.

The Kavafians' safety worried me. They should be safe, yet what if a neighbor there betrayed them? A watchful widow ruled the house on one side, a family of weavers had the other. Well-occupied dwellings overlooked the courtyard. Whatever hour, the neighbors' windows never lacked for eyes. Father warned the Kavafians to be invisible or we'd all be ruined.

The first day there, the family slept, exhausted. That evening, Father brought them a full sack of coins and IOU's. The day's customers had been excited and impatient, almost as if a snowstorm was coming. One red-nosed customs clerk demanded his boots "right now, before trouble breaks out." Did the refugees create those rumors, or was it Zeki and his staff who promised loot? Most likely both.

Many hours at Nazar's side trained Father well. He proved an able stand-in, locating boots, writing bills, stuffing the strongbox. The Kavafians' absence he blamed on a belly flux that strikes when seasons change. Plausible a few days, at least. He gave my brother a string of chores to keep him silent; both relished being useful.

On Tuesday I led my patrol through Rose Bush quarter, then Iron Foot. We saw few Ermeni, with more and more hamidieh riding slow through Armenian neighborhoods and many gangs of roughs and homeless swaggering around the Armenian bazaar. All assessing their prospects, silent and furtive like street-mimes sharp-eyed for coins. Preparing for a signal.

In barracks, I overheard one private, name of Tahsin, brag to another, "I know an Armenian house's got silver flasks and cups of gold. You wait, I'll be a rich man soon!" Their eyes gleamed. My lectures against thievery blew past their ears. How otherwise? That pittance wrested from the Imperial paymaster last spring was at most a month's wages: three minutes' worth of meat and dice. We officers fared better although still in arrears.

Simple lads mostly, good farm boys. Mothers and sisters cooked and did their washing before the army claimed them. Recruits could boil their wheat soon enough, but laundry was a slower lesson. Shirts got rank and stiff with sweat. When the weather was right I'd make them scrub their uniforms, mend them, bathe. They played naked by the stables while their clothes dried in the sun. Few had warm underwear or a second blanket for the iced dark already choking Erzerum's daylight. Was it any surprise they craved treasures, clothes, foodstuffs? I'd few illusions about them once action started. Shakir and a couple of others could be counted on, but the rest would steal. My best real hope was to forestall murder.

Although much relieved as to the Kavafians, I was uncertain as to warning others. Every Armenian warned increased the risk for me and those already hiding. If word spread, forget easy pickings, forget control. Soldiers and rabble would pry out their plunder, killing and maiming in their frenzy.

Two families weighed heavy on me: Giragos the goldsmith, my father's friend, and Grandfather Shabanian, our hospitable near-neighbor. Both were bright targets, the one's shop with its costly inventory, the other's handsome dwelling, sure temptations to men lacking possessions.

Troubled, I'd decide one way, then the other, so absorbed that Shakir, grinning, re-buttoned my tunic. I over-wound my watch because its hands seemed stuck in place. Finally it was mid-afternoon, too late for the dreaded order. Ruffians crowding the streets added to the barracks' fevered conspiring and persuaded me to warn Giragos and Shabanian.

Riding towards jewelers' row, considering what to say, I came upon the jeweler himself, trudging homeward. Two heavy sacks hung from a pole pressing into his neck. Shoulders bent, head down, Giragos was deaf to my call and was halted only by Keyif in his path. My effort was superfluous, for Father already had warned him.

"My wife wants this. My flour's valuable," Giragos winked at me and chuckled, mindless how each lurching step proclaimed hidden treasure. I urged he return, both to lighten his load and to put back some gold. His shop must look normal.

"Take care not to attract attention! Do nothing suspicious! Be discreet," I warned him.

"Surely, surely," he replied, without changing course.

Should I have insisted he go back? Might it have saved him? Perhaps I gave up too easily, anticipating Krikor Effendi Shabanian's common sense. Turning Keyif's head left, I went to find the banker.

Two

The Incident

October 29, 1895 through late January 1896

The Incident

Hamed   October 29-30

M ajor Rustem showed scant relish for his task, yet he was a
smart and able military leader. Seeing the risks, it followed
that he saw the need to organize deployment. He presented our
assignments early so we had some hours to absorb them. Our
strategies, though imperfect, kept chaos from consuming Erzerum,
and importantly, forestalled still greater suffering.

The Major expected final orders within two days. For now, with
boots firmly planted, he traced out our respective territories on a
rough-drawn city map. His copper-tipped pointer wore through the
Armenian quarters first. The two sub-lieutenants holding the sheet
up tried hard to see the details.

The Major insisted we control the population as well as our men,
warning us sharply, "Contain the mobs, else this city will be cinders!
Keep the assault orderly! Don't allow another blood-bath! This isn't
Trabizond or Gemush Khaneh, don't fear our minorities, they're
peaceful, by and large. They're <u>unarmed</u>! Don't shoot unless you have to!"

Zeki had claimed the Armenian market. None of my fellow
officers grumbled, we expected it. There'd be great resentment if one
of us got the juiciest plum.

Major Rustem followed sound principles, weighing each officer's
abilities and defects against his purpose. He applied mounted
squadrons where horses are most effective. My assignment suited
military ends and my character. He saw I'd do better at defense
than assault and respected this in giving me responsibility for the
consular district.

My assignment irked some men under me. "Why's our squadron deprived when everyone else gets rich?" groused Fikret.

"Officers got paid three times this year. Remember it's our soldiers want wages," I told the junior lieutenant.

I repeated Major Rustem's warning: prevent harm to foreigners and their property, protect our Imperial interests. Fikret and I divided our ranks. His were to protect the lower stretch of Customs House Street; his other troops could seek their opportunity once all was secure. My chosen squad was to cover Customs' adjoining length but my other troops were released. High moral ground, I've learned, can be lost to resentment.

Two horses proved their value the next morning, as messages streamed from telegraph office to Governor's office, City Hall and Citadel, between and back. Then the final order came.

Civil officials still claim that an unplanned incident set things off. A village priest entered the provincial government building, seeking redress after hamidieh robbed him. The priest was most probably a poor man, artless, as some said. He'd two or three other Armenians with him. A sentry said the infidels drew guns and wounded a guard before they died. I knew the sentry; he was a mean one and a liar. Unlucky timing for those Armenians, arriving when a scapegoat was needed.

"Save your bayonets for resisters, spare folks fleeing home. There's no need for slaughter—they'll reward you for letting them pass," I told my men. I made clear their main duty was protecting foreigners and their property. Yet their attention was divided, as if dodging cannon fire, and they heard only parts of what I said. To catch their ears, I called a sergeant by name. "Omar! Have you ever walked on broken glass?" I asked. The man reddened, confused.

"Now listen, soldiers! We want no windows broken this time!" In riots a few years before, every glass pane in the English mission was stoned.

Fikret and I divided our work more specifically now, with some groups to guard the consulates and U.S. mission. Shakir with me to head Customs Street, five pairs of trusted recruits behind us, and Fikret with two sub-lieutenants and 10 soldiers to block that street's foot.

We were in place when the signal shot skywards at the Holy Mosque. That harsh crack was echoed by shouts and gunfire, the mixed sounds spreading fast from Plaza to Armenian bazaar close by.

Our small force succeeded at first. Once Keyif reared at a pitched stone, but I held firm. Shakir struck the brat with his rifle butt. We discovered some stalwarts defending the Health Office from Armenians seeking refuge, firing at anyone crossing the street. Unbelievable! Fikret's men.

Forget plans—a battle has its own momentum, its own course. I regret my men did no better. Some ran off to plunder, faces expectant as gamblers casting dice. Soldiers forget their orders from cowardice and greed. They follow the worst among them, like uncontrolled children.

Could we have done more to check the rampage? I've thought hard on my orders, how tied my hands were even from protecting the Armenian cathedral. Unless the priests hid their treasure, how long would the faithful stay pious? My 36 years taught me that a show of wealth gathers allegiance.

Shakir pointed toward the U.S. mission. Not far down the street, one of our recruits was rifle-butting someone. As the victim fell, we saw a second soldier slash him ear to chest. "Let's pray it's not a foreigner," I said.

Investigating, I found Tahsin pulling a pocket watch from the man's vest. "A resister. Armed with a cudgel," his false excuse. His face was oddly satisfied; I recalled the same look when he bayoneted a bitch's swollen belly.

"Turn him over." I knew the man by sight. His brother Mikael was one of our city's few Armenian policemen. The man was unconscious, his blood spreading across neck and chest.

"You've made a mistake—this man's a Protestant. He teaches at the mission school. That's a classroom pointer, not a cudgel!" I stifled my scorn by pounding on the mission door. "Open up quickly!" I shouted. "Your teacher's been wounded!"

The slender boy opening the door was pale with fear. This was tough duty for a lad no older than my Ehsan, yet he handled it well enough. When he saw who lay near the steps he shuddered and nearly fell.

"The Professor! No!" he gasped, voice trembling. Then he drew breath and shouted for Reverend Chambers. "Professor Megerditian's been wounded, come quickly!"

We laid the teacher on the carpet as two women rushed shrieking to his side. Mr. Chambers gave me a nod of recognition before pulling off the man's jacket. He began at once to tear the teacher's ruined shirt into bandages, then the women took up the task.

"It may be too late," he said, but he was already pressing a wad against the teacher's throat. Blood rapidly soaked through the cloth, replaced again and again.

"I hope you can save him."

One of the women looked up. "Thank you," she said.

The boy looked directly at me as he pulled the bolt to let me out. "Please," he said, with deliberate irony. In that moment arrogance eclipsed his timidity and I made a promise to my son.

Tahsin avoided my eyes as he helped me mount. Perhaps he was chastened, yet he made no offer to return the watch, nor did I ask. That Tahsin was as canny and brutal as a bobcat.

"So far they're leaving this street alone. Let's hope they'll be content with Iron Street," Shakir said when I reined beside him.

Armenians streamed from all directions to the mission door. Their clothing placed them: a few rich, more poor, most in between. Some women had children on their backs or trailing after. Some were entire families of three and four generations. Some were men alone or in pairs, sometimes doubled ape-like by bundles. Some wailed or groaned as they ran. Others were soundless but for heaving lungs. They looked at us with terror before seeing we let all pass. None got shunted from the door, though few of those desperate Christians looked like Mr. Chambers' Protestants.

A cluster of ruffians ran towards us holding weapons of impressive variety. They carried daggers long-bladed and short, curved and straight, along with heavy cleavers, double-edged hunting knives, thin skinning knives, tapered melon cutters, axes, awls, picks, swords, sabers and various kinds of cudgel. Two old pistols. At the front trotted the blanket-thieving, white-haired Circassian, looking as wild as any holy man. Shakir and I arranged our horses chevron-style to block them from the slope.

"No harm to foreigners or Protestants or their property!" I shouted at them. They surged into the street below. We heard doors broken, windows smashed, shooting, blows and screams. A voice yelled, "Kill Ermeni only!" and another took up the cry.

An Armenian darted from an alley that leads to Rose Bazaar. An infantry officer shot his rifle close to the man's ear. The unlucky fellow dropped to his knees as if praying, whereupon his enemy pressed a revolver to his chest. The man threw his arms around the officer's legs. Though too far to hear him, surely he was pleading to live, sobbing that children, wife, sisters, mother depended on his life. Wasting his last breaths. That officer put his revolver to the infidel's forehead and jumped back as he fired to avoid splatter. Then he looted the corpse thoroughly, as if well practiced. Shakir cursed our passivity, yet they were outside our area.

"The wretch was ready to hand over his gold teeth," Shakir lamented. In battle, I remarked, officers often fail to think.

Screams, yells and gunshots rained from the Armenian market southeast of us—Zeki Pasha's preserve. His chosen men were tilling the richest garden in the eastern provinces. Zeki's favored would return to Erzincan heavy-laden even after Erzerum officials took their share.

From every direction came sounds of assault: cries and shrieks, gunshots, hatchets striking gates and doors. At moments a high-pitched whinny, a piercing screech from the next street over. Neither Fikret nor his detail was in sight.

A crone clutching a bundle in each arm struggled past, eyes fixed on the ground. Chanting a sort of prayer over and over, "God help us, the mission, Holy Jesus, the mission."

Now I saw her bundles were infants, fully wrapped except for their noses. The woman was blind to us until Keyif started, clattering his new iron shoes, forcing notice. She shrank against the wall as if I'd ride her down. I motioned her forward.

"Make haste, grandmother. Go in peace," I called out. She gave a shrill cry as she staggered to the mission door and disappeared with her babies. Many others followed in that long afternoon, yet I remembered the old woman for her terror-gripped purpose. Weeks later she reappeared among a pack of destitute, flailing and screeching for bread. She was puzzled I took her first.

A man dressed English-style watched us from the mission roof.

"Get down before you get shot!" I shouted.

He stayed motionless, apparently transfixed by a fire to the west whose faint glow was all we could see from the ground. For this heedless foreigner's safety, I left Keyif with a seasoned private and again banged on the mission door. I waited inside for Mr. Chambers.

Perhaps a hundred Ermeni jammed the main room, covering every bit of floor. My ears soon rang from their wailing. Parcels and baskets climbed the walls. A few men stood at the doorway to gain some small relief, watching me with narrowed eyes, hiding their apprehensions no better than their weapons. Two rifles and one revolver were visible, some bundles suspect. Cause for arrest, even hanging, by law: their carelessness a sign of desperation.

I told the American priest to clear the roof. With his habitual firm bearing, I thought he'd make an excellent officer if not for his thick spectacles.

Outside, Shakir waited with my mount, the recruit having gone to the Christian quarter two streets over. "Said he'd help keep order there, he wasn't needed here, this street being so calm…"

"He'll make bad worse with no officer holding him back." For a few moments I burned with helpless anger. With our last soldier now party to the looting, how could we two be effective?

"We'll manage without him. If you haven't caught the fever too, Shakir?"

"Our horses are safer here," came his answer, joined by a teasing grin. A good man, one of the best, and the finest soldier in Erzerum city and province.

Taking opposite ends of the street, Shakir and I used tricks to seem a platoon, not a pair. We shouted threats, fired rifles, waved sabers enough that marauders saw more profit elsewhere. Several Persians approached, including two of the Consul's staff. I told them Shabanian's house was empty, its goods safe-kept at his friend the Governor's. They believed our lies, knowing the banker's connections, and turned their feet west or south.

Sun still colored the mountains when a bugle signaled an end to the rampage. Then a muezzin called the faithful. Looters dropped their spoils to pray in the street. When they rose, we shouted, "Go home! It's over!" They dispersed, docile as lambs.

A few of my men reappeared. "Permission to return to the garrison, sir," said a spokesman, as if they'd been on duty all along. Their horses were laden with sheepskins, sacks, boxes and clanking kettles. Brass cutlery peeked above socks. Strange bulges under tunics made them look like clay figures children make. Fikrit rode up, oddly tidy at first glance. Then I noticed bags roped clumsily to his saddle.

I kept the ablest, directed the rest to barracks. They hurried off eager to savor their profits. Working with my six nearby, we flushed two men from one house, a youth from the next, a man and his mother from a rear dwelling. These looters all denied hearing a bugle, while their arms stretched over every manner of goods. A brass brazier crowned one man with a mis-rolled carpet hanging from his shoulders to his feet that likely weighed what he did. We sent a few shots skyward to scurry them. By now, streets were quiet, windows dark; female wails told of occupants within.

Heading north we came upon two women beside a drainage ditch, comparing copper pitchers as if their own hands engraved them. We chased them off with threats of jail.

Smoke stabbed our nostrils, eyes and throats. From the hilltop we saw flames along the far side of Holy Fountain Street, perhaps engulfing the Armenian theater. Fire could spread beyond the Armenian district, endanger even the Dog Street barracks. I left two sergeants guarding the missions and took my other men to see what we might do.

Smoke clouded fading daylight. Our horses stumbled and startled at forms running past: two-legged humans misshaped by burdens.

Heat struck in heavy gusts at 500 meters. Closer in, a frenzied pack of Armenians filled buckets at a fountain and dumped them at the fire's edge. Men and boys kept bumbling into slower women and girls. Some Armenians took fright as we advanced. Seeing no threat, they resumed dousing the flames.

A foot soldier trotted towards me, holding his rifle forward like a shield. This was the sergeant medaled for valor. I pressed the Izgirli with questions. Evidently his squadron went back to the Citadel on hearing the bugle, leaving this lone man behind to keep order. Too much for one sergeant, able and intelligent as he was. His officers were at fault. It made me suspect jealousy.

Fire was spreading as we watched; obviously the present efforts were inadequate.

"The water will do more good further from the fire. It should soak in before it evaporates," declared Shakir.

"They need more hands. Round up more buckets. Go find soldiers to help us—quickly!" I shouted to my unit and was soon alone.

Keyif was snorting and skittering at the flames. I wrapped his eyes with a scarf and drew closer. "Empty your buckets here, wet it down!" I directed the firefighters to a dwelling in line to catch fire next.

"But that's not burning yet!" objected a sturdy matron who was keeping up well with the men.

"Shut up, foolish female! Do you want him to shoot you?" cried her husband. Too overwrought to grasp reason, they complied.

Within moments, Sgt. Mohamed returned with two buckets and an Armenian lad. "I've promised we won't kill him if he works hard!" the soldier called out and winked.

One fire fighter ran headlong into another, spilling all four pails. The Izgirli helped me rearrange the workers. The new relay doubled their efficiency.

Soldiers arrived with buckets and helpers, some willing, some impressed. I positioned them into another relay with its two end men dousing walls. Soon common purpose created enthusiasm, a good thing to see.

As fire neared the fountain, heat slowed the laborers. Noticing a well-frame behind a broken gate, I routed the brigade to that cooler source and put some to watering dwellings near the well.

We shouted to figures watching from rooftops, "Come help us save your houses!" I rode about the district yelling, "The violence is over! You're safe! You must help check the fire, it's spreading!" Several looters ran by, bundles on their backs, headed for the Turkish quarters.

More Ermeni joined in, as did a few more soldiers. Nearly as many left. New water sources served us—the creek, other fountains, horse-troughs. We soon soaked every wooden gate, doorframe and overhang near the conflagration. Because sparks still flew, I had the relays drench the joined houses on the far side of one street, from as high as the water was throwable, on down. Sometimes Armenians within hauled water and poured it onto their rooftops.

In due course we moved to the next street, with its own water sources, then the next. Finally the fire was held on its southeastern-to-south perimeter. The relays had worked steadily and even late arrivals were exhausted. Over the Black River hill, flames singed the sky. Others must fight that one, if they would. Shakir and I got to the Citadel just before midnight prayers, utterly worn out.

Men who hate each other one afternoon work side by side the same evening. How does it happen? People of both races blinked in wonder at Armenians and Muslims laboring together like friends or family. Could it be? Some Ermeni muttered curses on us, understandably. Some soldiers formed their own relay, then quit early. But all in all, the relays showed reconciliation is possible.

Soldiers gambled, lit by stolen lamps long after the regular-issue candles burned down. They stayed up joking, trading and comparing loot, too excited to sleep. Some spoke of gunfire from Armenians, which I doubted.

After rolling dice with officers from another platoon, Fikret told me my neighbor Shabanian was shot dead on his doorstep. Fikret's companion affirmed this sad news. It didn't surprise me. From great fatigue I put my sorrow to one side and slept.

Giragos

Hamed   October 31

Major Rustem summoned us at first light. The Armenian
district's northwest sector burned all night, the flames
finally quenched at Amber Creek. His next words were tinged with
sympathy: "These people will be beggars through the winter now."
He laid no blame. A nod acknowledged our fire fighting, so I gave it
brief mention.

A captain reported three distinct sources of gunfire, perhaps four;
illegal weapons recovered from dead resisters included two old army-
issue Peabodys. At this, Major Rustem clamped his jaw in anger.

"Find out who's been selling their rifles! This is a capital offense!"
He was exhaling fire so fierce the officer began to quake. Rustem's
anger shifted as the hapless captain continued.

"We found four homemade guns as well—a new design that
makes no smoke." He related his siege of a priest's home. Two hours'
gunfire led to cutting a hole in the roof. This giant-like priest was
holding two novel guns in his dead hands. His wife and five young
children were hiding in the basement near an anvil, bellows and
molds for making guns and cartridges.

All were amazed to learn of a weapon factory in range of Erzerum
garrison, jail and police. Moreover, to discover that the priest, named
Vemian, was arrested twice for suspected revolutionist activities and
released when no evidence was found.

Every officer was confident no resisters survived our superior
firepower. The Major accepted reports of fatal fires and piles of
corpses as inevitable. His present aim was restoring peace.

He instructed us to prevent further violence, restore total order, treat Armenians with normal respect. Two lieutenants standing near me exchanged winks, amused at carnage assisted one day, prosecuted the next. Major Rustem was emphatic.

His orders worked imperfectly. We heard a few rifle shots that morning and one dwelling burned. Hamidieh were to blame, not regulars.

Assignments changed, and in my case expanded. My platoon was to maintain order in my own mixed neighborhood east of the Armenian quarter, as well as the consular district.

This day my men were boastful and generally satisfied with their new apparel, quilts and edibles—and oblivious to the suffering, hatred and mistrust so recently created. One soldier got four gold lira for his booty on the street and all cheered him. Our soldiers were not especially greedy by and large, merely a mix of selfish and unselfish ways, like most humans. For breakfast that day, three comrades shared sweetmeats from a confectioner's kitchen. A single tidbit persuaded me to seek out and buy his wares: one sack for my dear Khadija and Huru; another for Herr Consul Behrmann's little Heidi at Christian New Year.

Allah be praised. We found Krikor Shabanian in good health at home, through unusual circumstances.

Patrolling Customs House Street east of the cathedral, I came upon the white-haired Circassian paired with knock-kneed Pohar. They carried between them a large chest handsomely bound in leather and brass. When they set it down its loud, metallic rattling made Keyif start sideways. Inside, we found goblets, platters and cutlery sufficient to furnish two shops. Amongst that hodgepodge were a Christian Bible, gold-tooled and pearl-clasped, and a leather case such as rich women use for jewelry.

Pohar grinned at me. "Infidel thieves, they rob us of what's ours by Allah. The filthy money-lenders deserve jail." He spat.

"I heard you were released," I said. "So, who did you kill for this plunder?"

"No one, my honorable captain, we harmed nobody. They let us take it without complaint."

"You didn't hear the trumpet end this business yesterday?"

"We heard another bugle this morning." Though the Circassian backed him, his red djinn's eyes shifted from my gaze.

"You're both liars," said I, and threatened to arrest them for law-breaking. Their swagger faded when I insisted they carry the chest back to its owner. We turned the corner of Iron Foot Street before I realized we were headed for Krikor Shabanian's.

An elderly maidservant opened the door. At sight of our uniforms, she cried out, "Please, go away, please! We've nothing for you! Everything's gone, it's all been taken!"

The room behind her held only a rough-made stool and a stained straw mat. Shadowy outlines where paintings and fine silk carpets once hanged signaled former opulence.

"Tell your mistress we're returning something." My sorrow for the Shabanians grew while I looked about. Only a few days before, the family had shared its joy with others here. Then footsteps sounded, and to my surprised relief Krikor appeared, not his widow.

He entered bravely, expecting (he told me) further persecution. His expression relaxed on recognizing me. He apologized for having no refreshments to offer. He asked about my health and my family. He seemed apprehensive while I apologized for the present difficulties and inquired about his family. He told me they were unharmed and hiding elsewhere. As was he until this morning.

"We heard you were killed!" I answered.

"A rumor I encouraged for my safety." His bow concealed a smile.

After explaining my purpose I led him to the entry, where the two thieves waited with his chest. He chuckled and became again the affable neighbor, host and banker of better days.

"You've done me a good deed, my friend. I'm deeply grateful. But you should know, in confidence, there's little of value here. Our most precious furnishings were safely hidden before the disturbance."

The chest was the last of what he'd set aside for looters. While its contents cost little, its return saved him the inconvenience of replacing many useful household items. "Who knows what can be found in the bazaar and what will disappear? There's no predicting," he said.

Who could foresee Shabanian's next move? He now presented a sack of coins to the robber pair, "With my gratitude for returning the plates and cutlery."

Pohar and the albino could hardly believe their luck at having their victim bestow a greater sum than his goods' worth! The pair were so startled, they bowed thanks to us both. After a stern warning I let them trot off.

My respect for grandfather Krikor multiplied that morning. He'd calculated what must be spent to survive, and spent it. At modest cost, he restored the chest-stealers' pride and nipped their grudge before it festered. He'd saved more coins for other opportunists, if pressed.

"You've prepared your strategy like a general," I told him. We bowed to one another.

We encountered no other looting that day, but sent home some young men without cause to be in the Armenian neighborhood. We saw much bartering on the streets and every sort of person carrying bundles and baskets, carpets and lanterns to the market.

The morning provided grim signs of the prior day's carnage: an oxcart brimming with corpses headed towards the Armenian burial ground; an odor of burned flesh fouled the breeze; ululations flowed from house after house, and Christians stared out with vivid hatred as we rode by.

At the Customs Street watering trough, an Armenian crone was speaking to a camel driver. She flinched at my gesture and scratched up the small coin I tossed her without returning thanks.

Soldiers stood about near Armenian shops to discourage further pillage. Many sharp Muslim eyes were looking about that area for gleanings. Near the Iron Foot fountain, a pack of old women bickered over a sheepskin like scullery maids over lamb bones after a banquet. Rumors of easy pickings unleashed their demons.

Excepting beggars and urchins, Armenians stayed home, fearing more depredations. Yet today, our soldiers seemed content keeping peace, as ordered. Like the hamidieh, their greed was modest. I asked Shakir why the hamidieh were so strangely absent.

"It's strange the hamidieh aren't around," I said.

"Gone home to flaunt their loot," Shakir replied. His eyes were tired and I doubt he'd slept well for some time, fearful for his Rosa.

Reverend Chambers came to the mission door with his secretary-interpreter. Inside were Armenians of all sorts, young and old, poor and prosperous, crowding every bit of floor tile. Perhaps 100 men, three times as many women and children, but I did not see the door boy. The noise and stench were appalling.

"They're afraid to go home. Might you reassure them?" the American asked. His assistant earned his wage, interpreting for us both that day.

"It's over. We're enforcing order. Anyone who harms you will be arrested," I informed them, adding, "You may be safer here for now."

The American priest now told the refugees they might stay, but there'd be little bread. The scholars and teachers must be fed from storeroom shelves that were nearly bare. At once I offered to find what food I could for them; I was sure Giragos would have grain to lend.

Shakir and I set forth at an easy pace, as Keyif was still over-tired from the long day before. When a cluster of my men reported widespread calm, I reminded them to watch for looting. Their reluctance to patrol was understandable, for Armenians were looking at us with obvious anger and hate.

"We weren't all killers! We didn't make this happen," I wanted to call out. As if they'd hear me or any other soldier. How many years before we regained their trust—if ever? Whoever planned the actions didn't care.

We passed many ruined dwellings, saw families picking through rubble that was home the day before. We were beset by children imploring food. Our presence proved useful when we caught three hooligans kicking in a doctor's house door. We got their names and let them choose between home and jail; they slunk away like sullen jackals.

My mission was worse than futile. Giragos' house was wrecked, windows, doors and doorways smashed, chairs and tables splintered. Giragos' wife and son sat keening on the bare dirt floor, surrounded by broken furniture. Their clothing was blotched with bloodstains. On seeing me the widow's shrieks of grief grew louder, while the boy fixed me with mournful eyes. With some effort, I calmed the woman enough to tell what happened.

Giragos had emptied his shop, leaving only some rolls of tin and copper. He'd brought home six sacks of jewelry buried in beans, rice and flour. Straining under the weight—three trips all told. Working together, the couple diluted this treasure with foodstuffs from their cupboards, then hid it here and there through the little house.

They were resting on the divan when they heard shouts at their gate, men calling Giragos' name. Her husband, frozen by panic, looked about for a hiding place. His eyes darted to a corner where a quilt concealed two sacks. At first glance, a low sort of divan.

"Quick now! When I'm under the quilt, set that tray on top!" Giragos curled himself between sacks and wall. His wife was arranging a silk doily on the tray when four flushed and sweating ruffians forced open the door.

"Where's the jeweler?"

"Where's Giragos?"

"Where's the gold?" Pushing her aside, they searched the bedroom, tearing down curtains, unrolling mats, shaking bed linens and flinging nightclothes and underthings onto the floor.

The wife's heart was pounding louder than her voice (she thought) as she told them, "Nothing's here! It's gone, we've got nothing! I don't know where his jewelry is!"

One of the intruders struck her hard across the mouth, breaking a tooth. "You're lying! Give it to us!" He was wearing her husband's new boots.

Twice, three times she repeated that nothing of value was there, that her husband was out buying topaz from a certain Russian miner, the story invented for just this situation. The intruders—men she was sure lived nearby—ignored her and kept searching.

Angry and frustrated, they hatcheted windows, carpets, even a bulge in the wall. Knifed open pillows and the divan beneath. Spilled a basket of dung patties onto the floor. As she knew they must, finally yanked the quilt off the lumpy mass of sacks and husband.

She shrieked as her husband threw himself across their feet. He cried out, "I'll give it to you! You can have it! Spare…"

At that moment, two hatchets slammed down. One rent open a flour sack, cutting apart a gold and onyx necklace and a silver casting. The other split Giragos' skull from ear to ear.

She wrapped both arms around their boy, huddled in the soft fill of the ruined divan. Silently they watched three or four more men barge panting into the room: Circassians, soon followed by Kurds wearing hamidieh badges. The room was now crowded and her head was spinning. One of the men, she thought a Kurd, grabbed her arm and tore the bracelets from her wrist with a whoop of triumph. Her twisted arm was still painful, though it hardly mattered.

Collapsed beside her son, eyes shut in terror, she heard the men arguing, shouting, scuffling. Then, talk, laughter, footsteps in the passageway and finally quiet. Drafts of cold air struck her hands and face. In the growing dark the boy was crying from grief and fright. She held him in her lap and crooned, shivering. Hours passed.

At last a neighbor came, a kindly old woman who sometimes gave the boy raisins from a two-color basket. "God has your papa in a better place," she told him. She got her husband to hitch his donkey and take the dead jeweler to the cemetery. She collected scattered fuel, blew on embers, got a fire going. Together then the two women swept up feathers, picked up what was left and set about cleaning the blood-soaked floor.

Giragos' wife looked at me with red-rimmed eyes. "If only I simply gave them my bracelets, I might have saved him! I was too scared to think!"

"They wanted his stock. Your bracelets couldn't save him," I told her.

It's best a woman not be told her husband's a fool. Half his stock might have bought his life, had Giragos not hid every paltry trinket, even gold-washed tin ankle-bells and polished glass beads. He threw junk into his sacks along with costly gold coins and necklaces as if he sought his fate.

Giragos had been a respected man with many friends. Father would miss him. But it was his widow and child I pitied. The goldsmith had been the pride of two poor families. The mother and child would now be poor relations among their poor relations.

Whatever wheat they salvaged from the wreckage here failed my purpose. Where next, I wondered—and an answer became obvious. Briskly now, Keyif took me to the Citadel.

※ ※ ※

Complicity in great harm must have weighed on Major Rustem. He agreed to a fine thing now: cooperation. A means—in whatever small and partial measure—to heal.

It was a fine thing as well to relay good news to the American mission: a cart-load of commissary flour would arrive by nightfall. The bespectacled cleric's Armenian flock need go hungry only a few more hours.

Not far down from the Citadel, I was heading toward Custom House Street when a banner fluttering from a window caught my eye. It appeared to be a green wool horse blanket with a strip of white linen stitched across the center and bordered by wide stripes of red wool. It was rough work intended as a flag of Greece, though it took me some moments to identify. The more familiar flag of Russia was often seen painted on doors and gates that week.

A man at the window, alarmed by my uniform, shouted, "Leave us alone, we're Greek!"

Then he flushed as we recognized one another from Shabanian's party. He knew I knew he was Armenian, married to a Greek. Who could blame him for not wanting her widowed so young—she was a pretty woman. If it was she sewed the flag, however, she'd be a hungry seamstress.

Of the street's seven houses, five had broken doors and doorframes. Every window had been smashed, glass, muslin or oilpaper alike. Women's wailing sounded through the openings. We rode in silence to a granite dwelling at the corner. Its wood trim was charred, its gate hanging on one hinge, the place evidently vacant. A dead cat was wedged between door and post.

On a nearby side street, the French tricolor was nailed to an undamaged door. Some small number of the city's Armenians held foreign papers. Most were businessmen who'd persuaded some consul of mutual advantages to trade. It looked as if their documents saved more than taxes.

An oxcart was stopped at the home of a less fortunate neighbor. As I rode by, its drivers carried out a grey-bearded corpse and flung it upon some others. Hands and feet protruded thru the slats. One of the drivers called out, "See this! It's fair return for staying out of the army!" His cohort's reply made both laugh.

Hiding House

Marjan   October 28 to around November 9

S omeday I'll ask our Bishop how the great Saint Noah could leave his friends and neighbors, those babies and children, to drown. It seems an unholy thing he did letting only his family on board. I wept that we could do nothing for my sisters and Varti.

At least Patriarch let us bring my mother, along with Toumia's younger sister Ardemis, her husband and their unmarried daughter. That was it. Altogether we numbered 31, counting infants and our servants Verkin and Ephraim. Our hiding house bulged past any comfort. Each person meant more chance the neighbors might discover us, yet I felt ashamed we brought no others.

Sleep was hard, so many in a room: upstairs were two, downstairs one besides the kitchen. Nerses and Arsha, so new to us, woke crying from dreams, Arsha calling out "Mama!" and her brother asking, "Will they kill us?" Sometimes Heranoush and I could soothe them back to sleep without our really waking up. Our children had bad dreams, too; I guess we all did, though I only cried out once that I remember.

No one slept well. When anyone moved, everyone felt it. We lay there endless hours kneading our thoughts, pushing here and there, not getting up either, because we'd nothing to do but sleep. Or try.

What a change for us! We'd little cleaning or washing, no cooking beyond simple soups and stews of lentils, bulgur, dried meat. Two turnips and one onion were quickly gone. We mostly sat about like rich ladies, embroidering and mending and playing with the children. We did our best to keep them busy and quiet. When a baby cried, it got tended fast. We were careful as a seamstress with a wedding dress not to give ourselves away.

The boys were kept at schoolwork so they wouldn't fall behind. Artashes laughed at the line of letters I tried to copy from a school book. I found it hard to hold the pencil right. Heranoush and Astghig sang. They taught the younger ones "Frere Jacques"—this was a good quiet song everyone liked. We told stories. Sako was better than any traveling story-man. He cast spells on all the children, big and small. He made up exciting stories and gentle stories too, sweet ones for the little children, songs as well, even lullabies. The children loved their Uncle Sako, just as he loved them.

Then Sako disappeared.

It was late morning of our third day hiding when Patriarch looked up from his reading and called for Sako so loud he woke Flora and set little Yefkine crying in Yiri's lap. When nobody answered, he started pacing from Toumia to the window and back. There was just enough light to show his anger boiling on his jaw. He shouted for Henza.

"Where's Sako? Where's my son?"

Henza looked scared as she worked her way across the room. We were sitting too close together for her to step quickly and by the time she reached Nazar, everybody was quiet. Her voice was so faint he made her repeat.

"He had to take something to someone. He'll be back soon." She held her head up bravely but I could see her trembling.

"By all the saints, he'd better! He'd better be back this hour, I say!" The old man rose up and grabbed Henza's arm.

"Taking what, woman? To whom? Answer me! Answer! I want to know!" He was red faced and kept slapping her with questions.

Henza said she knew only that her husband left by first light and promised to come home soon. She faced Nazar with proper respect yet she was firm. She held steady though his barking made her flinch.

At last our Patriarch gave a grunt and sat back down. He opened his book and seemed to read it, still scowling. Henza came back to her place beside me. The rest went back to their handwork and schoolwork and chalk-drawing. Sarah turned her face away from me, too late to hide a little smile. Deep inside her was a loving heart, but sometimes jealousy made her mean.

We were fixing the noon meal when Levon shouted for us all to be still. He thought he heard a bugle, from a distance. Moments later, we heard gunshots. Certainly distant, but loud enough for us to know what they were.

Henza dropped a plate and we picked the pieces up with shaking fingers. She seemed about to faint.

"More shooting!" someone cried, and after a while, others called out, "More of it!" and "Again!" We all knew it had started.

As hard as I tried to stay calm for Henza's and the children's sake, I got more anxious as the hours grew longer. Petros, Martiros and Levon moved a heavy chest against the front door and stayed sitting on it with cudgels close to hand. They spoke little, only listening for noises from outside. Petros winked once at me and Heranoush, but mostly he was blind to us. We mothers tried to keep the children playing finger games and stringing yarn through buttons. Every outdoor sound made us freeze like statues in church. Again and again we held our breath for Sako's footsteps, praying he was at the door.

We sent Artashes to the roof so he could see the streets nearby. He was excited, scrambling down the ladder every few minutes with another report—never one we wanted. Just the same, it was important. He told of people running to the market and back, men on horses, wearing uniforms and not, with and without bundles. Armed soldiers and others. We knew they were looting, for sure. As Yiri said, "Booty is a sop to wicked thirsts." We said it meant less danger to our Sako—as if we knew anything about such things.

As each hour passed, our fear for Sako grew. We tried to cheer each other, saying things like "He's safe as a duck in a well" and "An angel guards his path." Years of hearing hopeful words from Yiri and her mother helped get us through that day of worry and fear.

My son spotted a plume of smoke to the west, then another. We told ourselves fire would draw danger away from Sako, wherever he was. When Artashes heard a gun go off, we still pretended. What I thought was, they must be shooting Armenians, but I held my tears and squeezed Henza's hand to reassure her. My heart was beating hard and my hand was cold as snow. Hers too. I couldn't fool her.

Night fell without a sign of Sarkis. We decided he'd been waiting for dark. My mother and the aunts agreed he must be hiding at a friend's. We prayed and waited. Artashes ran several times to look out in the moonlight. Twice he saw a lone man hurrying in our direction and we dared hope. We said Sako must be safe with his employer—or in a church. He was too smart to put himself in danger. And it was quiet now, he must be safe. Yet Toumia was short-tempered with Martiros and Nazar smoked himself into a coughing fit. Henza grew more silent by the hour.

Of course the children fretted, too. It took forever to settle them to sleep. Vagram woke during the night asking where was Uncle Sako, and though he woke his cousin Arsen, the older boy for once didn't scold.

We were so sure he'd come back that night! When dawn lit without him, Aunt Zabel reminded us of places he might be safely hiding. "Now it's over, he'll hurry home, for sure!"

"That's it, he'll be back soon!" I said, lifted by her words, as if wishing makes butter.

Half-way into the morning, Nazar decided it was safe to send Petros looking for his brother. There was no smoke by then, and no noise from guns. Yet we were anxious for Petros. He put on Ephraim's clothes, muddied so he looked like a Turkish laborer. Everyone called it a clever disguise. He had his Spanish dagger under his belt. I tried not to show my fear for him. Many times that long, long afternoon, Henza and I clasped one another's hands. Hers were as cold and damp as mine. She knew I loved her husband almost as much as my own.

※ ※ ※

My husband's face was turned away as he took off his shoes, but I could tell from how he barely moved his hands and from the slump in his shoulders. My relief gave way to horror.

Henza came behind me and put both hands on my arms without speaking. I think she already knew.

"Did you find him, Petros? Is he—?" I asked.

In answer, Petros took one of Henza's hands. His eyes were the blackest and saddest I ever saw. "Henza, I—" He stopped. "The bastards killed him. He's gone," he said.

"Dear Jesu, take pity," she whispered. She closed her eyes and bit her lip. Petros took her by the shoulders and kissed her forehead, then stepped away. "Help her," he told me. I put my arm around her back to stop her falling. Her body felt limp as unbaked dough.

I reached to comfort my husband, but he drew back, at the same time shaking his head at Martiros and Nazar coming towards him. Petros looked past us into the sitting room. "I must tell Mother," he said.

Matriarch Toumia sat knitting far back in the faint light from the only uncovered window, high above. Petros made his way to her and we followed, though my head was spinning and I nearly fell with each step. Every tongue stopped as Petros got near her.

"Hannum Mother, I found him. They've…"

She began shrieking before he said more. "Sarkis!" she wailed, "Sarkis, no! No!" Then again, "Not Sarkis! No! Not Sarkis! Not my Sarkis!" She rose partway from her chair, reached to grab my husband's—Ephraim's—tunic, then fell to her seat. She stayed still a few moments. Then she began to sway and keen, eyes rolled sightless. She didn't beat her breast or tear at her hair as some women do, but she shut us out just as tight with her white-eyed keening. Her chair creaked each time she rocked and I waited for it to fall apart and throw her to the floor. Despite my own weeping, I remember thinking that would end her trance.

After a while Toumia grew still and she looked about as if the room was empty. Finally her eyes fixed on the son who stood beside her. She groaned, caught her breath, and said, "Tell me how."

He went on one knee and took her hand.

"This much I learned. Yesterday morning he went to the pharmacy to warn his boss to close. He told Khagorian he was going home from there.

"It was right after he left the bugle sounded. People started running from the Plaza in every direction. Armenians were fleeing for their lives, chased by riff-raff and soldiers and half the Great Mosque. The whole mob was shouting "Infidels!" and "Dashnaks!" and falling on every Armenian in sight." Petros turned to his father to show he recalled the old man's warnings. The church history was still open in Nazar's lap.

"You know Sako is…was…a fast runner. He probably tried to get to the church…I found him in the cemetery. He was stabbed."

"You found him? You saw…?"

"Yes."

Petros blinked hard with a deep breath as if he had to pull his body into place against its will. Matriarch gave a long groan that rose into a flutter and soon the other women took it up, filling the air. Sometimes a shriek cut through the crying, as if someone was being stabbed or was watching the murder.

My husband held his father, then Martiros, then Miron, then Levon. They murmured in deep male tones and shook their heads, helpless.

Cries from the women and children joined Matriarch's keening to bury every other sound that day—Flora's coughing, dogs barking outside, a kettle boiling on the brazier. Our ears, eyes and noses were taken over by mourning.

Henza somehow kept steady as I pulled her along. Each time Toumia took a breath, Henza started towards her. But the old woman's grief made a wall too thick for us. Each time Toumia threw out another wail, Henza quivered. She didn't weep, yet I felt she pitied Sako's mother.

Martiros left his father's side. He stepped carefully over little Sahad, who was crying without knowing why, and put his arms around Henza. He spoke kind words to her. Miron, Petros and Levon did much the same. During this time, Nazar stood stony faced, staring at us, wordless. Then he looked behind a window-cover into the late afternoon light.

The women came to Henza now, one following the other. First, Aunt Zabel, then her daughter Yiri, next Sara, next Aunt Maxime. Then came Ardemis and her daughter, then my mother. While they murmured, Aunt Flora tried to rise. The effort was too much—she could hardly move from rheumatism. Later, when Henza passed near, Flora took her hand and held it to her cheek, and spoke into the pale young widow's ear.

It grew dark and the room got chilly in spite of our numbers. Someone lit a candle and Nerses added fuel to the brazier. Some of the children went with Heranoush and Astghig into the kitchen. Toumia paused in her wailing to visit the privy, moaning as she staggered stiffly from her chair. She took Arsha along, as she often did, to help her. When she returned, I went to her, drawing Henza with me. I knelt beside her feet and wrapped my hands around hers.

"Hannum, this is a great sorrow. I pray for you in your grief," I said. She looked past me, silent. I thought she might stay silent. I squeezed her small hands gently in mine instead of speaking.

I felt her tremble before she spoke. "My first born! He was my joy, my dearest, my best!" Tears filled the creases under her eyes and her nose dripped into her mouth. I pulled the handkerchief from her sleeve and pushed it into her hand. I made room for Henza, but Toumia drew back from her touch as if a hornet stung her, and screeched, "Sarkis! Oh beloved son! Oh dearest heart!" She began again to wail and rock, white-eyed. As if the sorrow was only hers. It was my mother-in-law's nature, she thought of no one's feelings but her own. I hoped Henza's grief numbed her to Toumia's rudeness.

At first it seemed simply grief for her favorite when Matriarch ignored his widow. "Best leave her until tomorrow. She'll be calm by then," I told my friend. We found space by the far wall, where Henza leaned back to rest. For a long while she barely moved. She seemed to doze, yet from time to time her breath caught or her eyes flickered. She made soft wordless sounds. She was thinking of Sako, surely. Among her murmurs I heard love words, and his name. I stayed close, aching for her.

I held myself back from weeping. I thought, *I must be strong, for Henza.* My mind made awful pictures of the knifing, the blood, the fear and agony of his dying, his Passion, for somehow the image of Our Lord on the Cross kept coming to me. I thought, *first his wife and daughters, now Sako himself. The light of our family is dead.* Grief pressing in waves was washing through me. A selfish thought: *where will we find jokes and songs now?* And a feeling of hatred toward the Muslims of our country, I knew it was wrong to feel this, but I could not squeeze it from my heart.

It seemed the sounds of wailing lasted hours, yet daylight still tinted the muslin curtains when the old woman exploded. They say a volcano explodes like that, no hint beforehand, not even a fiery trickle, no warning until JAKKAM!! It turns inside out, and pity the creatures in sight! Suddenly she was shouting curses across the room at the bereaved bride. Thankfully I was there beside Henza when it happened. It was startling as an earthquake, or a bat that swoops in your path, its poison wings scratching your face.

"You widow! You got what you deserve, widow!" She hissed and spat the words like a madwoman. "You worthless empty basket! Fool! You couldn't keep him home where he belonged! You're useless, worse than dog dung, no good! A no good wife! It's you I blame! I curse you!"

The family let out gasps and groans. No one could manage to speak. I did not even think to shield Henza, to put myself between her and our mother-in-law. Petros stood in place, mute as his father. Then Martiros seized his mother's arms like a child's. "Be still, Mother! Stop your railing! It's not for you to judge his widow! It's his murderer we should blame, not her!" he cried.

"She let him go! She knew! Did you?" she shouted. "No, you didn't watch him sneaking off by night! You didn't bless his going with farewells and kisses! You aren't to blame!" She was breathing heavily, staring angrily at him. Then she turned her face back to Henza. "Kisses of death! Kisses of death!" she screeched. Here and there in the room, children were crying, voices murmuring.

Martiros turned to Nazar, still silent. "Father, please, will you try to calm her?"

The old man stood. His body seemed to grow bigger as we waited for him to speak. "Your mother's said it well. I agree! Have we not lost the first of my seed, the first fruit of her womb?" He pointed skyward and glared straight at Henza, all the while stamping one foot after another until the floor shook. No one else made a sound.

"Is not the first-born son held precious in the eyes of Our Father and Son as he is cherished by his father and mother on earth? Is the son we nurtured, the son we taught and cared for each day, to get a mere hour of wailing? No! No! No! We will mourn until our lives on earth end!" Patriarch was shouting. I half expected him to call down a thunderbolt. Henza was shaking now and pale as milk.

Nazar went on accusing. "I don't know what that woman knew, how could I? Some things she must have known, with her husband gone from her bed at night…" He was snarling, a total bully now, and I felt hate grip my heart. Barely stopping for breath, he pointed at Henza and yelled, "Woman, I hold you to account!"

Patriarch stared at her with eyes afire, face flushed, his chest heaving. Here and there, a child whimpered, a mother murmured, someone whispered. I could not move.

Nazar turned back to Martiros. "Now his duties are your lot in life. This means you take no risks! No risks of any kind!"

At once he turned to the younger men. "It's up to you, Petros, and you, Miron! Levon too. Learn why Sako was killed. Why he is dead! I charge you with that task! I –"

His next words choked him. He clutched his chest, tottered and collapsed onto Aunt Zabel, ending with his head on her lap, his legs bent against Yiri's. Yiri and her mother, with Maxime and Ardemis on either side, all began flapping in confusion. It took awhile to clear space around Aunt Zabel before Nazar's sons and Levon could come to his aid. The way Nazar lay there made me think of our Holy Mother holding our crucified Lord.

All this time, Henza stayed leaning against the wall beside me. I felt her flinch when Toumia began and again when Nazar blamed her, but she kept her eyes bravely on him. She was trembling and gasping like a finch you trap in your hand. I thought she might faint. I wasn't sure she took in Patriarch's collapse.

We did our best to comfort her. "They don't know what they're saying."

"They don't mean it. Pay no attention, it's nonsense."

"They'll be ashamed they said these things once the pain settles."

And so forth. She thanked us with a lifeless face, her eyes fixed on air. Why listen to our wishful words? No one of us expected Nazar and Toumia to apologize. They never admitted wrong. At last my mother was seeing why I disliked this woman. Yet Toumia asked a troubling question—did Henza know why Sako went out that night, did she try to stop him? Maybe everyone supposed Henza deserved some blame. I made myself not think about it. What matters is to help a friend, give her love, ask no questions— it's what a friend must do.

The men lifted Patriarch to a divan. He lay wheezing, eyes half shut, deaf to all around. Toumia keened in bursts, stopping every two minutes to ask if her husband was awake, groaning at the answer. I heard whispers of a heart attack, a stroke, a seizure. Aunt Zabel and Yiri rushed for Aunt Flora's smelling salts. "What's wrong? Who's got the vapors?" the old lady asked.

Patriarch woke confused and couldn't talk. For once he let his sons tell him what to do. Martiros and Petros carried him upstairs that night between them. Toumia was close behind, complaining they were too slow, too quick, too rough. From then on, Toumia gave her husband all her attention.

For weeks we could hardly make sense of what Patriarch was saying. No doctor need say he had a stroke. We long expected it.

Many nights I prayed false when Martiros led our prayers for Nazar. My secret heart was hateful, asking the Almighty to let him die. The thought was unholy and sinful, yet I let it warm me over and over. May God forgive me.

The children turned into "what-hows", Sako's name for little Arsen, years before. They wore us out asking how and what and where and when for Heaven and dying, killing and God—questions too important for teasing.

Vagram asked why I was sad, since Uncle Sako is with our Heavenly Father in a happy place?

"I'm sad because he brought us happiness and now he's gone. We miss him."

"Oh yes," said Vagram, solemnly. "But maybe I'll go to Heaven soon, then I can be with Uncle Sako again."

I kissed his soft sweet cheek. "No, Vagram, you're much too young and healthy to die," I told him.

"Vagram, that's a silly thing to say," said Heranoush.

"No, it's not!" answered Vagram. "I could get killed! You don't know everything!"

"You promised to keep a secret, Vagram!" scolded Nerses.

Koren and Artashes called out warnings, too. "Be quiet, Vagram!" "Shut your trap!"

"I didn't say anything! I didn't tell the secret!"

No secret could last with us so tight-pressed little Hamajah's hiccups led us into sleep. No space to scratch, my father used to say. We kept a night-lamp lit for visiting the chamber-pot, but even so, Miron stepped on Artashes, or someone else tripped on an arm or a foot. The old folks were almost as crowded in the back room.

When I bent to kiss him, Vagram whispered, "I'll tell you the secret, Mama, if you'll promise not to tell."

"I can't promise if it's dangerous."

"There, you see?! Keep quiet now!" hissed Artashes.

"Not a word!" ordered Koren. In a small voice, Vagram promised not to tell. Reason to worry, if my head had room for one more.

Heranoush asked if we'd see Uncle Sako before he was buried, "Like we saw Grandfather?" Only Petros knew then about the huge and awful grave at St. Azdvadzadzin's, though I think he told his brothers and Levon later that night. We women were spared until we were home. Yet I suspected other killings from how Petros cried out in his sleep and lay tight and wakeful.

"Will we find out who killed him?" asked Astghig.

"That's what my father's supposed to do. Grandfather said so," said Artashes.

"He won't find out! No Muslim's ever going to tell!" said Arsen.

"Your grandfather told them to find out <u>why</u> Uncle Sarkis went out. What his purpose was," I said. "We all want to know."

"He was going to kill our enemies!" Vagram's little voice was strong.

In the kitchen, Aunt Zabel was pressing Henza to eat.

"At least, some sweet tea, dear! You'll be too weak to stand! Here, try a bit of bread," Aunt Zabel coaxed.

"I can't." Henza's voice was faint. I put my hand on her shoulder.

"Just a taste, sister. You'll get too weak to walk if you don't eat."

"Like Oskee and Arpeh, remember how they could barely walk, before?" put in Yiri. "Our good food made them strong!"

Then Henza took a few sips of honeyed tea. She ate nothing that day.

Zabel and I became twin sentries protecting Sako's widow from his mother. We kept a wall of children round us, so when the Captain and his father called they had to step like herons along the banks of the Araxes to get to Henza. They stayed only a short time and I supposed they were uncomfortable visiting us unveiled, Christian women.

Upstairs at night, Zabel and I lay with Henza between us on the crowded floor. The bride-widow never closed her eyes that I saw, but she must have slept sometimes. It was a wonder anyone slept an hour, with sounds from 21 live bodies in a room. Grief tired us—and there was little else to do but sleep. And grieve. And worry.

Of others, all we knew was from Petros: my sister Nora's house still stood, my mother's was ashes, things were bad. We women must guess the rest from tea leaves.

As mothers we teach children to ignore rumors, yet rumors passed amongst us, frightful rumors that twisted my throat against my stomach. Were rumors worse than truth? Yes and no.

We all were uneasy in that house, fearing the neighbors, closed indoors, our children like caged dogs. The children needed to yell and run. They missed friends and outdoor games. They missed Shapundi with his funny bray. They played with their food and slept poorly, they whined and annoyed each other. At least we married women once knew another home. We could mold ourselves to change.

Only Henza and my poor homeless mother stayed silent when we spoke of missing this and that at home. I wanted to change clothes, bathe, wash underwear in a proper tub, cook and serve real meals again, put my children to sleep in our family's room. How we love our habits! Yet they weigh nothing balanced with a beloved lost.

Days later, when at last we were told it was safe to return, my face ran with tears I couldn't stop. Most of the women were wet-eyed that hour, though we laughed and chattered and hugged the children and one another. We seemed to forget our grief as we thought of having our rooms back, our old places and routines. Later, packing, I was afraid. What will we find? Will we be safe? Ordinary questions. Another one was worse: *how long safe?*

We set out once more in darkness, my stomach turning so I could barely whisper to the children, and wishing we could walk more quickly. It felt good to be outside.

As we crossed into the Armenian quarter we paused to thank the Almighty for His mercy. A thin moon let us see burned buildings, many broken gates and ruined doors. We walked in silence through the darkness, listening for danger. We heard two horses passing nearby and held our breath until the sound faded. A patrol, most likely. A cock crowed, as one always does, whatever the time, and here and there, I saw the pale shape of sheep on a roof. It was just light by the time we got home.

We went in through a new front door, rough-hewn by someone learning his work. Its iron bolt was heavier than before. Inside looked strangely bare and clean. Someone had broomed the floors and tacked cloth across the windows. The tacks stuck out and the orange muslin made the rooms oddly foggy. At least, it kept the worst cold outside. Braziers warmed the parlor, but it did not feel like home.

Yiri said, "We have a good neighbor."

"May it be no worse for your sisters," my mother said. It was days more before we knew.

The Captain's little girl ran in and dropped a bundle at our feet. Behind Huru came her mother and a stable boy, bearing platters of bread, cheeses, olives and yogurt decorated with leaves and dried flowers. Khadija was truly gifted with food, and our appetites awoke for the first time in weeks as we helped spread the cloths. The breakfast drew our family into the room the way a magnet draws pins.

Once Khadija was done with condolences, I persuaded her to sit with us, the men feasting from the other platter, two circles of Kavafians around woven squares of blue.

The children were soon running in a pack through the house and into the courtyard, excited and happy. Their joyful cries when Ehsan jumped through the back gate made us think it was a candy-seller in the courtyard.

Ehsan's grandfather brought in some sort of box wrapped in dark cloth. He gave this with a bow to Nazar, who was sitting on a barrel near the kitchen door at that point, though he soon tired and had to lie down again. The mystery turned out to be a birdcage holding a yellow warbler. You couldn't lift the cover without scaring it into the farthest corner, and I know how it felt because the sight of a uniform still makes me tremble. A warbler has a shorter memory, and later it sang nicely for us.

Our husbands and Levon worked to exhaustion that day, carrying baskets from our neighbors' cellar to every corner of our house. Toumia bossed them from a kitchen stool, like a queen, deciding the place for each bundle.

In silent trade, Henza tended Yiri's infant while Yiri worked with her mother and me in the cellar, glad to escape Toumia's eyes as we weighted shelves with jars of fruits and vegetables preserved weeks before on our stove. By the time we returned to the kitchen to unpack pots and dishes, braided onions hung from the cellar beams and baskets and barrels lined the store room walls. It was a pleasing sight.

We made the children stay outside while we did all this. They didn't complain, they liked being children again. The big girls set up a circle game for the young ones, including Khadija's shy darling Huru.

We were still putting kitchen goods away, thinking of the good stews and pastries we could make now, when that flow stopped. Instead rugs started coming through the kitchen into the parlors. Three soldiers were now helping, likely the captain's men. They were polite and seemed good natured, yet I had to wonder what Armenians they killed and wounded and whose homes they looted.

The soldiers unrolled the rugs with great grunts and show, proud and pleased at their own manly strength. Our husbands decided the right place for each, sometimes pulling and heaving to help the humps disappear.

Yiri and I were taking cherry juice water to the children just as a Persian carpet woven in many shades of red and blue was spread. Pasha Berci praised its unusual design of running deer and roses. Then Nazar made some growling sounds, juice dribbling into his beard. Martiros took his meaning and at once presented the lovely rug to our neighbors with a little speech about our family's gratitude. The Captain and his father both tried to refuse the gift, but in the end, gave in.

Martiros left them stored foods as well—a half barrel of rice, basterma, dried eggplants, fruit leathers, rose-hip jelly and more things we'd preserved. Our dear neighbors did not make such foods themselves, for their cook was old and Khadija spent every moment tending her husband's mother. Food cost more than ever that winter, with so many crops and stores ruined and looted. Thanks to our neighbors, we'd food to spare when many starved.

Martiros also gave our neighbors a chest from the Caucasus mountains, its outside carved with birds and flowers. We'd kept it in the women's parlor, for it looked delicate though it weighed a lot. I hoped the Captain's father would give it to Khadija.

They wouldn't let our family do more to shrink a debt too large to measure. We sometimes say, "How can I ever repay you?" after some kindness, not a question so much as a way to thank a person. There would be another great kindness done by them for us, as impossible to repay as this. It seemed to me that the friendship between our two families would last forever. What I didn't yet know was that the friendship was already hurt by Sako's death.

Tour Guide

Hamed

R ustem had me guide a few consuls through damaged areas. Their dispatches require sound information not found in Constantinople's newspapers. How better for a consul to prove his value to superiors?

The foreigners must be spared undue distress, of course. No suffering, no scenes of carnage: Rustem insisted this was possible, I hoped it was. Tewfik Bey of Shakir Pasha's staff would accompany us. As military officers, we'd watch for signs of persisting rebellion. Regrettably, only this part of the Major's charge was fulfilled.

Already I'd met some of the gentlemen: British consul Cumberbatch, the Italian consul, Reverend Chambers, the German Behrmann. We used the British consul's assistant, a Greek fluent in several languages. He struck me at first unpleasantly, due to an ingratiating manner plus a habit of clearing his throat incessantly. However, he translated steadily and well. My problem was the immoderate willfulness of the foreign Christians in my charge.

First I took these dignitaries through the mixed neighborhood where most of us lived. Damage here was comparatively slight. Next I led them to the ruined theater where well-armed radicals fired on our soldiers. The Italian asked to tour the Armenian bazaar. He'd heard it was a total ruin.

"Not that bad," I told him, not expecting so many wrecked shops. Activity was nil along Iron Street except for an occasional shopkeeper or carpenter making repairs. They eyed our entourage warily, with two of us in uniform.

There was no dissuading the foreigners from the Armenian quarter on the same road. My best efforts were as useless as my experience and training once we got there. Concealing my shock was impossible.

The western part of the quarter was in shambles, as if a carefree giant skipped upon its roofs and gates. Men were struggling to right collapsed beams. Women were dragging out branches and baskets of dirt and grass. Only labor would make these houses habitable and roofs safe again for sheep.

On Pine Tree Street were three rectangles of burnt rubble where houses stood two days before. A family was picking shards of charcoal from the ruins.

"I've heard there's no kerosene left for winter," the Italian consul said. "If it's true, how can we manage?"

"Bread will be a greater problem," said Rev. Chambers.

There was resistance here, I explained. Gunfire from windows and roof until fire engulfed the walls. The nationalists were obviously insane, their destruction inevitable. Soft young soldiers sometimes kindle their brains with holy fervor and burn their lives to ashes. Some like fever must have gripped these Armenians. We'd soldiers in the thousands, rifles, endless ammunition, cannons ready by, and they knew it. They chose to die.

"You've seen the penalty for insurrection. A sad fate, but justified. I'll lead you back now. We'll find nothing worse." My words were sincere.

The foreigners seemed to acquiesce. Just then, a wail surprised us. Consul Behrmann pressed toward it, deaf to my calls. On the next street, a handful of joined one-story houses stood lifeless, abandoned even by dogs. The German, determined, proceeded through a broken gate and I followed into a stable yard where a solitary hen scavenged. From the nearest house came lamentations rising from a low, male register to a high pitch almost inhuman in tone.

A woman answered Behrmann's knock. She watched us coldly as Cumberbatch's assistant explained our purpose. She looked us over, her hands clasped across a streaked apron, hatred for us writ plain on her pock-marked face. With something like contempt, she said, "Come and see."

This woman, apparently a relative, led our file into the dark main room. Here keening overwhelmed us, blocking speech. The air smelled foul; remnants of wood caught at our feet; the room was bare. An elderly woman crouched, swaying as she wailed, turned in upon herself, eyes unseeing.

Mother mourned like this for my grandmother. As a boy it confused me. Who was this stranger, deaf and blind to me? Where was my beloved *anne*? I cried for my lost mother, her lost succor. Not for my grandmother. Now I shuddered with foreboding of unanticipated, undeserved death.

"We must leave," I said to my companions. We were imposing on this family, they needed privacy. The group declined politely several times: they must see this situation for themselves. The British consul bade a lamp be lit.

"She won't allow it." A statement, not a refusal. Soon the sister (as we learned) returned with a lit candle. "I've kept a fire in the kitchen." Her voice and face remained impassive.

The candle showed bullet holes marking the walls, and shattered windows. Nothing else remained, no pillow, no rug, no icon.

The woman raised her light. She examined me and Tewfik Bey in our officers' dress uniforms with eyes as fierce and bitter as I ever saw. Disgust stained the words she spat. "You want to see what your brave men have done? What heroes march in your army? Then look in there. On the floor. See why a mother weeps!"

Pushing past us, she pulled aside a curtain and motioned us into the next room. Here too, a broken window and shattered cupboards told of intruders. Against the far wall were shadows and two male shapes, crouched, arms around knees. One was mature, some years my senior, the other young and slender. Father and son, I guessed. They looked at us without interest, faces blanked by misery. Between them and us was a low, uneven heap I first mistook for bedding.

"You must witness this and tell me why." The sister-neighbor set piercing eyes on us for long moments. She handed me her candle, then bent to gather first one, then another and another blood-stained mats. This revealed a pair of bodies.

Can any of us yet wash our minds of what she showed us? I'd imagined I was inured to mutilated flesh until a candle lit that ghastly bedroom floor.

Two young women lay on their backs in disarray. Knees splayed, dresses torn and blood-stained. Blood-crusted stab wounds on neck, breast, belly, limbs. Both delicate bodies swollen with child, as if they must be twin sisters alike in all things. Mere girls—from their unlined soft faces perhaps no older than 18 years. The living here must be father, grandfather and grandmother of the never-born. And aunt.

The Italian muttered a few words. Another consul said, "Such villainy…" I knelt near the girls' feet, pulled their skirts down and their ankles together. When I tried to stand, my muscles failed. I bent my head and swallowed, fighting nausea. My skull was pounding. Tears smeared my vision.

"It is…" I could not finish.

"Unbearable," said Cumberbatch, voice catching. He helped me to my feet.

"What animals can commit such atrocities? I'll kill them! We must find and kill them!" The Italian threw his arms about, weeping in gasps. Moments later the interpreter made choking noises and ran from the room. Sounds of retching mixed with groans. Presently the man returned, his face grey.

I struggled to find words of solace for the mourners, knowing my uniform made it impossible. Could anything have helped? The foreigners proffered sincere, well-intentioned phrases, useless to the grieving if they heard.

We were near the front door. Suddenly the bereaved matriarch broke off keening and fixed eyes on each of us in turn. Her face was kindly in repose. She drew her sister-in-law close and whispered in her ear. The woman sighed and straightened before addressing us.

"She wants you to know her husband and elder son Digran –" here she nodded towards the next room "– owe their lives to a Muslim." I recalled the name from stories told by Martiros. True tales, he said.

"My brother and nephew were at the shop," the sister went on. I'd seen their sign, grain sellers. "Thank God Garabed, the other son, was at the American school delivering bulgur. He sent word home that he's all right. He doesn't know yet –" She halted with a short gasping cry.

"His father will go now to get him. First he must find Father Ashod. He cannot tell his son alone. Also, you see—we want a priest here!" Her eyes glistened. "We sent for Father Zaven. But he was murdered, too." This added with closed eyes, a deep breath. Plainly she was putting effort into self control.

"Let me tell you the rest. My brother and his son Digran heard the trumpet in the Plaza, and right after that came shouting and gun shots. They were expecting something, they knew right away they must run for their lives. They grabbed their coin box and ran out the back of their shop, desperate for a place to hide.

"Just then, not far down the alley, a Muslim friend appeared and beckoned them inside his store. Made a place for them under a pile of …" Here she checked herself from betraying the friend to her listeners. "…his goods. The men hid there all day in fear, making no sound. It was hard not to cough or sneeze from the dust, especially as the hours passed without water. They were choking from dryness.

"The shop was in fact searched three times that day, but never through all its corners. Someone caught sight of two Armenians in the alley, but didn't see where they went. Their friend said they must've run out the other end of the alley. He held to his story…"

"He took a great risk for them!" While her story was translated, the woman stared in turn at her nephew, her sister-in-law and each visitor. Like an officer challenging his troops before a battle. Then she sighed and held her eyes closed tight. Moments later, she resumed her story.

"If they were found, he'd be killed! Or beaten, his shop looted.

That's what happened to the Muslim baker on Olti Street. He was hiding his Armenian fire-tender. They killed the helper and nearly killed the baker. Perhaps you know?" I nodded. We waited while the translator caught up.

"Other shopkeepers closed up, went home or ran along with the mob. This Muslim stayed to protect her son—he's my nephew—and her husband—my brother. She is grateful."

For telling this I admired that woman as fully as I pitied her.

One or two of the consuls said something inconsequential. Then we excused ourselves as speedily as courtesy allowed. None of us wanted to linger in that tragic house. "I will pray for your nieces. May God be with you," Chambers told them. None of us could add anything.

We rode past more houses flooded with wailing, but the foreigners showed no interest. They were as preoccupied as I. Even the talkative Italian said little. We passed many beggars, a few wearing disbelieving expressions and clothes too good for beggar-wear. Surely the well dressed ones never went hungry two days before this.

Sometimes a horse's hooves scattered flakes of dried blood in all directions. Keyif's forelegs were dark with them when I dismounted. Within a broken gate a large woman was scrubbing front steps—perhaps it was a son's or husband's blood there.

An odd sound made me turn in the saddle when the third horse behind me reared full up. It took effort not to smile as Consul Cumberbatch gained his feet. The unfortunate consul rubbed his soft places with gloved hands. He blustered as his dragoman helped him back on the saddle. It can happen to anyone, I told him. He was embarrassed at muddied trousers, spoiled dignity. Dirt patched one side of his narrow nose.

Now I advised an easy route past the Armenian church and two Armenian schools for our return to the missions and consulates. Tired, the foreigners agreed. My relief was short-lived, for noises from behind the church drew their interest. Tewfik Bey trotted to stop them.

"Armenian religious services," he told them, "Armenians only!"

"We only want to see. We won't interfere!" The consuls rode past him, through the cemetery gates. The American led.

Tewfik Bey drew me aside. "It is unfortunate they see this. However, I believe many of the dead are already covered by dirt."

"We've no way to blindfold them."

A team of Armenian laborers and beggars was digging a deep square trench. Beside it lay a disorderly heap of corpses. More bodies formed double rows along the cemetery wall. Old bones, skulls and coffin-bits were strewn about, all crusted with dirt.

Overseeing the diggers were twice as many soldiers, all but one standing on the upwind side. A priest helped three sturdy Armenian youths pull a body off the gruesome pile and heave it to the second row. An officer preened, shouting at the diggers to work faster.

A few men and women searched the rows. Here and there, someone knelt beside a body. Paired priests stood head and foot to one corpse, black headgear hiding their faces as they prayed. We watched without dismounting, keeping our distance from the distasteful scene. My hands trembled from shame and helplessness; I was grateful not to have to speak.

Near us a woman was washing blood and soil off a corpse. Likely it was dragged face down some distance, as little face remained. The body was paunchy, middle-aged—a man who enjoyed his meals, probably her husband. The woman's face was haggard, her hair disheveled and hanging about her shoulders. She must have overheard the consuls' French, for suddenly she stood, still clutching her bloody washrag, her desolate expression replaced by fury.

She stretched an arm towards the foreigners. To our astonishment, she began castigating them in a shrill, hard voice. "God's curse on you English! Give us back our husbands! Give us back our fathers and brothers and sons! Give us back our homes and our belongings! You are to blame for this!"

A startled silence. The interpreter whispered to his employer; the others seemed to grasp her message without her words.

from the thick neck, his skilled hands now missing fingers. The artisan's rings adorned others now. Strangely, I hoped he'd marked them, made his genius evident to posterity. And I thought, at least one ring is with its rightful owner.

I took a cloth from Keyif's pack and wrapped it around Sako's mutilated groin. His bloated belly was at odds with his wiry limbs. His eyes stared up horribly. I closed them with a pained heart, angry and regretful, then pressed closed the eyelids of a man beside him. That body appeared intact except for a bullet into his forehead.

Silent figures searched the rows. A man approached, bent down to see Sako's face, fell groaning to his knees and gathered the body in his arms. The man was wearing servant's clothes. This misled me until he glanced up. As I recognized Petros, distress put my first thought into words.

"What was your brother up to that he wasn't with you?"

Enormous grief filled his face. "Forgive my thoughtless question," I said, at once offering condolences from my family.

His reply was to the question I regretted asking. "I intend to find that out," he said. He looked at me intently, jaw set like we were schoolboys racing our horses. I turned so he could not read my face, embraced him and drew back to leave. Only then did his self-possession falter. He gave a sob, tears washing his eyes.

"He was the best of us, you know. The smartest and most gifted, the least selfish. Our whole family looked to him...

"I loved him with all my heart. If I find out who took his life—whoever it may be—I'll strike him down and gladly hang."

"Please be careful," I said. It was not the time or place to suggest the dead brother was a traitor.

Sorrow

Marjan   November 10

Our people came to call it a massacre. Already we knew he was one of many, our beloved Sako, son and brother, bridegroom and uncle. My husband saw 200 more or less, laid out and dug into a single grave. That meant 200 other families, grieving like ours, numb and drowning, half blind, half deaf. Fear and anger poisoning their sleep. And longing.

What friends and neighbors were among them? I unfolded a coverlet Nora gave my newborn Heranoush and felt my fingers ice. I must find my sisters.

That second day home, I begged Petros to take me and my mother to the Armenian quarter. Yiri and her mother pressed Martiros. No, the brothers said, it was dangerous—the Captain just that morning met armed Kurds heading for the Armenian quarter. He made them leave the city.

The next day, we nagged at the men, refused to let them go without us. "We're not Muslim wives for you to keep locked indoors!" I said to Petros. Poor man, my outburst almost knocked him sideways.

We made a pack, the men carrying cudgels. My mother came, of course, Henza, too, looking for her parents and brother. Of the adults, only Nazar, Matriarch and her sister stayed behind. My daughter and Yiri's sulked at being left with the children, though our retelling brought tears enough.

We came first to Zari's, and found Nora there as well—both exhausted from nursing Asadur. Looters left Zari's husband cruelly wounded and nearly dead. At first no one knew if he'd live, but now his chances looked better. Mother stayed to help, for my sisters were shaking from need of sleep. We thanked God the families were mostly well. Asadur's father and brothers were also beaten, but though one lost an eye, they'd survive. My fears lifted as we went on to my friend Varti's house.

We could see a new front door, like ours, in new framing. Rough-cut muslin was nailed up to block the winter wind. Underfoot, bits of glass brightened the ground. My breath caught when Varti herself answered our knocks. Her face was colorless and thin, her eyes sunk deep. Her feverish look made Petros gasp. She looked as troubled as Oskee did at first, yet also frantic, like a captured crow.

"What?!" she said—already, a strange response. I wasn't sure she knew us.

"Dear Varti, my friend, may we come in, Petros and I?"

She drew back, puzzled. The figure of her father-in-law took shape from a shadow.

"You are most welcome to enter, good friends. Please, please, come sit with us."

"Yes, sit, sit," said Varti, as though she only now recalled our faces and a proper greeting.

Looking around, I saw axe holes, but none of the familiar fine furnishings. The walls were bare and on the floors only dhurries. Most startling, barrels and a board stood for a table. It was as if the house re-furnished itself in sympathy to Varti. While we answered Papa Meserian's questions about our family, she walked back and forth behind him like a caged dog. Already I felt ill with fear for what might have happened here.

It was Papa Meserian who told us. Varti was pacing behind him. She often cried out as he spoke.

"We heard them coming," he said. "What could we do? Soldiers broke through our door and swarmed in before we could move. They knocked me down, shoved my wife and Vartouhi against the wall, started looting. Three of these thugs…"

I cried out, afraid to hear more. My heart was pounding fast as four. Papa Meserian held up his hand. "Let me continue...these thugs they call soldiers went upstairs, we could not stop them. How did they know our children were hiding there? Except for Marta, praise God, she was visiting her friend..."

Varti broke off her moaning. "The twins!" she cried.

The old man looked at his daughter-in-law with sympathy before going on with his story.

"We heard cries and shouts and many thuds and footsteps. Then the soldiers came down, with..." he hesitated.

"Sacks! Sacks with faces!"

Papa Meserian shuddered at Varti's wild outcry. "What she means is, they wrapped the twins and slung them over their shoulders like sacks. Their faces weren't covered, so they could at least breathe."

"They looked at me! Zeput's eyes, Rebecca's, too!—they blamed me!" Varti shouted, almost in my ear. As I drew back, I saw her slippers didn't match.

"They went out the door into the street. We heard horses riding away."

"Sacks with faces, gone where? Sacks to market—" Varti's eyes shone as she said these strange words.

"The looting seemed to last hours, and we were... sometimes pushed and knocked down. We were terrified they'd kill us or take more children. Finally, they all left...

"We don't know if they're alive." He stared at the wall over our heads as he spoke. "We don't know, and it's hard."

"They'll want a ransom, don't you think?" I thought, *I sound like Yiri. We must find hope. We need it.*

"We pray so. But we've had no message..."

"If you saw their faces! They blame me! I had bracelets!"

"She's been like this ever since..."

"Bracelets!" Varti came at us, shaking her wrists, and I understood before Papa Meserian explained,

"The soldiers took the twins so fast, I doubt they'd have traded. But Varti blames herself. Please, come sit, take tea with us."

He called into the next room, and we heard a woman's voice call upstairs. In a moment his wife, his son Karekin, Varti's husband and his brother Manik, the twins' father, joined us, then little Rupen and Souren, with their sister Marta following. I caught her eye and a moment's loving smile went between us.

Then, to our surprise, Katoon came shyly to stand near Marta, her eyes fixed on our feet. She seemed calm and ordinary, not someone who needed watching. It was Varti you'd mistake for a madwoman, or at least for the bereaved mother. It made sense, Katoon's calm—I don't suppose she really felt what Varti felt, how could she? All the years Varti was mother to the twins and Marta was older sister, the woman who gave them life lay resting and weeping in a dark room.

Petros and I said the usual things meant for comfort. One or another asked after our families and gave condolences at our news. They knew they were not the only ones suffering. Papa Meserian might be (Varti said) too strict with his grandchildren, but he was not a selfish man. He saw beyond himself. Not like Nazar, for all his prayers. Grandfather Meserian said, "So many murders, so much ruin. Why? What made them turn our peaceful city into a battlefield?"

"A question we all ask," said Petros.

As you expect, the boys played, the women watched. Grandmother Meserian and I talked together about (of all things!) winter colds and how to treat cracked fingers. Meanwhile the grandfather spoke with Petros out of our hearing.

Varti looked a bit calmer as we went to leave. She stared hard into my eyes when I hugged her. "Bring them back," she said. Her mind seemed clear at that moment. Then her face changed and she became a wild woman again, feet and arms and eyebrows dancing about.

"Their faces! They're looking at me!" she cried, holding up her hands as if to hide.

We said have hope, but our hearts' grief lay heavy on our shoulders. Walking home I had to swallow acid hate each time we passed a Muslim.

Council Meeting

Martiros

M y brother. Father Zaven. The Council's own Giragos. Bedoian's daughters-in-law. It was weeks before new names stopped tearing at us like crows. The newspaper claimed a priest provoked it, as if a puppet kicks without a master, as if no telegraph wires tie Constantinople to Erzerum. It put the dead at 293, "most of them revolutionaries." That story was for fools and foreigners. We who paid witness in the sharp November wind counted 503 bodies at least in the new-dug trench. An awful burial, those battered corpses piled on one another head to foot, unclothed and uncoffined in the dirt, but that grave could serve a while. Better trenched than left for dogs, like the dead beyond the city gates. The dead are indifferent, yet the living choke to picture curs and raptors feasting on their flesh.

No Council member lacked for killed or wounded relatives, or relatives made destitute. Again we shared condolences. Even three weeks after the rampage, every face in the Prelacy meeting room showed signs of strain and sleeplessness. And anguish. And anger.

Their stories made you curse the waste of lives and property. There was Haroutoun Sabatian, hiding in his shop's loft, hearing his son scream before his throat was slashed. His trembling hands were unfit now for tailoring. Masis Timaksian was knocked flat just as his mortally wounded brother collapsed upon him, drenching him in blood and thus taken for dead. Saved. This within their shop while his lame-legged step-father was being struck down in the street. Zareh Kapikian's house was torched, as was Sempad's in-laws' home.

Arson destroyed half of Drikian's house, as well, and his servant girl was raped. Berj and his father were beaten, their house looted. It was something with every man around the table. I looked at Bedoian, whose unborn grandchildren perished with the mothers, and marveled that he and his sons stayed sane.

It seemed the violence was over—the mayor and police chief both gave many assurances. They counted on us as good citizens! We should resume business, re-open our schools and church, return to normal habits. Discard the hate we felt towards these murderous, thieving, devilish Muslims. Yet our beloved Father Zaven was dead, our Bishop gone to a distant jail, our choir master ill, our choir decimated and many church members either dead or destitute. I couldn't trust these devils now, who could? Fear made some talk of leaving for western provinces, even Syria and Russia or Greece.

Meanwhile, St. Asdvadzadzin's treasury waited largely intact in its Imperial German Bank vault, gold bars and coins along with four gilded candlesticks and 12 silver salvers. I take some credit for this. Later that winter we managed to ransom our great gilded crucifix and two of six large candlesticks. Some precious items never turned up—most likely melted, the artisans' skills no more valued by the looters than the Christian lives they wasted.

The meeting was my first as a Councilman, and also Masis Aghabalian's (replacing his brother) and Kapriel Baronian's (replacing his step-father). I welcomed this added duty, first as an opportunity to assist the Council, second to escape another evening of gloomy recollections and red-eyed women. Officially, I was a "spokesman-member with no vote," it being understood my father and I would vote as one. They were aware the church treasury survived on our advice. Though some resented us, they knew the Council might yet gain from our abilities.

Resentment is as ordinary as desire. I've concluded we must harness such feelings, else live as hermits. Successful men become used to resentment from those in lesser circumstances. Our family was long accustomed to some measure of it, as is any family more comfortable than poor. That's why a man's friends are generally of like means, though he may seek a varied inventory.

After the carnage in Erzerum, our family sensed new resentments that we could hardly comprehend. Why? For the simple reason that we were with one exception uninjured and our worldly goods largely intact. We kept quiet about being hidden. Each day I warned the family that secret held our neighbors' well-being as well as our own. Although our shop and home were looted and axed on that terrible day, and although we grieve and shudder to recall October 30, the fact is that we'd fleshly comforts few other Erzerum Armenians enjoyed through that harsh winter of '95-'96. Sako's death in some way served us, or sparks of hateful envy might have flamed and burnt our family. Losing Father as we did, through incapacity, served too.

Those who asked why our brother was on the street were told simply, "he was on his way home from the pharmacy" a simple and seemingly sufficient answer for them—not for us. Petros told me the Captain's terrible question at the cemetery: his accusation lingered in the air we breathed. We must find the truth. I was determined.

I must admit to resentful notions towards those few Armenians unscathed in the incident. And the Russians, why were they spared, supporting revolution as some did? Certain Syrians also favored carving the Sultan's territory, and they were left alone. And if it's Christians being persecuted, why overlook the Greeks, the Europeans? Such reasoning was useless, I let it drop. It was not so easy to overcome my hateful feelings towards every Muslim I saw, except our neighbors. Fury, too, even rage.

Once new members were elected, the meeting bobbed about like a wind-blown raft. We were agreed some tangible memorial was needed to solace the survivors. No Councilman cried "Let's do nothing!" What dragged this Council meeting out was deciding that memorial's form. Although Father Ashod was an adequate assistant priest, he lacked experience running a meeting. The Council was used to the Bishop taking charge and doing most of the talking.

How they wasted time! Again and again as the evening ran on, I stifled my impatience and reminded myself the goal was worthwhile. I find committees tiresome and aggravating. Besides, as I later said to Petros, I prefer producing money to spending it. Ideas piled high with little agreement. Yet at the end I was satisfied with the decision. Also, although I didn't expect it, I picked up information that proved useful

This one proposed we build a grandiose monument, that one favored a simple plaque, others wanted to purchase a fountain or a new gold crucifix and candlesticks to replace those plundered. While half the Council blathered on prices, Hovannes' son Harout interrupted. "We must ransom the captives! Armenian wives and daughters are being violated! We must save their honor!" He had the earnest face and voice of someone pounding at your door to say your roof-beam is burning. An understandable suggestion, stupidly expressed. His elder brother's girl was one of only four or five still missing. They'd be harem wives by now, if alive. Soon after that meeting, sadly, his niece's body was found. What was left of it wasn't worth a ransom.

Lawyer Sempad, a relative by marriage, twice removed, made a poor attempt at wit by telling the man beside him, "They've no honor left to save, they're either dead or Muslims." Principal Drikian rambled against the Council's paying ransom, saying it would encourage kidnappings, although if a family could afford it, paying was advisable. Less wind might have improved the principal's logic.

Whether it was merely Harout's foolishness or the dishonor to his family, his suggestion was ignored. The Bishop was still new back when Hovannes—a long time Council member valued both for his sense and generous gifts to the church—succumbed to pleurisy. Within months of appointing the son, the Bishop apologized to Nazar, saying our example misled him in his expectations of Harout. Even the man's wife thought him a fool.

Someone called for a special month of mourning, someone wanted a concert, someone else an annual mass in honor of the dead. Someone wanted to honor the school baker who ran to the Russian consul for help. Dr. Tashjian proposed establishing an infirmary for the destitute. This inspired considerable discussion until he acknowledged that a shortage of medical supplies and the danger of contagion made the thing unworkable.

Next, Sako's friend Ardavast Khagorian advanced a proposal for providing orphans with scholarships in memory of the dead. He argued fervently in his rasping voice. I thought this an excellent concept and said so. At this point, Principal Drikian began a lengthy monologue on the necessity for "high educational practices" that made plain he expected to administer the program. This turned a number of the members from pharmacist Khagorian's proposal onto other paths. Berj spoke forcefully for re-opening the schools at once, to show our determination to survive. I led several voices in agreement.

After some time without speaking, Harout now asked, plaintively, "Can't we get our stolen candlesticks back? And the crucifix?"

"How exactly would we do that?" asked Sempad in a mocking tone.

"Give a reward," said Harout.

"Sounds like ransom again!" I couldn't resist saying, drawing laughter around the table.

Harout looked unperturbed. "A Muslim can't use a gold cross!" he exclaimed.

"Muslims use gold ingots," Krikor Shabanian pointed out, sensibly.

"But the candlesticks could be bought back!" Harout persisted.

Though Harout's remarks got small respect, they primed a flow of new suggestions and debate. Poor Onnik Bedoian sat mute in his rumpled suit, wiping his nose and eyes with a large black handkerchief and whispering "yes" to every proposal, lame-brained or not. The rest argued over four ideas at once. Even Krikor Shabanian, normally a man of sound judgment, worked up such a passion over his desired fountain that he was ineffective. I will say for my friend, it was the single time I've seen this flaw in him.

Now and then I've all but sold a piece of boot-leather, only to have the buyer's companion spot some minuscule imperfection and start praising a hide rejected earlier. Just like that, some Councilman would polish up an old idea, someone else would take it for new and wave it, another would object, and we'd be back where we started.

Nobody heard that much contention since a meeting forced by the so-called 'Minor Incident' in '91, when our noble Principal Drikian proposed daily searches of his scholars to satisfy the police. Soon everyone was shouting, Dr. Tashjian knocked Drikian's glasses off and Father tried to punch him. It nearly became a riot before our former Bishop smoothed things over. In my opinion, he should have replaced the Principal.

Though that meeting turned into a melee, it was short, at least. The famous meeting of '92 lasted seven hours without resolving the matter of a memorial to the cholera victims. It was our dear Bishop Ghevont's first Council meeting and came soon after the fever tore so many from their families, including ours. Certain Council members are rankled yet from it. I recall Father saying Ghevont Shishmanian was probably fortunate to learn the human shortcomings of his Council early.

We waited up, expecting good news as to the memorial. Father finally came in the door at midnight, seething so from anger and disgust it took an hour to calm him. Our grief for Sako's lost wife and daughters made the Council seem worse than heartless: rather, absurd, inept, incompetent. It took two more meetings to bring agreement. The resulting memorial looks well, at least, and has (to my surprise) stayed undamaged.

Now I suspected the Council was tuning up for a repeat performance. The absence of Petros' brother-in-law, Asadur Melikian (whose survival was still uncertain) made no difference. Lawyer Sempad and Principal Drikian, not to mention a few others, were self-important enough to petrify the chamber. I watched and listened in silence for some time, as a newcomer ought. It was plain to me the Council was treading a circle without the Bishop and my father for guidance.

Father Ashod let things run on far too long. At last, when I was resigned to hours more of futile bickering, the priest took his first step toward leadership. He began to negotiate a solution, and though it came slowly and needed a measure of my indirect persuasion, he led us there. His feet grew to fit the shoes, you'd say. Three hours later he had the councilmen marching in one direction.

Nor should I slight my father's contribution. He followed every part of the discussion, despite his half-open mouth and half-closed eye. He was, at that point, still interested in church affairs. More than once he croaked good sense in my ear, for me to put into words they could understand. He couldn't bring the group together—he was no longer capable of that—yet the plan agreed to owed fair measure to him. He knew each member's temperament and what might best persuade him. With his help, I produced an excellent proposal.

"Speaking for my father," I said, "This isn't the time for a costly memorial. Members of St. Azdvadzadzin's are living in rubble heaps, without quilts, without comfort. They're hungry and cold. It's their tithes as well as ours fill St. Adzvad's treasury. We can't shirk our obligation. What if your house was burned up, Sempad, or yours, Ardavast? Do you think we'd turn our backs on you? Our Most Holy Bishop (may he and his good works prosper in Jerusalem!) would have us do good with our funds. Look at what he's got the Widow Sharopyan doing! We should apply our resources to a similar purpose."

I was gratified to see them listening closely. I let my voice fall. "I propose we help rebuild the homes of our destitute church members. Moreover, that we set up a shelter for orphans, where our wives will assist in their care. It's what the Bishop would advise, if he were here."

That's the essence. Of course I decorated my proposal with elements that would appeal to certain councilmen, such as Khagorian, the principals Madatian and Drikian, Dr. Tashjian and Krikor Effendi Shabanian, and so forth. I controlled my natural inclinations and kept my words relatively brief.

Fortunately, Father Ashod guided the group toward using memorial concerts for raising funds as we progressed, and meanwhile deferring construction of a carved monument. In due course the group accepted my proposal, adding a pair of memorial scholarships for orphan boys, one at Ardzenian, the other at Sanasarian, which most considered the better school. When Father Ashod announced the ballots, smiles lit the table and chairs were abandoned for hand-shaking and back-slapping. No doubt everyone was relieved to have the matter resolved.

Selecting a place was our next task. Various liabilities pertaining to certain unoccupied buildings were pointed out, and I offered the obvious thought that if nothing better was available, we could choose from among numerous burned out houses. The pharmacist Khagorian called out, "Yes, most definitely!", then fell to coughing and arm-waving. Finally his fit ended and he managed to suggest in a faint, hoarse voice having some members search out the best site. Without discussion, Father Ashod appointed him and me to do so and adjourned the meeting before Sempad or Drikian could object.

Late as it was, few hurried away, but stood talking about their affairs, too excited by the long discussion to go home to bed. I think all were gratified by the Council's decision. It was an ambitious new undertaking, and more complicated than many. I hoped Berj would do it justice on his next rounds.

I was pleased to collaborate with Khagorian. I knew him to be a sensible businessman and a fair employer. He was a bit older than me, but not yet 40, the age when men settle into their habits and grow blind to new approaches. Sako once told me Ardavast was always trying out new medicines on himself before offering them to customers. True to a family tradition: some said his father died from a dose of strange powder.

The pharmacist and I were deciding when and where to start, when One-Ear Manoug heard me mention his neighborhood, Black River (Chay Ghara), almost wasteland now. The creek that named it curved down a hill near his house. At its far end had stood the home of Father Karekin Vemian, a gigantic priest with an exceptional gift for gun-making. The priest's stone dwelling was solid as a fortress until the violence. One corner, tall as a man, still watched over the flowing rivulet.

"My house is nearby, I could throw a rock from my roof to his," said Manoug, as if he were young still. "Believe me, I heard every gunshot that day they killed Man Mountain Karekin! Out the windows, in the windows, shooting you can't imagine! ...in both directions! And hitting my house, too—a wonder we survived it. Bang!" He made a series of shooting sounds, enjoying our attention. "For a while, it was an equal fight...but then so many troops infested the street, anyone could see the priest was doomed. No wonder his wife lost hope and killed herself!" He paused to gain effect. "... and the baby!"

The man's mouth was flowing as if it couldn't close. I wanted to finish with Ardavast and get home. Most of the Council had dispersed already. The pharmacist waited patiently as Manoug babbled on.

"It's incredible his sons escaped alive! It's a credit to Karekin he made them go, they were every bit as brave as their gigantic father, may they live long and grow fat, though there's a bounty makes that doubtful. Their father did them proud, and we should thank God he got three soldiers before he fell!" Manoug cackled and slapped his hand gleefully on the table, then recalled his purpose and took on a serious tone.

"Did you know Sarkis helped me one day with my mule? Just a few days before ..." He caught himself before speaking of my brother's murder. "Ah, my mule, a ridiculous beast, she gives two hours' trouble for 30 minutes' work, what can I do? My point is this: I won't forget your brother's good nature, nor his skill with my mule. The sort of man who makes an effort to help others. May he rest in peace!" Manoug added, in a quiet voice, "He didn't say where he was headed, though of course, I've my own ideas..."

Seeing Khagorian conferring with Father Ashod, I left my father dozing in his chair while I put questions to the miller. His answers tended to drift, yet by interrupting I extracted useful information. One Ear was no liar, although inclined to fool's blather in company, excited perhaps by attention. His eyes were sharp, and since it's true that millers grind news and wheat in equal measure, Manoug learned some things before the rest of us. He got facts when we got rumors.

He'd information, for example, that certain Armenians were acquiring guns wherever they could, despite the risk, preparing for trouble. The miller happened to know, he was not free to say how, that the very best guns were not military issue (some of which inevitably strayed into civilian hands) but rather, manufactured by the giant-priest Karekin, whose canniness had kept him from arrest—so far. I felt my head buzz as I considered the coincidence of my brother in the gunsmith's neighborhood so soon before the rampage.

Surely Manoug must be mad? Yet his eyes were clear and his words had logic. I listened closely as he described the priest's stealthy visitors. Some posed as carriers or beggars and others were dressed like tradesmen, as they most likely were. He thought no guns changed hands in such meetings, for anyone walking from Black River Street with a firearm could as well pull open the jailhouse door and ask for the Commandant's firing squad.

I supposed this was all Manoug had to tell me, but he seized my arm as I started to turn away. "Wait! There's more you should know!" he said. He glanced about for eavesdroppers, then told me this: The night before my brother helped bridle his mule, One Ear (being a light sleeper, he explained) awoke at some slight noise, and from an upstairs window saw my brother emerge from Black River Street. "No doubt who he was, we'd a moon you could throw dice by, it caught him full in the face."

He often saw people heading to and from Vemian's at night when patrols were infrequent. Manoug supposed anyone visiting the neighborhood had business with the giant. He was sure Sako's purpose was the same, because he was carrying a bundle..

I said nothing to disturb my father, of course. It was for Petros to find out whether our brother was in fact linked with the dead gunsmith priest. Perhaps Manoug's story was only his imagination—or perhaps it would dispel the mystery surrounding Sarkis's last hours. I made him promise to reveal none of this to others, lest my family suffer consequences. I hoped his word was sincere.

The Lovers' Secret

Marjan   late November

With school re-opened the house was almost quiet. I tried to keep my daydreams pleasant while we plodded through our chores, told Heranoush to turn away dark thoughts. We must take the goods we're given, do our best with them, I told her. It's something we all must learn. Yet her nature's like mine, we have eyes and ears for others' suffering. There were rumors, too, of more to come. I tried to hide my worries, but any girl of 13 kept inside day on day will get fearful and downcast.

I was mending Artashes' best shirt in the window light, when Heranoush burst out at me, "It's horrible, how can you sit there humming as if everything's fine, you don't care!" in one breath ending with sobs and sniffles. I sat dumb, head spinning before I tasted her grief and rose to take her hands.

"Tears shed for others are blessed by God," I told her. She couldn't shut her mind to Rebecca and Zeput any more than I could look at her sweet face without seeing theirs and aching for Varti. I wondered how my friend's family could bear not knowing.

"They may be all right. Whoever has them will want the reward…" Yet weeks had passed. I doubted they were still in this life. Four kidnapped girls now lay buried behind the church. One was found drowned at the mill dam below Iron Street the day the boys went back to school.

Keeping busy got us though the days but nights were hateful. Horrors scratched at our eyelids and churned our sleep. Petros sometimes moaned aloud. I no sooner fell off than a child's cries stabbed me awake. Even Artashes, at 12, sometimes needed my comforting. Of everyone in our room, it was my daughter slept the worst. Oddly, the Trabizond orphans slept the best.

By day, stitching a quilt with her cousin Astghig or helping me wash linens, Heranoush sometimes fell still, deaf and blind to us for long enough to boil a kettle. Other times she looked for Henza or Maxime. She found more comfort with her aunts than her mother, as girls her age do.

One afternoon Toumia wanted a sheet mended. Since Heranoush was not in the usual places, I tapped on Henza's door. The girl was there often enough to be a burden, yet Henza said she felt better for her visits.

Henza was stretched out with her eyes shut. I started to back out, but she called me over. Heranoush, she believed, was in the courtyard. When she sat up, the dark skin under her eyes made them look large as a mule's.

"Are you ill? You look tired."

"No, it's just—" She reached for my hand, pulled me beside her. "Dear Marjan, I want to tell you something. It…" She looked uneasy. "I…first you must promise me something."

A thought sprang up—*she'll tell why Sako was out that night.* "Anything, dear Henza."

"I need your solemn promise, heart and hands, promise you'll keep a secret." She touched her breast and held her hand out to me.

"Yes, of course, I promise." I copied her sign, then took her hand in pledge. Something eager in her face made me blurt, "Is it what we've prayed for? Henza, are you—?" Her smile made me laugh aloud.

"Yes. I'm quite sure of it. I thought of telling you before, but –" She bit her lip. "No one else must know. Please, don't tell Petros. Or Heranoush."

"I won't—but they'd be happy for you! It's just what Sako wanted! Oh, Henza—did he know, or was it too soon…?"

"He knew. For two weeks, more or less. May God forgive me, he knew...." She wiped a tear, then reached for my hands. "He was like a priest at Easter with his rejoicing! He said he felt like the crowned king of Ancient Armenia!" She smiled, remembering. "We were so happy! And he spoiled me so, once I told him."

I'd seen him cut an orange for her the day before he died, watched her eat it. Maxime winked at me. We both were delighted by the newly-weds' ways.

"Aunt Zabel wonders why you barely touch your food."

"Sako asked me to eat more, but I was queasy...Then of course I was too sad."

She took a deep breath. Tears shone in her eyes. "That morning he promised to bring me a tonic. 'Don't worry, I'll be back before you know it,' he told me." She bit her lip so blood wet the cracks.

"I suspected he meant to do some secret errand as well. I explained this to your good husband, except about...the baby." She was almost whispering now and her voice began to tremble. "He... after the quarrel with his father, Sako was afraid his father would make me tell...if I knew what he was up to ..."

"But before that, Henza? The night Patriarch came here looking for Sako, where was he?"

"That was the night I told him about our baby. I was finally sure, and we were giggling like children... He said he was going out to do some business with a priest..."

She broke off and for a few minutes, simply stared at the far wall. There was a bright shawl hiding a damaged cupboard. She wiped her eyes. "I was thinking, 'Of course, he needs to arrange for the christening!'—imagine him seeing our priest that time of night!" We avoided saying Father Zaven's name as if it meant bad luck.

"...Sako was playing with my sleeve, smiling. I thought he was teasing." She bit her lip and it bled again. I thought—forgetting—Sako must give her salve for it.

She went on, "Problems with his father were troubling him. I couldn't worry him with more questions. He told me he'd explain some day and I must be patient. 'It's important, or I'd not be going out.' " She fell silent. In another room, a baby cried and a woman called out for Verkin to fetch water.

"I really didn't know. I still don't—I can only guess..." Her expression changed and she looked at me directly. "Did you notice a stranger speaking to me after last Sunday's service?"

An unfamiliar young man stopped her as we were starting down the cathedral steps. In those days it was nothing remarkable for a stranger to offer condolences.

"He told me Sako was a hero. 'Brave and determined.' That he helped avenge the hay carriers. Sako never said this, yet his hand had bruises, he was tense..." She shook her head. A sorrowful sigh gave way to a rush of words. "But I know he'd never kill someone. Never!

"That man wouldn't answer my questions, either. He said it would be more dangerous for him if I knew."

"You should tell Petros about that," I said.

"Can it matter? Are we making tangles into knots?"

I squeezed her hand. "The important thing now is the baby."

Henza began to cry softly, then with great sobs I was helpless to soothe. *She's weeping for Sako at last,* I thought.

When her tears stopped, she asked, "Will we ever be safe? Why do they kill Armenians? Trabizond and Erzincan and Bitlis and Baiburt and Urfa ...and other places, village after village...Where can we live without fear? How can we be safe now in Erzerum? Who's to say it won't happen here again? What kind of a world is this, to bring up children?..." Her voice broke and I put an arm around her shoulder, waiting for calm.

"It may be awful to say this, but is it right—do you think it's right, Marjan?—to even bring a child into this hateful world?"

"I don't know the answer, Henza. Some things make no sense. We must have faith in God's mercy. We're in His hands."

"It's hard to believe that any more."

We talked about God, wickedness and faith, as seriously as talking with a priest. It did us both good, though we never agreed on whether God was helping us or not.

The gate slammed—the schoolboys were home. Time for kitchen work. As I got to my feet, my daughter appeared in the doorway. She looked excited as she glanced from me to Henza and back. "The Captain's wife is the sweetest lady in the world. She's so nice!" she said.

None of us went from one sunrise to the next without tears in those weeks, and my daughter probably wept most. It turned out Heranoush was in the rear yard, crying, when Khadija's gentle voice invited her into the next courtyard. The woman welcomed her with outstretched hands and led her to a bench in the mid-day sun.

"Your eyes are very sad." This tact soothed the girl, for her brothers and Toumia made fun of her crying.

"You're mourning for your uncle," the captain's wife said softly. "You must miss him. My family and I are very sorry."

"It's more than that –"

"Your mother's brother-in-law—he's Asadur Melikian with the kerosene shop, is he not? They say he was badly wounded. It must be sad for –"

"No. Yes. It's partly that, but—Oh, Hannum Khadija! Something much more terrible!!" Sniffling and sobbing, my daughter told about the twins.

Our neighbor had questions and they talked a good while. At the end, the woman offered to find out where the girls were. "They can't be far, we're sure to know someone who knows something," Khadija told her.

I tried to hide my doubts. The child glowed with new hope. She was smiling for the first time in weeks.

"Mama, I can tell Astghig, can't I? Please!" She dashed from the room, slamming the door behind her.

"Your daughter is a credit to you and Petros," said my friend. "You must promise to bring her along when you visit me."

"Please don't desert us, Henza!" I wailed out—yet why should Henza stay with hateful in-laws when her own loving family longed for her return? A foolish envy tied my tongue. I heard the boys shouting, Aunt Maxime scolding, then silence.

"If Matriarch finds out, she'll make me stay—I'd have to appeal to the Holy Primate in Etchmiadzin! It could take a year, and then the baby…" She took my hand. "I must go back to my parents very soon. Where I'm loved. Before my belly shows."

Nothing I said could change her plan. She felt badly judged. "Perhaps not Petros, but all the others…" She pressed my hand to her lips. "Sister, imagine what it's like to feel, every hour, their blame…

"And everything here reminds me of him. Every day, I ache for him worse than the day before. At night, it's…dreadful. Forgive me, it's wrong to feel sorry for myself."

She made me too ashamed to speak. I looked at the flowers woven into the prayer rug beside the bed and thought *how many pretty things she'll be taking from the bridal chamber.* Finally I said, "You've been truly brave, Henza. I'll always love you like a sister."

She made the same promise, smiling sadly. A moment later she said, "Before Sako…died, Toumia never scolded me—it was the rest of you who felt her tongue. Sometimes it amazed me! She was rude to Sara and you and Yiri, she even went after the aunts. No wonder Sara resented me for marrying Matriarch's favorite…And may God forgive me, I liked my place of honor. It felt good!"

"Poor Sara resents everyone. The first son's wife gets favored in any household—why resent it, that's how it is! Yiri and I weren't jealous, we were used to Toumia." I sighed and thought of the day she slapped me for not leaving baby Heranoush to cry while I mended something for her. Another time she gave me Dela's chores just for being…powerless. "We only wanted Sako to be happy again. You made him happy."

"Did you know we quarreled over my going to Berthe Sharopyan's? Sako was afraid I'd catch some frightful illness from the refugees. 'I can't go through that again!' he told me. He was being reasonable…" She closed her eyes and breathed deeply.

"You can't imagine what I said! 'As if you were the only one ever bereaved!' I'm ashamed such words came off my tongue! But I didn't think first. Then Sako said, 'My daughters were 7 and 8, they were people already!' and I said, 'My son was almost 3, he was a person already too!'

She looked up with a hint of a smile. "Can you believe we squabbled like that, Marjan? We were two idiots trading foolishness. Which is what he said. 'This is stupid.' And he kissed me...

"I told him, 'At least you loved your daughters. Your family doesn't give much value to females.' And he said, 'You are valued by me.' And then..."

Henza paused, remembering. Her lovely eyes shifted from her hands back to my face. "He said, 'I want you and need you.' I told him, 'I'll give you a child.' And he said, "Let's make two, a boy and a girl.' Then he said, 'You know, it's alright if we've no children, as long as we have each other.' Oh, Marjan! I loved him so much!"

"And he loved you just as much, you know."

"Would he mind my deserting his parents...?"

"He wouldn't want you here, with Toumia your enemy. She treats you unfairly."

"Life's not fair."

"We must learn that."

"Your daughter's beginning to learn it. She's growing up."

"She needs to learn patience."

"She learns from your good example."

"I pray for calm. For courage to accept what is and will be."

"As I must also do, dear sister." She embraced me with tears thick on her eyes.

Did anyone suspect? Sara never kept a secret, and every time she opened her mouth, I was afraid she guessed. I was ready to lie, to say Henza had cramps and needed rags when she was only resting, but she asked me to keep quiet. All week I forced myself to act as if nothing worried me. Little Artashes got spanked for some mischief— and (may Christ Jesus forgive me) I was grateful it drew attention from other things. Thankfully, Sara never went beyond complaining about a rash on her hands and her trouble sleeping, what with infant Hamajah's teething.

Fortunately Heranoush and Astghig were fixed on different matters and noticed nothing changed in their Aunt Henza. Later Aunt Maxime told me she knew from Henza's peaked look, but kept quiet from compassion. Yiri also guessed, but decided Henza would be happier back with her own people. It reminded me not to underestimate Martiros' wife, as trying as she was sometimes.

Henza waited until the day before to tell our family she was returning home. I held my breath all evening, scared Toumia or one of the men would propose the widow wait a bit longer "to be sure". It seemed a blessed miracle that no one did! Everyone else talked about being sad to lose her, and Toumia only snorted, as if to say, "Good riddance!" It was hard to understand the old lady's rudeness. Maxime said that Henza reminded Toumia of Sako, and it was pain made the old woman so harsh.

That Sunday was the celebration of Holy Mary's conception, and all through the service I had to fight back tears thinking about St. Elizabeth's holy womb and the marvelous gift of God—mixed in of course with Henza's leaving, and her secret, and the gift of life that Sako's child promised. They are a gift, our children.

After church, Henza's father and brothers came with an oxcart for her things. Their good manners sealed Toumia's thin lips as she bowed to Henza's father, yet anyone could tell she was glad Henza was going. Nazar said something more or less proper, as best he could, leaving Martiros to offer a gracious speech about our departing sister-in-law and her sorrow. When little Sahad understood his aunt Henza was leaving our house for good, he let forth a great wail, and soon all the younger babes joined in. I didn't weep, knowing her house was close to Nora's and I could stitch a secret visit onto the one allowed.

Petros The Detective

Martiros late November

Soon after the first Council meeting, Berj stopped in at the shop. "I've information bearing on your martyred brother's final hours," he said, with typical drama.

"Wait!" I held my hand up. "Let me get Petros to hear this." My brother joined us a moment later.

Berj told us Sako had been seen by two Muslim acquaintances familiar with the pharmacy, running along Cotton Street toward Lilac, just after the violence broke out. Berj was usually more voluble, but this time his message contained few unnecessary words. He came to the point with little time wasted.

"They lost sight of him at the intersection, most likely when he turned down Lilac. So many people of all sorts—thugs and ordinary Muslims along with hamidieh and soldiers—were crowding the streets leading from the Plaza that they couldn't be sure. But if he did turn onto Lilac, Armenians live there: Sharopyan, Tarbasian, Tashjian, Madatian…someone just may remember seeing him.

"I suggest you talk with the people living near that corner. Who knows? You might learn something useful from them," said Berj as he left.

Petros went out that afternoon.

The Widow Sharopyan, dignified as always, hoped to help his investigation. However, she'd seen nothing whatsoever, nor had others in the house, for all were hiding in the cellar or behind mattresses upstairs. She'd made sure, days before, they knew where to go if the violence that had already struck other provincial cities struck ours.

When the noise started, those refugees scrambled to their hiding places, as did the widow and a trio of churchwomen working in her kitchen. A few of the women became aware of shouts outside the door, but nobody opened it because nobody was anywhere near. Petros gathered they were too terrified to go to the door in any case. The widow promised to tell him if she learned anything to help his search.

Petros' inquiries round the neighborhood turned up a woman who'd seen a man running past her window. She couldn't describe the man and seemed slow-witted, so he wasted no more time on her.

On the opposite side of the street, at the intersection of Cotton Street with Lilac, stood the Tarbasians' two story house. Its front windows offer a good view of the route Sarkis must have run, and the thought gave Petros hope. His knock was answered by the tailor Diran, as crisp and practical a man as his brother Boghos was preoccupied. Neither tailor nor mother had anything to add, while Boghos was too ill to speak, having contracted pneumonia (perhaps consumption as well) in prison. Petros heard his ceaseless coughing from the entry room. The mother complained it was still worse at night. Petros said she looked worn to exhaustion.

Nothing more came from Petros' inquiries, but he refused to quit. "In time, we'll find answers to our questions. Someone knows," he said to me.

Then I was astonished to get a message from someone we long avoided due to his reputation for reckless talk. He supported Armenian independence just like a Hunchak, whether or not he was one. Father predicted this man, Memmik, would shiver in jail, and the dog-hunt after the so-called uprising in Constantinople proved him right. The surprise was his release three weeks later, "still warm, still breathing!" as Rooster said—though with feet too raw to walk on.

Then as now, the police were harsher with Armenian nationalists than most other so-called criminals. Saying Christians deserved the same rights as Muslims was as dangerous as touting a separate Armenia, and beyond monetary remedy. A bribe wouldn't suffice, in other words. I reasoned that either the police turned Memmik into an informer, or they had spies watching to trap his colleagues. Or possibly, as Sako half-joked, they'd decided to let Memmik be slaughtered at home. No point wasting a safe jail cell. In any event, we had no dealings with the man in years and expected none now.

I was flabbergasted when this Memmik sent a boy to the shop to confide, "Memmik has something to tell you. Privately. It's about your murdered brother." He proposed a secret meeting at a site as safe as any I could think of. It never occurred to me to refuse.

I provided myself with an honest errand close by our meeting place, so I could say I'd entered the chapel on impulse, to pray. St. Barkevadu Chapel was an ancient sanctuary most unlike our St. Adzvad's. "Cramped, primitive, useless"—these were the words some people (including Father) used when they questioned the cost of its caretaker. Others (among them was Mother) were aghast at this, revering it as a holy place. My few visits over the years helped me see why ignorant people hold superstitions. Its very austerity gave St. Barkevadu's a primitive kind of spiritual power.

It was said this sainted lady wrought miracles. She was a wet nurse, poor and humble. Mothers prayed to her statue for breast milk. Parents brought sick children to touch her feet. Sako's first wife, Dela, claimed St. Barkevadu cured her four-year barren spell.

My eyes were still useless in the dim light when Memmik stepped from the shadows. Even out of the morning wind, the air was frozen as the stones we stood on. I had to wriggle my toes while he spoke or they'd have snapped off. I could feel the heat evaporating from his well-rounded body into the heavy, damp air.

"I am sorry about your brother. He was a fine man—and a close friend." He spoke in an odd mannerly way that reminded me of my first schoolmaster. I remembered then, Memmik's father was a school teacher.

"A great loss," I replied. "I knew nothing of your friendship."

"A necessary secret." He looked around him before whispering, "It must remain so."

"I pledge discretion. Sako kept his secrets close—as will I."

"Our work requires trust."

"We must learn why he was killed."

We spoke in quick bursts, pausing to listen for danger. A loud noise on the street pressed us into shadows against the wall. We waited wordlessly until quiet returned outside.

"It was dangerous, we all knew that. We couldn't <u>not</u> do it. We believed—we'll <u>die</u> believing—Armenians must stand against oppression! We will <u>not</u> be treated like <u>slaves!</u>"

I was fearful already of spies who might see me with that man. Now a boulder seemed to block my windpipe. Each gasp rent tissue, my head pounded, my balance faltered. I'd heard the identical words from Sako in private.

In the next moment, a flood of light silhouetted two women in the doorway. They were lighting candles in the far corner as Memmik whispered, "Stay hidden," and disappeared. I did not see the door open again until the women left many prayers later, nor did I glimpse my informant again until three days after.

During that interval I gnawed at the little Memmik had told me and felt my chest vised, my head hammered. I blamed these symptoms on not knowing what my brother was up to that day he was killed. I detest uncertainty, and now it seemed probable he'd been carrying guns. Already I was suspicious he was tangled with revolutionists. I found it hard to meet eyes with Hamed the evenings—less frequent since our return—he and his father visited. I sensed some separation on his part. I still hoped it was my imagination.

The messenger found me as I left the shop on some errand. I was to meet Memmik at the St. Dajar Chapel at noon, a time when we might be inconspicuous among many visitors.

The muezzin's call had barely faded when I entered the shrine behind an elderly couple and two women with a child holding hands between them. I bought and lit a candle, prayed a moment, then stepped into a shadowed alcove where a figure waited.

"We've more privacy than the last place—more people," he said, close to my ear.

"It's good. You have my confidence."

"Some facts should be kept from your family."

"Understood. Please go on, we've little time." Nerves stirred my impatience.

Memmik was guarded, yet passionate, his spittle-spray gleaming in the light. I wondered if he might be trying to recruit me to replace my elder brother—but he said nothing directly.

The man sketched a picture of what Sako and he were up to (together with others, not identified), consisting sometimes of messages relating to gun deliveries, other times actual deliveries. It meant enormous personal risk, obviously. What angers me yet is their risking their families without our consent. What right had Sako to imperil our household? Nowhere does it say anyone, first-born or otherwise, has that privilege.

For years the authorities had been quick to confiscate property "as a warning to others," turning entire families into street beggars. The property, of course, was soon in other hands—an official's relative or friend or business partner. It was state-licensed theft, corrupt and cruel. I was appalled that Sako placed his secret political activities before our family's well-being. Henza could reside with other relatives, but how could he dismiss the danger to his parents, his brothers and cousin, our children? Was he blind to the rest of us? I seethed. *The reckless fool!*

Memmik must have felt my anger, for as I began speaking, he put his hands on my arms. "Wait. Hear me. Your brother did this for love of his family. He told me, 'I have no children. I do this for my brothers' children, so they can hold their heads up without shame, proud they were born Armenian. If I give my life it's for them.' Those were his words. For you all, in case …" his voice broke off. When he spoke again, his tone was grave and sorrowful. "He wanted you all to know why he helped us."

I needed to know more of my brother's last hours, why he was running down Cotton Street instead of safe with his family—and I must learn who killed him. I pressed Memmik further.

"I still couldn't walk any distance, after prison…Guns had to be delivered, a few last guns for the cause. It's no secret where—- the building's gone, but what a great fight our heroes gave! They killed 18 soldiers and wounded 40 more before it ended!"

"So he went from Black River Street to the Armenian Theatre …?"

"With two bundles of costumes in his hands. Weapons sewn into sleeves, and so forth. After he delivered them, he was going home. To wherever your family was hiding."

"Did he make it to the Theatre? Do you know?"

"He made his delivery. He wasn't there more than two minutes. Then he struck out down Cotton Street. That's all I know, God help me."

"Did someone follow him from the Theatre?"

"I cannot say. I'll tell you this, I had a rifle and put it to good use until they torched the roof."

I shared this (without naming my informant) with my brothers and Levon. In due time, we shared it with our sons. It did the boys good to know we were proud of their uncle even though (we took pains to make this clear) we scorned his heroics. I did not tell Father. It was better he mourned without the added weight of anger.

Martiros Learns More

※ • ※ • ※ • ※ • ※ • ※ • ※ • ※ • ※ • ※

Martiros   December

N ot long after my meeting at St. Dajag, our family went to a special Advent concert in memory of the martyrs. As Father insisted on attending, my smart Arsen proposed a chair-sled, which Levon and Miron helped us construct. The contrivance proved useful the entire season. The concert was his post-stroke debut and also provided two significant facts in our quest for information.

The family had already entered the hall when a voice called out, "Please, wait!" and Diran Tarbasian ran up and pulled me and Petros aside. He understood we were seeking information connected with Sako's murder. His brother Boghos had now recovered sufficiently to tell us something potentially important. We arranged to talk with Boghos the next day.

The second development came with Berthe Sharopyan's summons during intermission.

"There's something I must tell you right away!" the widow told us. "My little Setrag woke me with his crying last night. He'd done this before, and his older sister, too—it's natural children have nightmares, especially the orphans…" Her prattle about childish bogeymen was interrupted by a welcome signal ending intermission. We agreed to call on her soon.

The following afternoon, Petros and I slipped out to visit the invalid Boghos. His mother led us up a narrow stairway to a room where he lay resting against an enormous, lumpy pillow. He smiled weakly and asked about our health, and our children, and dismissed our questions as to his health with a simple, "Better, thank you. Glad to be alive and <u>home</u>." (Seventeen days in prison nearly killed him. The reason he was jailed was never explained.) He proceeded with his story directly, in a weak but steady voice, wasting no words on inessentials.

Shortly after the violence began, alarming noises outside drew him from his sickbed to his bedroom window. He watched someone (certainly Sako) pound on the widow's door. He saw two men fall upon this person with knives. Boghos was transfixed, yet faint from fear and illness. Before collapsing on his mattress, he saw that one of the pair was white-haired. Not, however, old, instead agile and swift. Boghos hoped his recollection would help us.

"Was he Circassian?"

"Possibly so." It was typical Boghos, this uncertainty.

By now we were well aware that a white-haired Circassian went thieving that day, along with half the city's Muslims. We'd no special quarrel with Circassians, though they are apt to be especially poor and prone to theft. Murder was something else. If Boghos' eyes and fever hadn't deceived him, we might identify Sako's murderer by his mane only.

Calling next at the Sharopyan house, we were announced as "Two neighbors to see you!" by a woman we took for a maid—in fact, her guest-refugee. She'd been at the parlor window as we crossed from Tarbasians'.

The Sharopyan lady poured the tea herself into flowered china cups. "My household runs differently these days," she explained. Its aroma was such that I relaxed and let my attention stray to a calmer time, when my father served on the Council with her late husband. He'd been successful trading in rugs and other goods and possessed at least two villages on the plains. His widow continued his substantial financial support to our church.

Her voice pulled me back to the frightful day. "Let me tell you why our refugee child Setrag is important to your investigation.

"Little Setrag was supposed to be hiding with his sister in the front room upstairs, behind the bedding, but he saw a pigeon on the window ledge and went to look out the window. He was too scared to move until his sister yanked him away. Someone was pounding on our door, and though he didn't see your brother, or see him being attacked—I'm thankful that part was out of sight, at least—he saw a man below, a man with a bloody knife in his hand and a head of thick white hair. 'A ghost devil man,' Setrag called him. He saw this man run away down the street towards the Prelacy. Another man was right behind him."

She'd little more to tell us, but it was sufficient to convince me the Blessed Father was at our side.

So, after weeks of inquiries, we came to possess useful information. We were heartened that it came from sources unknown to one another but in agreement. If ever God's will was evident in human affairs—and who cannot have times of doubt—then these clues were proof He willed we know.

I was filled with hopeful expectation, even confidence. I read excitement in my brother's face, and something else, a mixture of determination and impatience that unsettled me.

"Go slow, Petros! Take no chances."

"Say nothing to the women," he replied.

Once again he was disappearing from the shop for hours on end. He'd return to work with only a terse "No progress" or "Perhaps a step." Much as I wanted an explanation, it was important Petros take his time, think carefully of consequences. Pressing him would defeat my intention. I warned Miron and Levon to be patient, to let Petros keep hold of the reins.

Meanwhile, a few at home guessed something was going on. Arsen and Yiri both pestered me for information, and I could see questions in Marjan's eyes. Not that I'd anything to tell them if I wanted to, being almost as ignorant.

It was nearly Christmas before Petros and I gathered sufficient evidence to decide what should be done.

Topol Reappears

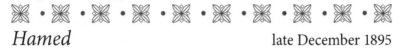

Hamed   late December 1895

Winters in Erzerum are bitter. Everyone complains, but we manage well. We wrap ourselves in wool, gather beside a brazier, sip hot sweet tea and keep ourselves comfortable. Little else is needed from October until May. It's the destitute suffer, clutching rags too thin to stop a breeze. Fighting over lumps of fuel-dung so they can swallow heated water—if they've a kettle.

Too many huddled among ruins in the Armenian quarter. They dug into snow-rooms behind the cathedral, camped behind the baths, in school yards, next to fountains. Listless in the cold.

A man's begging shows his character: pleading, pathetic, annoying, rude, proud. Alone or together, beggars made a constant, unwelcome chorus. We passed them with ears closed and eyes averted. Wishing them gone.

Food this winter was especially scarce and costly, with a wheel of bread priced at 60 piastres, not 10. Here's a riddle. Say your hunger's so great you'll pay any price, now where would you find coins to buy bread?

For much of December, a thousand beggars camped outside the city walls, another thousand on streets within. Many good people helped. Muslim and Christian, giving clothes and quilts, food and fuel. Khadija had the maid put out kitchen leavings. Likely my tender-hearted wife added pantry stores now and again.

Yet how could so many be fed? Officials promised grain was on its way in mid-November. More weeks passed, and each morning frozen starvelings were carted from the streets.

Late December, our lookout at Erzincan Gate sent word: grain at last! Three government wagons were progressing to Municipal Plaza with a growing wake of beggars. Nine cavalry from Erzincan protected that convoy. Two, better three times that number was needed here, else the least deserving would empty the wagons. I welcomed this assignment.

Keyif was ever ready to gallop 40 miles of plains, but never liked patrol-walk. A brisk trot got us to the Plaza before the grain was plundered. My men were slower, so it was good my rifle and pistol were fresh-loaded.

It was the usual wintry morning. Low clouds roofed the city and clean white coated the season's platter of muddy layers. Wind swirled under collars and caps, up sleeves and nostrils, biting.

Shouts from the Plaza reminded me hunger overpowers cold. The mounted nine were ranged loosely around the wagons, their circle already breached by some 20 beggars and more arriving every moment. The soldiers were impotent and seemed plainly confused at losing control.

The lead wagon's driver stood on his seat. One hand brandished a cudgel, the other an ox-whip. "Come back tomorrow!" he cried.

Supplicants pushed forward and back shouting for food, screaming and yelping at whip cuts. The driver lashed earnestly but clumsily at every head and hand in range, seldom scoring flesh. His thick wool coat took most of the backlash but his jawbone was red-welted through his beard. Other drivers were no more competent. They flailed whips, jabbed staffs, yelled at beggars to disperse without effect.

I fired my pistol skyward. "Clear away before you're shot!"

My ears rang too hard to hear my own shout, but some beggars fell back at my warning. As my militia arrived I organized an armed rectangle enclosing the wagons. Hundreds of beggars and opportunists ranged outside pleading, complaining and cursing. Their clamor rose and fell and gradually diminished. How long could the militia control the crowd?

"Capn! Capn! Come here, I must talk to you!" the lead driver called.

Turning, I saw a man I thought well settled in Gebizeh.

My former tenant was delivery master! Voice confident and clear of whining, he said he carried documents needing signatures. Proper authorities must approve before grain could get distributed.

Topol was pleased I'd guide him to the mayor's assistant's office. "You mustn't waste your time over my paperwork. Feel free to leave me once we're there," he told me. He proposed we meet for coffee when his tasks were done. He'd much to tell me.

As Abdi was engaged, I introduced Topol to the first secretary, explained the matter's urgency. Topol was all but dancing on well-booted feet. The once lazy Gebizehli was now an energetic, bossy man of purpose. The transformation puzzled and gratified me. Of course, no man changes his nature. His was cunning, sly and selfish. He'd take the short route to any sack of gold, ignore what might sit in the way.

Topol acted jumpy as a jack-in-box. Dropped his glove, exposing a gold ring set with a cut red stone; it looked expensive. "Handsome, ain't it?" he remarked. "I'll give it to my son someday."

Minutes later, he suggested I leave. "You may be needed outside. Don't let me keep you. No reason to burden yourself with a tedious wait." Topol still had subtlety to master.

I nearly laughed. However well-cloaked and thick-booted, anyone prefers waiting indoors an hour or two. The hardest bench is better than facing a mob of beggars in a blustery snowfall. Although I wondered what other business Topol was up to, my responsibility was outside. I knew the supplicants were more apt to storm our guard as the snowstorm abated, so I was glad to return to my horse and men.

The guard was still in motion, the crowd under control. The horsemen shaped now an ellipsis, now more a hexagon around the wagons, their motion gaining both order without and warmth within.

Perhaps 250 civilians clustered just beyond the mounted boundary. I called over some lads to unhitch and water the oxen, walk them as well, to keep their joints loose. The ox-drivers were enjoying a nearby café—and why not? The trip from Erzincan's no holiday.

News of the grain was spreading, drawing even some who looked well fed and wore presentable clothes. Many more looked destitute. Newcomers surveyed the scene and then hunkered into the crowd, waiting. They'd forget self-restraint once distribution began.

Someone tugged at my stirrup. "Cap'n!" It was the ne'er do well Pohar, leering as remembered. "I got a message from the Gebizehli, telling me to meet him here. You seen him?" He claimed he'd no idea why Topol wanted him.

Pohar drifted away. The wind began to soften. Shakir returned to the garrison to fetch more militia; I saw no reason for the same 26 to shiver all day. Once fresh cavalry were in place, I went home for a brief look at my mother, who lay failing.

I returned to find innumerable supplicants thronging the Plaza. Only two wagons were in view. Shakir was walking his horse around the mounted guard, no easy task. All the grain-seekers were on their feet now, pressing against the horsemen on the packed snow, imploring sustenance.

Snow was falling more lightly now. Fearing the militia would lose control, I signaled my junior lieutenant and together we fired our rifles skyward. The sound shoved the closest beggars back. Another signal got each soldier's rifle ready for transgressors. Our threat sufficed for now.

Topol stood on one wagon-bench. He turned backwards to shout at Pohar. That fellow squatted atop the grain sacks. Presently he sliced between his feet with a short blade. The sight of grain brought cries that spread like wind through the crowd. Young toughs shouldered forward amidst wails and curses. A thousand hands waved bowls and baskets overhead, every mouth called, "Here!" and "Me!"

Two fur-capped Lazes passed a tin cup between grain-seekers and Pohar and back. I saw weapons under the Lazes' belts, both dagger and cudgel. Pohar had engaged them, I supposed.

"They haven't thought this out, from the look of it," I said to Shakir.

"They mean to give one measure to everyone who comes, until it's all gone." His voice echoed my doubt. This process rewarded the strong, not the needful. Our armed guard was powerless to help.

"Wait! Wait!" I called, making my way to Topol.

"Something wrong, Cap'n?" He was frowning at my intervention.

At hearing my thoughts, he shrugged. "Do it your way, Cap'n, if you want. It's no matter to me, so long as the grain gets out." As hours followed, Topol put his energy into cracking his whip at anyone close to his wagon.

I positioned Keyif between a mounted sergeant on my left and Pohar's fur-capped Lazes on my right while I directed which supplicants were served in what order. The civilians did as I said. It helped to have Shakir facing me diagonally to the right with 34 mounted guards nearby.

Almost the first beggar I singled out was the mother-crone I'd last seen struggling towards Chambers' mission. Now without children under her arms, she was forcing herself forward step by step. In another hour or two, I calculated, she'd reach the wagon. Her effort stood out where many women lacked strength to push forward despite desperate tries.

Aware this woman's need was genuine, I called her to advance, motioned others to give way. She seemed perplexed at her priority but stayed firm in her purpose. She was the only one I knowingly allowed a second measure.

Selection of this sort is knotted. I looked around for the most gaunt and ragged among the crowd. Did my best to keep off strong-muscled men and women, both infidel and Muslim. Nonetheless, some undeserving forced their way in and took away a measure from a fast-decreasing supply. We faced a noisy, confusing, rowdy scene, tough on horses, tough on soldiers. We cheered for the replacement force that arrived mid-afternoon when the second wagon load was already half gone.

My eyes were focused on the supplicants besieging my side of the wagon, thus I failed to notice Pohar's steady chicanery. As each 50-kilo sack shrank to manageable size, Pohar grabbed it up and tossed it to his fur-capped cronies on the other side. That pair—one protecting the other—made their way to the north end of the Plaza, then vanished with the half-full sack into an alley.

Unsuspecting me, an innocent who never thought to watch the other side of the wagon! If I'd simply looked over my shoulder—yet I was absorbed in selecting the neediest beggars. I learned of the fraud that evening from one of my men. A casual remark—he supposed I condoned the arrangement.

I'd have stopped them, made the cheats share every bit out. Too many supplicants got nothing that day. Cynics called this grain-giving a futile sop. A thousand grain-loads would have fallen short. What difference, two wagons or three or one? So Topol justified himself. "What matter, a beggar croaks this week or next?" His shrug revolted me, yet I found no ready answer. Later I thought to remind him we all will die some day, and meanwhile, our Prophet commands us to help those wanting.

The second wagon empty, Topol proposed refreshment at one of the cafes nearby. I went, curious to learn how he got this contract. Such business requires money or family connections or both. Moreover, I wanted to learn what stopped their shipping home. He in turn was eager to show his success since departing so unpromisingly from Erzerum.

Topol told me he hung around Trabizond's Plaza after my contingent left. He waited for the military show while the place buzzed about Armenians assaulting the Palace. He and his boy were well back in the crowd when gunshots erupted. Tales of assassination raced about, everyone saying "Armenians!" He saw nothing, but heard the criminals escaped with police in pursuit. Some Armenian lads in the crowd near him were beaten flat and bloody.

Topol shrugged as he spoke, as if a gunshot in a city plaza must mean beating up Armenians. He described how rumors changed that day, from an official killed and another captured, the assassins escaping, to two officials killed, the assassins caught and jailed, no, executed, no, beaten to death. Yet another claimed the miscreants were Russians, not Armenians. One rumor blamed Jews, another, French Catholics. Arguments heated into scuffles and a policeman's guess became fact. Soon it was generally agreed the assassins were Armenians still at large.

Men cursed Armenians for trying to defile the Sultan and kill the Empire's leaders. Idlers mocked the traitors' incompetence, clowned inept shooting and bragged how they'd torment the murdering infidels.

"We'll catch the scum and cut out their eyeballs!"

"We'll teach a lesson with our knives!" Such boasts sounded up and down the hills of the harbor city. Heroic outrage filled half the Muslim populace. Men sharpened daggers and talked of assaulting the Armenian quarter.

Topol drifted about the Plaza trading rumors with the city's adventurers and riffraff, then struck a friendship with a mule-drover, Fasad. Both figured on raiding Armenian dwellings and taking any other opportunities for gain they found.

Topol kept trying to sell off his goods. Backed by his new buddy Fasad, he visited various merchants and struck deals for some of his fabric. During these hours he traded opinions about the Palace assault and the rumored assassination in Trabizond's plaza. Everyone agreed the wicked deserved punishment even if the entire Armenian quarter was shredded in the process.

Topol listened closely. By the time he disposed of his mules, he'd gained a rough sense of where the wealthier Armenians lived and which houses might be less protected than others. He'd also replaced his old curved knife with a sharper, shorter one. The new weapon's carved ox-bone handle fit comfortably under his belt and into his palm.

Topol and Fasad heard angry shouting. A mob formed, preparing to scourge the Armenian quarter. Topol promised his wife great gains to make up for a short delay getting home to Gebizeh.

"No danger to me, none at all," he told her. He had her stitch four sacks of muslin, two apiece for him and Fasad. These they wrapped around their waists under their shirts.

The pair discussed sack-filling strategies, even whether to do so. Fine large carpets fetch high sums from the right buyer. They considered the relative value of women's jewelry over men's watch-chains and watches, gold goblets, silver vases and other objects a rich family must possess. First grab the cash box, no question. Avoid men. Women wear more valuables and surrender them faster, all a-tremble at seeing a knife.

Finding fur coats, take them? Topol knew well off people in Constantinople prize furs, yet the fashion differed this far east. A good price was unlikely. Also, fur coats were too bulky to sack, too cumbersome to wear. Best ignore furs unless fine and small, a hat or muff; other clothing was not worth taking.

Relating these preliminaries, Topol was relaxed and confident, savoring his story. Chuckling at favorite points, pleased with himself. At last getting to the assault on the Armenian quarter, he spoke feverishly, happy and excited like a soldier after battle,

Hearing an Armenian shot a Muslim youth, Topol and Fasad passed the tale along, not caring for its likely untruth. Relating this, Topol shrugged.

"Everyone was saying the same. We wanted to wipe out those damned Ermeni!"

Next morning, Trabizond's Plaza crowd was larger by half, all armed, angry and impatient for revenge. As the sun lifted between the minarets of the main mosque, everyone started running toward the Armenian bazaar.

Topol and his friend were trailing the pack, mere witnesses to mayhem with no shot at first pickings. Instead they raced to the Armenian quarter west of the market. Already, soldiers were pounding on doors, shooting at will. The pair passed many broken gates, heard countless screams and gunshots as they stepped over bodies in the street. While others stopped to pillage, Topol and Fasad kept heading straight for certain houses on the hill.

They were first to reach one fine home. Here a quivering, bearded Armenian offered a gold-filled coffer to leave him be. They accepted readily. Topol began stuffing the box into his sack when a soldier shoved him aside and drove his knife into the Ermeni's throat. The coffer spilled. Topol and Fasad snatched up some coins before soldiers pushed them away. The coins were warm-coated in blood.

They went on to other dwellings where success out-balanced disappointments. Finding a house occupied only by two lifeless Armenians, Fasad guarded its door while Topol rushed off to settle a gold piece in his landlady's damp palm. He borrowed her donkey and collected his family and goods.

They took up residence in the deserted dwelling. They marveled at its airy rooms and fine view of the bay. Looking out an upstairs window, his wife and son gasped to see a mass of figures struggling against currents roiling the harbor. People drowned as two boatmen poled their craft away. "The owners of this place may be gone for good," Topol told his wife.

Fasad went scouting new prospects while the Gebizehlis made themselves comfortable. Portable items of value were already gone, but some clothing, heavy pots and urns remained. Topol met all comers at the front door knife in hand. With Ahmet's help he'd stripped the rooms behind him to discourage interest. He promised everyone at the door they'd find superior takings down the street.

At nightfall, Topol dined the best since leaving Gebizeh. The pantry could sustain them months, his wife said. They found three trunks of clothing, bedding and furnishings, as well. They might sell various paintings, mirrors, brass trays and such. Topol figured these comforts would last the winter.

"Then the very next day, well and good got better. Ahmet's smart as his father!" he bragged, grinning. "Just listen to this!"

Ahmet was fetching onions for his mother from the root cellar. His bare feet felt a changed texture through the thin straw mat. The curious boy pulled mat aside. A large chipped tile was set into the dirt. Underneath it were round indents pounded by a pole or ax-handle. At once he guessed valuables were buried there.

The hard clay almost broke Topol's knife. Sweating and breathless, Topol cut himself first on the knee, then on the palm. He hardly noticed, while cursing whoever had buried whatever so deep. Then his knife hit metal. A lot of trouble if it proved to be a family bible or a stillborn's grave!

By now his wife stood close by with the babies. He shut his ears to their crying, levered up the strongbox. Ahmet brought the lantern closer as Topol forced the lock—and there it was, <u>real treasure</u>! A pirate's hoard of gold coins and bracelets, necklaces, hair ornaments! The jewelry finely worked, mostly heirlooms of special value.

"Believe me, Cap'n, we praised Allah for his benevolence! Truly God is great!" To which I readily assented, for different reasons.

Thus my hapless tenant gained means to stay in Trabizond. He could buy his son a school uniform, dress himself as befit new circumstances. Whereupon, hearing of the possibility from his tailor, he secured appointment as a grain agent. The position promised to repay its price tenfold. It took his clever handling to overcome the Commissary Master's claiming two of Topol's six allotted wagons.

What of the wagon removed in my absence? Merely locked in a guarded warehouse awaiting the Mayor's decision. Topol's smug reply whirled inside my head.

First I felt shock at my friend Abdi for colluding in such arrangements. Reflection granted him common failings. Abdi was relatively scrupulous within an unscrupulous cadre. He neither lied nor cheated and was reputed to deal fairly with servants and laborers, even beggars. He'd a family to support, a negligible wage, no prospect of inheritance.

Topol chuckled at my question. Two wagonloads for beggars were enough—no need to sacrifice the third. Nor did he sense wrongdoing in the pilferage I learned of that evening.

"It's how it's done. Why not?"

"Because people are starving. <u>And dying</u>," I answered.

"Traitors."

Missionary Chambers bought the third wagonload as sustenance for scholars and staff. A group of bakers bought the pilfered grainsacks, so perhaps a little of that bread reached starving bellies.

Trabizond transformed Topol. He was no longer spineless, but firmed by stolen gold into a man of business and ambition. He saw two or three more grain expeditions ahead, then he planned to buy another, more profitable post. His ambition was to be uniform-supply agent for the Fourth Army.

"Then I'll be rich and respected. Just wait 'til my brothers see me!" Anticipated triumph lit his face.

An unpleasant, shameless man, unfit for shopkeeping. Inept in Erzerum. Yet events revealed a head for business—perhaps for better, more likely for worse. No doubt our kick in the ass did him good.

The Stolen Ones

Marjan   January 1896

O nce Henza left, I brooded every moment over the twins. Petros said, "You worry as much about one thing as others worry about 20." Whatever number, he wrapped his worries tight. We both slept badly, and Heranoush, too. One night I decided on a step.

In the morning I searched out Khadija and we sat whispering over spiced tea while her mother-in-law slept nearby. I told her about the Halebians' offer of ransom and their disappointing visit to the Mayor. We talked a long time before we agreed on a plan. We must talk to every Muslim we knew, ask every Christian who'd anything to do with Muslims. Sooner or later, this must turn up something helpful.

My father used to say, "To catch a small fish, cast a wide net," and that was our plan. If nothing else, it helped me wake each day thinking, "Today we may get an answer!"

Toumia kept her bad temper after Henza left. Now this, now that displeased her. She asked God's wrath on the ruffians who damaged her cupboards and more wrath on the ditch-digger-carpenters who mismatched the repairs. With great care as to my words, I suggested she get Martiros to hire a good carpenter. She said only "Humph," yet soon after that she did so.

The carpenter was a slow-moving, well-fed man with an easy manner—a surprising thing for a Muslim in a Christian home. Osama was as talkative as the Bishop and our boys made fun of him, with Arsen especially copy-catting his lisp. We had to laugh. Before Osama shed his cloak he told us he'd no quarrel with Christians and was sorry for the suffering his people caused ours. He seemed sincere. He was training a fresh lad because his former apprentice had set up on his own. Almost anyone could find work as a carpenter that year, as our ill-mended cupboards proved.

Elim came from an Armenian village near Baiburt and was the oldest of three brothers. He was quick at fetching more nails from the smithy or a tool from Osama's house, though he was as slow as his master in woodwork. He took pains with whatever he did, so the smallest task took a morning. I liked hearing them talk and I enjoyed watching them trim and fit a piece of board, shaping something rough into something fine-looking. They were a well-matched pair, taking pleasure from their work and careless of passing hours. Osama must have chosen Elim at just the right time before the lad fixed habits of his own.

Every afternoon, one or another of us would bring the pair fresh boreg and hot tea, and they would stop their work.

"Best tea in the city! Best boreg in the province!" Osama always said.

"Yes, it's so," Elim would agree in his sing-song village accent.

Sometimes Ephraim joined them for the refreshments—though not the praise. "My grandmother made stronger tea and lighter boreg," he'd say, and wink.

By the second week we felt easier with these two men in the house. I was able to ask the carpenter, without blushing, if he might have heard any word of two Armenian girls taken from their family. Their story made him sad and he promised to find out what he could.

※ ※ ※

Toumia got me to massage her neck. She sat upright and watchful while I kneaded the knots of spite under her skin. She was as cross as ever afterwards.

Some days Toumia served her husband like a slave as if no one else was there. Other days she screeched like a demon at anyone nearby, even Maxime and Zabel. Only young Arsha and old Flora could be sure of a kind word. We stayed out of Toumia's sight as best we could, leaving poor Verkin to take the worst of it. Listening as Toumia scolded Verkin one day, Heranoush said, "Poor Verkin, she's Matriarch's first target. Sometimes her <u>only</u> target."

It helped just laughing about her. The children found ways, as children do, to sweep aside her ill temper like snow off the front steps. In time, it drew us closer.

Toumia showed none of the usual female weakness. She gave in to weeping only once that I know, and I only found out by chance. We were on our way to church, it was Advent, and Toumia stayed behind (a rare thing) with a sick headache. I ran back through the gate to get a scarf for Vagram, for the air was suddenly bitter with sleet. Passing the ladies' sitting room on my way to our cupboard, I heard her weeping. She was lying on the divan, her moans far louder than my footsteps.

"Sako, my son! Oh, my dear boy!" she cried out. Pity came over me such as I never felt for her before or since. I tiptoed out without her noticing me.

The stroke turned Nazar into a cripple. He needed help with everything—walking, dressing, sitting down or rising from his chair. It was peculiar to see half his face shift and bob like a paper float, while the other half held still as a wood carving. He struggled to tell his mind while his tongue twisted and flopped. Heranoush said it was like a dying fish, and after that I always saw a flopping fish instead of an old man's fat tongue. Strange sounds came from his mouth. Martiros and Petros usually got the sense on his third or fourth try. Then the half-frown would fade and a small half-smile would appear.

I give Toumia her due. It was not her nature to nurse anyone—she disliked illness. She kept away from anyone unwell, even a newborn. She might have got us to tend Nazar for her, but she hardly ever asked for help. She tended him faithfully. Hardest was patience while he tried to make her understand his grunts. He talked less as the weeks wore on. He lost interest in our family.

It was the same at the shop, Petros said. Patriarch started out watching the men work and trying to tell them what to do. Gradually he spent more time watching the street from the doorway, or dozing. He stopped making suggestions. He seemed to stop caring—easier for them, yet pitiful. He seemed only half alive.

Sorrow washed away his interest, I think. Now and then we saw tears flood his good eye, one shoulder heave. Did he weep for his lost son? His lost health? Before, he never cried, was never ill.

Though the whole family grieved for Sako, I think my husband took it worst. In bed he woke shuddering from a dream and only sometimes let me comfort him. Petros did his best to play and joke with the children the way his brother had. This new child's side of him was his way of honoring his brother, though it made Toumia look sharply at him. Seeing my husband act light-hearted when he wasn't helped me see how Sako's play could cover hidden thoughts.

All the brothers, Levon, too, spent more time with their sons after Sako died. They were better fathers, mostly. On bad days my husband acted so much like his father, it made me shiver. He scolded the children for making noise and reminded the boys over and over to take care what they said and did, as if they were deaf. It must have calmed him. He didn't hear how harsh he sounded.

Martiros honored his father's rules but set lighter punishments. He was fair, usually—except with Arsen. The first-born grandson was spoiled early and never grew past starting fights to get his own way. His parents never interfered. Playing after school with the other youngsters, he was soon throwing pebbles at the little ones or shooting dirt clumps over the wall. Fortunately he never hit one of our neighbors. Our wall kept dirt marks long after the sling broke. Or he'd take a writing book from Nerses and hide it in the donkey hay. You expect some mischief from a boy, but Arsen was mean. He got meaner with Sako gone.

One day my Artashes was playing with our neighbor's boy Ehsan in their courtyard and Arsen climbed our roof and started throwing stones and insults at them, until finally Artashes came home raging. Arsen mocked him for being soft. Arsen liked attention.

We'd still no news of the twins. Heranoush cried for them and Astghig tried to cheer her. The two were lucky to have one another close by. They seldom argued. The other children studied and played as before, did chores and squabbled, got underfoot because it was too cold outside. The sunless winter pressed on us all especially without Sako, and we could not forget our fear. Christians young and old were chilled by the great grave near St. Asdvadzadzin's.

Nerses joined the other boys at school and made a good impression on his teachers. They said his mind was quick. Toumia wouldn't let his sister go to school. Instead, she taught Arsha fine handwork and had her help with the younger children. In the girl's free moments I helped her practice reading. She was too young still to want to read on her own.

Both orphans seemed content. They seldom talked of their life in Trabizond. Once when I was tucking Arsha into bed, and another night, when she had a bad dream, the girl asked when their mother's cousin was coming for them. I said I'd no idea and also told her, "Our family will always have a place for you and your brother." She said it was all right, yet her eyes seemed troubled.

We read to the children from torn story books, making up the missing pages. I remembered Sako's gift for this with a fresh taste of pain. One day my friend Sophia brought a French magazine to the baths in the bottom of her basket. At home, Artashes translated some of the words, though it hardly mattered—we loved the pictures of elegant ladies in fine silk gowns and huge hats. It was beyond me, how women can dress that way or make their hair look like carvings. Heranoush and Astghig daydreamed about going to Paris someday.

For weeks, bitter cold kept us home except for church, and twice blizzards kept us in on Sundays—we couldn't even open our door. Snow fell every day, and from the window I saw only Vagram's cap when he went through the gate to school. The boys built a huge fort. Khadija gave Ehsan a sack of candle stubs so they could play there after dark, but the cold soon forced them back indoors. My husband made up a riddle: what falls down but grows up?

There weren't so many soldiers around, but we still needed escorts when we left the house. On every street, beggars shouted curses and threats to make you give. Hunger made them desperate, I suppose, but it was terrible how the strong robbed the weak, even the most ragged and helpless women and children. One time Petros gave some bread to a beggar family at the fountain, and the father tried to snatch the child's share for himself. She bit his finger and got her face slapped! Anyway, the bread got to her stomach. I'm sure he wasn't her true father.

Another time we took clothes to a grey-whiskered beggar living in a snow-cave in St. Adzvad's cemetery. He couldn't stop coughing. Our castoffs didn't warm the poor man long, alas—our husbands saw the same wool cloak and trousers on a younger beggar a few days later. We never saw the old beggar again and feared our gift caused him harm. How do you ever know you are doing the right thing?

One day I found the children kneeling in a circle. Artashes was scolding little Yefkine for wiggling. "You're spoiling it!" he told her. I asked what they were doing.

"We're praying to Uncle Sako!" came the answer.

Then my Vagram burst out, "We're calling his spirit down from heaven. Nerses says he'll come, so long as we do it right."

"We have to hold hands in a cir-circle or it won't wo-work," said Nerses. I figured it must be a custom from Trabizond, then I found out he learned it from a classmate here.

I left them to their hope and disappointment. It took two more weeks before they gave up trying to call down Sako from the sky. It was years before Vagram gave up. I used to find him on his knees, hands together, eyes tight shut, pleading to his uncle's spirit. He held fast when Artashes made fun of him. Sako often visited his dreams, and Vagram was sure this was in answer to his prayers.

Around this time, I looked where the Spanish dagger was kept and discovered it missing.

Fighting Boys

Martiros January 1896

Something happened that fixed my attention on Arsen. My elder son, our pride and joy, was not an easy boy to raise. In my opinion, he'd too much spirit for his own good still, at 13. Yiri'd say, "That's what he'll need to be a man." I'd answer, "He must learn self-control. You're too soft with him." What I saw as over-willfulness she saw as merely youth.

Petros and I bear blame for not better concealing our hope of avenging our dead brother. We shouldn't have been surprised the boys made a pact to track down their uncle's killer. "But do you know who it is you propose to murder?" I asked, after the harm was done. Arsen shrugged as if it hardly mattered, and my nephew Vagram said, "Not yet, but we will!" The boys evidently kept their secret some weeks before we found out.

What they couldn't conceal was the nasty cut scoring Artashes' palm, creating a flap of skin like an uncooked piroshke, and staining clothes, quilts and carpet with blood. He was lucky the knife missed his vein. Dr.Tashjian sprinkled powdered sulfur into the wound. He wasn't always gentle, and his probing made the boy cry out. He was a good physician and familiar with our family from many years attending first births and serious illnesses.

"Unwrap his hand and look for pus," he told Marjan. She was to wipe it out, apply sulfur, put on clean wrappings. She did this carefully, yet a few days later Petros and I were summoned because the school sent Artashes home early, whimpering with pain, his wrist above the mummy-wrapping red enough to burst. We hurried him to the doctor. I half expected Mother to object to the expense, but she kept silent, seeing his arm red-streaked to the elbow. He was already starting a fever. I was afraid he might lose the arm, though I didn't say it.

As to how Artashes got wounded, I had to threaten beatings before any mouth opened. Then the boys let out the story in little pieces, taking turns and looking to the others for a sign no sacred secret was divulged.

To put it simply, the boys decided they needed Petros' knife for some enterprise. Since young Vagram was still hurting from his recent punishment for that same crime, he refused to steal it. However, they persuaded the child to point to its hiding place. It was Arsen took the dagger from under Petros's linen in the cupboard. Arsen concealed it under his folded nightshirt until bedtime, then under his mattress. My son couldn't resist telling the other boys what he planned to do with it once they found Sako's killer. Well, his bragging made his cousin Artashes jealous, Artashes tried to take the knife from him, then one accidentally stabbed the other.

On hearing what happened, Father panted and sputtered, shoulders shaking with anger. He'd have had me whip Arsen's back raw as a brigand's, but I refused. "It was only a schoolboys' quarrel. Ten lashes are enough. He'll get two weeks of bread and water," I told the old man. He started to argue, then let the matter drop.

Arsen was a plump lad who liked his meals—I reasoned going hungry would chasten him more than any lashing. My solution struck me as wise, and I'm certain it improved the boy, though he sulked and moaned the entire fortnight. As I told his mother, "It's not as if bread's not food. It's got no mold or dirt; a lot of folks are making do with worse."

I gave Artashes and Vagram the same 10 lashes for good measure and morale. My strokes drew no real blood, which bothered Father and gratified my brothers. Having felt the strap as boys, we know that its benefits arise from shame and indignity, not pain.

Grace

Marjan

A sadur's suffering did not improve him. His first time at church, Petros told him, "You're a fortunate man, Asadur, to have such devoted nurses! They wouldn't let you pass away!" What Asadur answered was, "God is merciful, thanks be to God." As if he was an altar boy! Zari held her face still and only blinked to show she wasn't going to let him upset her. Asadur never admitted his debt to Zari, never thanked Nora and Mother for their nights and days of nursing. They were his subjects, he was their sultan. A boy-sultan who yelled and hit when something annoyed him. A selfish tyrant who gave his sons nothing to respect. Yet God's light shone sometimes on his face. He gave generous gifts to the church that winter. He let needy families take kerosene from his barrels without charge. He provided for his family and educated his sons. He was respectful to his half-blind mother. Also, in the three years Mother lived on with them, he never raised his fist to her. Maybe he knew she'd shame him quick as you swat a fly.

The men came home smiling one evening. "Is it the twins? Have you heard something?" Heranoush asked her father.

"No, dear girl, there's no news of them," he told her.

Astghig cried out, "What is it? Please tell us!"

"It's nothing of interest," teased Martiros. Little Serop and Rafael were jumping like sand fleas.

"It's only that 50 fine lambskins were delivered," said Miron. For the first time since the Awful Day, his eyes twinkled.

"You've promised me gloves, don't forget!" said Sara.

"First your father's and my own. And Flora's," said Toumia.

"We know, be patient," said Miron, in the calm tone he used when his wife and mother pushed.

"Something else," said Levon. "An order for a child's saddle like we gave Shabanian's grandson."

"From the Police Director, yet!" said Petros, smiling at our surprise. Yet I knew from the men's faces they'd other news to give. I walked over to him.

"Do tell what you're holding back! You're keeping something secret!" I said.

Petros put his hand on my shoulder, letting me settle against him. "You're right, clever woman, we've another secret to tell. Perhaps you can guess…"

"Wheat and rice!" said Yiri. "At last it's come in, and we can…"

"Meat! Russian basterma!" Aunt Maxime always chose that over meats dried nearby.

"You ladies must think beyond your stomachs," teased Martiros. "You'll never guess it—and we want our dinner. We'll tell you."

"It might…have something to do with your stable family. With one of them…" put in Petros, giving me a wink. He was enjoying this.

"Humph." This from Toumia.

"Perhaps you won't care…"

"Oh, please!" I begged. What could possibly be better for our refugees than living with the Shabanians?

At last the men let on that one of the girls had a suitor. I guessed it must be Arpeh before my husband said, "Not the one whose baby died. The shorter, younger one." Arpeh carried her sorrow less heavily.

The man came from a farm village near Baiburt. His wife died on the way here, a daughter needed care. The widow Sharopyan was glad for his help in her house of mostly women and children. In fact, he was carrying a sack of turnips up from the cellar when he first met Arpeh in the widow's kitchen. Most Tuesdays, Souren took both girls to Berthe's. It got them out and let her daughter-in-law have the baby to herself.

Had he called on Arpeh? How many times? The men laughed and waved their hands at our questions. Krikor Shabanian hadn't bothered them with those small details. "You must ask someone else," our husbands told us.

"Humph!" Again from Toumia.

Souren gave us answers at the baths soon after. The suitor was healthy, of an agreeable nature, mature but not old, and not bad looking. He was indeed serious—he'd called on Arpeh three times, with her husband's permission. His child was four or five, "a sweet girl" with a nice smile and bad eyes. Everyone liked both father and daughter. Berthe Sharopyan called him "a helpful, decent man." He was handy with a hammer and did much to make her house livable after the looting.

There was, alas, a problem. The would-be bridegroom was looking after an aged uncle, feeble and addled. Demands and frets poured from his mouth. Although Arpeh liked the suitor and his child well enough, she detested the uncle. She meant to refuse the proposal.

Souren sighed. "It's not that I want to lose her, we'll all miss her. But who knows when she'll get another offer this good? And the uncle may not last the winter!"

"I'll talk with her," I promised.

We watched the women scrub one another's backs and rub themselves with towels. We waved my pretty friend from Smyrna to a cushion at Souren's feet. Sophia soon had us laughing at how she'd fixed a fine lentil stew that her mother-in-law called too peppery to eat. "His mother tells him we Smyrnalis have no taste, we must be savages!"

Our cackling brought Aunt Maxime and Yiri from the next room, but they barely smiled at the story before going back. This broke our mood and led Sophia to something more important. While she talked, I saw that her fingernails were bitten short, the skin around them rough, as if she picked at her fingers. Either she was homesick, or life with her husband's family was less than easy.

She talked of searching for a fine silk handkerchief for her husband. After trying the better shops, she came upon one she liked in a cluttered stall at the bazaar's edge. The shopkeeper was Persian, with goods from everywhere—leather cases from Morocco, painted boxes from Russia, slippers from China, ivory carvings from India.

The handkerchief was woven of bright blue Chinese silk, bordered with red and finely hemmed with matched thread. It was much like a handkerchief she'd noticed at the Shabanians' party, tucked in someone's top pocket. His nose and eyes were like my husband's— might he be the brother lost in the violence?

For a moment, I remembered Sako so clearly I couldn't speak. Then I said, "Yes, the man with the blue silk handkerchief was our dead brother Sarkis."

"I'm sorry." She pressed my hand. "Perhaps I shouldn't tell you—I was about to buy it when I noticed a dark stain in one corner. It looked like blood..." We fell silent.

At last I said, "His wife ordered the handkerchief from Draji's, there was no other like it in Erzerum. We must get it back."

Sophia explained how to find the shop. It lay outside the Armenian bazaar.

When my husband brought it home, we'd no doubt it was Sako's. I felt a strange comfort from touching it, almost as if—forgive me saying this—as if it was cloth worn by a saint.

More important, the Persian was talkative—and not ashamed about trading in stolen things. Shops were fat with looted goods at bargain prices. Some of our friends were buying back most everything stolen from their homes.

This Persian remembered the handkerchief's seller because he first tried to sell a gold watch for way too high a price. After that failed, he pulled three handkerchiefs (two silk, one linen) from under his turban. "One price gets you everything!"

Whatever else he bought that week from a hundred thieves, the Persian recalled this particular deal, for the young man's hair was white as new snow. Another thing the shopkeeper remembered—the man was Circassian. Already, Petros was fixed on finding this freak even if he'd got the handkerchief second hand. It had to do with Sako's murder, was my guess. I reminded Petros his three children needed him. He promised not to do anything dangerous. When I woke in the night I felt for him with my hand. When I was sure the others were asleep, I made him know I was a loving wife.

※ ※ ※

Souren Shabanian welcomed me with a hug, then took me to adore her fat grandson in his crib before leading me to the refugee family. They were working hard at a loom that Krikor Effendi had brought from his village. The thing was as tall as they, and wider than they could reach standing at either side. They had to step sideways to see one another's faces while they threaded the shuttle back and forth between them.

Serop sat cross-legged behind, firming the threads with a comb. Orphans are often taught the trade of rug weaving, for small hands are well suited to tying small knots. He ran to me at once and pulled me over to see a small carpet of the sort you put over a worn spot.

"See what we've made! Hannum effendi can't believe it's just our first try! Do you think it's good work?"

Of course, I praised it.

"No, no!" said Arpeh. "It's loose in places, we're still learning. But we're doing better each day. The weaving's different from what we used to do. We made cloth that's better than you buy here. Not the same pretty colors, but a lot stronger." She was embarrassed at talking so much, and she flushed. She was losing her village accent. Bruises no longer marred her face. Only a thick red line on her neck gave hints of her suffering. And the fact she rarely smiled.

We chatted together, Serop asking about Vagram and the other boys, his sisters asking about others in my household, and me asking how they fared.

"It's good here. We're content," said Oskee, Arpeh agreeing.

"I want to stay here 'til I'm big!" Serop made me smile. "Why not?" I said.

Arpeh remained serious. "Who knows?" she said. I started to say, "We must trust in God," but held back. Perhaps they no longer trusted in God.

Instead, I drew Arpeh aside so we could talk about her suitor. She liked him as far as she could tell—and was fixed on refusing him.

"The old man is dreadful. I can't stand him!" she kept saying whenever I pressed her with her suitor's good points, the blessings of marriage, and the daughter's need for a mother. She wouldn't budge, though I didn't give up easily. I even said, "His uncle may not live long."

"And is it right for me to wed this man, wanting his uncle dead? God would punish me for it!"

So much passion soaked her words I gave up, sighing. It came to me it was her father-in-law to blame, his hateful dying curses, not this uncle. I suggested only she wait to tell him.

"No, now!" was her reply. "If I never have another suitor, so be it! At least I won't have to nurse a horrid old crow!"

As I started for home behind Ephraim and his cudgel, a man passed us and knocked on the Shabanians' door. He was sturdy and neat-looking, with a kind, pleasant face something like Miron's. I took him for the suitor and felt pity for his coming disappointment.

His disappointment was brief. Arpeh's suitor continued to call after she rejected him, and within a fortnight, offered marriage to Oskee. She didn't hesitate.

"He'll be a good husband. I don't mind the old man so much," she told me soon after. Her face was softer and her eyes brighter than before, a good sign. It shouldn't have surprised me.

They were married at the altar of Surp Asdvadzadzin's at Easter. The newlyweds looked happy and so did Arpeh. The Shabanians gave a small party in their honor, inviting the Kavafians and the widow Sharopyan and a good part of her household. Toumia wore her best dress and a self-satisfied face, as if she deserved thanks for the happy result of her evicting them.

As a wedding gift, Krikor Effendi gave the couple use of a piece of farmland and a vacant house in a village that's only three hours east of the city. He promised to let Serop spend the summer helping them farm, if the boy wanted, as of course he did. All in all, it was a fine outcome for Oskee, for Arpeh, and for their suitor with his little girl and sick uncle. For Serop, too.

Doing Business

✻ · ✻ · ✻ · ✻ · ✻ · ✻ · ✻ · ✻ · ✻ · ✻

Martiros   January 1896

O ur business was in leather—making boots, shoes, gloves, more recently, saddles. High quality products a skilled craftsman could be proud of. Father's father trained him as a boy. Father said it was reading the newspaper aloud while his father worked made him a good reader, for his own father could read only common words. Father himself went just three years to school, despite his ever-present books. He insisted his sons complete their academics.

We went directly from school to shop to practice leather craft. No play time, yet we liked it well enough. Excepting Sako, who showed an early aptitude for chemistry. Father said three sons were enough in one trade.

And so we each in turn took up our father's craft. Because business is seldom steady, we'd time to expand our line, to offer fancy tooling on some boots, lamb's wool insides and heavy soles as well. One slow period led Miron—who ran short of the mark on boot craft—to try his skill at glove-making. His aptitude for fine stitches brought customers seeking his gloves.

By 1890, we'd five men in the back room with Miron and Petros, working shoes and boots. We also employed our neighbor's boy Khalil, a simple lad who swept and ran errands, little else. Father, me and two brothers, five others and Khalil—that made 10 all together. Seven Armenians.

Muslims drawn by the superiority of our goods were pleased to find other Islamists working for us—not only Khalil, but craftsmen, skilled cobblers, some with us for years. The day one left to join his brother's harness shop (we shed no tears, he was unreliable), we hired the other's nephew to replace him, as I recommended. The boy soon outshone our Armenian apprentice.

One thing is true of human experience: no circumstance will stay unchanged. Just as a child is helpless without you one month, then turns away the next, or as dislike may overtake you for a friend formerly held dear—so the conditions of one's business and residence are always shifting, sometimes in small aspects, other times in large. We are adaptable creatures. How else would we survive? We make the changes required while expecting we can soon resume our habits. We may not perceive that clouds and gusts and a drop in temperature presage a thunderstorm.

After the Incident on October 30, I and some others could look back on missed warnings of a cataclysm. Rumors of harm to Armenians elsewhere had made us increasingly anxious, yet we failed to see a threat to our own well-being. Wishfully, we overlooked the implications of changing policies.

A significant example: rifles began to multiply among the Kurdish tribesmen. These Kurds had habitually accosted travelers and preyed on villagers, particularly Armenians. It was their means of livelihood. Attacks on Armenians increased, thanks to the Kurds' new arms and the Sultan's blessing. Only the spring before the "incident" here, Kurds plundered the Armenian village of Arek, within our province.

Another: censorship of Armenian writing tightened, first in Constantinople, then in other cities. Censors went after anything Armenians might have printed, scouring textbooks and hymnals even, for words like "Armenia" and "Armenians". Our presses were prohibited.

Again: the slightest whisper that an Armenian had a hidden weapon, or that firearms were hidden in a school or church, brought sweaty Muslim hands pawing through our trunks. Folded ecclesiastic robes, stored blankets, even our women's underwear. Later they searched our persons, too. It was insufferable—and we held our tongues still.

And of course Armenian agitators were hunted down as traitors.

Muslim friends have told us the Sultan and his ministers were frightened by Armenian revolutionists and nationalists fresh-hatched from Russian eggs. Most of us considered these radicals worse than foreign missionaries. They tried to join every Armenian to their demands for "rights" and "freedom" and even a separate territory for Armenians. Their notions were preposterous. I asked in amazement how the Ministers could take them seriously?

Yet these lunatics gained followers. In 1890, they instigated a demonstration in the capital that accomplished nothing but bloodshed for the fools who joined them. Some radicals wanted this, some wanted that, and before long there were three groups making trouble, calling for different changes as if a dream world is waiting only for Armenians to ask. From what we heard, one bunch or another fired up rebellions in villages some distance from the capital, in Zeitun and Sassun. The outcomes were bloody, predictably, for how can villagers succeed against our Sultan's mighty Army? These rebels brought horrors down on our people in the eastern provinces.

First, we assumed only Kurds were to blame for assaults on Armenian villages. In October, we realized the Army was contributing to the carnage, and moreover, that we could not expect our city to be spared.

And so with our neighbors' guidance the family went readily into hiding. That first day our neighbor filled in for us, our workmen more or less believed we were ill, as he said. Yet they knew we expected trouble and they couldn't miss that half the stock had been removed. The second morning, the Armenian cobblers voiced suspicions. (Said the old one later, "I thought, '*First they hide the goods, then they hide themselves. We better do the same.*'"). Pasha Berci told them, "Who knows what will happen? Suit yourselves." I commend their using their brains, for they headed home and took their knives with them. By then, Berci and Ehsan were done delivering finished work. At the first gunshot, Berci saw it was pointless trying to save what merchandise remained. He put a couple of hides inside his shirt and sent the two Muslim shoemakers home with their tools.

That's why our losses were no worse than benches smashed, doors broken, a few shelves emptied, a table and cushions taken, general wreckage. No, Kavafian & Sons was fortunate and we thanked the Almighty for providing us a caring neighbor. Nor were we unique in foreseeing a Devil's Day and placing goods safely with a Muslim friend or at an embassy beforehand. Some larger number also took precautions without thinking them through. They hid their merchandise at home, in cupboards, or on a roof, never imagining the rampage would spread beyond the bazaar. Luck is improved by an intelligent use of imagination.

It was a good four weeks' time, nearly the end of November, before we restored the shop to working order. We didn't rush to re-open, not wanting to magnify our countrymen's resentment.

Rumor had it—trust eager Berj to crow this to me—we'd colluded with the governor and police, helped plan the devastation for our profit. Even—he shook his head in apology—let our brother be murdered in a Judas bargain. I ask, can sane people believe such vicious propositions? Do they ever hold up mirrors when they hiss such accusations?

Like judgments circled Shabanian, whose only sin was the foresight to send his family to Consul Bergeron's and the wisdom to sacrifice many valuable furnishings (saving the finest items) to ruffians. Similar lies cut at the Armenian policeman Mikael despite his roof being smashed through and his father crippled. Think idiots are few? Some months later, at the baths, Yiri heard a woman complain how the Manoogians, my brother's widow's family, had held off looters. The brainless cow blamed them that a mob plundered her neighbors. It's simple jealousy. Henza, poor lady, was fortunate her family managed to protect itself, or she'd never have escaped my mother's grip.

I see no point losing sleep for whispers—we'd no cause for shame. Yiri and her mother held their heads high and praised God for all to hear. My mother crossed St. Asdvad's lobby blind to whoever failed a greeting.

Few set themselves against us long. Those with sense could see it is self interest lets any beast, whether four-legged or two-legged, survive. They realized nobody came through the violence without some measure of selfishness. Others, lacking sense, wouldn't speak to us, though they might send a school boy son to our house to ask for rice and lentils from our pantry. However much they may have hated us for coming through it well, they didn't hate our food.

It was nearly Easter before the missions' own caravan got in.

Despite its rocky soil and harsh climate, our city has natural advantages. Its main features (as my friend Hamed taught me) are strategic: The place can be defended readily, being on a height encircled by mountains. Erzerum was a fortress before anything else. It still defends the Empire from its greatest fear, Russian invasion.

Soldiers need water, which abounds here—the stuff pours in from all directions, from springs, streams, river and rain. With cliffs and mountainsides well suited to sheep and goats, the city can feed its soldiers meat and their horses, grain. The plateaus beyond boast decent soil, and though altitude shortens the season, yield good food for trade.

Erzerum's other good fortune is its situation on a well-established, centuries-old trade route extending north to the sea at Trabizond and south to Damascus, Tabriz, Mosul and Baghdad. The northerly mountains discourage virtually all passage from mid-autumn to late spring. Five months of the year, however, we saw at least three caravans a week. These diminished once the Germans built railroads south of the Caucasus through to Constantinople. For some time even then enough camels passed to furnish the city with merchandise for its bazaars, according to plan, or not. Inevitably, I saw stock that cost a drover almost nothing traded to a merchant's gain. Coins spent for food and lodging added to the city's prosperity.

It may happen a lead camel driver, having traded successfully here, chooses to send a loaded team directly home. Rarely does a caravan come north from Basra or Damascus to Erzerum without any further destination. To get such a caravan here in winter, even following an exceptional harvest, would cost a recipient dearly. Anyone should appreciate, then, the difficulties Shabanian and I took on knowingly when we formulated our plan. Mid-October was already late to attempt such arrangements. Shabanian's financiers were doubtful any camel drover would agree, or if he did agree, would in fact materialize before spring.

In this matter, my neighbor's connections through his caravansary proved helpful. Berci knew a Damascene drover who could be relied on and whose price would be less than exorbitant. We ordered a massive quantity of foodstuffs, mostly Russian wheat and basterma, Indian rice and Moroccan fruits—a matter of 70 camels. It took faith on our part, for the broker required an outrageous advance payment, a full two-thirds the total price. He knew his advantage.

We financed more than half of it between us. The rest we borrowed from the Imperial German Bank, the Guild of Christian Merchants, two of Shabanian's Muslim friends in the Debt Administration Office, the American pastor Chambers, and Mazjur the Bald, a Jew made rich by leather in the war with Russia before I turned 20.

We negotiated a reasonable rate of interest, not too high, for our investors could see that recent depredations meant worse scarcities to come, whether or not our city suffered its own violence. Except for Pastor Chambers, who required foodstuffs for his staff and scholars and sought no monetary gain from his investment, these men were more than ready to glean profit from our business. In fact, they were delighted at the chance. We got hearty handshakes and coffee in delicate porcelain cups, sometimes fine brandy, in every office. Whatever injunction as to spirits is written in the Koran, I did not see it applied to business-contract brandy.

❈ ❈ ❈

Even when snow blocked the streets, Mazjur stopped in each morning, week after week, to ask about our shipment.

"No word yet, but it won't be long now!" I'd respond with a

show of confidence, as if I was blind to the hazards for any caravan in a winter of great scarcity. Already by then three wagon loads of wheat had been sent by the Governor to feed the starving. Part was distributed to the strongest among the beggars, and the rest, inevitably, to profiteers. It was an insufficient quantity, in any case.

"Those Syrians are slow!" Mazjur would mutter, then walk to the doorway and spit in the street. I think he was ready to spittle the face of any Syrian who walked by—fortunately none ever did. That done, Mazjur would accept a coffee, grimacing with each sip as if he disliked the taste. I liked to remind him it was Turkish coffee, not Syrian, invariably causing him to snort and clatter his cup on its saucer.

One January afternoon, not long after New Year's Day, Mazjur arrived perspiring.

"It's here! Your caravan's coming through the South gate!" he gasped, his message broken by a heaving chest. "My boy counted 46 camels, all heavy laden, and more still behind!" Rooster flew in just then to confirm it. The lead drover, he reported, gave my name.

I clapped for Khalil to fetch coffee and pastry for everyone in the shop, front and back. Imagine my relief! I'd kept my fears close even from Shabanian. Through Advent my wife kept asking why my lips were drawn so tightly, until she got to saying simply, "Must be another blizzard coming." Many nights I lay wakeful, apprehensive lest the caravan come short and late. Today we'd celebrate, whatever those 46 beasts carried.

It's a rare shipment matches its order closely, and this was no exception. More than half the wheat that Syrian sent was coarse, unmilled—a minor inconvenience. Thankfully the quantity of milled wheat was adequate to meet our immediate needs. On the other hand, the sugar was scant and most of the basterma was poor in quality, made not of sliced lamb, but of inferior goat cuts. We got olives in place of water eggs, no butter but twice the rice, two barrels of brined cheese instead of 12, and five barrels of pomegranate syrup, thick and dark, never ordered. We groaned on discovering this luxurious flavoring and were astounded when it proved as easy to sell as the rest of the shipment.

The caravan was barely through the gate, much less unloaded, before the first supplicant pressed me for a bushel of wheat. I knew Principal Drikian's even, small handwriting. "Tell him the shipment may be dung-straw, for all I know! First, I inventory. I have to know what these camels have brought me. He must wait!" I told the messenger.

The lad's face brightened when I gave him a hunk of fruit paste from a sack I kept under the table. Quietly I praised the Almighty God for letting us foresee such a letter, for it was no casual thing to defer a request from a man of his position.

That Krikor Effendi Shabanian and I were awaiting a food caravan was no secret in our city. We'd informed the council without requesting, or expecting, stitched lips from Rooster or anyone else. We'd each had many callers hinting—not always subtly—of charity expected when the food arrived. At home, Yiri asked me outright to save ground wheat for a beggar family camped behind the baths. I told her we'd see, she must leave me in peace. Several times after this, the women let me overhear pointed talk of worthy uses. My brother Petros brought up the widow Sharopyan's needs, reminding me how her refugee household owed its creation to our misguided Bishop. Krikor Shabanian's family pestered him likewise, before he lost patience with them.

Krikor and I were long aware that whether one camel came or 105, we'd be besieged for contributions. Together we prepared in principle, deciding our obligations as Armenians, Christians and heads of households. I was gratified to find this friend looking at the same scenery. Upon due consideration we agreed to set aside one-eighth of the foodstuff as outright gifts and to let another eighth be bought at cost by certain charities.

Yet how could we apportion this quarter among the numerous supplicants? A week or two before Christmas, I'd stood warming my hands over the brazier in Shabanian's office while we tossed the problem back, forth and sideways. The solution struck us both at the same moment—let the Council disperse our tithe among the sundry Christian charities, thereby deflecting the rancor we'd earn by deciding each contribution ourselves. Sense and self interest combined, as they often do, in an excellent solution. We promptly called on Father Ashod—whose charities would take first hand in any event—and got his pledge to convene the Council the moment goods arrived.

And so it happened that the Council gathered the next evening with much preliminary hand-shaking and pleasantries that only halfway disguised the determination on many faces. Father Ashod's prayer for heavenly guidance in our proceedings struck me as especially apt. Then, while Krikor explained the tithe, I wrote each food with its tithed portion of bushels or pecks or quarts on a schoolmaster's blackboard. I redid smudged lines from time to time as necessary. In the course of things, these notations answered many questions.

Krikor and I gave explanations when asked—and we listened. Otherwise, we relished each plea, every argument and protest, knowing this route was necessary. Berj surprised me by requesting aid for a few female refugees from some mountain village, now living among ruins near St. Dikran fountain. His persistence scoured my patience. Masjur and Harout began testifying for other needful refugees, Harout favoring a blind-deaf beggar, surely pitiable, yet I guessed smarter than he, having survived this long. I had to intervene to restore procedures. Who would have expected such pleading from these men?

With a mere three hours of debate—a short period, considering the passions exuded—an agreement satisfactory to most of the Council was reached. It apportioned free foods in a certain quantity to the Church pantry and our orphan shelter; in a lesser quantity to the various Armenian schools, based on pupil numbers. This ended objections from both school principals, St. Asdvadzadzin's being as large as Sanasarian and the other schools smaller. Sales at cost (factoring in only usury fees; we took no profit) were divided among these and other charities supported by our Church. The Council secretary copied the figures in his careful hand and later posted a copy at the Church.

Those allocations relieved us of a burden, and were fair, not profitable. What with food we gave free or at cost to charities, grain we sold bakers at a whisker's increase, and usury fees, our gains were modest. Nonetheless, some fools complained we enriched ourselves while beggars starved. The Council's endorsement saved our good names. It helped also that our financers included both the Christian Guild and the American Mission, whose generosity was now well proved by the refuge given many of our countrymen.

The wrong hands got some foodstuff, as will happen. I learned that an unsavory pair of beggars who frequented the church kitchen-yard took double their entitlement and sold it for a high price at the market. Several merchants, one a baker, grew sleek on the charity of others that winter. Erzerum housed profiteers in number, but we were not among them. Times of shortage reveal character.

We were fortunate to see the opportunity and make plans for it before prices rose like startled quail. Our arrangements took skill, cunning, and a measure of God's will, and many folks thanked God for what we did. Many more would have died of deprivation without us. We disposed of that shipment with great care over four weeks, distributing portions each day, securing the remainder at the Bank under guard. Meanwhile, the city rejoiced at the arrival of a second caravan, this one financed by certain Muslim merchants, certain Greek and Jewish businessmen, and the Christian missions. This second caravan was the last to get through until nearly Easter. By that time, many families who formerly provided for others had to choke on pride at the missions. The Kavafians and Shabanians were thankful to avoid paying exorbitant prices to eat.

Doing business is my born aptitude but at times it's far from easy. Those first weeks after Sako's death, I'd have suffocated from anguish if not for obligations. Those who can be occupied during days of grief should be thankful. Resting like an invalid only makes one suffer worse.

I told Mother, "I know Father needs your care, but don't let the women sit idle. Keep after them with tasks, make sure they keep the children busy." I arranged for Nerses to attend school with our boys, which stitched him to our family like sole to shoe. School suited him. He proved a fine student once he caught up in history and French. He found the math and biology familiar, no wonder he excelled with them. It bothered me to see him outperforming Arsen not long into the new year.

Connecting With Henza

❋ · ❋ · ❋ · ❋ · ❋ · ❋ · ❋ · ❋ · ❋ · ❋

Marjan   late January 1896

I t's not laziness. Something else makes a woman want to stand by a window watching nothing or to lie under a blanket instead of working on breakfast and getting schoolboys off. Winter's a gloomy time anyway with its long dark hours and having to stay indoors. Added to that we had our Sako dead, the twins murdered or slaved, the Bedoians. So many bereaved friends, so much grief. So many begging and cold and hungry. For weeks that winter I could hardly think of anything good anywhere, aside from the suitor calling on Oskee. I did my best to pretend a cheerful face.

Often I missed Henza. I thought of her with longing and pain. For half a year she was my dear friend and cheerful companion in household chores. Until Sako died.

We had a special understanding between us. A loving bond I could think of when winter gloom weighed my shoulders. Thinking of Henza consoled me especially because Varti, my oldest, truest friend, was too desperate, too wounded for friendship. I must love her—this I did—knowing she'd no way to love me back. How could she?!

All the women—leaving out Toumia—missed Henza. She used to cheer us with her sunny ways. Even Sara told me she missed her, forgetting her jealousy when Henza lived with us. I guess we all imagine yesterday better than today.

Sometimes Henza and I found a few minutes to talk together at church. One day she reminded me of my promise to visit. Her parents' house was not far from Zari's, so Toumia didn't have to know. Toumia of course was furious that Sako's child was going to be born at Henza's parents' house, not ours. She threatened to take the baby back, with help from—but the Bishop was gone! And Father Ashod was not going to take sides no matter how loud she shrieked. At any rate it would have to wait until the baby came. If it was a girl, we supposed Toumia wouldn't try too hard to claim her.

Henza asked why I hadn't come to visit, and I reminded her how difficult Toumia made it to get out of the house—had she forgotten? Yet thinking later about her question, I knew something else held me home. Suspicion? Doubt? Unease? Fear? I had to study my feelings like letters on a page to figure out why hearing her name made me anxious.

In fact, I was beginning to suspect Henza hadn't told us the truth. Once I said something to Petros before we fell asleep, about missing Sako, and he whispered back, "He put us all in danger. It was wrong."

What did he mean? It startled me to wonder, was it possible Toumia was right? Once I picked at it, that hateful thought turned me wakeful, night after night. I nearly fainted and had to take a nap the day before I went to visit Henza.

She saw it in my face.

"Dear Marjan, your eyes are hollow, you must need sleep," she said. "Tell me what's troubling you."

"First, tell me how you're feeling. Are you well? And your family?"

She gave a happy laugh. "Not too tired. The baby's kicking. We're all healthy, praise be to God. And what of your mother and Petros, the children, your sisters, and all the others—Tell me how they are, leave nothing out!"

And so it went for awhile, the pair of us floating calmly on safe water, as if doubt wasn't scorching my heart. She asked me again why I wasn't sleeping.

I went directly to it.

"I must ask you Henza, about your husband, our dear brother, and what you knew and when. For we know now he was helping the Hunchaks, bringing them guns from the priest gunmaker."

She shuddered as if I'd slapped her.

"My husband heard a rumor..."

She looked away, then back at my face. "Yes, I understand. Please believe me, Marjan, when I tell you this." She took a deep breath. "I never knew what Sako was doing. He wouldn't tell me. I only guessed something illegal was going on, maybe something to do with a free Armenia."

"So you knew he was up to something illegal."

"Is a guess the same as knowing? He never explained why he was going out."

"But you did know it had to be secret. That it had to do with politics, so it had to be illegal."

"One time he said we must not let them treat us like sheep. Except for that, he wouldn't talk about his politics."

"But didn't you even ask him?"

"He wouldn't tell me. 'The police can't make you tell what you don't know' he said." Henza looked away. "I knew whatever it was must be important to him. I couldn't ask him. I had to leave him alone."

By now I felt pounding in my head and I could hardly think. I had to close my eyes and count my fingers the way I learned as a girl. Then I said, "So you knew it was dangerous. That he could be arrested. Killed..."

"I was frightened for him. I didn't want him doing those things. He knew that—and made his own choice."

"But don't you see, it wasn't just his choice! What he was doing put us all in danger! His brothers. His father. Levon. The women, the children! If a man is a traitor, they can put his family on the street. Or in jail. Take over his property, his business! Think of it!"

"I tried to tell him. He would not listen." She started chewing on her lip. "I loved him."

I couldn't speak. My heart was beating fast and making me dizzy. It came to me that she knew what her husband was up to when she helped him sneak in and out of their bedroom at night. And yes, I told myself, a woman's first duty is to her husband. But when he puts his family in danger, isn't her duty to the rest of us? To all those who will suffer, maybe die when his treason is discovered?

I wanted to shout—and couldn't even swallow.

He should have stayed behind! Never come to our hiding house! He was wrong to throw doubts on his family and our neighbors! He was wrong! I thought, then: *And you, Henza, should not have let him come to our hiding house. And you should never, never, never have let him leave it.*

For several minutes I only sat, staring at Henza, and at the flowered cushions on the divans. Then I took myself out the door where Ehsan waited to walk me home.

Sadder even than before.

Three

Revenge and Resolutions

February 1896 through March 1896

Finding A Killer

Hamed   late February 1896

S ignificant events continued to unfold for me that winter. All season my mother chased my thoughts, for she was dying. A man has but one mother. It saddened me to see her interest weaken, to know she'd soon leave us. She was well cared for, there was no need for me at home.

A man is fortunate. My father had his business. My son his school and schoolmates. Even my brother had a job to give variety. A woman has few diversions. After my mother died, I expected Khadija to turn more to Huru for company. Khadija might welcome fresh purposes. Beyond that, we all would miss Mother. I was especially glad to have military responsibilities that winter.

One morning at the garrison, I saw a figure trotting from the south ramparts. Most men, pursuing or pursued, stumble in snow. This soldier kept his balance. Without seeing his face I recognized the Izgirli sergeant.

He intercepted me half-way between stables and officers' entry.

"Captain Hamed, sir, a soldier's face-down past the east rampart, near the shed there. He may be dead!" A clear report despite excitement. Mohamed explained the situation as we went.

Minutes before, on watch, he'd come upon footprints that climbed steps to a blind section of the ramparts. The section lacks scope of city approaches so it's rarely patrolled. A snowfall the evening before meant the marks must be recent. He went to investigate.

Footprints proceeded east from the top step to the ramparts' edge. Crust unbroken until almost the edge, then rough gouges, craters, dark splotches. The Izgirli looked below to see a body.

The sentries were perplexed. Why would we or anyone venture into drifts behind the ramparts? Fortunately a firm crust underlay a hand's width of powder. By walking deliberately, we stayed upright.

We found the body face to crust, encircled by clumps of dark-stained snow. Blood attested to death from a beating heart. When we turned him over his eyes stared at us in rage and pain. A ragged polo ball held his jaws apart. It was impossible to identify him at first.

A moment's pause and we said the name together: "Bekir." Exclaimed together, "His fingers!" for they were gone. The left hand looked a fairly neat job through the frozen paste of blood, its fingers severed at the lower knuckles. Rougher work on his right, those digits hacked crudely from the base. You'd think some wild beast fed there, but what animal is that brutal?

"I've seen gruesome deaths but none more painful," I said. Although I despised the blackmailer, I shuddered at his agony in dying. And at the nature of his killer.

"Truly, the worst," agreed the sergeant. "What mother's son could...?" His query went unfinished. A sentry arrived, freeing us to report the matter.

Some questions I can never answer. What makes a human capable of cruelty? What creates the will to inflict agony on another being? Might such a brute ever have suckled on a loving breast? Are such brutes motherless? The puzzle absorbed me as we walked to the command post.

Major Rustem grew hard, even angry at our report. Unspeakable, such disorder under his command. He'd not tolerate inadequate control—nor its appearance. His concerns surpassed management of ranks to bear on his future. The murderer must be caught without delay, and most especially before word got to Erzincan headquarters. There must be no scandal.

This murder was hardly important compared with some. The Incident here, the innocents, those pregnant young wives. He'd had me go back to that house, question the women. Ascertain if it was soldiers, not hamidieh, not street thugs. Answering, uniformed men for sure. Then not so sure. Nothing clear or credible beyond the crime itself. The Major's informants heard no bragging of it at the garrisons.

Standing at attention while he studied my diagram, I worried he'd assign another officer, perhaps Fikret. The Major had passed me over twice since the Incident. Unhappily I considered my prospects less secure than weeks earlier. Within minutes he lightened this weight.

"Question everyone you need question. Let nothing interfere, not rank, not exercises. Find the killer quickly!" he instructed.

Already I foresaw my need for help in the investigation. First, scores of soldiers must be interviewed and their information followed like so many rivulets into a stream. Too much for me to do alone. My helper must be discreet, also probing and also intuitive, to toss ideas with me.

Clearly, the best man for this was my adjutant. He was totally familiar with garrison life. Our eight years together would ease our collaboration; we build on one another's thoughts, yet often reach divergent insights. Assisting me would be a good experience for Shakir and improve his prospects.

Shakir at first demurred, as I half-expected. Although brave, Shakir avoided certain situations. He tried to keep himself distant from the ranks. He was self-conscious about his wound, especially on first meetings. Sometimes he wore a leather patch that took three strings to hold in place and looked uncomfortable. He disliked wearing it and dismissed its possible benefit, claiming he'd no desire for promotion.

"I'll hinder your investigation, not assist it. The men recoil at me face to face—how can they speak openly, without holding back, when they are close enough to hear me breathe?" he said. He knew his whistle-breaths made some uneasy. "Let me help you in the background."

"No, I want you asking questions, so we can resolve this matter fast. We'll dig out the truth together," I said. My tone and expression told him my decision was fixed.

We planned our strategy quick as mind readers. Which questions to ask Bekir's officers, which among his ranks? Which questions of other officers, other soldiers? We divided our work and arranged to meet at intervals that day. Almost by chance found we both suspected the same private—the only soldier we knew who'd a taste for painful killing. We each decided silently that his name must come from others.

The suspect's commanding officer was Fikret. His bristly reaction made my first interview needlessly difficult. Fikret disliked seeing his authority weakened (his words). It took considerable tact to guide his childish resistance into helpfulness. At last Shakir and I were able to conduct inquiries within his ranks.

Fikret insisted nothing unusual existed among his charges. His nature was more self-absorbed than observant. Self-protective too, as later information proved.

Fikret's sergeant told Shakir of several late night absences by Tahsin and another private. In little more than an hour we each heard the name confirmed by his fellows. I took Shakir with me to confront Tahsin.

Predictably, Tahsin denied any blame. "Look, my hands are clean!" he proclaimed. Thrust them towards us. Their impressive cleanliness belied his claim of innocence. His other visible body parts had obviously gone unsoaped for weeks. Only officers went to weekly baths in those days; Tahsin reeked even worse than his fellows. Shakir got very quick to smell even faint odors after his nose was damaged.

Tahsin's coat was smeared with dried blood. So was the knife we turned out of his bedding. If he'd a mother, she'd never judge him innocent. Tahsin kept protesting after we showed him the bloodstains. He hardly took breath between rants, cursing me and Shakir, Fikret, the Army, Erzerum and everyone in it. The murderer still shouting as the guard pulled him away.

Major Rustem's scowl vanished at my news, sure to gratify superiors. Nonetheless, we must keep investigating so as to explain the motive firing it.

We now questioned every soldier in both Tahsin's and Bekir's units. Plainly no one cared for either man. Answers nonetheless came slow and reluctant, for self-protection stands before honesty. Convincing the men to speak freely took effort.

Shakir's self-consciousness diminished hour by hour. His wound reduced his distance from the ranks, even helped him draw better answers. He gained confidence. The inquiry was, I saw, good for him.

Our second day of interviews was encouraging. Answers were more relaxed by now and sometimes even laced with laughter. First one fellow, then another gave us clues. These led to more. We learned of several quarrels, one the day before the killing. We found witnesses but not explanations.

The chain of clues was not easily linked. Our efforts were futile for two long days. On the third, a soldier steered Shakir to a stable-boy. This lad was recently reassigned from our Citadel to Ghezmahali Fort. He connected certain links later expanded and tightened by Tahsin. That criminal blamed Bekir for most of the wrongdoing. It was an ugly and appalling chain of the sort that keeps a captain humble.

Horse dung! That's what the chain was made of.

Tahsin had caught a stable-boy bagging horse-fruit. Mixed properly with straw and then sun-dried, it burns with little stink. Almost everyone uses it for heat. Wood's priced like gold in these eastern provinces. The boy was making profit on what cost him nothing. A common custom in anyone's army, yet theft, nonetheless. Dung was our fuel. An army drover carted our horse-fruit off to some plains village twice a month or so and returned it to us once prepared.

The boy begged Tahsin not to tell. He was only 10 or 11 and helping support his family. Tahsin would keep his secret for a price: certain favors they might both enjoy, watched only by a horse or two.

After the first time, the lad wanted out. Tahsin refused. The devil's bargain continued some weeks. Finally the boy plucked at Lt. Fikret's sleeve and pleaded for a place at another fort. Four forts ringed Erzerum.

"Please, could you find a stable boy who'll trade places with me? Someone who wants to work at the great Citadel?"

Fikret might easily have dismissed the plea. To his credit, he got the boy's story. The sobbing child begged Fikret not to confront Tahsin.

"He'll kill me!"

Fikret took in the boy's predicament and sent inquiries at once on his behalf. Learning of an opening at Ghezmahali Fort, he dispatched him there that day.

The boy was now out of Tahsin's reach. Fikret figured the problem was past; he chose not to discipline the soldier, nor to report the situation to Major Rustem. Tahsin was left unpunished without even a frown of disapproval. Later Fikret acknowledged poor judgment.

Shakir saw Fikret flinch at the killer's name. Fearful, he surmised, not of Tahsin's proclivities but of his lack of scruples. If a man killed stray dogs and cats for pleasure he was capable of any outrage. Every soldier feared his ruthlessness.

As did the other stable boys. They kept quiet as to Tahsin's secret trade in horse-fruit. His middleman, small surprise, was often Pohar. Sometimes Tahsin bartered dung for a stable-boy's favors, gaining both variety and profit, and so improving on his prior deal.

Enter Bekir. The blackmailer sniffed Tahsin out—or sniffed out the dung-sack where he was thumping the bowels out of a street urchin late one night. Not only were unauthorized visitors strictly forbidden, but the Commandant particularly opposed child-fornication. Any miscreant got flogged.

Bekir confronted Tahsin with a malevolent smirk. For his silence Bekir took payments several times; he bragged he'd got the meanest man in the citadel tied to a cannon.

Perhaps the extortionist raised his price; perhaps Tahsin grew dissatisfied; perhaps both. Observers termed their quarrels one-sided: Tahsin raging, Bekir smug.

We found no witness to their final meeting. First Tahsin denied luring his enemy to the ramparts. Once he admitted the murder, his boastful nature cut him down. Few men can resist well-worded flattery. I pretended surprise Bekir would meet in so remote a place. "Was it simply a chance encounter, something you never planned?"

Tahsin grinned, proud. He'd convinced his blackmailer of rich rewards if utter secrecy was maintained. I nearly left it at that, needing nothing more. Yet I wanted him to answer another question.

In the Incident, when soldiers attacked the Armenian quarter: Did you enter a house with several women in it? Two were big with an unborn child—do you remember?"

"Sure, I remember." A smirk. "Something different. But listen,Cap'n, I didn't kill them! They were already dead when I had them. You can't say I did harm."

He could not or would not describe the soldiers he followed, except for being Zeki's troops, apparently the Erzincan battalion. Although I duly reported this to Rustem, the matter was not pursued so far as I know.

Court martial came swiftly. No tears were shed for Tahsin as he fell—indeed, some called out taunts. It was Tahsin's good luck to die by gunfire, kinder than his own methods. The recruits forgot their dislike for Bekir and shuddered when speaking of his awful death.

The fingers melted out months after.

I made clear to Fikret I expected changes in his leadership. Shakir and I would stay close by as models and advisers.

A great deal can be said indirectly about authority and duty, honor and heroics. The necessity of telling the whole truth to one's superior without dissembling to protect oneself. Truth must be served first—and will come out.

I learned that Fikret was brighter than he appeared. He'd been tossed responsibility prematurely, without enough experience. He began to realize how little he knew. He wanted to do better, longed to prove himself. To advance on merit.

I spoke to him in broad terms about military discipline, particularly the need for mutual respect between officers and ranks, between the Army and civilians. Although I spoke of the value

Erzerum derives from its Christian citizens, I kept to myself any question of Armenians' loyalties, a sensitive matter for me.

We reached an understanding. I'd not implicate him in the Tahsin affair. He'd strive to support my command, not undermine me. He'd attend to how I handled my authority, learn skills military leaders require. Fikret proved trainable, in time. It took a year before I felt confident of him. His arrogance wore off slowly. Eventually he became a decent officer. One known among Armenians here as even-handed.

In digging that maggot out from its feast I drew favor around the camp. I no longer sensed doubts of my commitment to the Sultan's military. Not from the ranks, nor the major, at least. Some fellow officers resented my recent decoration. Always, I regretted receiving it, although the more egregious medal was Bekir's. Ridiculous awards undermine the base an army stands on: troops' respect for their officers may never be entirely restored.

※ ※ ※

My mother died the same week as Tahsin. She spent her final days without talking or eating, simply gasping to breathe. She was blind to us, looking only inward. I kissed her farewell that morning knowing she'd few hours left.

Since Ramadan past we'd seen her death advance. Each bad spell was worse than before, with less time between. She knew the end was close. "When I'm gone, you'll be glad, I know," she'd say. She was partly right.

It was Father came to tell me with his customary composure. We rode home without speaking. Home was a mournful scene flowing with sad memories.

I'd grieved already for the loving mother who laughed and sang and made up far-fetched stories, who comforted childish scrapes and worries and read our faces before she spoke, as women should. That mother was long gone, drained first of patience and laughter, then tenderness. Then of eyes for anything beyond herself. Drained by a bad heart that chained her to her couch.

We'd try to draw her thoughts to the children, their small discoveries and accomplishments. Father would talk about some neighbor she knew and I'd try to amuse her with some Army matter. Ehsan would talk about some boyish this or that, Khalil would offer something. No matter what, she showed no interest, simply resuming her complaints. She wanted constant attention and behaved unpleasantly, whoever gave it—even Father and me. Illness sapped her best qualities. It had turned her long since into someone far different from the mother of my childhood and young manhood.

A man owes his mother love, not pretense. Near the end, I realized sadly that filial duty must serve when love cannot. My affection was a debt to memory, devoid of present feeling. I pray she didn't know.

I knew this wheezing invalid was not our mother and grandmother. Yet the day she died, grief numbed me. It cut me through and made me shake unexpectedly and forget what I was saying. I recall kissing her limp, soft hands and weeping heavy tears. It is wrenching to lose a mother. It takes a year, I found, for unpleasant memories to fade out and be replaced by memories framed with good health.

Her death was a relief for everyone, I suspect, though no one said it. We spoke of her suffering. Khalil surprised me by saying, "It won't hurt her any more to breathe."

Strangely, Khadija seemed most grief-stricken. The children (I include Khalil) were done mourning soon after the burial. Father and I and Khadija spoke of her often—then less often. I can think of my Mother now without sorrow.

Khadija was haggard after weeks of nursing. She and our cook took turns at night. By day, Khadija dealt with most of Mother's demands. I assumed it was fatigue made my wife weep so ardently. Yet a week later, she was still red-eyed and preoccupied.

One night in bed, affronted at Khadija's passivity, I chided her. This drew out an apology of sorts: "I can't help it, I miss her," she said. "She needed me."

"I need you too, dear wife," I told her. "You must take comfort in having been good to her. Now let me be good to you." Then I pulled her into my arms, for I'd resolved on a solution. Within moments she let herself give warmth. We conceived our second son that night or the next.

A household must change when the matriarch dies. Yet I couldn't have predicted the changes, scarcely noticed them occur.

Father encouraged Khadija to make household decisions. She did this readily. Before, change came only with her most subtle persuasion. Mother might accept small alterations in household habit: more cut flowers in the sitting room, apples for the boys when they got home. Khadija now introduced improvements without asking: for example, the soft Bulgari cheese my Father liked for lunch.

"What's this? Bulgari for breakfast? Who likes it?" Father complained at the table. The third day, he took a tentative bite. The sixth, he asked why it was missing from the breakfast tray. Another example: fruits served with honeyed yogurt, Smyrna style instead of plain.

Khadija also brought more important changes. The sitting room got two chairs of strong oak carved by a Kolyan carpenter, a great convenience that Mother firmly resisted. The chairs eased hospitality.

Father and I held back as to the Kavafian menfolk, however. Our doubts lingered. We hosted other friends and neighbors occasionally. Khadija began visiting the Kavafian women—this Mother never allowed. She held such enjoyable activities unnecessary.

Maybe it was the child she carried. Perhaps relief from Mother's demands, or the pleasure of new authority, new responsibilities. Khadija grew more confident, more given to laughter. Even when she scolded, rarely, her voice was graced with gaiety.

In new recruits, confidence can be threaded with defiance. I watch for it and make them learn to conceal it. Khadija's ways were a lot like theirs, something I never imagined in her. When I told her what to do, I'd see her shoulders set and her eyes flash, as if objecting, yet silent. I learned a new game. "Serving Khadija" I called it. "Placating Khadija" fits as well.

The household grew more relaxed, happier. The air often flashed with humor, so long subdued. I teased my children, joked with Khalil—two real pleasures of family life. A different humor occupies a barracks. It is sometimes enjoyable, yet not half so precious.

Eyes and Ears

Marjan   February-March 1896

A t last a clue brought me hope. Ephraim arrived a little late that
morning, panting. Toumia began scolding before he was done
explaining. "Someone stopped me, I ran the rest of …"

"You fetch the water! We've been waiting! See you work quick,
now!" She clapped her hands.

Two hours later, when we were alone in the kitchen, Ephraim
whispered, "Osama gave me a message for you!"

Between the carpenter's lisp and his making the lad promise
we'd keep his part secret, telling his message took a while. My throat
was too tight to swallow by the time Ephraim set the meat on the
platter, as they say. Osama thought he discovered where the twins
were hidden! He wasn't sure, I should keep my hopes wrapped close,
still he wanted me to know.

First, Osama told Ephraim, we should know that he and Elim
were working now for the Provincial Customs Director, a man
named Genghis Bey. This official had a large house on a hill, tended
by many servants and gardeners. Some carpentry tasks were indoors
(a few new window frames, a child's cupboard, a kitchen bench),
others outdoors (replacing steps to the back door, adding stalls in
the stable) and either way, he and his helper took their meals in the
kitchen, the weather being bitter. Several times they'd seen the cook
fix a tray that a servant took away.

"Two cups, two bowls, two spoons—two people with tiny
stomachs, there wasn't food in those bowls for two field mice," he
told Ephraim. He heard the housemaid anger the cook by saying,

"They don't like your cooking." Osama ducked a flying onion as he fled the kitchen.

Ephraim's news raised a sprout of fresh green hope in my heart. First, I felt sure the two small tummies belonged to Rebecca and Zeput—only one other girl was still missing by this time. Then I lost hope, thinking the cook was feeding sick children.

I saw no way to find out. "Don't fret, we'll find answers if we keep asking everyone we meet," Khadija said. A week later good news set us both laughing. Khadija learned that her cook—a fussy little dark-skinned woman named Husneh—was a cousin of Genghis Bey's cook. Khadija told Husneh the problem, making much of the twins' love of birds and singing, for Husneh herself loved to sing and always scattered breadcrumbs for the sparrows. Husneh promised to do her best to find out.

While I waited, I took some flannel our neighbors gave us and cut new nightshirts for the children. I basted and stitched these carefully. Next I cut a new shirt for Vagram because he tore his sleeve in two places. Sewing helps me get calm when I'm nervous.

Some days later, Khadija met me with a downcast face. "Husneh's cousin was sworn to secrecy. If she tells Husneh anything, Genghis Bey will beat her—and then dismiss her."

Her words made me dizzy. Then I felt a glow of joy in my heart. "That's very good to know," I said.

"I don't see what's so good," she said.

"This shows there's an important secret! It's not just his own children, sick in bed," I said.

"Even so…" said my friend. "There's nothing we can do."

"There is! Husneh must make her cousin understand we'll never say anything to get her in trouble. I haven't said a word, even to Heranoush or my husband, not a word. May God be my witness!"

"That's what I told Husneh already. She said her cousin won't change her mind. We must find some other way."

We spent an hour or more trying ideas. Something occurred to me. "Is it possible to offer a gift…?"

"I don't know." Then Khadija slapped her hands together with a laugh. "I have it! You probably never saw Husneh's earrings because she wears a scarf. Her earrings are made of gold and jade, carved into a fig-leaf. Lovely earrings, truly.

"Well, she was visiting her cousin the other day, and since the kitchen was hot and they were alone, they went bare-headed. The cousin made a fuss over Husneh's earrings. Her cook said the woman was almost rude, the way she praised them, as if she was waiting for Husneh to pull them off and give them to her!"

In a blink we agreed on sending Husneh out to buy a like pair with some coins I'd put aside. It was no great price for the answer we needed.

A second week passed and a third began before Husneh brought an answer. Yiri and her mother both caught influenza so I was too busy to lie awake worrying. Even so, my head sometimes simmered. One time Vagram corrected my story-telling when I mixed up what Vartan bravely did with how David outwitted a giant. Petros noticed my odd temper and came close to guessing why.

"You must try not to brood so much about what you can't change," he told me. I pretended calm to keep down questions. I was glad Varti still avoided church so I wouldn't be tempted to add false hope to her suffering.

At first, Husneh kept her eyes on the floor to keep from giving away the answer. We had to show we knew the trouble she went through. It was no simple bribe! On top of the lovely earrings in a silken pouch, she had to pledge her own silence—and ours. Then she had to promise—her mistress must see she'd no choice—to help her cousin with the coming Ramadan feast and two others. Hannum Khadija must hire another cook for those feasts, unfortunately. Husneh hinted she might know someone able to help out. Khadija agreed to everything three times over. Her cook stretched out the story to get all our attention without ever looking at us directly. I wanted an answer to our question! My mouth was too dry to speak or even swallow and my hands shook.

At last, Husneh looked up. The lines beside her mouth held a trace of something smug and so I guessed a good answer was coming.

Like a butterfly unfurling her wings, Husneh proudly and carefully told us what she learned. There was indeed a pair of Armenian girls, thin as sticks because they ate almost nothing. Her cousin never saw them herself, but the housemaid told her they were sisters, maybe twins, and sometimes they sang songs she didn't know.

Even before I told Heranoush, I sent Ephraim into blowing snow to give Varti the message: "They're alive!"

Getting the twins safely home, of course, was another matter. We could see no way without help from our husbands and who knows what others. Soon! And so it happened that Petros and Martiros excused themselves early from family prayers, leaving Miron to lead the service while they called on Berci Pasha and the Captain.

Ransom

Hamed   March 1896

O ur neighbors asked to speak with us. We knew the essence already from Khadija, the matter's importance to her friend and most especially to that other family. We must help if it was not too late. We put aside our misgivings and stepped over the rift in our long friendship. This had nothing to do with loyalty to the Sultan, only with human decency. We welcomed the two men in.

I'd seen this Genghis Bey on those occasions when civilian officials come together with the Garrison command. He was late 40s in age, a heavy man who favored European tailoring that somewhat concealed his paunch. Weak eyes got him a habit of squinting, while at the same time tilting his head back so his chin stuck at you. It almost forced your attention. On visiting his office once, I found him in spectacles. Genghis held his head straight without looking over his chin and he spoke in normal fashion. It was vanity caused his squint.

"We must be especially careful how we go about this," I warned Martiros and Petros. "He strikes me as a proud man. The mayor holds him in high regard."

"I'd be careful anyway with the head of licenses," said Martiros.

My father resolved it for us. Raise the offer by 20 percent, enough to catch the captor's interest and let him save face, not so much as might impoverish the twins' family or encourage fresh kidnappings. Declare the offer void unless the girls are returned in good health.

Time was on our side, Father pointed out. "This fish will be hungry for bait by now—he can't still want the girls for bed-play.

Not skinny 12-year olds with bad breath, no breasts, no hips… no pleasure, just trouble!" We all laughed at the picture.

"Besides, he'll be afraid they'll starve themselves to death. You can be sure his wife's spoken on that point, whatever else she's held her tongue from saying." He raised his tone to mimic a nagging woman. "They'll die here, I won't have it! Look out, you'll bring disgrace and ruin on us! Your sons will be ashamed!"

Trust my father to bring laughter to a worrisome situation. Trust my father also to know (somehow) the man had sons. The sons played a part in the story, though they were blameless.

We discussed how to move forward: whether to spread the ransom terms throughout the city or instead get a message directly to this Genghis Bey. It was essential we protect the woman from the least suspicion. The captor was sure to beat and sack her if he knew. Khadija insisted on this point beyond imagining, even standing in the kitchen doorway to make sure I made this clear. Truly my docile, compliant wife surprised me that month. She attacked a problem and persisted to its end, like an eager recruit who knocks an enemy off his horse. She'd no idea I'd find her steel enticing. After 13 years married, I was astonished at my renewed passion.

To protect the cook, we leaned toward the first approach. Yet spreading the terms around the city takes time—the girls might die before he responded.

We decided the better strategy was the direct one. Someone aside from the cook must know he held the twins. Ignore the soldiers, they'd have traded their prize early on, mindless where it might end up. We must find an intermediary who knows Genghis Bey's secret— surely it was possible, yet was there time?

Infrequently a reluctant mount breaks into a gallop. That's how the solution came to me. Abdi knew everything happening in Erzerum city before it happened. He'd know who had the Armenian girls. Better still, Genghis Bey would expect he'd know. I need only ask Abdi to take a message to their captor.

He was a skilled negotiator, known for trading frugally, whether information or getting a thing done. He never acted without necessity. Yet I was confident he'd help me with this matter if he could, and without reward. Beyond our lifetime friendship, I'd done him favors related to the Garrison that put him in my debt.

The next morning I started drills, then went to see him. Fortunately, government officials tend to relax in deep winter. Business slows, only moon-heads travel, few licenses or permits need be issued, taxes dwindle. Not that Abdi was idle when I got to his office, but he set other tasks aside.

Abdi listened thoughtfully while I described my Armenian friend's connection to two kidnapped girls whose family wanted to increase the reward—provided the girls came home healthy and <u>soon</u>. I spoke of the family's fears for them, fears shared by many prominent friends, both Christian and Muslim. He nodded agreement as I spoke of the importance of restoring trust.

When I told him later, Father said he could have done it no better.

Abdi replied with generalities about the demoralizing situation for the Armenian millet. How we all must strive to restore harmony in our city so that Armenians will continue to rebuild their businesses rather than move away, as a few have already done. He spoke of the excellent conditions for trade owed to Erzerum's strategic location on the major north-south and east-west trade routes; of the security provided by its military fortresses and garrison; of how the prosperity of all was a fabric woven of trust and confidence among the various threads.

I waited quietly while he expounded. His words held nothing to raise an eyebrow.

After a time, Abdi came to the matter at hand. He said, as I expected, that he knew nothing about any kidnapped Armenians. A man might brag of such a thing. A wife might complain to friends at the baths. He'd heard nothing. However, for the sake of conversation, of good philosophical argument such as we enjoyed in school—just what was meant by "healthy"? What if one or both were pregnant? Some of these young girls were surprisingly fertile.

"I assume they'd not be returned, were that the case." It was impossible to imagine otherwise. No Muslim would let his child be raised out of the faith. He'd be scorned, a pariah.

"Still, what if—" he pressed. "Hypothetically speaking, of course."

"Their parents will take them back and make good on their offer."

"Indeed? It would be a matter of great shame. Can you be so sure?"

"I'm certain," I told him. "They will not cast their daughters out."

"The gold paid in full weight?"

"Providing the girls are in reasonable health, it will be paid."

"Just hypothetically, of course. It's useful I know this, in case the mayor, in his dealings—which are entirely unpredictable—happens to discover such a circumstance." Abdi leant to flick a bit of mud off his boot. "It's possible the matter will come to my attention. I promise to do what I can, if I should discover a pasha with a fondness for Armenian girls."

If he already knew, he concealed it well. Still, I suspected he knew more than he admitted. I chose my next words carefully.

"As you explained so well, this matter is important to our city. It should be resolved with utmost speed. More time can only bring more difficulties. As you said so wisely, Abdi, reuniting the girls with their family will most certainly be a public service of great value."

A squall of snow that night was followed by a clear sky and bright sunshine, a common event in mountainous places. We exercised our ranks and horses that afternoon in muddy slush. Afterwards I rubbed Keyif down and fed him a shriveled apple.

"You're fortunate not to mind some mud on your haunches," I told him. It was a particular nuisance to get one's boots off, remove one's trousers, put on clean ones. I hoped my valet had them dry from the day before. I'd slept poorly the prior night on account of Khadija's restlessness, and when I'm tired, small irritations become troublesome. My mind was on small inconveniences instead of larger matters as I crossed the stable yard.

My thoughts scattered when a curly-haired boy ran at me from the center gate.

"Sir, are you Captain Hamed, sir?" Panting, he flapped his woolen vest to cool himself. "Abdi Pasha asks to see you!"

I gave the boy a coin to tell his master I'd come shortly. Then I shouted for my valet and grumbled aloud at the mud.

⚜ ⚜ ⚜

The clerk led me at once into Abdi's office. My friend gave a mock salute and signaled for coffee. With the briefest of smiles, he said, "Sometimes progress can be quicker than we expect." He leaned back in his chair and pressed his fingertips together, hand to hand. The clerk set a tray down and began to pour our coffee. Abdi waved him off.

"Leave us!"

His phrasing now became almost formal in tone. "Through my various sources, a series of inquiries has allowed me to locate your girls." My eyebrows rose at the possessive, drawing a chuckle. "It's fortunate they're in the city or I might never have found them."

I murmured something appropriate, attempting patience.

"Moreover, by changing another appointment—and you are one of the very few friends I'd do that for—I was able to call upon the individual who is keeping them."

Men of power and influence are skilled at concealing emotion. Abdi's face was a mask. His voice was deliberate and without warmth. I felt a rising apprehension. "I'm in suspense. Don't keep me hanging, friend."

Abdi seemed in no haste to ease my mind. Perhaps his authority, limited like mine, made him savor his control over the conversation. Perhaps I do it too with my subordinates. At the time I recall thinking that if Abdi wasn't a friend, I'd detest his manner, his near arrogance.

"You understand, I'm sure, the need for absolute secrecy. The man in question insists on anonymity. Without identifying him, I can say he holds an important office and fulfills its duties commendably. Because of this, and because his character is of the highest standard…" I heard no trace of irony in his words "…he enjoys wide respect among both true believers and the faithless millets."

It was too much! This praise for vile behavior defeated my efforts to stay impassive. The moment Abdi paused, I interposed, "I'm pleased to hear he's above reproach, like Caesar's wife." His eyelids flickered at my meaning and his next words remonstrated.

"It's essential you understand the need for circumspection. The individual in question demands we exercise the utmost discretion."

Self control kept my face calm, though my body was taut under my uniform. Had we not discussed the need for secrecy two days before? I never expected him becoming the captor's spokesman. Yet I saw the balance in this: the captor's voice must be heard or there'd be no resolution.

"I've explained the benefits of resolving the matter. Benefits both for the city and for him personally. I'm glad to tell you, he's not a narrow-minded man. He's able to see a wider field than many. He values Armenians. Moreover, he's a good citizen, of the first order. He does not put his own advantage over the public good. He sees and appreciates the beneficial effect his sacrifice will have on those Armenians doing business in our city."

This last gave me the first clear clue of a favorable outcome. "I gather, then, he will release them," I said.

"Remember our logic lessons from Teacher Ismir. 'One must not reach a conclusion except by a straight path.'" His steady gaze held a faint smile.

"Remember another lesson he taught us. 'Clear glass is best for seeing truth,'" I countered.

"I fear your patience is shrinking. Therefore I'll tell you this. The news is good, though not entirely perfect." I reflected on the pleasure we all take at having knowledge others seek.

"I'm glad you say this. Please continue to explain." It took effort to keep my tone neutral.

"So far as the girls are concerned, it's an incredibly fortunate circumstance. In fact, a cause for much rejoicing."

"So he'll give them both back to their parents?"

Just the night before, my good wife Khadija confided her fears that one or both might be pregnant and would remain captive until the birth. "It would be dreadful if one had to stay without her sister for comfort! She couldn't bear it!" she'd fretted, preparing for bed.

"Don't look for rain clouds," I chided. She tossed about half the night, pulling our bedclothes off and on and back and forth. I finally calmed her in a way that always leads to sleep.

"Patience!" Abdi was enjoying his advantage. "Let me tell you the most important thing first."

He poured the last gritty drops of coffee into his cup while I waited wordless.

"In brief, not only are the girls not with child—they've not been harmed! It's amazing, truly—both are still intact!"

"It's not possible!"

"They are virgins still. So their good uncle tells me."

"Uncle? I'm confused! You must explain!"

"If you're truly interested," he said, now smiling. "The man intended to give them to his sons as brides this summer, when the young men finish their university studies. But they've written from Constantinople most adamantly, saying they prefer to marry Muslim girls, moreover, brides who are more mature, not so young and ignorant.

"And these Armenian girls are thin and undeveloped—who knows if they'll be well-shaped women?" Standing, he moved to the far corner to flatten a bump in the carpet. "He'd just as soon be rid of them. However…"

I braced myself for the rest.

"As he sees it, he's paid good money for these girls, and what's more, fed them these past four months. He wants to recoup his costs, of course, then to be properly rewarded for protecting them from the harm they'd have suffered from other hands. He argues that the ransom was offered in expectation that the girls would have been defiled, yet he's restrained his manly person beyond any normal expectation."

"His demand?"

"A modest increase only." He named a figure exactly double the second ransom offer.

"It's impossible. The family's shop was emptied, their business destroyed, their house looted. Furnishings, jewelry, all gone. Repairs have been costly..."

And so we proceeded to negotiate, with me overstating the family's penury, on one hand, while he (surely) overstated the other's insistence. Like any negotiation, it took time. We drank coffee and invented fresh arguments. We talked a bit about the food shortage, our families, our school days. Eventually we arrived at a figure we thought both parties might accept. It was about 20 percent over the family's recent offer and depended on finding them in health and unmolested.

Enough to buy a decent house or two excellent horses.

"He said we must accept his word that they are well enough. Thin, but able to speak and move about."

His words fed my suspicions. From my wife I'd learned the girls were barely eating. Disease and illness follow starvation, whether caused by blockade or willful choice. The girls might be dying.

"You have a gifted tongue, Abdi. Persuade him to let you see them as soon as possible. I will not create false hope." He agreed to do his best.

In my absence that morning, two privates under my command had quarreled. Each claimed to own a certain pair of boots. Different friends supported them and soon the two groups were hurling insults, heat growing. Shakir found a temporary solution by sending one group to drill outside while the other cleaned rifles.

The dispute would be trivial to a general, but as a captain, I wanted it settled. Good boots matter greatly to a man treading winter snow. I soon learned that both men already had boots, but old and cheaply made, soles worn nearly through. The boots in question were not new, but of fine quality and still in good condition. Scant wonder each wanted them.

I decreed a trial, one man to wear the boots all afternoon, the other to wear them the next morning. By noon, that second claimant was tense from pain and limping. The boots were too tight for his toes and grated both heels, especially his right. He gave them over grudgingly.

With a glad heart I drew Martiros and Petros from their warm sitting room that evening to relate the good news. Together we called on the captives' family. Such joy and surprise, you'd think their holy Jesus stood before them! Imagine the weeping and embracing, the many times my hands were kissed! Once assured the higher figure was possible, we accepted a single glass of the Meserians' potent cognac. The brothers and I were eager to join our wives for further celebration.

The Bey insisted—Abdi sighed in explaining this point of pride—that only soldiers come for them. "No Armenians! Soldiers brought them, soldiers will remove them," he'd said. He set an early hour when few people are about. Only at the close of these preliminaries did Abdi use the name known to me for days, 'Genghis Bey.'"

※ ※ ※

Shakir and a junior officer stood with me just inside the door, our rifles upright beside our boots. We watched in silence while Abdi and the Bey took positions at the table. The Bey gave no sign he saw us. His eyes focused on the velveteen coffer that Abdi withdrew from a leather sack and emptied onto the table. Lanterns hanging on each wall twinkled the big man's spectacles. Outside, the dawn was grey and little light came through the windows.

Abdi first spread the coins, then divided them. Equal stacks of 10 formed a line across the table. "It's good," Abdi announced. We all drew a deep breath together. The kerosene smell that struck my nostrils on entering the house had now dissipated.

Abdi stood while the older man repeated the process, still more slowly and carefully. Next, he scooped each pile into the coffer. When he'd made sure the table was cleared, he nodded in my direction.

"It's satisfactory," he said. He looked directly at me for a moment. Then he slid the coffer into its sack and the sack inside his shirt. He removed his eyeglasses and slipped them into his belt before he spoke.

"I've treated them well, even though they are homely, skinny creatures. I can do far better for my sons. I'm glad to be rid of them!" He turned and disappeared into another room.

We waited, chatting above worry. It seemed a long time, yet likely but a quarter hour passed. Abruptly, a woman servant appeared out of a dark doorway. Behind her walked the two girls, holding hands. Each clutched a pauper's shawl cut from a blanket. Better than nothing against the March wind.

Although I expected they'd be thin, I gasped aloud at their shriveled faces and hollow sockets. Thankfully, their eyes gave us a quick bright glance before returning to the floor. I was uncertain they had strength to get home without a litter. I thought of houses we could rest at if we must.

Genghis Bey held up a hand to command quiet. He walked in a circle around them. It was odd, as if he was inspecting them for purchase. No one else moved. The girls quivered with each heavy footstep. When he stepped back, they turned to face him. This man still controlled their destiny. He began shooting questions at them.

"Have you been mistreated?" was the first.

"No." The word was soft but clear.

"Have you been given enough food to eat and water to drink?"

"Yes," they whispered together.

"Are you able to ride home now, without falling off?"

They lifted their eyes from the carpet at last. "I think so. Yes," said one, and "Yes, yes!" the other.

"Be gone, then! My sons won't have you!" shouted the Bey, as if anger conceals wrongdoing. He clapped, making the girls flinch.

They looked bewildered and ready to crumple at his feet. I stepped close and held out my hand to the nearer one.

"I'm a friend of the Kavafians. I've talked with your family and they are eager to get you back." They blinked their cavernous eyes and nodded. "Come, follow me and my lieutenants outside to our horses. We'll put you up behind us. The ride is not too far. In half an hour, you'll be home."

Revenge

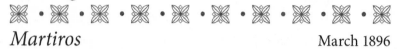

Martiros   March 1896

usiness had slowed, not that our shoemakers fell idle, but we stood nearly even with orders. Petros' daily absences let me turn my mind from conversation to the business of trading. I studied an official report on Russian commerce provided by the Czar's consul, and while the information could not be taken as fully accurate even had it been up to date, it helped me ascertain which foods were in most ample supply and which were short in recent seasons.

So I was deeply dug into calculations concerning Brazilian chicle, with a lamp and brazier warming my hands and legs, when a cold draft stirred my ledger. I saw my brother's fur-caped form in the doorway, his face lit with anticipation.

"Everything's ready," he told me. His mouth formed a peculiar smile. His voice was grim. "Tonight, justice. They won't escape."

He meant to leave it there, in case police should press me. Nor did he intend to add me to his cohort of avengers—as head of household, I ought not put my life at risk.

Indeed, my responsibilities as head of household were themselves in conflict. Obviously, I should be ignorant. Yet I felt compelled to make sure he'd set up everything properly. What if Petros had overlooked some essential detail?

I am a man of action as well as intellect. I was pulled by my obligation to Sako, what some would call honor or familial duty or even love. The more I considered it, the more clearly I saw my path. My elder brother and I were too closely linked for me to leave the task to others. I was equally obligated to set the right example for my sons. Actions teach deaf ears, Mother used to say.

Thus I insisted Petros tell me everything he knew and planned. It took some argument, but I prevailed.

Petros never said directly where his knowledge came from, nor did I ask. One allusion to the spymaster of the garrison and another to a felon named Pohar (a cloth-trader) led me to conclude our friend Hamed had provided assistance.

This helped soothe an unspoken unease I was feeling as to Hamed's friendship, a feeling I found profoundly unsettling, for had we not been close as brothers since boyhood? I'd sensed a distance between us when we came back from hiding, as if Hamed no longer cared to know my thoughts before I voiced them or to let me think his.

Was it my imagination or was he holding himself apart, closing his life to me? Of course, our circumstances were altered by my brother's death, my father's stroke, his mother's final illness and the unusual difficulties for the city that winter. Evenings together were reduced to once, sometimes twice a week and ended early.

"Do you feel a change in them?" I asked Petros one night as we delayed retiring. My question baffled him until I explained I felt Hamed and his father were more reserved these days, less cordial.

"It's nothing to worry about, just ordinary preoccupations. Nothing personal," Petros said.

"I fear we've offended them."

"How could we—??" Petros shook his head. "Look at how they found the twins for us, how Hamed brought them back! No friends could do better!"

"It's made your wife and Hamed's into close friends."

"But…as I consider this, you may be right that they've been holding back from us. I figured it was the matriarch's dying, other family matters, business concerns…the garrison murder."

The murder story Berj told was even more gruesome than Hamed's. "I want to think that's all, yet I've begun to fear it may be something more," I said.

Petros pushed up from the cushions and stretched his arms forward and back. "Have you spoken to Hamed about…" he drew a deep breath before going on. "…about Sako's reason for being on the street that day?"

My reply was a frown, a headshake. I could not bring up words. In all my recent anxieties about our friendship, I'd avoided examining this possibility. If the family's first-born son was helping traitors, would our friends assume we encouraged him? Did they conclude we were disloyal too?

"If they doubt us…" I began.

"We must allay their doubts," said Petros, nodding.

"Somehow."

"Somehow."

※ ※ ※

How long before one's birth name, bestowed by loving parents, gives way to some nickname reflecting the child's looks or character? This "Cowbird" (white hair) and "Crow" (black hair) were nothing but scum-coat thieves with bigger eyes than brains, friendless but for one another, loyal only to profit.

Like their countrymen, I supposed, they came to Erzerum dreaming of land and steady work, then made do with occasional day labor and larceny. They were braggarts telling how they'd teamed to pick an Englishman's pocket, how they'd filched a few buttons from a tailor shop, and one day, how they'd murdered a pair of Armenians. Yes, those luckless peasants who brought us hay. The buddies strutted all about camp, so brave and clever, such big men! I give the other Circassians credit for avoiding their company in the months since they arrived.

Although ignored, Crow and Cowbird were tolerated as fellow countrymen managing as best they could. A week or two before this, we heard, the situation changed. Their campmates kicked them out and nearly killed them. It seems they pilfered a sack of trinkets from somebody's aged mother, right there in the camp. They were trying to trade them in town when the woman's son chanced to see their booty. Those brainless birds spent all their buried treasure to buy their lives. Moreover, they were no longer allowed within the warm circle cast by the main campfire. From that time on they had to stay down along the swampy south edge of camp, where it was hard to stay dry because deep slush lay below the surface snow.

Muslim witnesses confirmed our prior information. My brother and I had no grain of doubt that Cowbird and Crow struck down our elder brother, nor any question they killed twice more that dismal day. They were seen attacking Sabatian's assistant as he ran for home from the Plaza. Crow was wearing his victim's boots before his chest stopped oozing blood. This was early in the day. Later, at Aghabalian's wool shop, a soldier saw them pull the pasterma-maker we called "Holy Francis" from under piled blankets. From beatitude, terror and a bloody death.

Surely Crow and Cowbird found pleasure in these acts, for their trifling gains hardly required murder. I suppose killing made them feel manly, like swaggering boys who fell a bird with a rock. They bragged without shame in the camp. Lives ruined for a few coins, a watch, a silk handkerchief, the mere pathetic pleasure of puffing out their chests and saying, "Look what we can do!"

Such men deserve a slow and agonizing end.

We were five in number and could have been an easy 20. Though you might think the recent depredations would impart caution, plenty wanted to return payment in kind. Angry men forget sensible restraint. Someone would greet us on the street or at church or stop by the shop, and whisper, " I've got a sharp knife, if you go hunting." Petros had his pick of helpers.

Memmik was his co-conspirator. Together they decided what and when, how and with whose assistance. I'd have questioned an alliance with any former prisoner except for Memmik's proven skills in subterfuge. He started devising plots when we were schoolboys, taking risks that awed us without his getting caught.

What got him arrested that one time was his Armenian fervor. Care and canniness kept him alive. He'd a rare ability to anticipate unexpected turns as a natural course, which enabled him to lead missions similar to ours in Erzerum and elsewhere. His feet would always be placed to outrun the next emergency. And finally, Memmik was as determined as Petros and I to avenge Sako's death. I accepted Petros' choice.

I'd let Petros move forward independently, until he and Memmik included Garabed and Aram Bedoian in their scheme. I'd have excluded the brothers for the same reasons they wanted to go. I feared anger and bereavement would make them reckless. And consider: if something happened to them, their parents would never, never recover.

Petros and Memmik maintained the brothers would take fewer risks, respecting their parents, and show more courage, lacking children. Moreover, that they were strong, fast, smart and determined. I saw contradictions in their logic but Petros and Memmik held fast.

We could have managed without them. But though three might have done as well, four was not an excessive number, and it was my participation made the number five. Five of us chanced discovery as we sneaked out the city and over the bridge into the marsh below the Circassian camp. Five were at risk, too many. I slept badly the night before, chewing on this. Yet we'd no time to refine our plan. Success depended on a partial moon and a clear sky. By the time these recurred our prize might have quit Erzerum.

In darkness we went alone to our rendezvous under the bridge. By various means we avoided the sentries, who at any rate dozed half the night. Petros and the Bedoians slipped through a break in the cemetery wall and descended a well-worn path ending at the Olti bridge, which they crossed separately without attracting attention. Meanwhile, I felt my way along a hidden passage my friend Hamed once showed me, just east of the garrison. I emerged beneath a granite ledge that shielded my route from eyes on the ramparts. Memmik was already at our rendezvous when I got there, though how he left the city, I don't know. He was a wily creature.

Memmik had scouted the camp some nights before, using information from the spy Pohar. He'd a torch concealed in a canvas-covered basket that also held a few small jade carvings for barter in a crisis. Fortunately unnecessary.

Memmik found the wanted pair encamped some 40 yards above this path, with twice that distance to the main camp. He drew a diagram showing the location. It was almost perfect for our purpose— close enough to the river for us to escape quickly, far enough from the slumbering Circassians to avoid being heard. We counted on finding our two birds in the same place when we made our move.

The best route for staying unseen was a sloppy course along a narrow strip of riverbank, wet and muddy most of the year, slick-sloped and unpredictably soft in some places, sometimes deep to the knees. I was glad to have well-made boots for it, though I'd have rather not plunged good leather into such muck.

We planned to attack our targets simultaneously and swiftly, before anyone raised an alarm. A trio composed of Memmik, Petros and Aram would silence the larger Cowbird, while I and Garabed handled Crow. We each had strong, sharp knives tucked into our belts. Memmik and I also carried short coils of knotted cord.

"Now," whispered Memmik.

"Now," we responded. And so we set forth along the river bank, running a few lengths at a time, then halting to look about and listen, with Memmik leading my brother and me, the Bedoians close behind.

Though I'd rehearsed this adventure many times through, I'd ignored the noise of throbbing blood behind my ears. The crescent moon above Palendoken Mountain cast dancing shadows on the snow crust but the light was too faint to read one another's faces.

Memmik held up a palm to us, then started up the slope. Half way he halted, crouching, then motioned us to follow. I felt for the knife at my waist and saw my brother do the same. "We're going to kill Sako's killers," sang through me. I felt no fear, no guilt, only fierce pride, excitement and urgency.

Within yards of a few recumbent figures on the rise, Memmik had us stop. We crouched and waited. Without shifting his feet, he turned his head compass-wise, scanning in all directions.

He hissed a word to Petros and flattened himself to the ground. "Flat!" hissed Petros to me before dropping down.

"What?!" I thought, at the same time I passed the message on and pressed myself into the snow. I saw then that only one of the blankets beside the fire wrapped a human form. The other blanket was empty. I realized we must wait for that missing person to return. Perhaps he'd heard us and had flown away.

My friend Hamed once said time becomes ice when you're waiting to attack, yet these minutes melted in the flow of possibilities. Meanwhile emotions from elation to anger to defeat pounded inside my head. I considered whether we'd best slip away immediately, postponing justice, or kill the lone man at once and go after the other when we could. Already, of course, Memmik had determined we should wait.

A momentary glint a few yards off told me my brother's knife was ready. I heard the sound of feet on snow and knew our wait was ending.

It turned out well we were five and no fewer, or they'd have cried out before we did justice. Had Cowbird shouted the instant he saw us instead of reaching for his blade, God knows what would have happened. Nothing good for us, for sure. As it was, that instant ended with Aram thrusting a wadded cloth into the albino's mouth so neither Memmik's garrote nor Petros' dagger could raise a scream. In the same moment, Garabed and I fell upon Crow. My cohort stifled the killer's voice with a balled rag as I stretched the cord between my hands. In the few blinks before that wretched creature took his final breath, the young widower applied his knife to the man's groin.

I remember an argument some years ago between Sako and our father when my brother was still a pharmacy student. Father said suffering changes a man's nature, Sako maintained it merely loosens his customary fetters. As I recall, we were discussing a man executed for some dreadful crime who'd been a respectable citizen until he lost his property and family in the Russian war.

The question has no single answer. At the time, I shared Sako's viewpoint—now I think both hold true for different people. I acknowledge the once gentle Bedoian brothers did cruel things after their wives were killed.

They showed no remorse or embarrassment at inflicting unspeakable harm to other human beings. They flicked it off as if torturing a man was schoolwork. "We had to teach those animals something about pain before they died," said Garabed.

I'd be a hypocrite to say I disagreed, though I couldn't have done such things to those Circassian birds. We could be sure one at least had murdered; we'd no report they'd raped. Yet I don't blame the Bedoian brothers for what they did. I pray most fervently that I never feel compelled to do the same.

We dragged the corpses in their blankets to the river, scouring our tracks with their weight. The bodies were light enough that two could manage to heave them by arms and feet into the moon-sparkled currents. Next we broke thin ice at the river bank to rinse hands and blades clean in the faint moonlight. Finally we filed back, Memmik leading, with me now the last. I pulled a snow-laden blanket over our footprints the remaining distance to the bridge.

The coins and boots we took from them, we promptly gave to beggars. Not knowing the rightful owner of a watch found in one boot, my brother passed it on to his informant Pohar. "Don't forget the Bedoian matter. They are waiting," Petros told him.

I arranged to call on Hamed and his father the next evening with Petros.

"A special matter has been weighing on us," I told them right off. "You should learn from us, not some police report." Then we recounted our resolution of Sako's murder.

We wanted them to understand that our vengeance was independent of our patriotism, that we have always been loyal to the Sultanate and will remain so. We admitted having sensed Sako's nationalist sympathies without knowing anything of his revolutionist efforts. We were close to honest in this, I think. I remember seeing his blackened finger, my suspicion. No moment passes clear of shame I didn't challenge my elder brother, didn't argue to persuade him from the Hunchak path. This sad fact is my business, not the Bercis'. The situation between us required repudiation, and God help us, we did so, putting it subtly this way and that, and then directly.

Whether we succeeded was not clear from their manner. They were courteous, as ever. I felt, Petros also, they were glad we'd spoken. Yet though they called us friends, and embraced us, we felt a lingering reserve in their response. Petros and I agreed we must keep fixed on one goal: Convincing them, as we truly believe, that all our interests rest on a stable balance between Muslim majority and Christian minority and that we have no appetite for an Armenian homeland.

It was spring before what was left of two mutilated bodies washed onto a riverbank at Ilidja, some miles west. We felt no remorse to hear that vultures feasted on the flesh. The bones were left to bleach in the sun. There was no investigation. My guess is that nobody at the Circassian camp cared enough to report those men were missing.

Reconciliation

Hamed   late March 1896

A rmenians endured many injustices. Unfortunate, even reprehensible—but not unique.

Wherever people live, so does injustice. I've read of natives and Africans mistreated in America; Irish starved by government decree; Jews exiled *en masse* from Spain; and Russian pogroms. The worst deeds here last fall owe to thugs and idlers, seldom the Army. I looked into this.

The facts are unavoidable: our government instigated the violence here in Erzerum and our military abetted it. Similarly, incidents in Trabizond, Baiburt, Erzincan, Bitlis and Urfa. Zeki's regiments assisted other incidents: they facilitated violence. These matters troubled Major Rustem, Shakir, me, Sergeant Mohamed and surely others who kept silent.

Granted, radicals exist within the Armenian millet. These criminals were and are hunted out, prosecuted. Why punish the entire millet?

Government decisions weren't mine to change. Even the highest rank of the Sultan's officers must obey. I considered resigning, then taking up some business or profession less constrained. Reflection showed me no clear path, although I sought one. Everyone must follow laws and accept government policies and programs, else a citizen must exile himself. Despite much thought, I was helpless to solve this riddle. My father helped me weigh the balance of Army and civilian life before I shook my shoulders and decided to stay put.

Another heaviness that winter was still more difficult. My father and I grew uneasy about our Christian friends next door after the incident revealed a revolutionist among them. The eldest son was smart and charming; he seemed loyal. Not so. He delivered weapons just before the bugle. He was killed running home, his death too easy for a traitor.

The discovery shattered a long held trust. We'd never heard a radical opinion from anyone of that family. From that brother, only the most ordinary complaints. We were astounded and disillusioned.

Information changed our first sympathetic grief for the family to doubt about their loyalty. The man's next brother was my closest friend from childhood. It made me nearly sick to think of his possible complicity.

Did the father of these brothers know? My own father denied any possibility and reminded me how often Nazar voiced contempt for Armenian radicals. Yet how could the father not have known of his eldest son's efforts to subvert our Empire?

Most important to me was my formerly beloved Martiros. How could he claim innocence of Sako's purposes? How could his two other brothers and their cousin Levon? How could these supposed friends let us risk so much to protect their numerous household? We'd assumed that family's complete loyalty to our government— and they encouraged us. We felt betrayed, duped, disrespected: stupid for endangering my career, my father's business, our family's well-being.

Inevitably our tether to the Kavafians was frayed by that traitor's death. Evenings together diminished in frequency, length and warmth of spirit. Our conversation lacked its former conviviality. Good manners replace affection at great loss.

Yet we let Ehsan continue his employment. It meant his life to him. Was this hypocrisy? Nor did I deny my wife her growing friendship with a younger brother's wife.

One evening a few weeks after my mother died, Martiros and Petros came over. It was our first time together since their condolence call. Their faces struck me as older, more lined than I remembered. I supposed they thought to resume our former backgammon tourneys and I was reluctant to agree.

Our usual courtesies were conducted with tangible reserve. Then the brothers' eyes met and Martiros spoke.

"We've felt the need to talk with you about our first-born brother." He frowned as he arranged his next words. "We sense that you (nodding to include both my father and me) may have misgivings about our family, in view of our brother's alliance with a revolutionary separatist movement."

"We can't deny that the circumstances have created –" I searched for a neutral word "discomfort for us." I sounded aloof, inevitably.

"You've been our close and valued friends for many years," said Petros. And that's the problem, I thought to myself as his brother entered in.

"The bonds between our families are too strong, too well established, and too important to let the gap between our families persist. Not if we can help it," said Martiros. "Please allow us to explain that our brother kept his activities secret from us."

I gazed at each in turn. "I'm sorry to say we find this hard to believe."

My father took up the reply. "We can accept he did not tell you directly, since you insist on this point. But surely you must have been aware that your late brother was involving himself in Hunchak affairs. Perhaps delivering guns, messages, whatever. How could you not have known?"

So our discussion continued. The two brothers were adamant as to their ignorance, their family's as well. They admitted uncertainty as to what Sako's wife knew. She later admitted to them she was aware he sometimes went to secret meetings at night. She insisted he never told her the reason. They were (they said) unaware he sneaked out after the family was asleep. The brothers more recently sneaked out to avenge Sako's murder: his killers were now dead.

We challenged them with many questions. We'd learned a secret group was set on avenging the murder of two Armenian hay carriers.

Martiros and Petros said they knew it occupied Sako certain nights but nothing more. They'd no idea of what his last hours demonstrated: his collusion with radicals and his helping them arm for so-called "self defense". Did they suspect? Did his denials fully convince them?

Other questions rose in silence: When a beloved brother chooses a traitor's path and you cannot dissuade him, do you betray him to authorities? Must blood ties always come first?

These difficult issues leave me uncertain as well. Our long discussion finally convinced me they sincerely believed in the need for a strong and well-established government such as the Sultanate. They were sure their business and community would collapse without it. They believed that if Armenian nationalists got some corner of the plateau for themselves, ruin would follow. The entire family shared these views, excepting Sarkis.

Not every issue was resolved. Yet the importance they placed on restoring our friendship persuaded first my father, then me, to accept their appeal. We were all exhausted and relieved when we finally clasped hands.

"We'll breathe more freely now," said Petros.

"We've missed you greatly," said Martiros.

"We too." And then more came to me. "And I must express something, for my father as well as for myself, and for my family. Our deep regret for the bloodbath here. The violence should not have happened. Much blame goes to opportunists. Your brother could have been arrested, tried in a court..." This wishful alternative was not altogether impossible.

We embraced.

A friendship is slow to build and breaks painfully. Trust cannot be restored overnight. But we were in a position now to begin rebuilding.

Astronomers with telescopes tell us winter's done, spring's here, disregard the snow and ice about us. However cold the wind, the vernal equinox lifts our spirits. I welcomed the end to a difficult season that stretched from October into March. I would savor the months into summer. The ease and pleasure of riding Keyif on the plateau, the shift in military routine. The men's fresh enthusiasm for their drills in air that smelled of earth and life.

Perhaps this reconciliation improved my father's spirits. Perhaps the change was destined anyway. He began leaving the house more often, meeting friends at cafes, exploring the bazaar, stopping in at provincial offices. He took summer excursions to the warm springs at Ilidja, visited the market fair at Erzincan, and in August sailed from Trabizond to Constantinople. He spent the next three weeks arranging an enterprise in woolen goods with friends in the Commerce Ministry—and returned with bright eyes and a springy step. He confessed to having met a pretty widow, was considering remarriage. Odd, his seeking my counsel on such a topic, yet our family was becoming accustomed to a new formation.

I advised the happy man to take it slowly. After all, Khadijah was matriarch now, and managing the household as well as any woman could. Much as she might welcome the right new mother-in-law, she might be happier without this change. It would wait, at any rate, until Father traveled again to the capital.

Four

Marjan Decides

May 1896 through September 1897

A Difficult Summer, A Decision and Delay

❋ · ❋ · ❋ · ❋ · ❋ · ❋ · ❋ · ❋ · ❋ · ❋

Marjan   May 1896 to August 1897

easons lined up like fence posts to keep us in the city. Nazar was half-paralyzed, hamidieh still roved the mountains, Martiros was owed a flock of sheep, Petros was trading in Russia. Most of our friends stayed home too, except the Shabanians. Their village was miles west of ours, a safer place, but too far for an easy visit. We did go see them once on one of those summer days that start out perfect and then dark clouds blow in. We had to have our picnic indoors, but the sky did clear for our journey back. We were glad to see everyone.

The family managed a few Sunday outings to the hilltop town of Hintzk. The old people took a hired carriage and the rest of us divided between Shapundi's cart and the usual hired horse wagon. But a few outings to play in a stream don't match having a pond and raft and running space. All summer I felt sorry for the children.

We did our best for the young ones, yet some days were misery. Toumia picked at Heranoush, scolded Artashes, sometimes even ill-tongued Vagram. She was never so ill-tempered to our children with Petros home, even when summer was hottest.

Once, carrying wash, I play-tripped to take her fury off Heranoush. I landed in a pile of stockings and underwear beside the basket and my knees wore bruises for a month. Another time I got Yiri to interrupt with some made-up urgent question and Heranoush was able to disappear.

Our staying in the city was good, as things turned out. My mother fell very ill in the heat. She grew worse despite the good rich broth we made her, the doctor's powders and tonic, and our care.

Was the consumption already in her lungs that week in the safe house? Before then we used to tease her for her appetite, how she'd eat half a bowl of stew, then finish off two pastries and a few sweetmeats. Not after. Still, we all were changed, we didn't think her sick. Seeing the skin below Mother's eyes turn dark as burnt walnuts, we blamed her nights of nursing Barsam. We thought her coughing was something ordinary. All winter in church you hear a concert of rasping and hawking. We call it "Lenten chest" because it's generally gone by Easter.

Lent was nearly over by the time Barsam first got himself to the privy with only a cane. He hardly moved for five long months, but now he began to shuffle this way and that. He shook Mother and Nora away from his arm, got deaf if they told him to rest. Some spider was biting him. I was afraid for his family, though I said nothing. Two days later, he called for his mule, climbed up, and fell right off onto a mud patch. I had to laugh, hearing about it. Before long he got his balance back, and rode off to his beloved shop without a thank you that I heard of. He said he needed men's company after too much of women. Men never think to ask women if they get tired of men.

By the time her nurse-work ended, Mother shrank to a bent old woman whose head no longer came to my shoulder. Her dress hung loose as if stretched wet on the bias. Simply making our tea wore her out—she could barely move the kettle from the back of the stove to the front.

"I'm just a tired old widow, let me be," she said, so we let her be. She stayed on at Zari's doing little, and seemed content. Weak bodies come with age, we told ourselves. I remember Varti saying, "She's lost her house, her neighbors, such things make people old. Look at my in-laws, they barely sleep, they don't look well…"

Varti herself looked far from well, I thought, but she was so much improved by then, I was amazed each time I saw her. It was as if she knew she had to be healthy for the children, must put away the mad woman and act like a loving mother-aunt again. Her husband told me how the day the twins came home, she bathed her body and her hair, combed it with Marta's help. They had to hold her down to get her clean before that. "We were startled at how fast she changed—it was a miracle!" he said.

❈ ❈ ❈

When we got the twins back safe, we thought the family would be happy again, same as before. As if what you want will happen! Truth was, all were miserable, fearful, the twins, the men and women, the other children. None of them could see a door open or hear a heavy footstep or a loud noise without turning into ice. One might freeze, another cry, another gasp and tremble. Different shapes, one dough. Others said it was worse for the girls than their family, but I'm not sure. Varti told me they were all afraid of their shadows. Any time the men went out, one brother stayed home with the rest. The women and children never left the house and courtyard.

Varti was still pale and drawn, though the wild look was gone from her eyes. Heranoush and I were on our way from visiting my mother on a fine spring day. My daughter was upstairs with the twins. When I asked Varti to tell me her worries, she surprised me.

"My biggest worry is Rupen," she said. "He comes home from school and doesn't want to play. He just sits by himself and says nothing. He doesn't laugh, he doesn't talk. He won't tell me what's making him sad."

She stirred a pan of sliced onions in oil while their house cat rubbed against our legs. Then my friend gave a sad, deep sigh.

"We are leaving Erzerum."

Her news came like a club against my forehead. I hardly heard her explain. I remember her saying the family decided they must find a new life somewhere free of reminders. Here, fear squeezed every breath. They would try Constantinople. If that didn't work, they'd go on, perhaps—tell no one, it must be secret—to Athens.

"You can't!" the words boiled out. I saw the cat jump to its shelf over the stove and I couldn't remember its name. My head was a stew. I was losing my friend, our friends.

Dear, beloved Varti wept with me—yet she showed no thread of doubt. She said they saw no choice: Erzerum meant only misery for them. Leaving for another place gave them hope for a scrap of happiness some day.

At home, Heranoush and I sobbed together. We went over Varti's reasons and what the twins and Marta told Heranoush. Some of the family were sleepless, some dreamt horrors, another trembled or choked or wept at a touch. All those reasons! In the end, this one: the family was too afraid to stay.

"But can't they see, they'll get over this, they'll forget it!" wailed Heranoush.

"I told her that but she didn't hear me," I said. I was not as sure of it myself.

Vagram told me Rupen wasn't still his friend. "Rupen won't play with me. He's changed." My son's feelings were hurt. I did my best to help my child understand.

Children play a game where everyone joins hands and follows the leader around the yard and through the house, turning here and twisting there. They finally make a big circle and then coil tight around the leader. Wherever you are in the coil, you can touch 10 friends. But if some giant slices a wedge out of the coil, a pit opens and some friends disappear. You have others, but it's not the same. Well, I was in that coil with a deep wedge where Varti and her family should be. I felt for my daughter. She must grow into a woman with a gaping hole beside her.

Many times I comforted Heranoush and then went off to weep. Sometimes I dripped tears in the middle of helping Vagram with his boots or filling pastries with Maxime. I tried not to think how hard it is to put true feelings in a letter and how much better to read a face. A letter can't match a visit. Yiri and Aunt Zabel, Sarah, too, would try to console me.

"They won't like Constantinople and if they do, it's not so far! Don't we know 20 people who make the trip every year or two?" Yiri said one time when I was red-eyed. We were all peeling turnips together in the kitchen.

"Think how nice it will be when you visit them in Constantinople!" Sarah said. Her face shone with longing, like a child hearing a fairy tale. She imagined lovely silk dresses with velvet capes and clean, paved streets—it made me smile at her through my tears. I'd promised Varti to keep her secret. Even Marta and the twins and Heranoush didn't know.

Many people we knew were getting ready to start over in Constantinople, or were already gone to its Armenian quarter. Everyone believed Papa Meserian when he said it was a better place to sell violins and flutes. Petros and Martiros talked a lot with Karekin and his brother about doing business there. I heard there were 20 times as many musicians as here.

Artashes has a book that shows it's not so far from Constantinople to Athens. From Athens you can take a train to France or Germany, or a ship to Italy or Africa and other places.

Their secret plan was America, or if not America, then France. Constantinople was only for a time, until they could travel on. Of course, I tried to change Varti's mind. If I could turn her around, she'd persuade the others. "At least stay in Turkey where you understand what people say!" I pleaded. It was no use, I couldn't move her.

"Dear Marjan, I hate to leave you. I will never have a better friend. But we want to live where Armenians are safe. Not afraid."

She took my hands, pressed them in hers.

"You should leave, too."

It was a strange idea to me just then. I only gasped and shook my head.

Of course, it takes money to move somewhere else, and 100 times more to get out of the country. And nerves, too, as it's forbidden. The Meserians were fortunate to get a good price for their house. I was glad my friend Sophia's family bought it, not strangers. Papa Meserian also sold a fine orchard not far from the city, to Garabed Shabanian. Papa M sold other property too, so they'd have quite a fine amount waiting at the bank in Constantinople.

The Meserians were smart to get away before summer. Later on, so many Armenians were trying to leave, they had to take next to nothing for their houses. The men talked of little else but who was selling what for how much.

It worried me how a family's life-long possessions could be sold away, like carpets woven with birds and deer and flowers, even signed to honor some special birth or wedding or prize. Familiar things that gave comfort and pleasure. Braziers handed down for generations, pillowcases worked by young hands for a dreamed-of wedding chest, necklaces and bracelets and ornaments that marked births and marriages. Precious things traded for cold coins and lifeless notes, things that can never be got back. Like being lost in the bottom of a lake. Or lost at sea.

Late May they joined a caravan to Trabizond—they planned to take a ship from there. The same week we waved them off, Mother fainted twice from coughing spells and we had to open our eyes to her illness. She ate a wren's meals, slept less than a fly. She barely moved from the Melikians' parlor divan. Even Mother was for having the doctor visit.

Doctor Tashjian said she was too thin and tired, needed rest and nourishment. He didn't let on how sick she was, though she worked to breathe. We set about lifting her appetite with special soups and sweetmeats. We got hopeful when she tasted tiny bits of anything. Her best days she took long naps or at least rested with her eyes shut. Then she'd be almost lively for an hour or so. She was coughing worse each day.

Sometimes she stopped what she was saying to make a rasping sound, then went on talking without seeing she'd scared me. She kept a scrap of linen in her sleeve to wipe her mouth.

One summer afternoon while we watched the boys playing ball-toss in the small kitchen yard, Nora told me Mother's handkerchief was dotted with blood. She woke from napping hot with fever. We got her to sip some water, then she fell right back to sleep.

From that hour, she was not only an invalid, but set on starving. Feeding should follow a fever, but she wanted nothing. Now and then, she swallowed a spoonful of broth or mulberry juice—mostly, she turned her head away. Bread didn't tempt her, with jam or without. Not raisins or beans, not the soft stewed lamb Doctor Tashjian said she needed. She showed no appetite for life, either.

I longed for Sarkis' way with medicines, for however I mixed Khagorian's powders, she spat them out. We thought her cough might turn her inside out. Her breath smelled like rotting cheese and what she brought up was horrible to look at. At first we had the children come close to greet her, but they made faces without thinking. They didn't mean disrespect. We let them only stop at the doorway and say "Hello, Grandmother." She showed no sign she heard.

We filled her ears with bits and scraps, family, weather, birds, what flowers were in bloom. She sometimes said a word or two and sometimes nothing. I don't think she heard much we said. Maybe she was thinking of more important things. She said little and made little sense.

When she was awake she sometimes watched us and sometimes looked at the picture on the wall or the brazier near her feet. One time I was talking about Heranoush's quilt-work and Mother began to mumble something about the tassels on her pillow. The girl still collected tassels then.

We knew she was going to leave us soon. In those last weeks, it was Heranoush who looked after the boys at home, while I stayed day and night with Mother at Zari's. How any of us kept from catching her illness is a mercy from God.

My husband was away three months so he missed most of this. By some small miracle I happened to be home the day he got back. My daughter was feverish with flu so my sisters were going to do without me for a couple of days. When Petros came through the door, tears poured down my face and kept coming.

"She's so happy you're home!" Yiri told him. His eyes were wet, too. That night in bed I was able to put aside my tired flesh and we became husband and wife again.

Near the end your mind grows clear, it's said. I'm sure it happened the day she reached up and pulled my face towards hers. "A better life," she said.

"In heaven," I answered, guessing at what she meant.

Her fingers clutched at my dress-collar. "No, no, for Varti! For her family, all of them!" She gave a few hard coughs and then her voice was strong again for a moment. "It will be better there. Happier."

"I hope so, Mother."

She mumbled something more before her voice faded into sleep. The only words I picked out were "...you too..." She started me thinking.

❊ ❊ ❊

It surprised me, the grief and shock I felt. For months we knew she was on her way to meet the Host, we knew it would be soon, and even so it felt like a cudgel knocked me down and left me broken. Bleeding. I strained to do the things I must do every day. For a long time after, I felt like I was really somewhere else, with her. I tried to pay attention to my tasks and my family instead of daydreaming. Sometimes Yiri or Sarah or Heranoush stepped close and clapped their hands the way we do with a child who doesn't listen. Toumia scolded me many times. Petros was more patient, and told me more than once to think of today's tasks now and save my memories for later. It was not just grief that came with my mother's death. It was feeling I'd lost my roof overhead, my guardian on the path to the world after this one.

All this helped change my mind about leaving. It was no new idea. I remembered Martiros and Petros talking for years about setting up a shop in Russia. They both saw business growing better with someone living there. What kept us home before this was me—I wanted to stay near my mother. And Varti, and my sisters, and other friends as well. Everything and everyone we cared for was in Erzerum. Petros understood.

It was different now. Mother with Sako in that place of grace (for surely such a good man is forgiven the flaw that killed him). So many friends now far from Erzerum. Most everyone dear to me except my husband and children was either gone already from our lives or uncertain. How long before my sisters' families, too, set out for a safer place? Even our dear Khadijah, who knew where the Army might send her captain? And life in this household was so bad, some days. Toumia worse tempered. Patriarch…

And of course, as days started getting cool, we recalled the October past, its good and bad. How Sako let the children out-race him on the Feast of the Holy Translators, how the brides and the twins poured joy on us. How could we quit thinking "just a year ago, he…, or just a year ago, she …?" I tried not to think back to anything that made me cry. That month was hard.

※ ※ ※

"Shall we all go with you to Russia next spring?" I was curled against him, warm, matching my breath. I felt his surprise before his soft laugh. Excited and happy, we lay awake whispering a long time. Petros had to talk over many things with Martiros before deciding. We kept our plan secret from the family. Heranoush read my face and asked why I looked about to fly around the room.

"You'll learn about it soon," I promised. It was different news I told her some weeks later.

Petros set off alone that spring to trade; the trip was too risky for a newly-born baby. All through the winter our eyes shared joy, knowing a fourth child was coming at last. God seemed to be favoring us again. I stopped my constant mourning. Instead I was often light headed, light footed, a feather—my thoughts lifted and blew away like lint.

Of course, many times I was weighted by longing to lie down, and must lift my legs to ease the throbbing. A chamber pot became my friend—and even so, I could not always get back to sleep, what with knots in my legs and back and kicks in my belly, and the worries that come loose at night. In time my belly got like a stone pulling on my back, as bad as when I carried Vagram, maybe worse. At least it didn't surprise me. I worked less and rested more. I was grateful for the kindly favors given pregnant women in a big household—it's different being pregnant with no other women at hand.

Toumia sometimes surprised me with words that sounded polite or grudging instead of harsh. Now and then she even spoke gently to me and Heranoush, showing something soft she kept hidden like a quail egg too small to share. My belly was only part of why she was kinder to us. She liked our plan to move to Russia. The men saw it helping the business. I think she saw it differently. A smaller household is easier to manage and less noisy. She'd get more rest. And I think without me to keep in my place, she hoped to show her soft part more.

We both were eager for a Sarkis to honor our lost brother, yet when the midwife told me, I laughed that the babe would be Virginie. Our fourth child was small and delicate, pretty to my eyes. She grew to look a little like her namesake—we saw my mother in the girl's mouth and chin and sometimes in her eyes. More than her looks, she showed my mother's spirit, following everything that moved with her eyes, refusing to sleep or nurse when she saw children nearby. Even learning to walk, if she fell she pushed up like a worm and kept on without a cry. I was sure she'd talk early, learn to read before she went to school. I was happy knowing she'd be home with me for years after Heranoush married. A daughter is a mother's blessing.

By late summer our babe was finally strong enough for the trip to Russia. Petros reminded me it would be difficult, risky, uncomfortable. I was set on going even so.

Journey to Kars

Marjan   late summer 1897

W e waited until bedtime to tell the boys, and even so gave them the same story as their cousins. That at dawn we'd set out to visit a long-lost third cousin who lived near the border. The truth was too dangerous if the wrong ears heard it. All summer I bit my tongue while Artashes and Vagram cooked plans for marsh-bird hunting in October and winter sledding parties. Then the older boys set Vagram fretting and moaning about the harsh-handed teacher he was supposed to get. My saying he'd be all right as long as he behaved didn't soothe him. I had to turn away from saying more.

With my daughter it was different. Heranoush came into this world only 15 months ahead of Artashes, but she was years wiser, able to keep the secret. I never thought of the burden for her. We'd been saving some pretty striped chambray for a new dress and I had to tell her why it must wait: fabric takes less room packed for a trip.

"This secret you must not tell even Astghig: Papa will be taking us on a long trip soon. If anyone finds out, we might all go to jail, so don't say a word."

Heranoush rushed at me with questions until she read my face. Then together we laid out our pattern to cut the proper lengths for folding into a chest with her quilts. That done, we returned to our quilt-making. I didn't tell her where we were going or for how long, yet she seemed to guess we were leaving Erzerum for a new place. I thanked the saints for giving me a bright girl who figured things out without needing every question answered.

Sharing this secret drew me and my daughter close as spoons

that summer. I didn't look at her when others talked about the fall and winter so our eyes couldn't give us away. Once Yiri made me promise to arrange a harvest party for when we finished putting up our preserves and pickles. Heranoush gave me a look that said, "How can you lie like that?" and I felt a flush heat my head and chest.

Knowing we'd leave by autumn gave me patience when Toumia scolded or Yiri chattered or Sarah sulked. And the joy my little Virginie gave me! They say there's nothing more content than a fresh-nursed baby, but I think a nursing mother, cooing into her baby's eyes, is even happier. So I paid little attention to what my elder daughter was feeling. Once after church that summer I heard her say to some of her girlfriends, "I think it's pretty stupid to leave here because it's never going to be better anywhere else!" At the time I thought she was clever at pretending.

Sitting one day in the sunshine, watching the children chase their India rubber ball around the courtyard, I heard Heranoush and Artashes quarrelling.

"Just wait, your friends will forget about you, next year you won't have any friends!" she hissed. Artashes hurled the ball at her, causing a yelp and a bruise, and I sent them both inside.

Later the girl boiled over like a hot stew spitting out a cold quince. "You don't care about me, you just want to go off with Papa, I have to leave my friends, I won't have Astghig to help me, there won't be anybody but you and my stupid brothers to talk to!" And so forth until she tired of complaints and cried in my arms. From that day until we left, I tried to make her see the best parts ahead, as if I was sure.

Petros decided not to hire soldiers for fear they might betray or rob us—or be jailed for helping us escape. Our route northeast from Erzerum was not one of the usual trade routes and should be safe for ox-carts and mules. The one bandit he knew of stole only horses. Petros was going to keep a loaded rifle under his seat—woe to a robber who came too close! And woe to my husband, if soldiers found it (though I think the Captain knew about it).

We told our good neighbors the safe story about visiting a cousin who lived near the border. Maybe Khadija guessed from my long hug, but I did hold back my tears. It was hard knowing I might never see her again. Saying goodbye to Nora and Zari, to Souren, Berthe and Sofia, all those goodbyes were hard. I told myself we'd be back to visit, just as we told the children. Who knew if we would, or not? Who knew anything for sure about the future?

The family rose early to see us off. They pressed gifts on us, mostly food, and we gave things back to lighten our cart. I gave my carved animals to the children. Little Arsha got my favorite, a small bird carved of ivory from India. I felt for that poor orphan girl with Toumia as stepmother. Her brother was fortunate, having Martiros for a guardian, and school. Boys are fortunate in many ways.

The hugs and smiles at our gifts reminded me how giving is more pleasing than getting, even for a child. Little Vagram was happy at making his cousins' faces shine.

Next came farewells, the men cheery, the women weepy, except Toumia. She filled the air with warnings of dangers and reminders to the children, though I cannot imagine why she chose that time to scold. Perhaps it was her only way to delay our leaving. When at last she kissed our cheeks, her eyes were wet. I felt sorry for her. She didn't know if she'd ever see her son and grandchildren again. She loved even me in her way.

Our leave-taking made me cry with the other women, but Heranoush seemed to be somewhere else, sleep walking. That whole first day her eyes stayed dry and she barely spoke. It worried me. The next day I heard her tell her brothers she missed Astghig and her other cousins. She held her tears back from us by day. Sometimes at night I heard her sobbing into her pillow when she thought everyone was asleep.

Once we reached the high meadows east of the city and saw the road rising into the distant mountains, Heranoush was as excited as the rest of us. Explorers must feel that way when they find new lands, excited by what may come and eager to keep going. I began to understand the joy some men get from danger.

Petros let Artashes take turns handling the two mules while the rest of us walked beside the cart. It was easy to keep up on level ground. When it sloped, we either held the cart back or else pushed. On steep slopes the driver walked beside the lead mule and someone carried the baby. Petros said the mules' health mattered more than ours. He took care they got enough rest.

Our first night we sheltered at a so-called inn that was more a stable than real lodging, in a village of seven or eight small houses. As Toumia predicted, we picked up fleas that tormented us for a month, even Petros and Artashes, who usually aren't bothered. She also warned us about lice that thankfully never found us. Fleas were trial enough, the itching night after night making us feel family to Job. I'd have traded a bracelet for a few sprigs of jewelweed, the remedy my mother taught me. I finally spotted some near the trail the day before we got to the border. I laughed aloud as I picked it, too late to do much good.

A young woman brought us a battered pot filled with mutton stew. We welcomed the warm food, stringy and salty as it was. We were used to like meals on our summer trips. The cherry juice was too sweet, and I warned the boys they'd be sick if they kept on drinking it. The spring water tasted strange and gave me belly cramps. All the same I think only Heranoush was unhappy that night. We were excited at starting our adventure and our discomforts looked small as our fleas.

The second night, a Kurd chief Petros knew let us sleep in a hut behind his own. His wife served us goat stew, beans, goat milk and hot tea. Petros showed us how to use a piece of flatbread like a spoon, but it's harder than it looks. A lot of stew fell into our laps before it got to our mouths. The chief's children got to giggling at us and before long we were laughing along with the Kurds at our clumsy hands. Petros gave the chief some green muslin in thanks the next morning and we parted like good friends.

Most of the next day Petros and Artashes pushed the cart from the sides while the mules pulled, helped a little by Heranoush,

Vagram and me pushing from the back. At day's end Vagram showed me a big blister under his left big toe. It must have hurt a lot, though he was too brave to let on. I rubbed the toe with a salve from my medicine sack and wrapped it with a rag. In the morning I wrapped it twice to hold the boot off the blister. By the end we all had blisters, even Petros. Our boots weren't to blame for the rough rocks or for whole days of walking. We longed to put on house slippers and we dreamt of good feet, healed of blisters.

We took shelter that night in a clump of trees too small to break a cold north wind, though we'd twigs to burn and leaves to spread under our quilts. Our meal was pasterma, dried apricots and hot tea. I wished for a stray goat to milk. Still, it was marvelous, with more bright stars than anyone can imagine. They seemed closer than at home. We sang a few songs before we fell asleep, our legs aching.

Petros promised us a village for the next night, and at noon pointed to a dark spot in the valley far below, saying "There it is!" Hours pushing along the trail seemed to bring the spot no closer. We reached it just before the sun dropped below the hills. We heard a rooster crow, sheep bleat, a woman calling a cow, and children's voices. Small children ran towards us, shrieking and laughing, then scattered as a black-bearded, barrel-chested man came forward, gripping a stave in each hand. Close behind was a pair of lads about Artashes' age, wearing the man's joined thick eyebrow and his same small nose. The boys looked from our family to their father to Petros to our mules and back, their eyes hopping from one of us to the next. What about us fascinated them? It must be strangers hardly ever reach their hamlet.

Petros bowed to black-beard with phrases I barely understood, pointing toward far off mountains. Soon black-beard led us to his home in the village. Entering, we were greeted by two veiled women I took to be mother and daughter, for both were short and heavy, and one moved as easily as a cat. They pointed us to floor cushions and gave us a towel and water for our hands. The younger one brought a tray with thinned yogurt in stoneware cups and a dish of salted chickpeas. We listened quietly while our host showed Petros this and that favorite object and showed how he would hang a curtain between our families when time came for sleep. Easier than in the Kavafian kitchen, for the rafter here was barely above my head. When the youngsters went outside, Artashes forgot to stoop—and bruised his forehead. He was already an inch or two taller than his father.

After Virginie was done feeding, the women invited me outside to see their cow, and then the toner oven where they baked their flatbread, their butter churn, a yogurt tub and a pair of large cheeses hanging from a roof-beam in the shed. These things were somewhat different from what we were used to and I thought interesting for Heranoush. I found her not far from the cowshed, with Artashes. He was chatting with our host's sons and a couple of other youths. It was almost too dark by now to make out faces, but none of them looked much over 20. I heard my daughter giggle. As I walked over, Vagram came tearing up, pursued by two others, all dripping wet and shrieking joyfully.

"We fell in the stream!"

Vagram ran galloping for his big brother. He nearly knocked him down, wrapping his arms around Artashes' knees and smearing his pants with mud while the other youngsters shrieked and shouted. Petros and our host laughed at the children, then our host sent them home to wash.

Heranoush and I gave the two women what help we could as they set out a meal of stewed mutton with beans, barley pilaf, pickled cucumbers, cheese and yogurt. My daughter helped serve while I went behind a curtain to nurse Virginie. Perhaps an hour passed while my baby fed and I drowsed contentedly with thoughts that the trip was going well. No illness, no bandits, no hamidieh, and in a few days more, Russia.

Suddenly, my daughter rushed through the curtains and flung herself down beside me.

"Mama! Something terrible!" she gasped. "I'm scared, I don't know what to do!" she wailed, the baby wailed, and for a time I felt like the woman with 15 children to care for. At last I managed to get the baby back to sleep so I could let Heranoush explain.

"They say Papa must leave me with them. They want to keep me here! Please, don't let Papa do that!" she cried. I promised to keep her safe. It was a custom in these places for girls to marry as young as 10 or 11 so they'd not get kidnapped. I suspected a marriage offer from one of the older youths she and her brother were talking with. It was time I warned her about the risks of flirting!

Handing the sleeping baby to her sister, I went to eavesdrop on the men. If they saw me standing in the shadow behind the big wood box, they didn't show it. They went on talking back and forth and around and back. I couldn't understand every word but it was clear Heranoush was right, she was wanted for a bride. What a tangle for all of us, city Armenians and country Armenians. Not all tangles can be combed out without damage.

My daughter's unwelcome suitor was not discouraged by Petros' tactful refusals. He was the host's eldest son and thought this gave him claim on any visiting maiden he chose. Whatever Petros said, the young man kept repeating that he was strong, of good stock, and ready to marry. He pleaded gently one moment, shouted at us the next. How could we refuse their happiness, he asked, when our daughter herself clearly wanted to marry him? He pointed again and again to his eyes and mouth, putting on a false smile to show the laughs and flirty looks our daughter gave him. He kept insisting she show him her heart was his. Whatever the son said, the father followed with like words. Both were surprised and angry we refused their proposal of marriage.

"We're the best family in these mountains!" they kept saying. They refused to believe Heranoush was too young to leave her parents, as Petros kept telling them. The discussion made me think of a cow tethered tight to its circle—it sees nothing new and does nothing new, whatever time of day or direction it faces. After a while I returned to Heranoush and my baby. I offered to bring her something to eat but she wanted nothing. For the sake of my baby I took some yogurt, but it tasted sour on my tongue.

We arranged our mats and quilts so hers was in the very middle. Though I said nothing, I shared her fear our host and son might steal her from us in the night. Vagram and Artashes whispered plans to stop any attack. When Petros finally settled into place, I whispered, were we safe? "For now, probably," he replied. His face was grim as he blew out the candle. It was not a good time to ask more questions. It was some while before his breathing turned steady.

When he shook us awake it was still dark. My first thought was that someone was trying to take our daughter. "Heranoush?" I croaked, seeing nothing in the dark. "Keep silent! Hurry! We must get away before they wake up!" he whispered. He held his hand across Vagram's mouth as he came awake. "Up, quickly!"

I rocked Virginie against me while the children gathered our belongings in darkness. For every little sound we made I expected a shout from the other side of the curtain. My heart was pounding so loud! Carefully as we could manage, we tiptoed out the narrow door. In the early light I could barely make out our mules with my husband just beyond the cowshed. Heranoush and her brothers were already running toward them. An angel must have kept them from tripping on the rocky ground. I held my breath until they'd thrown the bed stuff into the wagon. I hurried to catch up. Petros was done harnessing the mules and now Artashes helped him fasten the cart-braces. Heranoush tucked in a quilt that was hanging over the edge. I knew she was frightened even before someone shouted from the house.

After the shout came many outcries—the whole family must have come awake.

"Quick! Run!" Petros sent the children along a path as he climbed to the driver's seat and pulled me up beside him. The jarring set the baby crying against my breast.

"Quick!" and so with hands and hearts cold and trembling, Virginie wailing, the children stumbling like blind soldiers and our host and his sons yelling for us to come back, we left the little village of our countrymen in fear and haste, rudely, like thieves.

I felt bad to leave without thanking the women for their kindness. They must think us rude big city Armenians! Their village would tell the story to future travelers. These thoughts weighed me until I chanced to ask for gloves (evenings and mornings were cold now) and Petros told me he'd left a fine set of them along with a bag of wheat as gifts for our would-be bridegroom's family. He'd seen a pair of tattered gloves hanging from a peg. I doubt the family saw the new gloves' good quality. My shame about the misunderstanding lifted whenever I warmed my hands inside my sleeves, and finally dried to nothing.

The next few days we kept looking over our shoulders to make sure no one followed. We barely stopped until we got well away from the valley. It was a great relief to settle into a simple travelers' hut in another small hamlet the next night and find no young men about. Just the same, I made Heranoush veil her face, and warned her not to even glance toward any males. She didn't need her father's advice on the subject. She hardly left my side until the day we crossed the border.

Travel grew harder further east. Sometimes huge rocks had to be heaved off a path, and sometimes a path disappeared or was blocked by a rockslide. Petros pointed out dark clouds one day, and not long after we were wet through and chilled, but we kept on, guided by his compass and eager to reach the next village. An important nail broke and we almost lost a wheel. Luckily he had a piece of nail-iron for this. The problem cost us half a day and much worry. It was raw, barren land little traveled even in summer. Petros said it was Kurd country, yet for two days we saw no one except a lone goatherd with three or four goats. It made me uneasy.

One day we had to cross the same stream three times, first on a fine arched stone bridge and later on a rickety bundle of logs. The last time we had to wade into rushing, icy water above my knees. Vagram wanted to wade as well, but was too small, and Artashes carried him high on his shoulders, Vagram crowing like a cock the whole time while his big brother scolded him to be still.

Once Artashes fished with a length of heavy thread from my sewing bag and a hook he found. While the family fed on bread and cheese, the clever lad caught a fine big trout, and how could we not make a cook-fire for it? The fish tasted marvelous, although we charred it, lacking oil for the skillet.

We saw no one for hours until we passed a woman working alone in a field. She stood watching as if we were the strangest sight in her life. A bony ram grazed near her. Soon after we came to a cluster of small stone and mud huts and stopped for the night. A man called out on seeing us, and in a moment we were surrounded by what seemed the whole village, looking us over with exclamations that seemed friendly, though only Petros understood them. They were as weathered and wiry as mountain people everywhere. The men wore baggy, clay-colored trousers that must have been great trouble both to make and to wash—and also to wear. The women's skirts were light, faded hues and prints, not the dark shades of our usual dress. Their feet were wrapped in bulky stockings quite unlike ours.

Two of the bolder children ran up to Vagram, said something, and ran away again before Petros even got down from his seat. Vagram began making silly faces, his favorite trick, and soon others were doing the same, giggling and hooting. Meanwhile, my husband went to greet the village elder, a little man leaning on his cane while chickens scratched around his feet. The scraggly-bearded old Kurd motioned to a younger man, likely his son, and the three men talked, with Petros pointing out our route and explaining his family. Soon everyone was bowing and smiling at us, and I murmured to Heranoush, it will be safe here.

A woman came over and waved her arm to have us follow her home. I hesitated at the door, ready to take off my shoes, but she waved us inside as we were. A rooster followed in as if he belonged and our hostess took no notice. Another woman greeted us, whether an older wife, or mother, was not clear. She sent the rooster and a chicken out the door with an easy push from her broom. That night we shared the room with many chickens, as well as the family. The fleas we brought in our bedding got new playmates that night. When we went on the next morning I hoped we left more than we added. It was the least of our worries, right then.

On our way to the house, we'd seen three young men idling against a stone wall, tossing pebbles now and then at a chicken. They showed no interest in us except for staring at Heranoush as if her body was bare as her face. Though we kept our eyes down, I saw tin badges on their shirts. At first it meant nothing to me—only later when I heard our hostess say "hamidieh" did my heart jump into my gullet. It was easy enough for me and Heranoush and the baby to stay indoors, but the soldiers would know our family was here, and Armenian, and headed for the border.

The soldiers, we learned, were resting a lame horse before riding on to Erzincan. They gave no sign of interest in our plans—they seemed only bored, lazy and indifferent. Yet we felt uneasy about them.

They say a guilty man sees only shadows. Throughout the evening meal I saw doubts in our hosts' faces and read unease in my husband's eyes. I saw him tighten at outside noises, as I did too—we pretended not to hear the shouts, running footsteps, thuds. Trying to sleep, I woke, dozed, woke again, like a ball of dough now kneaded, now left to rest, now kneaded, through the night hours. Aloud, I blamed our fleas. In my head were jabbing pictures of soldiers arresting us and worse. Petros, too, barely slept until nearly time to rise. It was the chickens that woke us when daylight finally came.

Petros gave the man gifts that pleased him, two fine sharp knives, and for the women, pretty combs and matched mirrors. For his children, an India rubber ball. For the family, to share out as they chose, a bag of dry apricots. Nothing expensive, but the whole family smiled at what he gave them. My husband was sure the family would cause us no trouble. The soldiers were reason enough to worry. Sometimes you follow your nose forward because you can't walk backwards. Some people never walk a new road. They live and die in the same place. Well, Erzerum had soldiers to worry about, that's why we were on this road. We weren't going to turn around now.

❀ ❀ ❀

We did visit this pretend relative, a small friendly man with a matching wife. Both laughed a lot so I saw they'd only five or six teeth between them. Their son lived nearby with his wife and wife's mother and two young children. Father and son embraced Petros warmly and the women fussed over Virginie. One of the grandsons followed after Vagram and it was good to see the two boys playing together without bothering Artashes and Heranoush.

The couple shared a thick stew of okra, mutton and bulgur with us, smiling proudly as if it was a feast dish. Perhaps they ate with special delight because chewing was so slow for them. Most people eat too fast. Smoke filled the air and I kept filling our cups from the pitcher, even knowing I'd be up in the night. The couple made space for us to sleep in their best, warmest corner.

It was our last night before the boxes, and I woke early, feeling already as if heavy sacks were pressing me down. I tried to think of happier things, just as I tell my children. It took some time before I was able to breathe slowly and raise my head and shoulders to see the rest of my family still asleep. I woke Virginie, for I wanted her awake until time for our box and her medicine.

Before we left, Petros talked for some time with our host as to what to tell soldiers who might come asking about us. The man saw no reason to worry, my husband told me. He gave them a generous supply of bulgur, rice and dry fruit. Our trip taught me to value the plenty in our Erzerum markets. I never expected so many people would prize a gift of dry figs and walnuts.

When we left Erzerum, the four boxes were filled with foods to trade and eat along the way. By the time we reached the border, eight days later, those boxes were still well filled with plenty for us to eat and trade at the end. We spent a good hour that last morning scooping dried fruit into muslin sacks, and then nuts, rice and wheat into burlap bags of various sizes. A merry task for the children. I tried not to let them see my fear of what was coming.

I've hated small spaces since I was five and my cousin Arten shut me in a blanket chest and sat on the lid while I screamed and sobbed myself sick. The whole trip I tried not to think of the day we must hide inside those boxes, wrapped in quilts and covered with rice and pistachios. I knew it was a good plan. I agreed to it. But now, looking at the box for me and Virginie, I almost wished those soldiers would come after us and make us turn back. I hated, truly <u>hated</u> knowing I'd be nailed into a coffin with my baby as if we were already dead. I was far away and chilled numb while we arranged the quilts. Petros teased the children, warning them what would happen if they ate raw rice or too much dried fruit. He got them all laughing, but I couldn't even smile. I couldn't imagine eating anything ever again. I cleaned and wrapped my little girl with my head throbbing. I didn't think we'd come out of the box alive. It was hard to hide my fear.

Heranoush and I had to arrange ourselves first, for our boxes had to lie under the boys'. It made my skin cold to think of being trapped in a box under a box, however good the reasons. Closed in by a lid, weighted by another box, then more sacks on top, under the canvas. I still shudder to recall it.

Petros said the border soldiers were usually easy and always lazy. If an officer wanted a box opened, it would be one on top, not under. There was room for a thick layer of bulgur over Vagram in his quilt, and room to cover Artashes with close-packed bags of dry fruits and pistachios. They'd be well hid.

I ran my fingers over the breathing holes, poked my finger tips into them, punched at the quilts, blew thru each breathing tube, checked the holes in my big daughter's box and rearranged her bedding. Trying for calm. Delaying. Finally, I waved bravely to my children and climbed into my box.

Heranoush blew me a kiss as she settled herself into place and I blew a kiss back, trying to smile. Petros handed me the baby, half-asleep. I curled around her, then thought better and lay on my back with her on my chest and a rice-sack for a pillow. I had to bend my knees, for the box was too short, though deep enough to let me move some. At least Heranoush and I didn't have bulgur and rice pressing down on us.

Petros fixed some pieces of wood next to the breathing holes to keep them clear. "You'll be all right, little mother," he said. "Want some bags of apricots?" He leaned over and kissed my damp forehead. "Try to sleep, mother Marjan. In a few hours, we'll be safe."

"God willing," I answered. With eyes still open, I began to pray.

I still remember Vagram's face just before they closed me in, his tender kiss. "Be brave, Mama. I love you."

"I love you too, brave boy."

Did you ever hear of someone opening a coffin and finding a dried up corpse inside with its clothes torn into tatters around the throat and scratches inside the coffin where the corpse scratched trying to escape, not being dead at all, only looking dead, like poor poisoned Juliet? God pity them, if the tales are true and not made up to scare us. Two or three of these stories came from serious people who swore their truth. It must happen sometimes. Though I tried to close those dreadful stories out, lying in that box with my baby, they kept coming like smells from the outhouse when the wind's wrong. You think awful thoughts, lying nailed in a box for hours and hours.

I tried to think of the future: making a home for ourselves the way we wanted, finding new friends and new places, being safe from Muslim soldiers. I imagined our church, wondered if the priest would be kind like Father Ashod, if there'd be good women like Berthe and Souren and Keghvart. Already we'd half-friends in Kars, the Madatians. Maybe others to come. Then I started thinking of my sisters and friends in Erzerum and other friends gone far from us like Varti and Henza. This got me crying until I fell asleep.

When I woke, my left arm was asleep and the cart was jolting over ruts that felt like so many boulders. The mules were struggling to pull all our weight over the rough ground. What if they collapsed, I wondered? There were plenty of what-ifs to worry through the next few hours. Some soldier grabbing Heranoush for his pleasure, Artashes shot dead trying to save her. Vagram somehow wounded,

Virginie suffocated. A mother's fears are endless always. For a time I was in a strange, hot bath room where my mother was telling me how to feed the baby and Henza was telling me what to say to Heranoush, and then my mother and Henza were chewing over some rude thing I'd said about Petros' mother that I never said out loud.

After this I made a game setting names of friends into different tunes. The baby, bless her, was smart enough to do her crying early on, before any soldiers were near. I didn't let her nurse until Petros banged on the lids to let us know the first border post was close. Thankfully, a sugar teat helped get us through.

Why is it we remember things we should forget? I tried to pull up happy thoughts inside that box, but I could only think of the nailed down lid and my long ago child's panic. May God forgive me, lying there I cursed my cousin for laughing when I screamed to let me out. Are boys always that mean if they get a chance?

I knew our breathing tubes were working, I could hear the cart wheels scraping. I knew safety was just a few hours away, yet I felt I'd be trapped there forever, I'd suffocate and die in that box. My throat tightened on my screams and my heart beat loud as a church bell. How stupid I was to let bad thoughts rule me! I took three deep breaths and started whispering all the Apostolic chants and prayers, responses and homilies I could remember. I told myself stories from the Holy Bible. I tried to remember everything I learned from my children's schoolbooks—arithmetic, alphabet, grammar. Geography, history. Finally, I made myself spell out every word I could bring to mind. At some point I managed to press back fears and fall asleep for a while.

I heard men's voices, though I couldn't say for sure if one was my husband's or what was said. How long the cart was still before I came awake, I don't know. More voices. I felt the cart shift as Petros got down. I was too scared to pray. I could barely breathe as long minutes held us in place. The baby stirred—and never before or since did she get to suckle so fast. More minutes, voices, another shift, and another. A shout froze my breathing. Then creaking cartwheels, thudding mule-hooves. Thank you gracious God Almighty! Thank You Lord!!

That was the Turkish border post, where my husband folded one last gold piece into his travel papers before passing them to the commandant, and also gave over two big sacks of high quality pistachios. The officer remembered Petros, or our story might be different.

It seemed at least an hour before we came to the Russian border station. Not so risky a crossing, though we must stay in our boxes. The Russians cared little for finding Armenians but must get a good share of whatever goods came in from Turkey. From there we rode another mile or so before our freedom.

Head, neck, shoulders, arms, hands, back, thighs, calves, feet, toes, fingers—every part of me ached from lying in that awful box. Add a bellyache from needing to make water. Now add to thick stale air the stench of infant shit. It's well said the last part of a trip is longest. Yet after the Turkish border post I felt less afraid.

I took three deep breaths and turned my thoughts to the house waiting for us in Kars. It might feel small, Petros had warned me. I thought it would be fine for us, whatever size. We'd have Armenian neighbors and a church nearby. Protection from a Russian garrison just up the hill. Downhill, a river made for skating. I didn't know we'd take a healthy newborn Sarkis to be baptized at that fine small church within a year. What I did know is that I was strong enough for almost anything now.

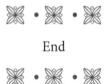

End

Glossary

baksheesh: a bribe or gratuity

caravansary: facility for the men and beasts of a caravan, providing food, water and a place to rest

Circassian: member of a north Caucasus ethnic group, mostly Sunni Muslims

Dashnak: member of the Armenian Revolutionary Federation. The ARF was an Armenian socialist party which advocated reform and defended villages from attack. It was founded in 1890.

hamidieh: para-military fighters, usually Kurds, invited to assist the regular army and given tin badges. Named for Sultan Abdul Hamid II (ruled 1876-1909).

hannum: wife or matron, honorific term of address

Hunchak: member of the Social Democrat Hunchagist Party, the first Armenian socialist party. It was founded in 1887 and advocated a national Armenian state independent of Ottoman rule.

khan: a no-frills hostelry or inn

Laze: from a village in Bosnia

millet: a religious minority under legal protection in the Ottoman Empire. The two main millets were Christian and Jew. Each millet was led by the recognized head of that minority in Turkey. A Christian would be tried in a Christian court; the Christian millet was subject to different taxes and restrictions from the Muslim majority.

pasha: term of respect; a man of property and position